" We have at least **i: this house together,"** Alex said.

H∘ was now using both hands to massage Joy's sh∘ulders. It felt so good, his fingers so strong and in istent, she wanted them all over her body right n∘w.

V th the two of them alone in this big, beautiful h∘use, it seemed like the best use of their time to ju t tear each other's clothes off and fall into bed.

"What should we do now?" he asked.

" don't know. You have any ideas?" she muttered. *Ju st kiss me.*

Vell, it's nearly Christmas and it's a little sad that ere are zero decorations up in this house."

e'd done her best to leave behind no trace of her- lf while she was here. She had to.

e smiled and she thought she might melt into a uddle right there on the carpet. The bed was ly paces away. He'd hardly need to do anything to ave her.

Get your head out of the clouds. She *had* to be ensible.

* * *

Snowed in with Billionaire

V eep it

SNOWED IN
WITH A
BILLIONAIRE

BY
KAREN BOOTH

HarperCollins
PUBLISHERS
— Since 1817 —

First Published in Great Britain 2017
By Mills & Boon, an imprint of HarperCollins*Publishers*
1 London Bridge Street, London, SE1 9GF

© 2017 Harlequin Books S.A.

ISBN: 978-0-263-92848-8

51-1217

MIX
Paper from
responsible sources
FSC™ C007454

This book is produced from independently certified FSC™ paper to ensure responsible forest management.

For more information visit: www.harpercollins.co.uk/green

Printed and bound in Spain
by CPI, Barcelona

Karen Booth is a Midwestern girl transplanted to the South, raised on '80s music, Judy Blume and the films of John Hughes. She writes sexy big-city love stories. When she takes a break from the art of romance, she's teaching her kids about good music, honing her Southern cooking skills or sweet-talking her husband into whipping up a batch of cocktails. Find out more about Karen at www.karenbooth.net.

Special thanks and acknowledgement are
given to Karen Booth for her contribution
to the Secrets of the A-List series.

One

Joy McKinley hated to lie to anyone, especially some-one as sweet as her fellow bakery worker, Natalie. But she had no choice.

"This is me. On the right. Don't bother pulling into the driveway. It's tough to back out. Cars whiz around that turn so fast." Snow was coming down like crazy now. By all accounts, they were in for one heck of a storm.

"Cute house." Natalie peered through the window at the rustic cabin Joy had driven past every day on her way up the mountain. Her blond curls poked out from underneath her gray-and-white-striped knit hat. It had a giant pom-pom on top. "You make enough at the bakery to live here by yourself?"

If Natalie knew where Joy was really staying, her eyes would have popped out of her head. This house wasn't nice enough to be the shed behind the one she was currently living in. "It's really not that nice. It's a total fixer-upper on the inside. And it's just until I decide whether or not I'm staying in Vail long-term."

Every fib out of Joy's mouth, however small, ate at her. That was the reason she'd kept to herself since coming to Vail—it was easier to live covertly if you never had to speak to anyone about the details of your life. It made for a solitary existence though, one that was starting to chew a hole through Joy's sanity and sense of self, especially now that Christmas was almost here. Unfortunately, lies and lone-wolfing were the best ways to keep her cover, and keep it she must.

Natalie's car quaked and rumbled as it idled, but at least it was still spitting out heat. December in Colorado was no joke. Although Joy had grown up in Ohio and had lived through her fair share of bitter cold winters, she'd lost much of her immunity to chilly temperatures while living in LA and Santa Barbara over the last few years.

"Which way are you leaning? Staying or going?" Natalie asked.

"I'm not sure. I need to weigh my options, find a permanent place to live. Let me know if you hear of anyone who needs a roommate. I'd love to share the rent with someone."

"I'll definitely ask around. We'd hate to lose you at the bakery. I love working with you."

"That's so sweet of you to say. I love working with you, too." Joy nodded eagerly. Those words were the truth. Still, her pulse was starting to thunder in her ears. What if the real owner of this house came outside, wondering what a strange car was doing idling out front? What if they suddenly came home? The thought put her too close to the edge, a place she'd spent the last several months. Someday she would get settled. Someday she wouldn't have to be a nomad.

"Just so you know, I'm not trying to guilt you into staying. Seems like you're pretty overqualified to work there."

"I'm really not overqualified. Pastries and baking are just as much work as French or Italian cuisine." Those were Joy's specialties, but if she started talking about food, she'd never get out of the car, and she was already tempting fate by sitting there. Needing to force the issue, she pulled the handle and opened her car door. "I should go. I'm beat from today and you should really get home before the snow gets any worse."

Natalie leaned across the seat and looked up at Joy. "Do you want me to talk to my brother about helping you with your car? He works cheap if I tell him it's a favor to me."

Even cheap is too expensive for me. "It's nice of you to offer. I'll let you know. Thanks so much for the ride. I'll see you at work tomorrow."

Of course, I have no clue how I'm going to get there, but I'll worry about that later.

"If the bakery stays open in this storm. I'd check in with Bonnie later tonight before you go to bed. She'll tell you what the contingency plan is based on the forecast."

"Thanks. I'll do that." Joy dawdled on her way to the mailbox, pretending to fumble with her bag, then stood with her hand on the pull, waving at Natalie. As soon as she was out of view, Joy pulled back her hand. Knowing her luck, she'd get saddled with federal mail tampering charges.

Joy waited another moment, standing perfectly still as snow fell all around her, collecting on her shoulders and her nose. As soon as she was certain Natalie was long gone, she doubled back to the end of the street and started her long walk up the hill to the sprawling luxurious mountain estate of her former employers, Harrison and Mariella Marshall. Landing the job as head chef at the Marshalls' estate in Santa Barbara, California, had been a dream come true. Now she was enduring a bizarre bad dream, one in which her surroundings were still luxe and of the Marshall variety, but the reality was decidedly less shiny.

Harrison Marshall, one of the world's original celebrity chefs, owned a global culinary empire. Working for him was the ultimate foot in the door when it came to being a chef. Unfortunately, Harrison had been in a near-fatal car accident soon after Joy began working for him. In the aftermath, Harrison's family unraveled, especially his wife, Mariella. She used Joy as a verbal punching bag, launching unprovoked tirades about things as minor as what type of table salt to use. One day, Mariella pushed too hard, and Joy quit. With little money and zero prospects, she walked away from the best job she'd ever had.

Only empathy from Mariella's son Rafe had saved her, and it was a temporary fix. He'd given her the keys to the Vail house, saying she was okay to stay until mid-January, when his siblings would likely come to ski. It was such a beautiful home, her stay was a respite, of sorts, but she still needed to work, and the only employment she'd found was at the bakery downtown. It was money and that was all that mattered.

Normally, Joy would be driving her beat-up car home from the bakery at this time of day, rocking forward and back in the driver's seat and praying it would make it all the way to the top. Not today. The cantankerous piece of junk had decided not to start that morning. This was after she'd just spent the only significant chunk of money she had, nearly six hundred dollars, on fixing it. She would've been better off abandoning the car and keeping that money for a deposit on an apartment. The clock was ticking on that front. Mid-January would be here before she knew it.

She'd considered borrowing one of the three cars in the Marshalls' five-car garage, all of which had to cost more money than she could make in five years. As someone who was supposed to be laying low, driving around town in a showstopper of a vehicle was a recipe for attracting too much attention. She'd attempted to borrow one of the family's bicycles, but she only made it partway down the icy driveway before nearly wiping out. At that point, out of options and on the verge of being late for a job she absolutely needed, she'd decided to spend her last available cash on a taxi. Hence the ride home from Natalie.

The storm seemed to be gaining momentum now. The fluffy fat flakes from earlier were turning to icy pellets. The wind was blowing like crazy, howling between the trees and rustling snow from the branches in dramatic swirls. With a deluge of frozen precipitation pummeling her face, she had to squint in order to see. Joy tugged her scarf up around her ears and over her mouth. It was hard work to scale the hill, and she was breaking out into a sweat, even in the freezing temperatures. The high down in Vail that day had only been twenty-eight degrees. She got off work from the bakery at 3:00 p.m. each day, and it was nearly five now. The sun had set. The brittle night air grated against her cheeks; it worked its way into her bones. Colorado was beautiful, but Joy wasn't sure she was cut out for being a snow bunny long-term. She would've done anything at that moment for a margarita and a beach.

She dug the toes of her boots into the compacted snow, trudging away, careful to stay as far to the side of the road as possible. So much snow had fallen over the last few weeks that waist-high banks lined both sides of the street. She zipped her jacket up around her face and focused on what was waiting for her when she reached the top. She visualized the unbelievable bed she'd been sleeping in every night, the fluffy king-sized pillow-top in Mariella's daughter's room. Climbing in and sinking into that luxurious mattress, swishing her bare feet against the fine sheets, was pure heaven. It was her reward for surviving every day. It was also her safe place, a place where she didn't allow herself to become mired in negative thoughts or worries about where she would go next or what she was going to do in terms of building a future. Yes, she was living a borrowed life right now, and a clandestinely borrowed one at that, but she had to be thankful for what she had. A roof over her head and a warm place to sleep were at the top of the list of her blessings.

The incline was getting steeper. She hitched her bag up on her shoulder. Her breaths came faster, icy air slicing through her lungs. Everything was freezing—her feet, her thighs, her fingers, and especially her cheeks. She started to shake from the cold. *Think of the bed. Think of the bed.* Just then a soft glow came from around the bend. Light bounced off the snowbanks and the snow-covered branches of the dense stands of trees all around her. The light became brighter. It swept from side to side. But it was the strangest thing. There was no noise. She'd typically hear a car by now. And then came a recognizable sound—the crunch of tires over snow.

The black car came into view, up at the very top of the hill. She inched closer to the side of the road to be safe. She waved her hand to make sure the driver saw her, and he seemed to, slowly moving to the center of the road. She looked down at her feet for an instant and the next thing she knew, the car was skidding across a patch of ice, drifting closer to the opposite side. She could see his exact trajectory. He was going to go into the ditch. The car turned sharply. An overcorrection. The back end fishtailed. The car slid sideways. The tires crunched against the snow again. The driver had slammed on the brakes. But it kept going. Coming right for her. *Run.* That was all she could think. But which way? Up seemed like the only answer. Her feet slipped. She fell forward, clawing at the snow with her hands, scrambling out of the way. The headlights blinded her. The car barreled at her. She righted herself and scrambled. Not enough time. She did the only thing she could do. She dove into a snowbank.

Cold shot through her entire body, like a tidal wave fueled by adrenaline. She took a sharp breath, her lungs filled with unbelievable iciness. Her throat tightened. She couldn't breathe. Snow was everywhere. Like she'd jumped into the deepest part of the ocean and was surrounded by icebergs. She flailed about, all arms and legs, struggling to stand. She couldn't get a foothold. There was no solid ground. Only snow to breathe and swallow. Did people drown in snowbanks? She was about to find out. Leave it to her to be the first person to accomplish such a feat. As she struggled with her arms, trying to push herself up, something grabbed her leg. *Oh, God. A bear.*

It was full-on panic—flailing, fighting and kicking. She screamed at the top of her lungs and managed to roll to her back. Whatever had her in its clutches was pulling on her now. She dug her hands into the snow, trying to stop her progress, but the beast was too strong for her. She couldn't fight it off. She was going to get eaten by a bear. Now she wished she was back to drowning in the snow.

With a thump, her butt landed on hard ground. The bear let go. She kicked and screamed. A dark figure loomed over her. It was lit from behind. *Wait a minute.* If this was a bear, he had very nice shoulders and an awfully nice head of hair.

"Are you okay?" the figure asked, desperately. "Give me your hand."

Joy was finally able to sit up, but she couldn't stand. She was still gathering her wits. She stared at the figure. A man. It was a man. Behind him was a car. *The* car. The lights beamed across the road. The man in the car had pulled her out of the snowbank. It was all starting to come together. He crouched down in front of her, grasping her shoulder.

"Are you okay?" he asked again. "Are you hurt? Can you hear me?"

She wasn't merely disoriented when her eyes were able to focus and he came into sharper view. For a second she thought she might be dead. *Wow. He's handsome. He's like a fairy-tale prince.* A real one, with thick dark hair that held a perfect wave. His eyes were icy blue. He even had a dimple in his chin.

That was it. She was dead.

The handsome prince dug in his pocket and pulled out a phone. "I'm calling an ambulance. You must be in shock."

Joy instinctively grabbed his wrist. "No. No. I'm fine." She took a deep breath and as the air fully filled her lungs, she realized she was not dead. Plus, her hand had landed on firm man. A real man. "I'm so sorry. I just... I didn't know what to do and it was my first instinct to jump into the snow. I'm sure that seems crazy."

"Do you think you're okay to stand up?"

"Probably." She nodded. As soon as she was on her feet, she saw that she had not been crazy to leap into the snow. The rear end of his car had stopped just shy of the bank. "Wow. I could have been hit."

"I'm so sorry. I ran into a patch of ice and lost control of the car. Sometimes these precision vehicles do what you want them to and sometimes they don't." The handsome prince had a very deep voice, rich and authoritative. He was probably really good at telling people what to do. He was tall. And good God, now that she could see his face in its entirety, she couldn't help but notice that he was unbearably handsome. He was all high cheekbones and full lips. A strong jaw and brow line. There was nothing soft about him. Everything was defined. He wore a black wool coat and black leather gloves. "Do you mind if I ask what in the world you were doing out here walking alongside the road in the dark?"

Oh, yeah. That. "Hiking."

"Hiking? In those boots?" He pointed at her feet, which were clad in her brown leather boots with the chunky heel. They were surprisingly comfortable and made her butt look damn good in jeans. She didn't wear them at work, though. She donned the chef's clogs that were currently in her bag for the long hours on her feet.

"Yeah, I know. I guess I'm just a slave to fashion." She tittered nervously.

He narrowed his focus on her, his eyebrows drawing together so tightly they nearly touched. "Okay. Well, I don't think it's a good idea for you to finish your hike. Why don't you let me drive you home?"

Home? *Oh, no.* That would never work. Her home was the Marshalls' home and absolutely no one was supposed to know she was there. For all she knew, this guy was a friend of the Marshalls. They not only knew a lot of people, most people knew of them. "I'm fine. Really." She waved him off.

He shook his head. "No way. You are not fine. You should see yourself right now. Your hair and your makeup." He drew a circle in the air in front of her face. "Plus, I'm not entirely sure you didn't hit your head. I'm driving you home. If my mother were still alive, she'd be horrified if she found out that I was anything less than a perfect gentleman."

Oh, sure. Bring your dead mother into it. "No, really…"

"No. Really. I insist. Either that or I call an ambulance for you. You're not walking home."

Joy blew out a breath and knew it was time to relent. If they got to the top of the hill and he said a peep about the Marshalls, she'd have to come up with a quick excuse. In the meantime, at least with Prince Charming around, she was fairly sure she wasn't in danger of being arrested. "Okay. Sure. That'd be nice."

Alex stepped ahead of the mystery woman and opened the passenger door for her. "I can turn on the heated seat for you in a moment." He took care when closing the door. He still wasn't convinced she wasn't in shock. He was certainly disoriented. One minute he was out for a drive, trying to blow off some work-related steam, and the next thing he knew, his car was sliding down a mountain and he nearly hit a woman. The scene that followed, the epic panic in the snowbank, was like something out of a movie. He could hardly believe what he'd witnessed.

He climbed inside and glanced over at her. She was using the visor mirror to wipe away the smudges of makeup beneath her eyes and smooth her hair.

"I wasn't trying to say you needed to primp."

"You were right. I'm a disaster."

Even though her hair had looked like it had been through a tornado, he couldn't imagine her ever looking bad. In the soft light coming from the mirror, only in profile, she still stole his breath. She was a classic beauty, like something out of an old Technicolor movie—creamy complexion, lively flush on her cheeks. Her now-tidier hair was long, rolling past her shoulders in gentle waves.

"If this is your version of a disaster, I'd love to see what you look like when you're going out."

She turned, sizing him up with her soulful brown eyes.

He reached out his hand. "Seems like introductions are in order. I'm Alex. Well, Alexander if you want the long version. Alexander Townsend."

She swiped off her fluffy mitten and placed her hand in his. "Nice to meet you, Alexander Townsend, although if this is your way of picking up women, I suggest you get a new technique."

Alex laughed. Beautiful and witty. It was his lucky day. "And your name?"

She flipped the visor up, tugging her mitten back on. "Joy."

"Nice to meet you, Joy. Just Joy or is there more to it?"

"Baker."

"You aren't a Denver Baker, are you?"

"Excuse me?"

"The Denver Bakers. I'm very good friends with Patrick. He and I both graduated from Columbia the same year." The look on her face said that she was not a member of the Baker family from Denver. "I'm guessing no?"

She shrugged. "Sorry. I don't know them."

"Ah. Well. Thought I'd ask. Where are you from, Joy Baker?"

She cleared her throat. "Santa Barbara."

"I'm from Chicago. Not nearly as picturesque as coastal California, but it's home."

"Sounds nice."

This conversation didn't seem to be going anywhere. Probably best to move along. "Where can I take you?"

"Do you know this road well?"

"Clearly, I don't."

She pointed up the hill. "It's at the top. Just drive and I'll show you."

He followed her directions, the headlights casting golden beams across the silver snow. That bit of friendly back-and-forth had been pleasant enough, but reality was sinking in. He could have killed her. For all he knew, she was injured. Bleeding internally? Head trauma? All possible. The thought set him doubly on edge. His protective side came out with all women, sometimes to his own detriment. It was a product of his childhood, years of his father mistreating his mother, and Alex having to be the buffer. He had to remind himself that he hardly knew Joy. There was no reason to protect her any more than any other stranger.

But there was reason to worry. With his money, and

his family name, he had been the frequent target of unscrupulous people. The most notable of which had been his former fiancée, and although that was a chapter of his life best left closed, it did make him wary of people and their intentions.

"It's up here. On the left. You can just pull up to the gate and I'll get out."

He crested the hill and the vista opened up, almost as if they were perched on top of the world. It was all vast blue-black sky and stars up here; the house Joy had pointed to a showpiece that seemed to go on forever. His shoulders lightened. He had no need to worry about her intentions. Joy, from the look of things, had more than enough of her own resources.

He pulled closer to the gate and rolled down his window. "Code?"

"Oh, no. It's fine. I'll just get out right here. You can go now."

Alex didn't know what to say. It wasn't like he saw himself as God's gift to women, but he was certainly not accustomed to getting the swift brush-off. Usually, women enjoyed being in his company. And it wasn't like he'd asked her out. This was a ride up the driveway. "I promise I won't memorize it. I work in finance, but I'm actually horrible with numbers. Well, small ones at least." He laughed quietly at his own joke, but she didn't. *Idiot.*

"I just… I don't know that I should let you in."

He nodded, trying to understand what sort of vibe he was giving off that made her so uneasy. Part of him wanted to tell her that he was the most trustworthy guy imaginable when it came to women, always a perfect gentleman, but what kind of guy says that? Someone who's the exact opposite, that's who. The trouble was, he wasn't entirely certain she was okay after her swan dive into the snowbank. "I don't want to bring up my mom again, but can't a guy at least drive you to the door? That driveway has to be at least a five-minute walk. Probably ten in those boots. Which are completely inappropriate for hiking, by the way. I can't believe you got in a single step before you wiped out."

"If you'll stop criticizing my footwear choices, I'll let you drive me up."

"Deal."

"The code is 6274."

He punched in the numbers and the tall wrought iron gate pulled back behind a towering stone pillar topped with a craftsman light fixture. The car crept ahead, but with this much power under the hood, he was careful not to gun it. The house was impressive as they approached, with tall windows peeking out from under at least a dozen gables, supported by honed timber trusses. The roof was blanketed in snow, the exterior clad in cedar shakes and trim. This gorgeous mountain lodge could likely sleep twenty people comfortably.

"Beautiful home you have here. It reminds me of my place in Switzerland. Of course, the skiing over there is better, but I wanted a quick getaway this Christmas, so my house in Vail seemed like the right choice."

"Oh. Um. This isn't my house. It belongs to friends of mine."

"Who are your friends? Maybe I know them."

"Uh. The Santiago family? They're letting me stay here for a while." Her voice was a bit shaky and unsure. Maybe she really had been hurt in the fall.

"Hmm. I don't know them. You're staying here by yourself?"

"Well, yes. Wanted some time to myself. Life gets crazy." Joy collected her things and opened her car door. "Thank you, again." She turned back to him only this time, there was a momentary connection difficult to ignore.

"Of course. It's the least I can do." Something about this wasn't right. "Hey. Is it okay if we exchange numbers? I want you to be able to call me if you aren't feeling well."

She pressed her lips together like she was trying to escape a deeply uncomfortable situation. "How about I just take your number?"

Fair enough. "Sure thing." He rattled off the digits and she put it into her phone, or at least he thought she did.

With that, she climbed out, closed her door, and scaled the grand sweep of stone stairs leading up to the front porch. Joy was tall, her legs long and lithe, but she looked tiny compared to the massive wood double door. She keyed her way in and as soon as she disappeared inside, he put the car into Reverse and backed up. Her sweet fragrance lingered—an aroma like spun sugar. It'd been months since he'd been on a date with a woman, and even just a few minutes with Joy was going to haunt him. He had a sense she was holding back or hiding something.

Hopefully, it wasn't that she'd been hurt in the accident.

Two

Joy flipped the dead bolt and collapsed against the door. That had been entirely too close a call. When Rafe Marshall, Mariella's son, had said she could stay in the house, he'd been explicit about one thing—no one could know she was there. His mother would kill him if she found out he'd given sanctuary to someone who'd dared to quit her employ, and the Marshalls knew a lot of people in Vail. A lot of very wealthy, powerful people. People like Alex.

Thank goodness she'd been quick enough to say that the house belonged to the Santiago family. Santiago was Mariella Marshall's maiden name, and luckily did not ring a bell with Alex. Joy despised these little white lies, but she was deeply concerned about her future in the culinary world. Mariella Marshall could kill her entire career, everything she'd worked so hard for, with one or two well-placed phone calls.

Joy raced to the window and pulled back the heavy gold tapestry drape, peeking outside. The red of Alex's taillights glowed in the dark as his car cleared the gate. As soon as the wrought iron barrier completed its trip back across the driveway, she felt as though she could breathe. He was gone. Unbelievably hot Prince Charming had flown the coop. And that was a good thing, however disappointing it might seem. She'd been lonely since she'd come to Colorado. She hadn't had a single in-person conversation that hadn't revolved around working at the bakery. Some time with a personable, good-looking man would have been welcome. It would have been wonderful, actually.

Not for you, she reminded herself as she dropped her bag, traveled down the hall, and walked upstairs to the bedroom she'd been staying in. Rich guys were just asking for trouble. She'd met her fair share working in the restaurant world. Whether it was wealthy owners, investors or customers, men with money were too accustomed to getting whatever they wanted, when they wanted it. Joy was too bullheaded to ever put up with that.

If anything, having a man make demands sent Joy running in the opposite direction. Case in point, her hometown ex-boyfriend. He hadn't had money, but he'd always had control. Getting away from him had been a harrowing experience. It still wasn't over. Money and her car were obstacles, but he was the big reason she couldn't go home at Christmas. There were no secrets in her small town. He always found out when she returned, and then he'd start circling in on her. It was best to stay away, however sad and lonely it made her to not be with her family.

Joy removed her work clothes, turned on the shower

and stepped inside, closing the glass door behind her. The spray was the ideal temperature, with the perfect amount of water pressure to soothe her aching muscles. Baking was hard work, physically exhausting, possibly even more so than being a chef. Taking a mile-long hike up a mountain and ultimately landing in a snowbank had been a less-than-ideal way to end her day. She felt every bit of it.

Even though this house had unlimited hot water, she decided she couldn't spend her entire evening in the shower. She climbed out, curled her toes into the plush bath mat, and wrapped herself up in the fluffy white towel. Everything in this house was the finest quality. Every element was chosen with an eye for luxury and comfort, and she would've been lying if she'd said that she didn't appreciate every second of it.

Mariella's daughter Elana's bathroom was a perfect example—marble-topped vanity with custom cherry cabinetry, a shower with a waterfall head and shimmery glass tile. There was even a towel warmer. Joy didn't use it often. It was more of a treat, which was a silly notion, but Joy didn't want to get too accustomed to this life. She wouldn't have it for long.

She grabbed her robe from the hook and towel-dried her hair, studying herself in the mirror. Some days it was a necessary reminder of who she was and what she was. She was Joy McKinley, a hardworking girl from Ohio. She did not come from a house like this, nor would she live in a house like this. Pipe dreams didn't get anyone anywhere. Hard work did. She most definitely was *not* Joy Baker, invited guest of the Marshall family and woman perfectly at home staying by herself in a sprawling estate. She'd only let Alex believe those things because she was covering her tracks and he was nothing more than an acquaintance. A ridiculously sexy one, but a stranger nonetheless.

The security system control panel on the bathroom wall dinged. Joy jumped. Someone was at the door. Her pulse took off in a sprint. Anyone who arrived on her doorstep had already passed through the gate. Had someone from the Marshall family arrived without their key? Had Mariella Marshall invited friends to stay here, leaving Joy to explain herself and hightail it out of there? She jabbed the button for the security camera. Alex came into view in pixelated black and white. Relief washed over her, followed by a jolt of excitement. But why was he back?

"Hello?" she asked into the intercom.

"Hi. It's Alex. From before. The car? The hill?" He was so adorable, talking into the doorbell instead of looking up at the security camera.

"Yes. I remember."

"I got halfway home and I had to turn around. Are you sure you're okay?"

She waited to answer. She really wanted to invite him in. She wanted to have a real conversation. If he didn't want to talk, she could just stare at him for a while or maybe she could convince him that a brief make-out session with a stranger was totally normal. "I feel fine. I think."

"See? That's a problem. I think I should call 911. This could be serious."

"No. Please don't do that."

"Can you come to the door and talk to me?"

He was the most insistent man she'd been around in a long time. "Fine. I'm coming." Down the stairs she thundered. She opened the door but quickly remembered she was wearing a bathrobe and nothing else, and stopped herself from flinging it wide open. She greeted him by poking her head out through the narrow opening. "I'm fine." The soft amber glow from the porch lights made him even more movie star handsome. It was going to hurt to tell him to go away.

"It doesn't seem like you should be by yourself right now," he said.

"I told you I'm fine." Except that she wasn't entirely sure she was. Her neck still felt tight, even after that long shower, and she had a headache brewing.

He pursed his lips and looked down at the ground for a moment. "I think you should see a doctor."

"That's not necessary. I just need to get some sleep."

"Are you positive you didn't hit your head? If you have a head injury, it could be a bad idea to go to sleep."

Good God, he was persistent. "It was snow. Nothing hard to hit my head on."

He moved his face closer to hers, studying her. The breath hitched in her throat. He had a really sexy mouth. Totally worth kissing. What if they ended up having that make-out session after all? "It seems like your pupils are pretty dilated."

"I don't even know what to say to that. It's not like I can see my own eyes right now. Nor do I even know what it means if they are, in fact, dilated."

"Can I please come in for a moment? I promise I'm not wielding an axe."

She sighed and opened the door wider, the brutally cold air rushing in behind him. The snow was coming down even harder now, which she hadn't thought possible. "Have you ever noticed that murderers don't carry an axe, they wield it?"

"It just occurred to me that I shouldn't have used axe-murderer terminology. I'm sorry. I swear I'm a good guy." His smile was extra convincing. Alex wasn't a threat, although she might pass out from how blindingly perfect his mouth was.

Joy couldn't imagine finding a reason to put Alex off, even when logic said she should. That smile had done something to her. It had left a chink in her armor. "Please. Come in. You must be freezing. It's horrible out there."

He shook snow from his hair and stomped his boots on the foyer rug. "Yeah, the forecast isn't looking good." His eyes dipped south, then returned to her face. "It's much nicer in here."

A vaguely familiar tingle zipped through her. Was he flirting with her? Was Prince Charming making the moves? A breath of cold air crossed her shoulders and she realized then that the top of her robe had gaped quite significantly. It wasn't a full-on wardrobe malfunction, but it wasn't far off. She quickly covered up and re-cinched the tie. Embarrassment covered her from head to toe.

"Can I make you a cup of tea?" She wasn't sure what else to offer the man who'd showed up at her door again.

"That would be great, but I was hoping we could call my doctor together. I'll feel a lot better about things if you just talk to him."

"So I don't have to go anywhere?"

"Nope. You can do this from the comfort of your own home."

My own home. If only. "Okay. Do you want to have a seat in the living room while I run upstairs and get dressed?"

"You don't have to change on my account. I think you look pretty amazing just as you are."

There it was again—that flirtatious lilt to his voice. Or maybe he was just one of those men whose every comment came off with an edge of innuendo. Regardless of whether he was trying hard or not, she had a deep desire to comb her fingers through his hair, if only to learn whether it was as thick as it looked. It'd been more than a year since she'd been with a man, and that one had been a deeply disappointing kisser—weak lips and a hesitant tongue. If a man was going to kiss her, she wanted him to go for it. Send a message. Alex looked like he could knock a woman off her heels with a single kiss. And here they were, all alone in this big beautiful house, she in a near state of undress.

"You're sweet, but I think it would be best if I was wearing something that more closely resembled clothes. I'll be right back."

She turned and darted up the stairs, mumbling to herself, "What in the hell are you doing? Why did you let him inside? That was really, really dumb. We're going to call his doctor? At night? How weird is that?"

Learning firsthand how adept Alex was at talking her into something, she needed to remain on her toes. She also needed to remain calm and allow him to leave of his own accord. Making a stink was a good way to arouse suspicion, and she didn't want to give him any reason to decide she was acting strangely or quite possibly didn't belong in this house. For all she knew, he'd call the police. Surely a guy as thorough and conscientious as Alex wouldn't even hesitate to turn her in if he thought she wasn't on the up-and-up. She had to do her best to appear to belong here. She had to make things seem as normal as possible, then hope he would leave so she could return to her sad, but relatively safe existence where she still got to sleep in an amazing bed.

Dressed in far less revealing pajama pants, tank top and hoodie, Joy hurried back downstairs. As she turned the corner for the living room, she saw the glow and heard the crackle of a fire in the hearth. She hadn't bargained on Alex making himself at home. "Oh. You built a fire."

"Well, yeah. Look at it out there." He tossed his head toward the long wall of the living room, where the windows soared to the top of the cathedral ceiling and stood in single file like soldiers. The night sky was a midnight blue, dotted with fat, glowing snowflakes. "That's half the point of having a mountain house. To build a roaring fire when it's snowing."

Except that building a fire created a wisp of smoke that trailed from the chimney, letting anyone who might happen to drive by know that someone was staying there. Sure, it was a long shot, but if that person knew the Marshalls and decided to stop by or call Mariella to ask how long she'd be in town? That would be very bad. She not only didn't make a habit of lighting the wood-burning fireplaces, she'd been careful to use as few lights as possible. "Um. Sure. It's very nice."

"I thought so." He plopped down on one of two sprawling sectional couches, each covered in plush tapestry fabric in shades of taupe and rust. He pulled out his phone. "Come. Sit. We'll call the doctor." He patted the sofa cushion right next to him.

This was officially the strangest situation Joy had ever been in, but she'd be lying if she'd said she didn't want to sit close to him without a car's center console between them. "Okay." She carefully took the seat next to him. It was impossible not to fixate on his warm and masculine smell, or just how big his hands were as he cradled the phone.

The screen came to life, showing a tiny picture of the two of them in the bottom corner. She couldn't help but notice that they looked cute together, even when he was dressed nicely in a black sweater and jeans while she was in her PJs. "A video call?"

"Well, yeah. He's probably going to want to see you. I figured this is easier."

Another face popped onto the screen, a face so familiar that Joy had to blink several times to be certain she was seeing who she was seeing. *Holy crap.* This was no regular doctor. This was Dr. David, the doctor who made a living on the TV talk show circuit. He was the guy every network called when there was a big health scare and people needed someone impossibly good-looking to talk them off the ledge. "Alex? Are you seriously calling me from Vail? Shouldn't you be hitting the slopes?" Dr. David asked.

Oh, great. Alex isn't just a guy with a super expensive car and a house in Switzerland. He's on a first-name basis with celebrities. What world am I living in, anyway?

Alex laughed. "I've been doing some of that, but I was calling because I have a friend who might have hit her head. I was hoping you could talk to her."

He tilted the phone in Joy's direction, and she had no choice but to wave and say, "Hi. I'm the friend. I'm Joy."

"Hello, Joy. I'm Dr. David."

Well, duh. Another wave of embarrassment hit her. She was sure his first question was going to be why her cheeks were flaming red. "Hi, Dr. David." She did her best to pass it off as if she chatted with ridiculously famous people every day.

"Tell me what's going on," he said.

Joy glanced over at Alex. He looked so uncertain and worried, it made it hard to know what to say. He was concerned about her. That was why he'd come back. This revelation was sweet, but dangerous. Joy needed to be invisible right now, not attracting attention.

Alex listened as Joy told the story of the near-accident. With every word out of her mouth, he felt exponentially guiltier. She'd really, truly been in harm's way and it had all been his fault. He quite literally could have killed her. He could have ended the life of this beautiful woman. The weight of that sat squarely on his shoulders. Call it his biggest fear, but ever since he'd been a kid, he'd worried about making a choice that would lead to an irreversible mistake. If he hadn't decided to go for a drive, Joy wouldn't have ended up in the snowbank.

As reluctant as she'd seemed to accept help, he would have to insist on whatever Dr. David's orders were. No ifs, ands, or buts.

Dr. David was nodding and writing down some notes. "Okay, well, it sounds to me like you're going to be okay. It doesn't sound like you've sustained any kind of serious injury."

Joy sighed and her shoulders dropped in relief. "Oh, good. Thank you."

"That being said, you should not be alone over the next 24 hours. If something crops up, you'll need help to get to the nearest medical center."

Now Joy didn't seem quite so happy. "I'm staying by

myself right now, but it's not a big deal. You said it yourself. It sounds like I haven't sustained any real injury."

"But I can't be certain of that without examining you
myself. I think it's best if Alex stays with you if his
schedule allows."

The ramifications of that sank in quickly, but Alex
knew David was right. She shouldn't be alone. Just to be
on the safe side. He would never forgive himself if something bad happened to her. "I'm on vacation, so I have
nowhere else I need to be. I'm happy to do it."

"We're supposed to get a lot of snow tonight," Joy
pled. "You could get stuck here."

Again, this was not the sort of reaction Alex was used
to. Most women did everything they could to spend time
with him. It wasn't a boastful bit of information; it was
merely the truth. "That's quite literally the last thing I'm
worried about right now."

"I'm sure you two can work it out," David said. "Call
me at this time tomorrow and let me know how the pa-
tient is doing. And Alex, if you need anything in the
middle of the night, don't hesitate to call. I'll have my
phone right by the bed."

"Thanks so much. You're a real lifesaver," Alex replied. "We'll call you tomorrow." With that, he ended
the call.

Joy sat back on the couch and wrapped her arms
around herself. "I'm fine. Really, I am."

"I know. I know. I still think we have to play it safe."

She twisted her lips and tucked her leg under herself.

"We could play cards. Or watch TV. Or talk. You
must get lonely living in this big house by yourself." It
occurred to him then that he'd assumed that since she
was alone, she'd always be alone. "Oh, wait. Do you have

someone coming to stay with you? For the holidays? A boyfriend? A husband?"

She cocked an eyebrow at him. "Is that your way of asking if I'm taken?"

He wasn't convinced it had been a bad approach. He shrugged and kicked off his shoes. Might as well make himself comfortable. "Well? Are you?"

"No. I'm not. I'm too focused on my career for a man right now anyway."

Judging by the generosity of the friends who were letting her stay in their house, Joy must have a pretty big and successful career. "What do you do? No. Wait. Let me guess." He studied her face, trying to keep his eyes from drifting to her other pleasing features like the graceful slope of her neck, her long legs. She was definitely serious. Focused. But she also had this girl-next-door vibe that was not only super sexy, it wasn't entirely congruous with being a bigwig. "Entrepreneur. You started some company that went through the roof. Organic cosmetics or maybe yoga wear?"

She shook her head. "You couldn't be more off base if you tried."

"Well, you're definitely a huge success, whatever it is that you do. That's pretty obvious."

"I wouldn't say I'm a huge success, but I get by."

She was modest. He liked that. Most people in his circles were eager to rattle off their pedigree and accomplishments, whether they'd worked hard for them or not. Joy was a lovely change of pace. "Oh, come on. You're spending time in this huge house all by yourself. You obviously have some very successful friends, and in my experience, successful people attract other successful people. Plus, you just have that air about you."

She narrowed her skeptical eyes. "That air?"

Alex let out a frustrated sigh. He wasn't doing particularly well for himself. Nothing he said seemed to be clicking. "You seem very comfortable here in a home like this, that's all. That's a sign of someone who's had some success."

Joy pulled her leg up and set her foot on the edge of the couch. Her toes were painted a deep red that made his pulse race. She was certainly a beguiling creature. She rested her chin on her knee and cast a thoughtful look at him. "What about you? What does Alex Townsend do?"

Part of him wanted to ignore her reply and circle back to her. She hadn't really answered his question. She might have an even greater sense of humility than he'd realized. Or perhaps there was stress and strain involved with her occupation, and now that it was the holidays, she simply wanted a break, a concept with which he was intimately familiar. After all, she was staying in this big house all by herself at Christmas. If anything said, "I need to be alone," it was that. "I work in finance. Investments. It's my family's business, but I'm running it right now. It's not the most thrilling career, but it's what my family has always done."

"Are you close with your family?"

"I'm very close with my brothers. We all work together. My dad retired last year and put me in charge, but he's not doing a very good job of being a retired person."

"Has to keep his nose in everything?"

It was a constant point of friction, the most difficult part of Alex's day. As the oldest Townsend son, he'd always been heir apparent to Townsend & Associates Investments. He'd looked forward to the day when his father would finally step aside and let Alex take the reins.

Unfortunately, his dad second-guessed him constantly, especially now that Alex was putting his own stamp on the company and changing things, making their operation more modern and more equitable among the employees. "Yeah. You could say that. I keep hoping it'll get better. It's only been a little more than a year since I took over."

"Sometimes parents can be overbearing. Mine were not happy when I decided to go to culinary school."

"So you're a chef? I wasn't that off base."

"You're were pretty off base." She nodded. "At the moment, my focus is baking."

"Hold on a second. You're Joy Baker, the baker?" He couldn't hold back his grin. There was something extremely adorable about this revelation.

"Yes, although I'm not sure why that is so funny. I'm classically trained. Cooking is my passion. My grandmother instilled that in me."

"I'm sorry. I wasn't trying to make light of it."

"Well, it's important to me."

Alex was again having a hard time not smiling. He loved her fire, and how nice it must be to have a family connection to a career that didn't involve money and was rather related to something homey or creative. "So if it's so important, why didn't you parents approve?" She averted her eyes, and Alex fought his first inclination, which was to think that a woman was hiding something when she looked away. It had become a habit, one he was desperate to be rid of. He wanted to trust. He truly did.

"They thought I'd never make enough money, which isn't exactly wrong. It isn't always a high-paying line of work. But I'm not in it for the money. I'm in it because I love doing it."

Joy was a breath of fresh air. He had to admire her bravery. She'd gone against her parents' wishes to pursue her passion, and she'd clearly done very well for herself. He wished he felt so strongly about something. "I think that's fantastic. It's very impressive."

"You know, you didn't say anything about your mom. What does she do?"

It felt as though the air around him had gone flat, which was too bad considering how sparkling their conversation had just been. "She passed away when I was in college." Even years later, the guilt over not being there when his mother died was immense. She'd suffered greatly and Alex had been hundreds of miles away in New York.

"I'm so sorry."

The pity in Joy's voice was a mixed blessing. It was genuine, and he appreciated that more than anything. So much in his life no longer felt real, not since Sharon had betrayed his love with lies. But he also didn't want Joy to feel sorry for him. He wanted her to see him as strong and capable, not weak or vulnerable. "Tell me more about your parents. What do they do?"

Joy closed her eyes for a moment. "You know, maybe this is a conversation best left for another time. I'm feeling pretty tired. I should probably head up to bed."

Was that deflection? Or was she truly tired? Alex couldn't arrive at a conclusion. *Stop with the paranoia.* She'd been through a lot tonight, all of it set in motion when he'd lost control of his car. "I hope you don't have a headache."

She shook her head and got up from the couch. "No. I feel fine. Truly. I'm just tired."

"Okay. Sure. Where do you want me to sleep tonight? I can crash on the couch if that's best."

"Don't be silly. There are a bunch of bedrooms up-stairs. You can stay in the first one on the left in the hall upstairs. I'm two doors down from that."

She'd been sure to leave some space between them, which Alex had to respect. He was a strange man staying in her house. It would set any woman on edge. "Thank you. I appreciate that. I'm also wondering if it would be all right for me to move my car into the garage. No tell-ing how much snow we'll get tonight."

"Oh. Of course. The door is to the left after you walk through the entry. I believe one of the bays is empty."

"Thank you so much. Good night."

"Sleep well." With that, Joy left him to his own de-vices.

Alex found the garage with little trouble and opened the door. The wind had picked up considerably, and the snow was already drifting in the driveway. There were three or four inches on the ground, and although his Bu-gatti had a lot of firepower, it wasn't a huge fan of the snow. It took a bit of convincing to get it into the garage. He grabbed his gym bag from the back seat. At least he'd have clean underwear and some toiletries.

He shook off the cold when he got back inside. He wasn't sure he'd ever gotten himself into a more bizarre situation. He couldn't bring himself to be upset about it, however perilously close the incident with the car had come to hurting her. At least he had a temporary inter-ruption to his very dull and lonely Christmas vacation.

Still, there was something about Joy that wasn't quite right, and that worried him. However much he hated walking around with his defenses up, he couldn't be the guy who could be fooled more than once. In his position, with a vast personal fortune and a professional reputation to maintain, he had to be leery of everyone. The one time he hadn't been careful, it had nearly destroyed him. If the unthinkable had happened and he'd married Sharon, his former fiancée, the woman who duped him into thinking not only that she loved him, but that they didn't need a prenuptial agreement, his face would've eventually been splashed all over the cover of tabloid magazines. Half of his money would've been gone.

Alex trailed through the foyer and back into the living room, dialing the number for Paul, the Townsend & Associates Investments staff investigator. His primary duties for the firm involved due diligence on potential mergers and acquisitions, but he was especially good at digging up skeletons. He'd been at the company for a long time, since Alex was a teenager. Alex's entire family trusted Paul implicitly. In some ways, Paul was like a dad figure to Alex. Alex could speak openly with him and have a real discussion without it turning into a referendum on Alex's style of leadership.

"Aren't you supposed to be on vacation?" Paul asked when he answered.

Alex walked to the far side of the room. He didn't want Joy to overhear him. "I am on vacation. And I'm enjoying myself. But I want you to check into something for me."

"Something or *someone*?"

Paul was a smart man. No question about that. "Someone. A woman."

"Oh, boy," Paul said. "I hope you aren't putting yourself into a delicate situation again."

Alex closed his eyes and blew out a breath through his nose. Paul had every right to be wary. He'd suspected something about Sharon from the moment he'd met her. He'd kept it to himself for quite a while, but when it got close to the wedding day, Paul had taken the initiative and started digging. What he found was a trail of lies. Alex had let his heart cloud the issue when it had come to Sharon, and he'd come close to paying for it dearly.

"It's not exactly a neat and tidy situation. I met a woman tonight, but only because I hit a patch of ice and nearly ran into her with my car. I'm at her house right now. I just want to make sure there aren't any surprises I should know about. She's lovely. I'd like to ask her out, maybe take her to dinner. But there's also something about her that seems off. I'm not quite sure what it is."

A few moments of silence played out on Paul's end of the line, and Alex knew he was thinking, hard. "Off in what way? I don't want you to be unduly paranoid because of Sharon. The vast majority of people are mostly honest."

"Mostly?"

"We all tell little lies. The question is how little."

Indeed. "Do you think you should look into it?"

"It can't hurt. What's her name?"

"It's Joy Baker. She's from Santa Barbara."

"California, I take it."

"That's what I assumed."

"Can you tell me anything about her family? Does she own any businesses?"

"I'm afraid I don't know anything about her family other than she's not related to the Bakers in Denver. And oddly enough, Joy Baker is a baker."

Once again, Paul was dead quiet on the other end of the line. "Okay. Got it. I'll look into her and give you a call tomorrow."

Three

Joy climbed into the bed she'd been fantasizing about during her trudge up the hill. It was just as heavenly as it had been the night before, and the night before that. This bedroom was gorgeous, and it wasn't even the master bedroom. Joy couldn't stomach the idea of taking Mariella and Harrison Marshall's room. She was already pushing things far enough.

She'd instead chosen their daughter Elana's room, with its beautiful cherry wood sleigh bed and richly colored tapestry carpet in shades of gold, cream and taupe. There was a gas fireplace in the corner of the room, lit with the simple flick of a switch. The flames would probably cast a golden glow and warm the entire room, but Joy was too nervous to turn it on. Windows spanned one wall overlooking the back of the property, which had a stunning view of the seemingly never-ending mountain vista. Being in this bed felt like being on top of the world.

The snow was still coming down. Joy picked up her phone and pulled up the weather app. They were predicting an unusually heavy snowfall overnight. It took a lot of snow to shut things down in this part of Colorado, but the reality was that the Marshall estate was at the very top of the mountain. Even if life was normal down in town, it would take a while for plows to make their way up here. Rafe had told her as much when he'd given her the keys to the house.

Bad weather or not, there was no way she'd be able to get to work tomorrow. Not with Alex and his 24-hour timeline, courtesy of Dr. David. She still couldn't believe she'd practically met a celebrity while she was wearing her pajamas. The Marshalls had lots of famous friends, some just as well-known as Dr. David, but she'd certainly never had a conversation with any of them.

She dialed the number for her boss at the bakery. "Hey there," Bonnie answered. "I take it you're calling to chat about this lovely bout we're having with Mother Nature?"

Joy smiled and sat back against the pillows. "In part, yes. But even if the weather cooperates, I don't think I can come in tomorrow. I had a small accident when I came home and the doctor wants me to rest for 24 hours. I'm sorry if that leaves you in the lurch. I think you know how much I hate to miss work. I love working at the bakery." *And I don't want to jeopardize my job.*

"I hope it's nothing serious."

"The doctor doesn't think so, but he's not entirely sure I didn't hit my head. That's why he wants me to lay low."

"What in the world happened?"

Oh, nothing. Just a super handsome man flew down

a mountain and almost killed me. "I slipped and fell. Stupid snow."

Bonnie clucked her tongue as if she was scolding Joy. "Ouch. Well, I wouldn't worry about work tomorrow anyway. I'm not sure we'll be able to open on time, and even then, I'm not sure we'll have any customers. This storm is supposed to be pretty bad. I think it's best you stay inside and recuperate. We'll see you on Thursday if all is back to normal."

Joy breathed a huge sigh of relief. Bonnie was a wonderful boss. After Mariella Marshall, this was one life change Joy was glad for. "Thank you so much. I really appreciate it. I'll be in touch. Stay safe."

"You, too."

Joy hung up and settled back in bed, her mind zeroing in on her other problem—Alex. It would've been so nice to stay up and chat with him, but he asked too many questions. It took a lot of effort to think about the ramifications of every answer she gave, and she knew it made her come off as someone who was hiding something. She didn't want to be that person. She was horrible at being that person, but such was the situation she'd gotten herself into.

Part of her wished she never would've given him a fake last name. It set a bad precedent, and she'd done a ridiculously bad job with it, to boot. *Baker? Seriously?* It was the first thing that had come to mind, a perfect illustration of how ill-equipped she was to go around the world being anyone other than herself. Luckily—or unluckily, depending on how you looked at it—she would only know Alex for a short time. Twenty-four hours. He'd never have to know she'd fibbed a few times. It certainly wasn't hurting anyone.

Despite her inability to lie for hours at a time, she would've liked to have talked to Alex more and at least find out about him. She was a naturally curious person, and he'd been almost as dismissive of her questions as she'd been of his. He hadn't made a big deal of his occupation, but if his car was any indication, he had to be an important guy… She didn't like the idea of snooping, but maybe one internet search wasn't too nosy. He *was* sleeping in the same house as her, after all.

She pulled up the web browser on her phone and typed in Alexander Townsend, Chicago, Illinois. As the results came back, it quickly dawned on Joy that she was in over her head. He wasn't merely Alexander Townsend. He was Alexander Townsend III. Joy had never been acquainted with someone with roman numerals after their name. Ever. Judging by the bio and photos that came up, her hunch about Alex being somebody had been absolutely correct.

The Townsends were one of the wealthiest families in Chicago and had resided there for decades. They were old money personified—houses all over the world, expensive vacations, lots of heavy political ties and famous friends. As she scrolled through the stories about Alex though, she learned that he was generating his own new money. He was responsible for taking Townsend & Associates Investments to a whole new level of success. According to several business publications, he was doing so with aplomb. Good for him.

Joy clicked on Images and she was glad no one was watching her while she did this. She got all tingly and hot-faced just from seeing pictures of him. She needed to have her head examined—it wasn't as if she hadn't just had the chance to look at him as much as she liked.

Most of the photographs were from big social events and fund-raisers, the theater, fancy dinners. He was in a suit in many of them, a tux in a few, always dashing and impeccably dressed. With every suit came a stunning woman on his arm. After a while, it became her mission to find a picture of him without a woman, but all she could find was his corporate head shot and a few of him leaving or arriving at his office.

Alex's parade of women was ready for the covers of magazines. They were ripe for the society pages or the red carpet—gorgeous hair and makeup, flawless designer gowns, long legs and perfect skin. None of these women, Joy was quite certain, was a baker from Ohio. She might have enjoyed her conversation with Alex, she might have liked riding in his car, she'd had a few minutes of fun with the fantasy of kissing him, but between these photos and her phone call with Dr. David, Joy knew one thing for certain—Alexander Townsend III was 100 percent out of her league.

They weren't even playing the same game.

Her number one job tomorrow, after assessing the road conditions and passing the 24-hour mark, was getting Alex out of this house. Joy knew rich people. She'd worked for too many to not understand precisely how they operated. They stuck together. If Alex found out she didn't really belong here, he'd call the police before she'd even have time to sputter out the long, drawn-out truth. She had to clean her mind of sexy thoughts about him and get rid of him. As to how she was supposed to sleep with this information fresh in her mind, she had no idea. She only knew that she was stuck in this room for now.

The trouble was, she couldn't relax. She liked Alex, but letting him into the house had left her exposed. She was vulnerable, and she didn't like it. Living on the brink did that to a person. If you spent enough days worrying about money or food or shelter, you eventually became territorial. You'd cling to every good thing you could find. She knew this house wasn't hers, and it certainly wasn't home, but it was all she had right now.

Her car was a piece of junk and a money pit. It had left her with eleven dollars in the bank. She had a job, but she wasn't sure she could afford to stay in Vail. And to make things especially heartbreaking, it was Christmas.

Embarrassment over quitting her job with the Marshalls was part of the reason she couldn't go home for the holidays. She couldn't admit to her parents that she'd not only failed, but her failure had been an implosion of her own making. They'd had enough reservations over her culinary career. She didn't need to add fuel to the fire. Her mother had always voiced the loudest concerns. She'd seen her own mother struggle to make ends meet, and she didn't want that life for her daughter. Joy understood, completely, but it didn't change the fact that her grandmother had lit a fire in her that would never go out. Everything about cooking appealed to Joy—the creativity, the connection to family, the sights and smells, the ability to bring pleasure to someone's life. There was absolutely nothing better than having someone eat your food and express their approval.

The other reason for not going home loomed like a dark cloud—her ex, Ben. Her parents had protested Joy's decision to attend culinary school, but Ben had flown into a rage. He'd never liked any sign of Joy improving her lot in life. He liked her best when she was down, when she was at a disadvantage. Of course, she'd enrolled anyway, because she couldn't bear the thought of *not* cooking, and she wanted to do it well.

She'd worked hard in the school kitchens and studied on nights and on the weekends. She'd been determined to prove to everyone that she could not only be extraordinary at cooking, she could make a life for herself—a big life without worries about money. An important life where people knew her name and regarded her work with high esteem. But as every day went by, and Joy became more immersed in her studies, it became clearer that Ben would not be a part of her life moving forward. He was too controlling. He didn't want what was best for her. Her parents saw it. Her friends saw it. Joy saw it, too, but it had taken a lot of nerve to sever that cord.

His response had been exactly what she'd expected— first rage, putting his fist through a wall. Then he begged her to change her mind, kneeling before her and clutching her hands. She'd cried her eyes out, wishing she could help him but knowing she couldn't. Then, finally, the anger came again, but it was different the second time, hate filled and spiteful. He'd called her trash. He'd said no one would ever love her. He'd said he would never leave her alone.

A judge had granted a restraining order eventually, but it did little good. Ben still drove by the house all the time. Joy would take pictures. She would call the police. Her dad would go out on the front stoop and yell. But in the end, Ben would only ever get a slap on the wrist. Ben had too many buddies in the police department. As soon as she was done with culinary school, she got out of Ohio. She went straight to Los Angeles and took her first job. She didn't look back. She knew Ben wouldn't follow her outside of his little bubble, but that didn't mean he was gone for good. Every holiday, he'd start stalking her parents' house. Hence, another Christmas alone. Someday she'd be able to afford to fly her parents to see her, but that day wasn't coming anytime soon.

Still unable to sleep, Joy got up to go to the bathroom. When she stepped back into her bedroom, there was a knock at the door.

"Joy? Are you okay in there?"

What the hell? Was he out in the hallway listening? Joy did not like overprotective guys. She could take care of herself. "Yeah. I'm fine. Getting a drink of water."

"Okay. I'm sorry. I was just on my way to bed. Good night."

"Good night." Joy headed back to her own bed, knowing what she had to do, even though she dreaded it. Tomorrow, she would thank sweet, handsome Alex Townsend. She'd probably employ her talents and make him a nice breakfast. He had been exceedingly kind to spend the night with her, all because he was worried about her head injury. Then, as soon as the twenty-four hours were up, sexy or not, Alex Townsend needed to go.

She didn't want some guy watching her every move when she was living in a house that wasn't hers, no matter how much he might be Joy's idea of Prince Charming.

Alex woke to the rich, heavenly smell of coffee and sat up straight in bed. He could muster great enthusiasm for his morning hit of caffeine, and knowing that Joy was downstairs making it only added to the appeal. If they were snowed in, he hoped she'd lose that skittish edge. He hoped Paul wasn't going to call him and tell him he needed to hightail it out of there.

Alex climbed out of bed. Outside, there was much

more than a blanket of snow on the ground. It looked as though there'd been an avalanche overnight, leaving behind endless billowing drifts. Alex pulled on the basketball shorts he had in his gym bag.

A few steps into the living room, and he caught a glimpse of Joy in the adjoining open-plan kitchen. His feet felt like they were in cement. He wasn't entirely sure he was, in fact, breathing. She was wearing an off-the-shoulder top that showed off the graceful stretch of her neck and just enough skin to paint a white-hot picture in his head, one that might require visual confirmation at some point. Her glossy brown hair was gathered to one side in a loose and sexy ponytail. She was pulling out a mixing bowl and some other items from the kitchen drawers, doing the most benign of tasks, and yet he couldn't have found her more enchanting if he tried.

"Too bad you don't have a housekeeper here to do that," he quipped, forcing himself to walk with a normal gait.

Joy shook her head and continued working. "I'm perfectly capable of doing this myself. No housekeeper needed."

He liked how independent she was. "I can see that."

"Coffee's on."

"I could smell it all the way upstairs. It's the only thing that could get me out of bed." *That, and the idea that you might be downstairs.* "That mattress is quite comfortable." He watched as Joy stood on tiptoes in fluffy pink slippers, plucking a coffee mug from the cabinet. She smiled when she handed it to him, but there was something about her this morning, again—that edge that left him feeling unsettled. He decided to shake it off and filled his mug from the carafe. He took a sip. It was strong and full-bodied, just how he liked it. "Delicious."

"No cream or sugar?"

He leaned back against the counter. "No way. I avoid that stuff at all costs. I've grown to like black coffee."

Joy visibly shuddered. She scrunched up her adorable nose. "Yuck."

"I'm guessing you don't take your coffee that way."

"Absolutely not. I will die without cream and sugar. And since I will die without coffee in the morning, it's necessary to have all three on hand at all times."

Alex made a mental note that if he ever got to make her a cup of coffee at his place, he would be sure to follow her rules. Making beautiful women happy was one of his favorite pastimes, mostly because it almost always paid off. "Have you checked on the weather at all?"

She nodded at the big-screen TV in the living room, which was on, but the sound was muted. "The storm is tapering off. We're just supposed to get flurries for the rest of the day, but it's going to take a while for everyone to dig out. We got almost two feet of snow."

"Wow." There was his answer—he would definitely be spending the day with her. How did he get so damn lucky? He'd nearly run over a gorgeous, smart, highly successful young woman. Hopefully one without a single skeleton in her closet, or at least nothing of huge consequence.

"I'm sorry you're stuck here in this house with me. I'm sure you have more important things to be doing."

Was his work more important? Technically, yes. But more appealing? Definitely not. "You know, I think a day off is going to be really good for me. I don't take nearly enough downtime."

"Workaholic?"

The last year at Townsend & Associates Investments had been absolutely brutal, but the workload was entirely of Alex's making. He'd been waiting for years to put his own stamp on the company and stop taking orders from his father. He could see now that he might have been overzealous, but he wasn't going to dwell on it. His hard work had paid almost immediate dividends. The money was rolling in and the world of finance was taking notice. Still, Alex had recognized two things over the course of the last twelve months—he never would've been able to work the way he had if he'd been married or had a serious girlfriend, and second, it was already getting old. If he didn't make a change, he'd burn out before his thirty-fifth birthday. "Something like that."

"Yeah. I can relate. I'm always working. But I love it." The wall oven next to the range top beeped. "Oh. Oven's preheated. I'd better get to work on breakfast."

"I hope you aren't going to any trouble. I don't normally eat before lunch."

True horror crossed Joy's face. "Didn't your mom ever tell you it's the most important meal of the day?"

Alex's mom had told him lots of things, but not that. In fact, the question of whether or not to eat breakfast had been answered when he was a young kid. His mother was a morning drinker and he couldn't bear to be around it. So he usually kept to his room until it was time to leave for school. But he wasn't about to share that with Joy. He never spoke of it to anyone, not even his brothers. "Sorry. No."

"Well, you haven't had my scones. I promise you will change your stance on breakfast." She measured out flour, added a sprinkle of salt, and unwrapped a stick of butter, cutting it into small cubes, then scraped that from a cutting board into the bowl.

Alex took a seat at one of the barstools across the kitchen island and watched intently. She was so comfortable and at ease in the kitchen, humming to herself as she worked. This was not a woman with a treacherous past. He was fairly certain of that. "Now what are you doing?"

She had pulled out a fork and was mashing the mixture in the bowl. "Cutting in the butter. You want it in tiny pieces the size of a baby pea. That makes a flaky scone."

"I take it this was part of your classical training?"

"I took a few baking classes, yes. A good chef has to be well versed in everything." She turned and fetched a bottle of milk from the fridge. She added a splash to the bowl and mixed with the fork again.

"You don't measure much. I thought baking was like science."

"Cakes and cookies, yes. Bread and other baked goods are more like art and science mixed together. You need to learn what to look for. You don't want the dough to be too sticky or too dry. With scones, you don't want to overmix. With bread, it's almost the opposite."

"Interesting." He took another sip of his coffee. He enjoyed being with Joy even when she was hesitant to answer his questions, but the times when she was chatty were certainly more fun and interesting.

"I'm sure this is boring to you." She picked up a glass jar that had been sitting with her other baking ingredients. "How do you feel about dried cranberries?"

"Honestly? I never really thought about them enough

to have a feeling one way or the other. But I like fruit, so sure."

"Good. Because I love them." She grinned and shook a handful onto the cutting board, chopped them roughly, then added them to the mix. She then pushed everything aside, sprinkled some flour on the counter and dumped out the dough.

"Now what are you doing?"

She picked up a rolling pin and shook it at him. "Please tell me you know what this is for."

"Depends on your personal preferences in the bedroom."

A smile played at the corner of her lips, making everything below his waist go taut. Finally, he was acting like his normal semi-witty self, not the idiot who asked questions she didn't feel like answering.

"I'm not much for pain," she replied, working on the dough. It was impossible not to stare at her shoulders while she worked. The display was poetry in motion.

"A bigger fan of pleasure?" He took a sip of coffee, happy he managed not to choke on it. Things were escalating, and he liked this new direction.

"Definitely." She cut the dough into triangles, transferred them to a baking sheet, brushed them with cream and sprinkled them with sugar.

"The triumphant return of your good friends, cream and sugar."

"Not a return, Alex. They are a fixture." She smiled, even more effortlessly this time, then put the pan into the oven and set a timer.

Damn, he liked hearing her say his name. Her voice was so sweet and soft. It was hard not to wonder what it might be like to have her moan it in his ear. *Down, boy.*

Normally, the thought of being stuck in a house with nowhere to go would bother him greatly, but not today. He had nowhere he needed to be, nobody he wanted to see, except Joy.

"So tell me why you're here alone in this big house at the holidays. Why not go home to Santa Barbara?"

She busied herself with cleaning up the counters and putting dishes into the dishwasher. "Why aren't you going home to Chicago? You told me yourself that you're close with your family."

There she was again, trying to flip the conversation so they ended up talking about him. Did the modesty she'd shown him last night when talking about her career cover all aspects of her life? Was she simply one of those people who didn't want to talk about herself? "I asked you first."

"I'm not sure you want to hear this. We hardly know each other."

"You can tell me anything. I'm a good listener. I promise."

She sighed, then nodded in resignation. "It's difficult for me to go home. I have an ex-boyfriend who's bad news. If he hears I'm around, he starts looking for me. It's easier if I just stay away." She seemed embarrassed, almost ashamed, and that made him feel horrible about having pushed the issue.

"I'm so sorry. I had no idea it was something so serious."

"It's okay. We all have our stories, don't we? It's not a happy subject. And it's the holidays. This should be a happy time."

Alex had to respect her plea for privacy. "I'm not at home for Christmas because I needed a break from my father and his wife, if that makes you feel any better. They're insufferable. My brothers are both off partying in the Caribbean. Call me old-fashioned, but I want snow at Christmas. I grew up in Chicago. I don't know any other way."

"I'm with you. I have to have snow, too, or it just doesn't seem right."

"I'm not a meteorologist or anything, but I'm guessing you don't get much snow in Santa Barbara."

She shrugged it off. "Oh. Of course. You know. Lots of winter getaways with my parents when I was younger." The timer buzzed. Joy stepped over to the oven and removed the sheet pan. She carefully moved the scones to a plate, then presented them to Alex. The smells that filled the kitchen were unbelievable—warm, sweet, and comforting.

He took a scone from the plate, opened his mouth, but stopped shy of taking a bite. "Wait a second. I don't know if I'm ready for this. What if you end up ruining me for all other scones? Then what?"

Joy brought two small plates and a stack of napkins, then took the seat next to him. "I can't be responsible for other people's shortcomings. If I blow your mind, I blow your mind. Not my fault."

All Alex could think was that his mind was already blown by Joy. He still didn't know what to make of her. She was so down-to-earth for someone who'd been born with a silver spoon in her mouth. Perhaps her decision to pursue her passion had helped to ground her. Or perhaps it was whatever had happened with her ex, a situation he couldn't dare let himself think about too much, lest his temper flare.

"Here goes nothing." His teeth sank into the flaky

pastry. As soon as he got a taste of the slightly sweet treat, he was a goner. It was buttery and rich, but light as a cloud. "Oh, my God. I have never had a scone that good. Not even in England."

She took a bite herself and dabbed at the corners of her lips with the napkin. "Told you so. I don't like to brag, but the customers down at the bakery are always raving about them."

"Customers at what bakery?" He pointed around the kitchen. "You practically have a bakery right here."

Joy coughed, almost like she was choking. Alex patted her back, then hopped up to fill a water glass. "Are you okay?"

Tears were misting her eyes. "Yeah. Just went down the wrong way." She took several long drinks of the water and slapped her hand against her chest.

"Better?"

"Much."

"So what bakery? Do you have your own bakery in town? I thought you were just visiting."

Joy cast her sights away, probably getting ready to be modest again. "I've been working out of the bakery in town. I'm working on a cookbook and it's good to do your research and recipe development when there are people around to test out your work. It's much better than eating it all yourself. I'd be the size of a water buffalo if I ate scones all day long."

"So you have writing aspirations. Sounds like being a chef goes well beyond just cooking for you."

"Definitely. I'm not the sort of person who sits around all day long. I'd like to have my own empire at some point. A little empire, I guess."

"Why would it have to be little? You could definitely

have your own TV show. You're more than beautiful enough to be on camera." Funny thing was, he didn't know her very well, but he could already see her doing those things.

Joy Baker didn't seem like the type of woman who failed at anything.

Four

Joy was taken aback by Alex's supportiveness. Sure, she'd had a lot of people appreciate her work, but very few acted as though her greatest aspirations, her biggest pie-in-the-sky dreams, might come true. And he thought she was beautiful? Alex was not only accustomed to beauty, he was apparently a big fan, judging by the photos she'd seen last night. The weight of the compliment did not go unnoticed. "Thank you. That means a lot to me. Truly."

"Good. I'm glad." He looked right at her, for long enough that she could feel their connection all the way down to her toes. His eyes were so breathtaking, the most vivid shade of sky blue. It wasn't easy to sustain a direct hit, but what delicious pleasure it was to stand firm and take it anyway. It left her feeling as though she was in the presence of greatness, and that was a wonderful sensation.

"You know, I'm sorry I knocked on your door last night," he continued. "I didn't mean to intrude. I just happened to come up the stairs for bed and I heard you up and about. This house is so quiet, it's hard not to hear."

So he hadn't been eavesdropping or checking up on her—he'd been concerned. She needed to stop being so silly. Every guy was not Ben. Alex wasn't even close. Hell, he'd expressed more enthusiasm for her dreams and pursuits in the last five minutes than her ex had been capable of showing in a lifetime. "Please. Don't worry about it. I'm thankful you were worried enough about me to stay the night. Most guys would not do that."

"The way I see it, I'm spending my day with a gorgeous future celebrity chef. I definitely won't get bored or go hungry. I'm not exactly suffering here." He picked up his coffee mug and took a sip, delivering a clever look that left her breathless. Alexander Townsend was supremely confident in everything he did. Probably why he was so tempting to spend time with. He set down his mug and raised his arm, giving his armpit a whiff. "Although you might be suffering soon, unless I throw in some laundry. I had some gym clothes in my car, but that's about it."

She hadn't considered that. "My friend's son has a whole closet full of clothes in your room. You're about the same build." She knew she'd made a mistake as soon as the words left her mouth. What was she doing? Offering to loan out Luc Marshall's clothes?

"Do you think he would mind?"

What was she supposed to say to that? "Of course not. He's a really good guy." He wasn't really. He was nice enough, but would he loan his clothes to a stranger? Joy doubted it, but she couldn't renege on the offer now.

"Any port in a storm, right?"

Joy glanced out the window. The sky was still gray and unsettled. "I'd say this weather definitely qualifies."

"Lead the way then."

With every step up the stairs with Alex, Joy's pulse began to pick up. She liked Alex. She liked him a lot. He'd been incredibly kind to her, and even when she'd worried that he might be getting nosy, she'd learned that he was being nothing of the sort. Did he like her the same way? And if he was interested, would they have a chance to pursue anything? She didn't know how long it would take a plow to get up to their house and clear the driveway, but Rafe had made it sound as though it might take a day if the weather was bad. At the very least, she hoped she'd get a parting kiss. She needed more happy remembrances of nice guys. There hadn't been nearly enough.

Now that they were alone in Luc's room, she had to admit that she was more than a bit curious about Alex and what his demeanor might be like in a romantic situation. He had this very smooth veneer, but there was an underlying wit that had her intrigued. He also had a tender and sweet side. After all, what man comes back in a snowstorm to check on a woman he hardly knows? So the question was, where did the passion lie inside Alexander Townsend? And how much was there? What would his kiss be like? Soft and polite? Or would he skip right to the white-hot part, where things became frantic, hands were everywhere, and clothes started disappearing?

Alex came up behind her and put his hands on her shoulders. "Ready?" He stepped around her and made his way to the closet. His touch was gone entirely too soon, but he left behind a lasting heat, like he'd branded her. She couldn't help but notice that the bed was rumpled, bedding piled up in a heap. There was something so intimate about the sight, it sent flickers of electricity along Joy's spine. Did the sheets still hold his warmth? Did they smell like him? A very big part of her wanted to experience the fantasy of being with Alex, have him take off her clothes and pull her down onto the mattress…put his manly hands all over her and give her the ultimate snow day.

Alex flipped on the closet light and stepped inside. Joy followed. The walls were lined on three sides with hanging clothes and rows of shelves topped with neatly folded garments. A round, tufted leather ottoman sat in the middle of the room. Why anyone needed so many clothes in a vacation home was beyond Joy. Plus, she had to wonder about the logistics. What did Luc do if he was getting dressed in Santa Barbara and remembered that his favorite shirt actually lived in Vail? Maybe he had two or three of everything.

"What do you think you need?" Joy watched as Alex perused the findings.

"Just a pair of jeans and a sweater for now." He glanced back over his shoulder at her, flashing her a sly look. "I sleep in the nude, so I don't need any pajamas."

Between that and the rolling pin remark in the kitchen—was Alex leaving her a trail of sexual bread crumbs? Did he want her the way she wanted him? And if so, who would be the first to give in, break the ice, and just kiss the other person? "It looks like the sweaters are there on the shelves. It looks like the jeans are hanging next to them." She sat on the ottoman, trying not to think about the fact that if Mariella Marshall could see her right now, Joy would never again work in the culinary world. Mariella was just that vindictive.

Joy instead tried to soak up the moment, being in this luxe setting with Alex. This was as close as she'd ever come to winning the lottery.

He pulled a chocolate brown sweater from the shelf and checked the label. "One hundred percent cashmere. Good. I can't stand wool. And it's a quality maker as well. This should work." Alex whipped off his T-shirt and tossed it onto the ottoman. It landed right next to her.

Joy swallowed hard, staring at the garment, preparing herself to look while her brain was telling her she was an idiot if she didn't hurry up. She planted her hand on the ottoman and crossed her legs, eying him as he threaded the sweater over his head. Wow. Alex was…built. Much more so than any other man she'd been fortunate enough to see without his shirt. She didn't need to touch him to know he was firm, but damn if her palms weren't itching to conduct a thorough inspection. He was solid. His pecs were defined, his abs a ladder of muscle. She wasn't about to tear her eyes away, but then he poked his arms into the sleeves and tugged down the hem. The heavenly vision disappeared far too fast. But she'd seen enough to know she wanted an eyeful a second time. And a third.

He looked down at her. "Well?"

Joy was finding it hard to breathe. "It's nice. That color is nice on you." That part was true. The warm brown was the perfect counterpoint to his steely blue eyes. It was like they were meant to go together. Fire and ice.

"It's a little snug in the shoulders."

"Yeah. You're a lot more muscular than I had guessed." She had definitely underestimated his build as compared to Luc.

"You guessed?" He cocked an eyebrow at her.

Her face flamed with heat. "Of course I did. You needed clothes and I was just thinking that the guy whose clothes you're borrowing is tall. Like you. And he's, you know…" She drew a line in the air to match the angle of his shoulders, hoping this would somehow illustrate her point and make her seem less hopelessly distracted by his beautiful body. "He's broad like you, too. But he's not anywhere near as, you know, built."

"So I could take him in a fight. That's what you're telling me." He winked and laughed. "Kidding."

You could take me in a fight. I would hardly fight at all. What had happened since she'd walked into this closet? She was struggling to keep up.

Alex pulled a pair of jeans from the shelf and she quickly realized what was coming next. She wanted to stay, but she didn't. Whatever shred of prim and proper resided in her body was telling her to clamp her eyes shut or get out of there. She popped up from the ottoman. "I'll let you finish on your own. You don't need me here." The next logical step was to walk right out of that closet. But her feet apparently wanted to stay for the show because they wouldn't move. Perhaps they'd cut a deal with her eyes.

He undid the button on his own jeans and stepped out of them. "I'm not shy, if that's what you're worried about."

Yeah, I'm beginning to understand that. "I'm not worried about anything."

Except that she was worried this was all a ruse. That it wasn't real. She didn't belong in this house or in this world or with this man. Hell, he didn't even know her real name.

He zipped open his gym bag and pulled out a pair of

black boxers. Her feet were just going to have to cooperate with her exit strategy. She pivoted on her heels and stared at one wall of Luc's clothes, everything hanging so neatly, so perfectly. There had to be tens of thousands of dollars of clothing in here, just waiting for the odd weekend when its owner would show up, but that excess wasn't enough of a distraction from Alex. It was impossible not to wonder about his state of undress. Just thinking about it made her body temperature spike a few degrees.

"It's okay to look now. I'm not naked anymore."

She turned back, but her face felt as though she'd just had a steam facial. "Oh. Okay. I just wanted you to have your privacy."

"I don't know you particularly well, but you seem on edge." He stepped into Luc's jeans, and she stole a look at his legs, which were as much a marvel as the other parts of him she'd been privy to—solid, with uncommon curves and contours. Somewhere there had to be a block of marble waiting to be carved into his likeness. If any man should eventually become a statue, it was Alex. "I hope it's not me. I hope I'm not making you uncomfortable."

"No. You're not. I'm fine. I've always been wound a little tight." The chronic worrier. If she ever got to a point in her life where she didn't have a care in the world, she had no doubt she could come up with new concerns. It was just the way her brain was wired.

He straightened the pockets of the jeans by stuffing his hands inside, then folded up his own clothes. "All better. I'll probably take a shower later."

A shower. Sounds nice. "Oh, sure."

He clamped his hand on her shoulder and gently kneaded. She was still in her PJs, not wearing a bra.

The heat of his hand sent a sizzle through her body that made her nipples tighten. Her shoulders caved in, if only to hide her body's response to him.

"You sure you're okay?" His voice was so deep and rich, it only made it harder to stay wedged in reality.

She nodded, hoping the movement would make her feel less out of place. She desperately wanted to feel at ease around him. She wanted whatever invisible barriers were between them gone. "Yep."

"So what should we do now? We have at least a whole day stuck in this house together."

He was now using both hands to massage her shoulders. It felt so good, his fingers so strong and insistent, she wanted them all over her body right now. She wanted more than anything to close her eyes, drop her head to one side, give him access to her neck, beg him to slip her top off her shoulder. With the two of them alone in this big, beautiful house, it seemed like the best use of their time to just tear each other's clothes off and fall into bed.

"I don't know. You have any ideas?" she muttered. *Just kiss me.*

"Well, it's nearly Christmas and it's a little sad that there are zero decorations up in this house. How are you going to get into the holiday spirit?"

That was quite literally the last thing on her mind. This year, December 25 was simply going to be the day after the twenty-fourth and before the twenty-sixth, except it would at least be a day off. "I don't even know where we would find decorations or if they have any."

"So, we'll look."

"Doesn't that seem a little bit like snooping?"

"I doubt your friends would trust you with their enormous house unless they felt totally comfortable with you using it. Nobody wants someone they care about to spend Christmas alone with no holiday cheer."

Why was it so easy for him to convince her of things that were essentially very bad ideas? Up until he'd arrived, she'd done her best to leave behind zero trace of herself while she was here. "Okay. I suppose you have a point." She turned, flipped off the closet light, and Alex trailed her out. "I should probably get dressed."

"I don't know. I'm a big fan of the pajamas." He smiled and she thought she might melt into a puddle right there on the carpet. The bed was only paces away. He'd hardly have to do anything to have her. *Get your head out of the clouds.* She had to be sensible. That would make for a less dramatic crash back to earth whenever Alex Townsend walked out of her life.

"I think I'll go for more traditional attire today if that's okay with you."

"Whatever you think. You're in charge."

Alex hung out in the living room, watching TV for the road conditions, while Joy took her shower. The general consensus from county authorities was to stay inside and let them clear the snow. Alex didn't have a choice anyway. They wouldn't hit the 24-hour mark until that evening, and his Bugatti had too little clearance under the car body to make it through any snow at all. He'd toast the engine before he got anywhere.

His phone rang. It was Paul, his investigator. Alex hopped off the couch and rushed into the foyer, taking a peek up the stairs before he answered. "Hey. Did you find anything?" He answered in a hushed tone, quickly distancing himself from the stairwell, walking across the living room to the farthest side. If Joy came downstairs, he could end the call if needed.

"Well, I don't know. I found dozens and dozens of women with the last name Baker and the first initial J. But as far as a Joy, the only one I found is a seventy-two-year-old woman from Flagstaff, Arizona."

"Seventy-two? Definitely not the same person." He leaned against one of the mammoth wood posts that held up the vaulted ceiling, looking out the window at the stunning mountain view. All except the highest rocky peaks were blanketed in white. "I don't know that it's really necessary anyway."

"Did you strike out?"

Alex had become especially close to Paul after he discovered the true identity of Alex's former fiancée. It wasn't uncommon for them to discuss personal things. "Strike out? No. But I'm not worried about it anymore. She's a nice, kind person. We're spending some time together." Alex stopped short of disclosing the details of the storm. If Paul knew Alex was stuck in the snow, he'd suggest something ridiculous like bringing in a helicopter to rescue him, even though there was nowhere to land. Alex did not want heaven and earth moved for him. He rather enjoyed the idea that nobody could get to him right now. He had the freedom to spend time with a singular woman, someone completely unlike most people he met. Sure, she had odd habits like constantly turning off lights, but he wanted to trust her. He *could* trust for a day or two. It wasn't like he and Joy were going to get married.

"Okay. Well, let me know if you change your mind. With the internet, it's almost impossible to hide, but some people are just squeaky clean."

"Are you worried that you couldn't find her?"

"I'm only worried if you are. Worry is driving all over town because you have a five-year-old grandson who has to have an action figure for Christmas that's impossible to find."

Alex laughed quietly, realizing how stupid this all was. It was the holidays. And he only had a few days with Joy Baker, whoever she was. He should relax and have fun. That was what his brothers had told him before they went off to the Caribbean.

He loved Christmas. He should be enjoying it. December 26 he'd be headed back to Chicago. He wasn't sure how long Joy was staying, but regardless, her life was in Santa Barbara, which was a world away from his. "Definitely don't worry about my stuff. As for the action figure, go on one of those online auction sites, pay whatever outrageous price somebody wants, and be done with it. I'll foot the bill."

"Are you serious?" Paul asked. "You don't have to do that, Alex. You pay me well."

"I could always pay you better. Seriously. My treat. I just want you and your family to have a merry Christmas."

"You're the best. You know that?"

All Alex could think was that Paul was the best. He'd saved Alex's hide two years ago. "You're worth it. I'll catch up with you after Christmas, okay?"

"Deal."

Alex got off the phone just as Joy walked into the living room. The notion of a woman making his heart race made him feel like a teenager all over again, but damn, she did exactly that. She smiled softly and wandered toward him. She was wearing a fluffy white sweater with a deep V-neck and a white tank top with skinny straps underneath it. The sweater fell off her shoulder even more easily than her pajamas. She had such beautiful bone structure—her collarbone and shoulders begged to be touched. That moment in the closet was still fresh in his mind. He enjoyed giving a woman a neck rub, but he'd mostly had a hard time letting go. All he wanted to do was touch her.

"More work?" Joy asked. "Being the boss must suck."

He laughed and shook his head, advancing on her, finding himself so drawn to her it was ridiculous. There was something very freeing about the fact that he'd decided not to look into her background, to just trust her. This might be a good way for him to regain his footing when it came to women. An experiment of sorts, which was perfect since it had a logical conclusion—the day he'd leave for Chicago.

"I was just catching up with one of my employees, but no more work calls today. It's our snow day and I'd like to have some fun."

She smiled sweetly. "Honestly? I could use some fun, too. It's been a really long time since I've done anything like that."

"Perfect. Then let's go hunt for Christmas decorations."

"Project Snooping is underway."

"Don't call it snooping. We're merely attempting some necessary seasonal redecorating."

"If you're lucky, I might make Christmas cookies this afternoon."

He patted his belly. "Between scones and cookies, I'm going to need to find some way to work off all those extra calories." He hadn't planned on the naughty overtones of the statement, but he meant it.

"Maybe a snowball fight?"

He grinned at her. She'd saved him from himself. "I'm not sure you want to challenge me to that. I have a pretty killer arm. I played baseball in high school and college."

She smirked and shrugged her one naked shoulder, making everything in his body a little tighter. "I'm sure I can kick your ass in a snowball fight. I have extensive experience."

"Growing up in Santa Barbara?"

"Nope. Just lots of wintry vacations like this one."

"Oh. Right. Of course. My parents used to take us skiing all the time. That's how I fell in love with Vail. Did you used to come here often?"

"Actually, this is my first time. We used to go other places." She slipped her sweater back up onto her shoulder, taking away the view he'd been enjoying so much. "Aren't we supposed to be looking for Christmas stuff?"

For someone who hadn't been that eager to pursue this project in the first place, she'd sure changed her tune. "Yes. Where do you think we should start?"

"I think there's a storage space downstairs. No clue if there's an attic."

"I vote for the path of least resistance. Lead the way."

Off Joy went, and Alex followed, down a set of steps just off the main staircase. They took a turn, the stairwell flooded with light from an arched window, then down another five or six steps to a hall that opened up into a railed walkway overlooking a beautiful indoor pool area with a fireplace and a hot tub at one end. "Wow. This is amazing."

Joy shot him a look over her shoulder. "I know. Right? And to think this is just their vacation home. I don't think they end up coming here more than once or twice a year at most. It seems like such a waste."

Alex got what Joy was saying. There were certain excesses that came with wealth that were, well, silly. "Someone should be here enjoying this all the time."

"I totally agree. I bet that pool and hot tub haven't been used in a year."

"You haven't used it while you were here?"

"No. I've been too busy, I guess."

She stopped at the end of the walkway, then they headed down some circular stairs, ending up on the pool deck, which was covered in honed flagstone. The snow was piled high against the windows and a pair of large glass patio doors. "We're going to have to change that. We can't let the amenities go to waste. Especially that hot tub. I'm telling you right now, later today, that has our name written all over it."

"Is that your way of getting me into a bathing suit?" Joy asked.

"If it is, and I admit to it, how does that affect your willingness to do it?"

She smiled and shook her head, a breathy laugh rushing past her lips. "You're terrible. You know that, right?"

"What? You're a beautiful woman and we're stuck in this big house in a snowstorm. I'd have to be an idiot not to try."

"I'd have to be an idiot to not want you to try. At least a little."

Bingo. Things were definitely looking up. "But just so you know, I will always be gentlemanly. Always."

"Good. I like gentlemen."

"But even a gentleman wants a kiss."

She slanted her head to the side and raised her eyebrows at him. Was she considering it? He wanted to study her velvety brown eyes, but the reality was that her lips, so full and pouty, were the main attraction right now. "And a lady reserves the right to tell a gentleman that she might make him try a little harder."

"Exactly how hard?"

"If we're going to discuss hardness, I'm going to need you to buy me a drink first." She knocked into his chest with her elbow and pointed to an alcove at the back corner of the pool area. "I think the storage rooms are back there."

Alex was stuck there for a moment. Every thought he'd had before about Joy being different from other women he knew? He'd been right on the money.

He caught up to her quickly. The first room they found was full of pool equipment, but the second room contained all sorts of cardboard boxes and plastic storage tubs. "Makes you wonder why they'd store so much stuff if they only spend a few days a year here."

"It looks like they have a lot of winter gear."

Alex scanned the room. "There. Christmas." He walked over to the boxes and opened one. Inside were gold garland and boxes of ornaments. "Yes. Decorations. There's even an artificial tree."

"I don't want to do anything too over the top."

"Think of it this way. The harder we work, the more time we'll need in the hot tub."

She lifted a box while rolling her eyes, but he could see that smile she was trying to hide. "Keep trying, Alex. Just a little more."

Five

Joy plopped down the plastic tote she'd brought up from the storage area. Thoughts of dips in the hot tub with Alex and gentlemen wanting kisses danced in her head. Time had stood still after he'd said that…and she'd been sure he was going to actually do it. But he hadn't. And then she'd had to go and be coy about it. Waiting was not her strong suit.

Of course, she could have made the first move, but that just wasn't her, even when she was not a shy person. Call her old-fashioned, but she wanted him to do it. And when he hadn't, and he'd only talked a big game, she'd felt obligated to give him crap about it. But maybe she'd scared him off. That was *not* her intention.

"Should we start with putting together the tree you found?" she asked. "No telling how long that's going to take."

Alex opened the box. "I'd rather have the real thing, but this should be nice enough."

"I love the smell of a real tree. It instantly puts me in the Christmas spirit."

He pulled out the metal stand. "Where do you think we should put it? By the fireplace?"

"Sounds good." She watched as he placed the stand and the bottom section of the tree. "I can't even think of the last time I decorated for Christmas. It's been a while." It was the truth. She'd been working so much over the last several years, she hadn't had the time. Plus, living with the Marshalls had meant actual servants' quarters—cramped and not holiday-worthy. "I used to love it so much when I was a kid. Trimming the tree with my parents and my sister, listening to them fight while they untangled the lights. We would drink eggnog and listen to Christmas music. It was so great."

Alex just stood there, another section of the tree in his hands, branches sticking out every which way. It was almost like he couldn't quite compute what she'd said. "Sounds like your parents were committed to giving you a normal childhood. Our Christmas was nothing like that."

"It wasn't?" How could that possibly be true? Judging by his family's history in Chicago, surely he'd had a charmed childhood.

He shook his head and pressed his lips into a thin line as he dropped the next section of tree into place. "No. My parents had someone come in and do the decorations for us. There was a new theme every year, so we never had any favorite ornaments. My brothers and I didn't even know what to look forward to. One year my mom decided on a Miami-themed Christmas. We had aqua tinsel and pink flamingos everywhere."

"Oh, no. That sounds decidedly un-Christmas."

Alex shrugged. "I don't blame her. She was trying to please my dad by being the ultimate wife and mother. He was the one who insisted on putting on a big show. They hosted a huge party on Christmas Eve every year and their friends all came and drank too much and talked about how much money they had."

Joy couldn't even fathom it. Not a cent of his family's money had been used to build beautiful memories at the holidays. What a shame. "I'm so sorry."

"The worst part was they used to make us wear these hideous red plaid bow ties. My brothers and I just hated the whole thing. We couldn't wait until Christmas morning." Finally, he put the last section of the tree in place and began connecting the cords for the lights.

"Lots of presents under the tree, I'm sure."

"It wasn't even that. It was more that it was the one day of the year where they were nice to each other. The strain of the party was gone. My mom was distracted enough by my brothers and I that she didn't tend to drink. It was the only time we were ever really a family. There was just a whole lot of unnecessary hoopla leading up to it." He plugged in the tree and the white lights came to life. "Voila. Instant Christmas."

She smiled. It was a little thing, but having a tree up really did deliver a welcome dose of cheer. "It's so pretty. It'll look even better when we put the ornaments on it."

Joy handed Alex a box of glass ornaments in festive Santa and snowman shapes, painted in bold colors. She took a package of gold and silver metal icicles. They stood side by side, her shoulder coming up to about his armpit. The tree was small. It was hard to decorate without touching each other. Their hands kept brushing. Their elbows kept knocking.

"You're not distributing the ornaments evenly," Alex said. He scooted around her from behind, placing his hand at her waist for a moment, sending a ripple of excitement through her.

"Wow. Somebody is a little particular about the Christmas tree." She bumped her hip into him. His eyes flashed with mischief. Joy felt as though her entire body was on fire.

"I'm only particular because I haven't had the chance to do this in two years."

That seemed like an awfully specific number. "Let me guess. Girlfriend related?"

"Worse. Former fiancée."

She'd seen a mention of a broken engagement in her online snooping, but Joy assumed that was par for the course with a man like Alex, a man who had no shortage of women in his life. "Ah, so you were more deeply invested. Had to decorate for the holidays."

"Of course. She was really into it. Had my apartment all decked out. Unfortunately, it ended and my enthusiasm for doing this on my own has been lacking since then."

"I bet it was nice while it lasted." Joy had a burning need to ask him more, but she didn't want to pry. Not when they were having fun.

"It wasn't. *This* is nice," Alex said. Again, his voice was doing funny things to her, making her chest flutter. "I think the tree might tip over if we load it down with any more ornaments. We need one of those things that goes around the bottom."

"A tree skirt." Joy flipped open another box and dug around. She didn't come across what they were looking for, but she did find a suitable substitute. "This is probably meant to go on the mantle, but it'll work in a pinch." She pulled out a long swag of gold and red brocade with tassels at both ends. She held one in each hand and gave them a little twirl like a burlesque dancer. "I can do a show later if you get bored."

"Have I mentioned that I'm really bored? Things around here are chronically dull. I'm going to fall asleep unless someone entertains me."

Heat plumed in her cheeks. "You're such a flirt." The truth was that *she* was being the flirt. She desperately wanted to kiss him. She was tired of the notion of anyone trying harder or waiting longer. "Are you always like this?"

He shrugged and took one end of the swag from her. "Never. You must bring it out in me."

Yeah, right. Joy wasn't about to believe that for a second, but she did love that he wanted to create an illusion that he did things with her that he'd never done with anyone else. There was something so sexy about it, she felt light-headed.

They crouched down by the tree and wrapped the festive fabric around the base. Alex's knee was touching hers. Their shoulders brushed. They were so close she was aware of the tempo of his breaths and found her own body wanting to fall into the same rhythm. "Works like a charm."

"You're the real charm." He turned to her, his lips a heartbeat away. Everything in that library-like house became even more quiet and still.

She didn't want to put up barriers, but there was a part

of her that was naturally defensive. She just wanted one more sign that this would be okay. One more clever bit of convincing. "You should talk. You and your flirting."

"I'm just wondering if you're ever going to take the bait."

She didn't give herself another second to question whether she should do this. She'd never have a better opening than the one she had right now.

She dropped to her knees, grasped his shoulder and leaned in for a kiss. His lips were soft and warm. She reveled in that glorious instant when everything was new.

Her eyes fluttered shut and he leaned in, also on his knees. She inched closer, pressing against him—stomach, chest and lips. His fingers threaded into her hair and he gathered it at her nape, cupping the back of her head. His hand urged her to deepen the kiss, their tongues getting eagerly acquainted. She pushed her hips to meet his and felt that magical moment when he got harder.

He eased them down onto their sides. The carpet was so thick and plush, Alex all firm muscle and a capable grasp. He rolled to his back, Joy on top of him. She loved weighing him down, mostly because she knew he was so strong he wouldn't have to work at all to have wherever and however he wanted. She spread her legs wider, her knees slipping to the floor, so she was straddling his hips. She rocked into him and he groaned fiercely, slipping his warm hands up the back of her sweater, sending a bright white thrill through her. This was not only escalating quickly, it was barreling toward somewhere she'd thought it might not go. She wanted him so badly the need burned inside her. Alex might end up making her spontaneously combust.

She planted a hand in the center of his chest and

pushed back, loving the feel of his solid muscle beneath her palm. "I want to see you again," she said. She threaded her fingers beneath that beautiful cashmere sweater only to experience firsthand something far more breathtaking. The landscape of his torso was a sight to behold, especially as he arched his back, raised his arms, and let her push the sweater past his head. She spread her hands across his chest. Every inch of him was rock hard, except of course, his lips. They were soft and welcoming and she sought his kiss again, if only to get lost in how heavenly it was.

"This isn't fair," he muttered against her mouth. "You got to see me. I haven't seen a single inch of you other than your shoulder and it's been killing me."

She bit down on her lower lip. He was so damn sexy, he only made her want to be free with herself and completely let go. "Do you want to be in charge?"

"Unwrapping presents is the best part of Christmas, isn't it?"

She giggled against his neck as he pushed her until they were both sitting up, Joy's legs wrapped around his waist. His fingers curled under the hem of her tank top and she drew in a sharp breath as he raised that and the sweater slowly, lifting the fabric from her skin, leaving her exposed to him. He flung her clothes aside and placed both hands in the center of her back as he kissed the tops of her breasts, making a trail along the edge of her bra cups. He unhooked the clasp and dragged the straps down her shoulders. He ushered in a new level of intimacy as he cast aside the bra and her breasts were left naked.

Their gazes connected as he lightly pressed his palms against her nipples, rubbing up and down. Her skin went impossibly tight, the heat of blood rushing to her breasts, sending her body temperature skyward. He molded his hands around her, then let go of one side, leaning down and drawing her nipple into his warm mouth. Her eyes couldn't have stayed open if she'd wanted them to—and she did. She wanted to watch, but the feeling was too amazing, too exhilarating, so she decided the visual would have to wait. She rocked her center against his crotch, relishing the unbelievable tension between them.

"Do you have a condom?" she asked between kisses. She knew she was making a leap, but she would've launched herself off a cliff right now for him.

"I don't." He looked at her with the saddest eyes, as if she'd just shattered every dream he had in his head. It was quite possibly the sweetest thing she'd ever seen. "I'm not really the guy who walks around with condoms in his pocket."

"Good. Because I don't want to sleep with that guy." She kissed the corner of his mouth. "Lucky for you, I have some upstairs in my room." It might have been a while since she'd been with anyone, but she had moved to Santa Barbara on top of the world and feeling optimistic.

The smile that broke across his face was nearly as adorable as his broken one moments before. "What are we waiting for?"

She hopped off his lap and stood. It was hard not to notice just how much poor Alex was straining against the front of his pants. Feeling impatient and wanting to put him out of his misery, she grabbed his hand and they stole away upstairs. He followed her into her bathroom and wrapped his arms around her naked waist while she rifled through the drawers, looking for the right cosmetic bag. He was running kisses along her shoulders and along her spine, driving her wild with desire.

"Found 'em." She turned in his arms and flipped the foil packet in her fingers.

"I have never been so happy to see one of those in all my life."

Again, she doubted smooth Alex's words, but she didn't really care. He was trying and that was all that mattered. He gripped her rib cage and kissed her again, pressing her against the bathroom vanity as she tore open the wrapper.

He broke their kiss and unzipped his jeans, shoving them to the floor. Anticipation was working its way through her and now she was feeling like a woman of action more than anything else. She dropped to her knees and tugged down his gray boxer briefs. She wrapped her fingers around his steely length, stroking firmly, marveling at just how ready he was for her. Alex groaned and dug his fingers into her hair. "That feels so good, but I want to make love to you. And those jeans you're still wearing are a definite problem."

She laughed quietly and rolled on the condom, then stood and let him be in charge for a moment, watching as he dispatched her jeans and shimmied her lacy panties past her hips. Finally, there were no more clothes to worry about; there were only frantic kisses now, tongues winding around each other, his hands grasping her bottom, hers roaming the muscled landscape of his back. She couldn't wait anymore. She rose up on her tiptoes and perched on the edge of the bathroom counter, raising one leg until her ankle was on his hip. He positioned himself at her entrance and drove inside at the same moment he pulled her into the deepest kiss yet, strong and passionate. Her body struggled with how perfectly he filled her as she wrapped her other leg around his waist.

He used his ridiculous upper body strength to boost her off the counter, his craving hands cupping her bottom. His thrusts were deep. They were slow. His breaths were short and ragged, but she definitely felt like this was all about her. He was so focused on their kisses, every moan she made was met with more intensity in his touch. The tension was rattling her body, toying with her—it built, then ebbed, over and over again.

She was close—it was as if she could feel it before she came—but when she finally did, it was more than she'd been prepared for. She pitched forward and dug her fingers into his shoulders, clinging to him for dear life, her body grasping his and not willing to let go. He called out and she felt every nuance of his release, heard every subtle gasp as it left his lips.

When the pleasure subsided, he allowed her full body weight to again rest on the bathroom counter. He kissed her softly. "Let me take care of this."

Joy didn't yet have words for what had just happened, so she nodded and walked into the bedroom, climbing into the heavenly bed, sinking into the pillows and curling up under the fluffy duvet. If she persuaded Alex to make love to her here, she might die from too much bliss.

He joined her moments later, slipping under the blanket with her. His warm body quickly found hers and he wrapped his arms around her, kissed her forehead. "That's definitely the best tree-trimming party I've ever been to."

She giggled into his chest, rubbing her nose back and forth against his smooth skin. "Very funny. Technically, we still have work waiting for us downstairs. We have to put away those boxes."

"Compared to what I would normally be doing today, what's waiting for me downstairs is nothing." He tucked her hair behind her ear and left a peck on her nose. "Although all I really want right now is what's waiting for me in this bed."

Six

Alex hadn't slept with a woman in his arms in eons, but an afternoon nap? Even better. He turned his head on the pillow, buried his nose in Joy's silky hair, which was in disarray. Now he knew what that spun-sugar smell was—it was Joy. He might not like sugar in his coffee, but this sweet fragrance? He might be able to live off it, at least for a little while. For fun. For the sake of enjoying the company of a beautiful woman, even when they both had different lives, far flung from where they were now. He could enjoy their few days in Colorado together, and parting would be sad, but hopefully still happy. They could be friends. That would be nice.

Alex's stomach growled loudly. It was nearly four in the afternoon, and not only had they spent the last few hours sleeping off the exhaustion of two rounds of making love, they'd skipped lunch. He was starving.

Unfortunately, Joy was still asleep. And mumbling.

"No. Mariella. You're wrong," she muttered. Her voice was halting and breathy, like a drunk who has convinced themselves they're sober. She tossed her head from side to side.

Alex pushed up on his elbow and rubbed her arm. "Joy. It's almost four. Probably time to get up." He kissed her shoulder, but made it quick. If he got too vested in his mouth on her body, he'd never eat.

Her eyes opened halfway, then drifted shut and opened wider. "Wait. What?"

"It's almost four. You slept for more than two hours."

She sat up in bed and pulled the covers up over herself. "I did? Seriously? I never do that."

"Yeah. I think you were having a bad dream, too. You kept talking about someone named Mariella. You were saying no. Who's Mariella?"

"Who? Oh, that's my mom's cat's name."

"Why would you tell a cat that she's wrong?"

Joy shrugged. "She's very vocal. Sometimes, talking to her is the only thing that gets her to stop meowing."

"Huh. Okay." That made as much sense as anything. He guessed. "Can we eat? I can only subsist on scones for so long."

"Of course. I'll make something." She climbed out of bed and grabbed a fluffy white robe from the chair next to the bureau. "I should probably get dressed."

"Up to you. I don't mind you being not dressed."

She smiled and rolled her eyes—so adorable. "I need clothes while I'm cooking. Meet you in the kitchen in ten?" She was being distant now and he didn't want to push her further away. He was starting to understand that distant Joy might just be regular Joy. He didn't like distant Joy as much as fun, carefree Joy, but he wasn't going to worry about it. Food felt like a more pressing issue.

"Sounds like a plan." Alex grabbed his boxers from the bathroom floor and headed across the hall to the room he was staying in for a quick shower. He scrubbed his hair dry with a towel and swiped at the mirror, leaning closer. He was getting downright scruffy, but he never shaved at the gym, so he didn't have his toiletries with him, aside from deodorant. Joy would just have to live with it.

His mind stubbornly wound back to her change in mood after their nap, but he could accept that they'd managed to put themselves in a bit of an odd situation. Sleeping with someone in the first twenty-four hours was rarely accompanied by being confined to the same house. She'd been living here alone, and maybe she was a woman who enjoyed her space.

"Hey," he said to Joy when he reached the kitchen. She was busy digging through the refrigerator. "Do you think we should call someone about having the driveway plowed? Is there a caretaker?"

"No. I think they're just supposed to come as soon as they can."

"Oh. Okay." That seemed odd, but he also lived in a gated neighborhood where things like snow removal were taken care of as part of the homeowners association fees. "What's for dinner?"

"I'm trying to figure that out. Are you okay with chicken piccata? Lemon butter sauce, a little garlic, some shallot. I was thinking I'd make it with a thin spaghetti on the side, maybe some wilted spinach? That's really the only vegetable I have in the house right now other than baby carrots."

"Are you kidding? That sounds incredible. Yeah. Make that."

"Do you want to help?"

"I'm seriously no good in the kitchen. I'll just end up putting paprika in the wrong thing and then you'll hate me forever."

"First off, I could never hate you. Second, if you know what paprika is, you're getting your butt in this kitchen and helping."

Alex had no answer for that. "Okay. But you're going to have to tell me how to do everything."

He stood next to her at the stove top. She leaned closer and kissed him softly on the lips. "Something tells me you'll be a quick study."

There she was again—happy Joy. She was going to be the death of him. That was all there was to it. He'd dated plenty of sexy women, but she was simply off the charts. And perhaps it was just that she was exactly his brand of sexy. Every minute they were together, she managed to do or say something that left him wondering where she'd been all his life.

He followed her around the kitchen as she showed him the proper technique for mincing garlic, breading chicken, and sautéing. It turned out that he'd even been making pasta incorrectly all these years, not that he cooked very often. Don't use oil in the water. Any Italian would have his head for that. The room filled with heavenly smells, and he enjoyed every chance he had to watch her while his hand settled in the small of her back, or she offered him a taste of something and she'd hold on to his arm while she did it.

As good as the meal looked, it really only took about thirty minutes to prepare. They decided to forgo the stuffy dining room, which had seating for at least twenty people. Sitting next to each other at the kitchen island with a bottle of wine Alex had found in the well-stocked wine fridge was plenty romantic for him. Joy had even dimmed the lights and lit a candle.

"This is incredible. Truly." He held out his wine glass to clink with hers. "To the chef."

She smiled shyly. "Cheers. But you did just as much work as I did. There's no big mystery to cooking. Once you learn to trust your instincts, you can just go into the kitchen and have fun. That's what I do."

Trust his instincts. That was something he might be rediscovering with Joy. He still trusted his business instincts, but it was the personal side that had been lagging. She made him so comfortable; it was as if they'd known each other for months. Years, even. "Well, I'm still in awe of your talents, and the scary part is you've shown me so much in a very short amount of time. I can only imagine what mysteries Joy Baker is hiding behind that beautiful face."

"There's no big mystery to me, Alex. I love to cook. I like spending time with you. That's all you need to know."

"I seem to remember something about threatening to kick my ass in a snowball fight. It'd be good to find out what that's all about. Sounds like a lot of hot air to me."

"Snowball fight? Alex, it's dark outside. And cold."

"I know. But I have an idea."

Joy shook her head and took another sip of wine. "If it involves trudging out in the driveway in snow boots and mittens, forget it."

"Nope. It involves putting on your bathing suit and meeting me downstairs."

* * *

Joy stood in the pool area in her bikini, wondering what in the heck Alex was up to. Outside, it was pitch-black. The snow was nearly waist high. "You are certifiable."

Alex was trying to figure out the locks to the tall patio doors. "Half of the fun of a hot tub in the winter is enjoying the cold first. My brothers and I used to do this all the time when we were kids. We had a pool and hot tub in the backyard and we'd run around in the snow, then jump in. It makes the water so much nicer."

Joy was thinking that Alex's back was so much nicer. He was wearing his basketball shorts, which hung a bit low around his hips. He had no shirt on, so she could see every muscle as it rippled and twisted when he flipped through the set of keys she'd given him, trying each one. Everything about what they were doing was crazy…using the house the way they were, putting up Christmas decorations and having sex on the bathroom counter. Still, it was the most fun Joy had had in a painfully long time. The last twenty-four hours might have been the most fun she'd had with a man, ever. Alex, for all of the syllables and roman numerals in his name, was at heart, a playful guy. It was just that nothing about his upbringing, his career, or his past romantic life hinted at any of it. She had to wonder if he felt as though he'd been living half a life. It was hard to fathom given every advantage he'd had, but perhaps it was true.

"Finally." Alex turned the handle and opened one of the patio doors. Cold air rushed in with a forceful gust. The snow that had been piled up against the glass tumbled inside onto the flagstone floor.

"Oh, my God. Alex. It's freezing." Joy wrapped her

arms around her waist and turned her face away from the arctic blast. "And the snow. It's going to make a mess."

"It's frozen water. There's a drain. It's a pool area. It's meant to get wet." He approached her with a huge smile on his face. "And stop being such a wimp. Come on." He took her hand and led her to the open door.

The cold air was more and more bracing the closer she got, but it certainly made her heart race—almost as much as Alex did. "Are we really having a snowball fight?"

"Nah. That doesn't seem very fun. We're just going to run out into the snow, stand there for a minute, and run back inside. Then get in the hot tub."

"In our bathing suits. And bare feet. Right now."

"Right now." He squeezed her hand and lifted it to his lips. Such a simple gesture, but she loved it. For a nanosecond, she couldn't feel the cold.

"Okay."

Alex tore off and Joy hustled to keep up. Her bare legs shuffled into the icy snow, cold shooting up the length of her body, but this was entirely different from being in the snowbank. At least she could breathe. In fact, frozen air filled her lungs readily, but it stung in a delightful way now that she couldn't stop laughing. She was into the snow past her knees. It came to Alex's shins. She hopped from foot to foot, trying to keep warm, not letting go of Alex's hand. They were facing each other, not far apart. His cheeks were bright red, his eyes piercing. Their breaths left their lips in puffs of white.

"Have we been out here long enough yet?" she asked.

He shook his head. "Nope. I'm not dying yet."

"Wait a minute. We have to wait until you're dying? I might freeze to death before then."

"Just a few more seconds." He bobbed his head five or

six times, his hair flopping into his eyes. "Okay. Now."
Still holding her hand, he bolted for the back door.

With their entrance came several cubic feet of snow
all over the floor. Mariella Marshall would literally give
birth to a litter of kittens if she saw this. Joy wasn't about
to ruin the moment with thoughts of being found out.

Alex didn't wait. He hopped down into the hot tub. Joy
took the steps. The water was impossibly hot. Alex sub-
merged himself to his shoulders right away, but Joy had
to ease in slowly, the heat prickling her back and stomach. She held her arms above the surface of the water as
she acclimated herself, gradually sinking down.

Alex had been so right, but she wasn't quite ready to
admit it. Her blood raced through her body. Her cheeks
and lips were still ice-cold. Her body didn't know what
to do about any of it—it only knew that whatever was
going on was exciting.

Alex dipped his hand into the water and ran his fingers through his thick hair, then settled back on the stone
bench, draping his arms over the side of the hot tub.
"Well? Good?"

No longer worried about surviving the freezing temperatures, she now had the chance to admire his chest
and shoulders. Every distinct contour, the way his muscles bulged and dipped, was familiar now, but that didn't
stop her from desperately wanting to touch him. Her
hands were alive with electricity. "Better than good. Fantastic."

"Told you so." He bounced his eyebrows in that cocky
Alex way.

Joy thought she might faint. This was certainly one
of those pinch-me moments, frolicking in the snow
and hanging out in a hot tub with Alex, the impossi-

bly handsome billionaire. "You were right. I fully own up to it. Between your genius at recreational planning, your Prince Charming good looks, and the fancy car, I'm trying to figure out how you're still single."

Half a smile cracked at the corner of his lips, but he quickly adopted a more serious look. The air stood still for a moment while the water swirled around them. Their gazes connected, his icy blue eyes making her feel exposed in a way she not only was willing to admit she liked, but that she also didn't want to end. "I can't figure out how you're single, either. You're literally one of the most beautiful and fascinating women I have ever met."

Alex's words were like a dream come true. Normally a compliment like that might make her blush, or possibly roll her eyes if it wasn't delivered with sincerity. But Alex was not like a normal man. He didn't warrant an everyday reaction. "That's very sweet of you to say. Today has been so amazing." The one thought that wouldn't leave her head at this moment was that she didn't feel like less than Alex. Not anymore. She was in awe of him, but she no longer felt as though they were on uneven ground. The realization made her keenly aware of every frantic beat of her heart.

He held out his hand, his eyes heavy with desire. "Come here."

She'd never followed a request so quickly. She slipped her fingers into his grasp and he tugged her closer through the water. His other hand cupped the side of her face. That single touch had the power to make her melt. His hand was firm and strong against her skin. He leaned closer and she shut her eyes, soaking up the moment when his lips touched hers. His kiss was like heaven, just like the first time, the perfect balance of

strong and soft. She tilted her head to the side if only
to get closer to him. Her lips parted, then his, and their
tongues found each other, winding together in a way that
was now beautifully familiar. Every inch of her body was
on fire now and not just because she was immersed in
the hot water. She had to be closer to him, and the second his arm wrapped around her waist, she shifted herself, placing a knee on the bench and straddling his lap.

He groaned his approval as her legs settled against
his hips and her elbows found his shoulders. Her fingers dug deep into his thick hair, their kiss never breaking. It only intensified. She gently nipped his lower lip
and he got harder between her legs. She rocked back and
forth against him, letting her body take over. His warm
and masculine scent filled her nose, his damp, silky hair
so soft against the tender underside of her forearms as
she dug her fingers deeper into it. His hands raced up
and down her sides, gripping tightly, pressing into her
skin, like he couldn't get enough. And she didn't want
him to go without. She reached back to the nape of her
neck and untied her bikini top. He was immediately on
board with her decision, undoing the tie across her back,
plucking the garment from the water and tossing it onto
the pool deck.

"Much better," he muttered, pulling her into another
deep kiss. His hand molded around her breast, his thumb
riding back and forth across her nipple.

They rocked against each other, her hips involun-
tarily bucking into him. She couldn't get enough and
she couldn't get it fast enough, either. "I want you, Alex."

"Can I say how much I love hearing that?" The words
were delivered straight to her ear, his rich voice only
deepening her need for him.

"You can if you make love to me. But we have to get out. Condoms and water don't mix."

"I realize that." He flattened his palm against her belly and slid his fingers down into the front of her bikini bottoms, finding her apex. "Just relax."

Joy gasped. She dropped her chin and nestled her face into Alex's neck. Her shoulders rolled forward and his hand did his bidding, fingers moving in firm circles. The rhythm did not waver. Round and round. The tension in her hips wound tighter.

"Kiss me," he said.

She dragged her cheek across his stubble, their lips joined, tongues even hotter than the steam swirling around them. The kiss was wild. Brash. Like they were trying to outdo each other, only Alex had the advantage. Joy was under his spell. The strokes of his fingers exactly right, the pressure in the perfect spot. The energy gathering in her belly coiled, mercilessly pulling at the muscles in her thighs. Her breaths frayed. Her mind juggled too much—heat and pleasure and Alex.

The peak slammed into her. Alex broke the kiss. His other hand clutched the side of her neck. His thumb raised her chin. Joy's head dropped back then rolled to the side. A squeak left her throat as the waves kept crashing. He stilled his hand. Her body tightened, then let go. Over and over again. When the final crest faded, she collapsed against his chest. He reined her in with his strong arms. She was as vulnerable as she could be, strength wrung from her body, but she'd never felt safer.

"That was so amazing." She dotted his wet shoulder with kisses, wanting to show her appreciation.

"I loved watching you at the end." One of his hands traced up and down her spine.

"Now we have to take care of you." She was surprised she could feel anything at all between her legs right now, but Alex was even harder than he'd been minutes earlier.

"Upstairs. In your bed. All night long."

She smiled, fighting back a well of sadness inside her. Tonight had been magical, but in Joy's experience, magic didn't last. Soon enough, the snow would be gone, and her real life, the one without Alex, would resume.

Seven

The *beep beep beep* woke Alex from a deep sleep. *What the hell?* His eyelids opened and closed. What was that sound? *Oh, right.* The snowplow. Careful not to wake Joy, he peeled back the duvet, padded down the hall and looked out through the Palladian window visible from the top of the stairs. The telltale scrape of metal against the house's stone drive served as further confirmation—his time with Joy was up. Another hour or so and they would no longer be snowbound.

Which left him with a quandary. He liked Joy. A lot. Last night had been incredible. They couldn't have gotten enough of each other if they'd tried. And they'd tried. They'd even broken a condom, a feat Alex had never before accomplished. Joy hadn't seemed overly concerned. She said she was at the end of her cycle anyway. No need to worry.

That wasn't heavy on his mind, but the calendar was. He was only in town for a little more than a week. Come December 26, he'd be headed back to Chicago. Just enough time to enjoy each other a few more times. The trouble was, he didn't want to seem like he was just after her for the sex, even when there was no blowing out that candle anytime soon. They'd fallen into sync with so little effort it was uncanny. Sex with Joy was fantastic, but it wasn't the only reason he wanted to see her. Never before had Alex wished, at least for a second or two, that he had waited or taken it slower. Even when he couldn't imagine any path other than the one they had traveled together.

The other concern was its own sticking point—feelings. Eight or nine days was just enough time to get attached. Alex was fairly sure he was capable of walking away with few scars. Not none, but few. She would always have a special place in his heart. He knew that much by now. And although he knew so little about her, he did know that while she was tough at times and fiercely independent, there was a sweet side to her as deep as the ocean. No woman cooks for a man the way she did without caring. He didn't want to hurt her.

"Hey. You're up," she said from behind him. Her voice was sleepy and sexy. She was wrapped up in her robe, looking as gorgeous as he could imagine, messy hair and fresh faced.

"Yeah. Good morning." He put his arm around her waist and kissed her temple softly. They settled against each other, both leaning into the railing, watching the back-and-forth of the plow in the driveway.

"Looks like they're digging us out."

"Appears so."

She looked up at him and licked her lower lip, but her expression was difficult to decipher. The trademark Joy wariness—it was the only way to explain it. What made her like that? Was it the ex she'd talked about? Her life, at least the career and family part, all seemed perfect. If anyone was following their bliss, she was. "I'll go make coffee and then I think I'll call the bakery to see if they need me today."

If she was going back to work, that meant he should probably do the same. It was Thursday, after all. He'd turned off his phone and left it downstairs. There was no telling what fresh hell might be waiting for him when he powered it back on. *Back to reality.* "What are the chances of scones this morning?"

A delighted grin spread across her lips. She'd converted him and she would gladly take the credit. "What happened to the guy who doesn't eat breakfast?"

"He's making up for lost time. I had absolutely no idea what I was missing."

She kissed his cheek. "For you, I will make scones. Different flavor, though. I have an idea after digging through the pantry last night." She flitted down the stairs, her hair bouncing behind her. Cooking was her happy place and he envied her for that. For him, work was work. Success brought satisfaction, and there was no question he relished any time he proved his father wrong, but he wasn't drawn to his occupation the way Joy was.

He ducked down the hall into his room and grabbed a sweatshirt, then went downstairs to spend some time with Joy. When they'd been stuck in the house, it had seemed as though time had stood still. Now that the plow was almost done, it felt as though the countdown had begun, their time together had a terminus. And he would've been lying to himself if he said that he didn't want to squeeze everything from it that he could.

Alex didn't put much stock in fate. He believed that a person built their own future, their destiny. But he had to wonder if something else was at work when his car slid down that hill and he nearly ran into Joy. Was she sent to him to help him learn to trust a woman again? He hadn't felt this at ease with someone in years. He hadn't felt an instant connection like this—a bolt from the blue—in quite some time. He wasn't sure the one before this came close to matching what he already had with Joy. So one woman had hurt him…he had to stop feeling as though he was doomed to relive his own history.

He could smell Joy's scone experiment from the staircase, although he wasn't sure what it was exactly. He only knew that whatever it was, it would be good, he'd eat too many, and with snow no longer an excuse, he'd need to drag his ass to the gym today.

"Smell good?" Joy poured him a cup of coffee and handed it to him.

"Amazing. But I can't figure out what it is. Cinnamon?"

She planted a hand on her hip. "Cinnamon. You honestly think cinnamon was my experiment? Give me a little more credit than that."

"It's my inferior olfactory skills, obviously. I'm so sorry." He bounced his eyebrows and took a sip of coffee.

"You can make up for it by raving about the finished product. I think it's going to be pretty damn good." The timer rang and her eyes went wide. "We're about to find out." There was so much pure excitement in her voice, it was contagious. It was impossible to be unhappy around her. She pulled the sheet pan from the oven and plated the scones. She settled into the seat next to him at the kitchen island. "Well? Go for it."

"Aren't you going to have one?"

"I am. I just want to see the look on your face. It's the best part."

A very naughty remembrance crossed Alex's mind. "Just like the hot tub last night."

"If my scones are as good as that, you can just declare me better than Julia Child and we'll call it a day."

"I didn't think it was possible to look forward to baked goods this much." He picked up a scone and took a bite. The texture was just as perfect as the day before, but the flavor was out of this world, and honestly, quite unusual. It was warm and sweet, with a spicy edge. "Ginger?"

"Ginger and…?"

He took another bite, savoring her wizardry with butter and flour, cream and sugar. "Ginger and delicious? I have no clue."

She elbowed him in the ribs. "It's okay. I was trying to stump you. Yes, crystallized ginger, cardamom, and the secret ingredient is a tiny bit of black pepper. Gives it a little zing."

"I love it. It's absolutely brilliant. You should definitely put this in the cookbook."

She tapped her fingers on the counter and stared down at her plate. "Yeah. It's not ready for a cookbook. I need to try it out down at the bakery and see how it goes over."

"You don't trust my taste buds?"

"Oh, I do. I just think there's a chance you might be biased. I haven't slept with any of the bakery's customers."

"I would never let sex get in the way of honesty." Alex was struck by a strong and undeniable realization—he loved the effortless back-and-forth with Joy. He could get used to this.

She got up from her seat and poured herself another cup of coffee. "Do you think you could give me a ride down to the bakery? I can get a ride home from my co-worker, Natalie."

"Of course. But don't you have a car?"

She started cleaning up the kitchen. "Not right now. I've taken a cab a few times, or bummed a ride. I'm afraid to drive one of the family's cars. I'd rather drive something with a little less oomph. I'm kind of an old lady when it comes to driving."

"Yeah, I noticed there's some real firepower in the garage when I put my car in there the other night."

"Too much firepower makes me nervous."

"No worries. I'm happy to drive you into town. But first, another scone."

After breakfast, Alex collected his things, not knowing if he'd be returning to this house. Joy had said not to worry about the sheets on the bed or the towels in the bathroom. She'd take care of it, which he assumed meant the housekeeper would deal with it when she came in to clean. Joy was focused on getting down to the bakery as soon as possible. She seemed almost anxious about it, but Alex understood. He had those days at work, too. Surely, something like a cookbook had to be a daunting task. As far as he knew, she hadn't even found a publisher for it, nor did she have a literary agent. She was thinking about doing it all on her own, which he found amazing.

He and Joy went out through the garage. On the far end, in a bay with two motorcycles, sat a car-sized lump under a tarp. "This family is even more obsessed with cars than mine. Is there another one over there?" Alex pointed in that general direction.

"Just a pile of junk." Joy opened his passenger-side door and climbed in.

Alex joined her. "Why would they have junk in their garage? They should have it hauled away."

"I'll be sure to suggest that."

Alex's phone chimed with a text. "One second. I should check this." It was from his brother Jonathan, a photo of him on the beach in St. Barts with a very young-looking, buxom woman. Wish you were here. Alex shook his head.

"Everything okay?" Joy asked.

"Yeah. Fine. Just my brother's misbehaving in St. Barts. This time of year is big for picking up women, but it's not my scene."

"Not your scene now? Or never your scene?"

Alex wasn't quite sure how to answer this. "I've gone down there with them before, yes. And I did meet a lot of women. But, you know, it just isn't smart. You never know who's going to glom onto you when you have money. And people take pictures with camera phones. Just too much potential for messy situations."

Joy nodded, but her lips were pressed together in a thin line. "I see." She started to rummage in her purse.

Alex set his hand on her arm. "Really. That's not me anymore. That was a long time ago. And surely you understand the need to protect yourself when you have money."

"Of course. Makes perfect sense." She pulled back the cuff of her coat sleeve and looked at her watch. "We should get going. They really need me today."

The drive into town was a relatively quick one, although entirely too quiet for his liking. He should've thought twice before making comments about picking up women in the Caribbean. He pulled over at the far end of Vail Village, one of two main business districts. It was like a charming European village, with cobblestone walkways and quaint shops. Also, no cars, which meant he had to drop Joy off here.

"How far is the bakery?"

"About halfway down. On the left. Have you really not seen it?"

He shrugged. "I probably have and just didn't go in. But now that I know I can get the best scones in town, I'll make a habit of stopping by."

"Thanks so much for the ride and everything. It was fun," Joy said.

Alex put the car into Park. "It was more than fun for me." He turned to face her, but Joy was looking out the window.

"You're right. It was more than fun. It was great. I'll always remember it." Still, she wouldn't make eye contact, and that really amped up Alex's nervousness. How would she react to what he was about to say?

"I'd like to see you again, Joy. Take you out for a real date. Spend some more time together. I don't go back to Chicago until the 26th."

"When Christmas is said and done with your family?" She glanced at him, but only for a second.

"To put it bluntly, yes."

"I'm sorry. I didn't mean it like that."

He shook his head and finally, out of frustration, reached for her jaw and urged her to look at him. Their gazes did more than connect—they locked. This was yet another version of Joy, one he hadn't seen before. She seemed sad. "Would it be okay if I called you?"

She sighed, then nodded. It was like she was resigning herself to something. Alex didn't want her to feel obligated to see him. "Of course it would be okay. I would love it. But I also don't want you to feel like you owe me that, or like you have to say it just because we slept together. It's okay if this is goodbye. I've said it many times. It's a lot better if a guy is just up front about it."

His heart was about to beat out of his chest while he took in her words. So that's what this was. She thought he was one of those guys, the ones who say they'll call, but don't. "I'm not just saying this. I want to see you again and I'd like to call you. I don't want this to be goodbye."

He leaned in and kissed her deeply on the lips. That moment when he felt her resistance melt away was sheer heaven. He couldn't miss out on that again.

She rested her forehead against his, their noses touching. "I don't want it to be goodbye, either." She reached for the car handle. "I guess I'll just say see you later."

He grinned like a damn fool. "Yes. I'll see you later."

She closed her door and he took the chance to watch her walk away, study the particular sway that came with her determined stride. Their kiss was still on his lips, the effect of it still making waves in his body.

Even if it only happened one more time, it would be worth it.

"So? Who's the guy with the fancy car?" Natalie asked the instant Joy came through the door at the bakery.

"You saw that?" Joy had been worried about that, but she'd figured she'd be okay since Alex had to drop her off blocks away.

"I just got in a minute ago. I walked right past his car. I would've waited, but it looked like you guys were talking about something intense."

Joy didn't like calling attention to herself, nor did she like it when someone took notice. Her whole future rested on flying under the radar, earning the money she needed to earn, and getting out of the Marshalls' house. "He's just a friend. You know my car still won't start." It was her car that was the pile of junk under the tarp in the Marshalls' garage. Joy had held her breath when Alex mentioned it. If he'd decided to go look? One glance in the glove box and he would know that it was hers. Or more specifically, Joy McKinley's.

What had she gotten herself into? The whole thing had spiraled completely out of control, and she didn't know what to do about it now. Alex wanted to see her again, and she wanted to see him, too. Badly. It made her stomach wobble just to think about his touch, his proclivity for fun. The kiss in the car had practically seared itself into her memory. But he deserved better. He deserved the truth. He needed to know that the cookbook was a pipe dream, that she was working at the bakery for an actual paycheck, that she was *not* Joy Baker, the baker.

Or maybe it didn't really matter. He was leaving in less than a week and she'd never see him again after that. She hated lying, but sometimes you had to do things to survive. She only had a few more weeks in the Marshalls' house and she didn't have the money for a security deposit on an apartment. She might have to ask for an advance from the bakery or maybe ask to crash on Natalie's couch. Either way, she would keep working to turn things around so she could return to her life as Joy McKinley, distancing herself from her unfortunate history with the Marshall family and putting her career back on track.

"You know…" Natalie looped an apron over her head and gathered the ties behind her back. "My brother is a mechanic. He sometimes fixes cars on the weekend. I could send him over to your place and he could take a look at it. As long as it isn't anything major, he wouldn't charge you much money to get it running again."

That was the exact can of worms she'd been trying so hard to keep sealed tight. She couldn't go around inviting other people over to the Marshalls' house, especially not in this town where everyone knew them. "That would be amazing. Let me see if I can get it to start tonight and I'll let you know. Sometimes it's just being temperamental." Maybe she could look up some possible fixes on the internet. She'd repaired all sorts of things over the years of owning that disastrous car. And if not, she'd figure out something else. She always did. She'd push it back down the mountain if she had to.

Joy and Natalie went to work, cranking out a limited version of the daily menu since the bakery had opened late. They were in charge of pastries and cookies. A whole team of other bakers was in charge of bread, which was a separate undertaking and required getting into the bakery in the wee hours of the morning. They worked out of the larger kitchen in the back.

Joy and Natalie, with some help from Bonnie, their boss, had the smaller front kitchen as their domain. Joy loved it because they could see the customers through a glass window. Customers could also see them, and there was a narrow platform for kids to stand on, so that was part of the fun as well. They would stand with hands and faces pressed to the glass, watching in awe as Joy and Natalie did their magic. Even better was the pure satisfaction Joy got when she saw a customer bite into a cookie or Danish and roll their eyes in ecstasy or smile. Making people happy was the number one reason Joy would never find herself doing anything else.

The shorter workday whizzed by. Natalie gave Joy a ride at three, only this time, the drop-off at the house that wasn't hers was a much quicker affair since Natalie had errands to run. With no snow falling and slightly warmer temperatures, the walk up the hill wasn't quite as difficult, but in an odd way, she missed the fact that Alex wouldn't be speeding down the road, about to slide right into her. It had been the start of something special. Something short, but sweet.

As she walked the final stretch up to the Marshalls' house, she saw it differently. No, it wasn't hers and it never would be. But something good had happened there, and in a world where there just wasn't enough good, she could hold on to that. She had memories to live off of, especially if and when things got tough again.

After her usual long shower, she didn't have the energy to make a real dinner, so she had a peanut butter sandwich and headed up to bed. Alex and work had worn her out. She needed sleep. So badly that she almost didn't answer her cell phone when it rang. But what if it was Bonnie? Or Natalie? A big part of her hoped it would be Alex.

The smile on her face when she saw his name on the caller ID had to have been ridiculous—her cheeks hurt from two seconds of it. "Hello there," she answered, cozying up under the covers.

"You have no idea how nice it is to hear your voice." This was a different version of Alex. Stressed. Not playful and fun. "Seriously. I've been looking forward to this all day."

"Oh, no. Rough reentry after our snow days?"

"Yes. Work sucks, in case you're wondering. My father is impossible. My brothers are goofing off and I'm stuck picking up their slack. I don't even understand why I do it. I could walk away and I'd still be okay for money."

Joy couldn't fathom what that must be like. She'd probably still be working when she was seventy, just like her grandmother had. Still, she knew that Alex worked very hard. Every business article she'd perused had said he was known for his relentless work ethic. "I don't know. I bet you'd miss being busy."

"I'd rather be busy doing anything else. Move to Mexico and run a bait shop."

"Don't drink the water. You'll regret it." She was prepared to say anything to improve his mood. She hated hearing him like this. This was not the guy who'd suggested they go run around in the snow in their bathing suits.

He laughed quietly. "I'd probably smell like fish all the time. Not super sexy."

"I'm sure you'd find a way to pull it off."

"Maybe a surf shop would be better. In Hawaii."

"Sounds nice. Maybe I'll come visit." What a lovely thought…palm trees, blue skies, ocean breezes and Alex. He'd probably walk around barefoot in board shorts all day, ridiculously tan and even more stunning. Now that would be a life. She didn't need some big fancy house, but a dream locale would be awfully nice.

A heavy sigh came from his end of the line. "Is it weird if I say that I miss you? I know we haven't known each other for that long, but I feel like I get you. I had a hundred things I wanted to say to you today."

"You can always text me if you really have something you're dying to say." Joy was sure her smile was about seven miles wide. It surely put the one from the beginning of their conversation to shame. "But no, it's not weird. I miss you, too."

"Tell me what you miss." His rich voice and suggestive inflection was about to lead her off on an entirely different fantasy than the life in Hawaii. Or maybe she should just combine the two.

"What do you want me to say?"

"I mean exactly what I said. I'm a man. I have a horribly fragile ego. We all do. Tell me what you miss."

She had to roll her eyes at that one. Did some men need ego stroking? Absolutely. She didn't believe it about Alex for a second. He was one of the most self-assured men she'd ever met. He walked around as though he had the world at his feet, and by most measures, he did. But telling him that wasn't going to improve his day, and she had a strong suspicion that was what he needed more than anything right now.

"I miss your eyes. They're amazing." *I'd look at them forever if they didn't make me feel so exposed.*

"Okay. I like it. Go on."

She giggled, smiled, and rolled onto her side. "I miss your laugh. I miss the way that it's easy to be around you. I don't feel like I have to try very hard. It's nice."

"I don't want you to try at all. I want you to be you, having fun, cooking up a storm. I don't think you realize how cool it is to see."

Goose bumps crept over her skin. "I think eating is a lot more fun than you realized."

"True. That would be the one downside of being around someone who is a genius in the kitchen. But seriously, it's fun to be around someone who genuinely loves what they do. And you create things. You make people happy. You made me happy and I don't think I realized how unhappy I was until I met you."

"The night you nearly killed me with your car?"

He laughed heartily. "I'm never going to live that one down, am I?"

"Probably not. Sorry." In her fantasy world, the one where she lived in Hawaii with Alex, the surf shop owner, she and Alex would tell their kids that story. They would giggle and think it was so crazy, that Mommy and Daddy must be making it up. And they'd tell them again that it was true.

"But seriously, I was so focused on work that I didn't stop to appreciate much of anything."

"But you're good at what you do, and you care about it. I don't think your father's attitude would bother you if you didn't care so much. You've obviously been super successful, and that doesn't happen by accident. Maybe you just needed a break."

"A fresh perspective. You gave me that."

He was acting as though she'd given him so much, but the truth was that he'd done the same. Possibly more. "You're sweet, but you know, you did the same thing for me. We had fun together. Do you have any idea how long it's been since I've had fun, aside from at work? It's been eons."

"Then let's go have more fun. The tree lighting ceremony is going on down in town on Saturday. We can do some shopping and I'll take you to the Four Seasons.

They have the most incredible hot chocolate. Even I've been known to indulge in it."

"Decadent hot chocolate? But isn't that full of sugar and cream?"

"Precisely why it made me think of you."

It sounded so wonderful, but she needed to work at the bakery that day. "What time would we go? I should be at the bakery until three. I might be able to skip out early."

"I could pick you up straight from there. I could even drop you off in the morning if I come over tomorrow night. But I don't want to invite myself or assume."

"Assume what? That I'll go to bed with you?"

"You are really good at asking the hard questions."

She laughed under her breath. She got that from her dad. He was as hard-nosed as anyone she knew. "Well, was I wrong?"

"No. You were not wrong. I just want you to know that all that stuff about being a gentleman wasn't a line. I'm serious about it. A gentleman does not assume."

She more than adored this aspect of his personality, she needed it. She needed to be asked, she needed to feel appreciated and valued. She hadn't had that from any man she'd dated. Her ex had made her so unsure of herself that she usually didn't last more than a few dates with a guy. The minute he started to assume that he could have her anytime, the instant he showed a blip of possessiveness, she went running. Alex was giving her the space she so desperately needed, and he likely had no idea what a gift it was. It was just Alex being Alex. Who knew she'd ever feel grateful that a man had nearly run into her with his car?

"Alex, I would love to go to the tree lighting. I'd love

to have you stay over tomorrow night. I'll cook for you and everything."

"That sounds amazing. I'm really looking forward to it. Can I pick you up at the bakery tomorrow afternoon?"

"You can just wait for me where you dropped me off today." She didn't want to put him off, not when he was being so romantic, but she still had to keep her secrets safe. "We can shop for dinner then. You'll have to tell me what you like."

"You already know what I like. I like you."

Eight

The bakery was adorable. With a high-pitched roof lined with Christmas lights and inside a row of bright red bistro tables and chairs along the front window, it was welcoming and cheery. No wonder Joy liked coming here so much. Alex wasn't sure how he'd missed it the dozens of times he'd walked through quaint Vail Village, but perhaps it was that he'd been too busy trudging through life to notice. Better late than never.

He pulled the door open and nearly ran right into Joy.

"Oh. Hi." She seemed flustered, hitching her bag over her shoulder and nearly pushing him back out onto the sidewalk. She had to have had a long day.

"We have to stop running into each other like this." His joke didn't seem to make much of an impression— Joy nearly bugged her eyes at him.

"Ready? Let's go."

Alex was looking past her. A young woman was busy behind the counter. The bakery case looked nearly depleted. "Busy scone day?"

She nodded. "Yes. And I need some fresh air."

"Okay. Sure." He took her hand and they stepped outside, where there were hundreds of people milling along the wide cobblestone pedestrian shopping area. The sun was just starting to set, and although the air was cool and crisp, it was pleasant. "Beautiful night."

"It is. Sorry if I seemed out of sorts back there. I just wasn't expecting you. I thought you were going to pick me up where you dropped me off."

"That made sense yesterday, but seeing as we're going to the tree lighting, I thought I should just park and find you." Funny how he and Joy had already adopted the sort of routines couples fall into. He'd picked her up after work yesterday and they'd gone shopping for dinner, then back to her place for an unbelievable meal and an even more out-of-this-world evening in bed. He'd dropped her off this morning, but that hadn't seemed right for tonight. "Plus, this is our first real date. I wasn't going to hang out by the curb in my car. A gentleman comes to the door."

"Or the bakery, as the case may be."

"Precisely."

"Well, thank you. I appreciate that." She stopped and kissed him. "I'm sorry if I'm a little tense. This is really nice."

He smiled. It *was* really nice. Christmas was looking up. Or at least the Christmas season. Alex could feel it in his bones.

"I promise that hot chocolate is the cure for all that ails you." Their first stop was the Four Seasons, where

Alex had reserved a small table in the corner of the bar. It was warm and cozy inside, just as elegant as Alex remembered. He wanted Joy to have every fine thing she was accustomed to.

"This place is gorgeous," she said, just as the waiter brought their order. It arrived in clear glass mugs. "Is that a chocolate orb in there?"

"It is, ma'am," the waiter answered. "I pour the hot chocolate over the top and give it a gentle stir. It's quite sublime."

The look on Joy's face when she took a sip was priceless. She held her fingers to her lips; her eyes were like platters. "That is crazy good."

Alex took his own sip, which he did enjoy, although it was far richer and sweeter than anything he would normally drink. This was all about Joy. Watching her sit back in her chair, her day melting away, he knew he'd done his job and he was nothing but happy for it.

"So, I was thinking," she said, licking her spoon and making him wish they were going home soon. "You aren't leaving until the day after Christmas, right? And we've been spending so much time together. It just seems like we should spend Christmas Eve together. You can stay over and we'll make dinner. I'll even make breakfast the next morning. It'll be a nice way to say goodbye."

Goodbye. That was a word Alex was coming to hate, although he wasn't sure what to do about it. He did need to be back in Chicago for an important meeting on December 27. Circumstances were standing in their way. Plus, his time with Joy wasn't supposed to last long. It was supposed to be a way for him to test the waters. Nothing else. "That sounds really great. I would love that."

"I have a dress I think you might like, if you want to dress up."

"You want me to wear a dress?"

She laughed and swatted his arm. "No, silly. I'll wear the dress. You wear a suit."

"And how long do I have to wear it?"

"Not too long. I won't torture you." She licked her lower lip, which was like completing a circuit in Alex's body. Everything was bright and alive. "No presents, though. That's my only condition."

"What? I'm not going to spend Christmas morning with you and not buy you a gift." An idea sprang to life… maybe there was a way to extend his time with Joy at least a little bit.

"Nothing big, then. Promise?"

"Nothing too big." Alex consulted his watch. "We'd better hurry down to the tree lighting or we won't be able to see anything."

"We'll be fine. That tree is really, really tall."

Out they went, tracking back past the bakery and on to the square where the tree stood. The crowd was easily in the thousands, but the space was open enough that people weren't too horribly crammed together. Alex found them a semiquiet spot off to the side. All around them was the steady hum of people talking while holiday music played in the background. Alex stood behind Joy and wrapped his arms around her. He breathed in her hair. He kissed the top of her head.

Joy gasped and pointed skyward. "It's starting to snow."

Alex looked up. "It is. It's so pretty."

It's so perfect.

It was so perfect he'd better not get used to it. Just

then, the music ended and an emcee stepped up on a small platform. She welcomed everyone and began the countdown. The entire crowd joined in, kids and parents, couples, and groups of friends, just like it was New Year's Eve. *Five...four...three...two...one.*

The lights came on in a flash and the crowd cheered. The music started up again.

"Hey. They're playing my song."

Alex laughed. "'Joy to the World.'"

She turned in his arms, looking up at him. Her cheeks were bright pink from the cold, her eyes happy. "It's not really my song. I just made that up."

"You know what? As far as I'm concerned, I think we tell everyone it *is* your song. Nobody can possibly prove us wrong."

"I like it when you're goofy."

Alex had been called many things in life, but never that. Being with her was like seeing a side of himself he'd never even known was there. "Good. Now let's get out of here."

Alex and Joy strolled back to his car, hand in hand. He couldn't ignore the way it felt as though his feet were hardly touching the ground as they walked. Joy was amazing. Spending time with her was so enjoyable, it made everything bad seem as though it didn't matter. Sure, he'd told himself he would never fall in love again, or at least not as hard as he had in the past, but he already knew he was too far gone.

He'd never expected he would feel this way again. In fact, he'd done everything he could to prevent this from happening, but then he hit a patch of ice on a snowy road, a beautiful woman ended up in a snowbank, and the rest, as they say, was history.

They approached the parking garage valet stand and Alex handed over his claim check.

"I'll have your car for you in a just a few moments, Mr. Townsend."

Alex's arm was already wrapped around Joy's waist. He pulled her closer when the valet ran off to get the car. "Is it too much if I ask to stay over again tonight?" He kissed her cheek, then trailed his lips to her jaw. Her sweet smell and soft skin were enough to drive him crazy, but the way she bowed into him when they were close was enough to send him rocketing off into space.

"Or maybe we could go to your place? I haven't seen it yet."

As head over heels as he was, there was still this voice in the back of his head that was reluctant to truly let someone in. The last time Alex had let his heart lead the way, rather than his brain, he'd nearly ruined his entire life. But he had to get past that.

Soon.

"Tell you what? Maybe we'll spend Christmas night at my house. Is that okay? It's a longer drive to my place and your things are all at your house." All a long string of excuses. He knew that.

"Okay. Sure." Joy gave him a reassuring smile, but he could tell she wasn't entirely happy about the answer.

Just then, Alex's phone rang. The caller ID said it was his father, a call he didn't want to take, but Alex had been putting him off all day and the man was persistent. He'd just keep calling. "I'm so sorry. I should really take this. The valet will be back in a second." Alex plugged his finger into his ear and stepped away. "Dad. Hi. What's up?"

"Alex, I'm not happy."

Surprise. Surprise. Thank you for ruining my evening with the world's worst timing.

"Okay. Why don't you tell me what's going on?"

His dad launched into a diatribe about one of the Townsend mutual funds, which was currently under-performing. Alex listened but didn't say a thing. His dad always had to just get it out. Then they could really talk. Alex turned to see a man enter the parking garage. He stumbled up to the valet stand, listing to the side, unable to walk in a straight line. He was nicely dressed, in a wool coat and nice shoes, but Alex knew from experience that a good wardrobe did not make a good guy, and he was standing entirely too close to Joy now.

"Dad. I know we need to talk about this, but I'm in the middle of something important. Can I call you later? Or can we just talk about it on the 27th? It's not that far away."

"Absolutely not. You're trying to shut me out of our business, Alexander, our family business, and I won't stand for it."

Alex couldn't take his eyes off the scene unfolding at the valet stand. Where was the damn attendant? The man's lips were moving. He was looking at Joy, his eyes half-open. He said something to her. She turned away from him, then took several side steps, deliberately distancing herself. Whatever he'd said was not good. Alex's breaths became heavy. He wasn't even listening to his dad anymore. The man turned back in Alex's direction for an instant, then returned his sights to Joy, advancing on her. The hair on the back of Alex's neck stood up. *Oh, no.* Whatever came next, it was not going to happen on his watch. "Dad. I have to go."

He hung up just in time to see the man grab Joy's shoulder. Alex did the only thing he could. He sprang into action.

One minute, Joy had been having a Christmas dream date, and now this—a drunk making a pass. He'd even swiped at her shoulder. Her mind shifted into defense mode. Her body responded. She jerked away. "Don't touch me. Get your hands off me."

"Stop being such a bitch," the man slurred. "I was just trying to…"

The next thing Joy knew, Alex had the guy in a head-lock.

"Alex! Don't!" Joy jumped back.

The man struggled, but he was no match for Alex. Joy's hand clamped over her mouth, not knowing what to do. It was all happening so fast.

"Let me go!" the man shouted.

Alex must've had some sort of martial arts training, because he seamlessly released his hold and grabbed the man's upper arms. He walked him backward to the cinderblock wall of the parking garage. "You got a problem I need to know about?" Alex's voice was a growl. He'd come a little unhinged. Alex pinned the man against the wall by his shoulders, which only made Joy's stomach sink.

"Get your hands off me. I was just trying to talk to her."

Joy's pulse raced, her chest heaved. Alex had saved her. That was what good guys did. But she also knew that good guys could turn to bad guys. Like her ex. "Alex, it's okay. I'm fine. He didn't hurt me." She stepped closer.

The valet brought the car around. She heard the car door open.

"It's not okay, Joy," Alex replied, not taking his eyes off the man. "He grabbed you. I saw it with my own two eyes."

The man's head was bobbing. He'd obviously had too much to drink.

"Yeah, and he's so drunk I could probably knock him over by myself. I'm fine. Just let him go."

Alex tightened his grip on the man, his knuckles bulging. "Don't go around grabbing women. Ever, okay? I don't care how drunk you are. There's no excuse. You're lucky I didn't take you out." He finally let go, but not without an unsubtle shove.

The valet attendant approached. "Sir, is there a problem?"

"This guy has had way too much to drink. Don't give him his car. You're going to need to call him a cab." Alex pulled a bill from his wallet and handed it to the valet.

"Yes, sir. I'll take care of it." The attendant took the money, seeming confused, and opened the passenger-side door for Joy.

Joy couldn't handle any more of this scene. She was too rattled. She climbed into the car and put on her seat belt, trying to ignore the memories that kept creeping into her head. Ben had done this sort of thing many times. All another guy had to do was look at her the wrong way and Ben was in his face. If there was alcohol involved, it was always worse. At first, Joy had thought it was just protectiveness, but after a while, it became possessiveness, and if Joy wanted anything these days, it was her freedom and independence.

They drove for several minutes in near silence, winding through the mountain roads, the sky pitch-black now. Alex's grip on the steering wheel hadn't loosened at all.

His knuckles were a hard line of ripples across the tops of his hands. She glanced over and could see the fierce tension in his face, the way his jaw was tight and his brow furrowed.

"I'm sorry about that back there," she said. "You really didn't need to say anything. I would've been fine."

"Don't you dare apologize, Joy. He could've hurt you. No man should ever, ever touch a woman like that."

The tone of his voice cut right through her. Tears welled in her eyes. He was absolutely right, but she hated feeling like this. She wasn't weak. She wasn't defenseless. Her mind struggled to find the right words, coming up with nothing. All she wanted to do was apologize again, make it go away, but she had nothing to be sorry for. She only wished that man hadn't made his stupid pass, hadn't had too much to drink.

"You're right. No woman should ever have to be in that position, but that still doesn't mean I can't take care of myself."

"Would it have been better if I'd done nothing? What kind of man would I be if I sat back and watched a stranger touch a woman I care about deeply? I can't even fathom being that person. If that's what you want in a guy, then maybe I'm not the right one. Because all I know is, the instant I saw him touch you, my blood boiled over and I had to make it stop."

Joy felt like her breath couldn't find its way out of her chest. "Do you really mean that? That you care about me?"

A breathy laugh left his lips. "Yes, I care about you. What do you think today was? I want to spend time with you. You're a breath of fresh air to me. You make me laugh. You have insightful things to say. You're sweet.

And you're so damn sexy. I'd have to be a complete idiot to not care about you." He reached over and placed his hand on hers. "I'm sorry if my temper got a little out of control, but this is my weak spot, and it's a big one. I can control it most of the time, but if I'm pushed, all bets are off."

What did he mean by that? Was he saying he had a problem? Because, if he did that was a nonstarter for her. "Weak spot?"

"It's because of my mom." He ran his hand through his hair, staring intently at the road ahead. The pain on his face was evident. More tension. More angst. "Or more specifically, it's because of the way my dad treated my mom."

The air in the car began to change. Alex's anger was something quite different from what she had worried about. "Do you want to tell me about it? You don't have to if you don't want to. I mean, I understand if we haven't known each other long enough for you to tell me."

Another frustrated laugh left his lips. "Does time really matter? Does it really matter that we've only known each other for a few days?" He looked right at her, his icy blue eyes penetrating her soul with so little effort. "You and I have talked about more in the last few days than I have ever talked about with another woman."

A smile played at the corners of her lips. They had shared a lot. Or at least as much as she'd been able to divulge. "You're right. You still don't need to talk about it if you don't want to."

"But that's the thing. I want to tell you. I want to tell you everything." He pulled up to the gate, rolled down his window and entered the code. The car zipped down the driveway and up to the garage. Alex put it in Park and turned to Joy. "I'm not going to sugarcoat it. My family was totally dysfunctional when I was a kid. My dad couldn't keep it in his pants. He ignored my mom except when he needed a beautiful woman to parade around at a business dinner. When he did pay attention to her, he was verbally abusive. So she drank. To numb the pain, I guess. And as the oldest son, I tried to protect her. I wanted to. But I failed. I couldn't get either of them to stop, and eventually she paid with her life." His voice wobbled at the end, his anguish bubbling to the surface.

"I'm so sorry, Alex. You told me a little about this, but I had no idea it ended so tragically."

Alex reached out and stroked her hair. "I don't want you to feel sorry for me. Plenty of people have much sadder stories. The point of me telling you this is that I don't want you to think badly of me because I flew off the handle at the parking garage. I think you know that I'm not always like that."

"I do know that. And maybe that's why it was upsetting. Just to see you be someone I didn't think you were capable of being."

He nodded slowly, taking it all in. "I can totally understand that. And I'm sorry for that part. You know, usually I just hide the ugly stuff in my past. Ignore it. Pretend like it's not there. I've gotten pretty good at it."

How could Joy's heart feel simultaneously so heavy and yet so fundamentally happy? Alex was baring his soul to her in a way few people ever had. He cared. And she sure as hell cared right back. But there was still a barrier between them—she'd put it there and it was hers to take away.

But if she did knock down that wall, it would destroy every beautiful thing that was already between them.

And since there was an end to their romance bearing down on them, she couldn't stand the thought of sabotaging the rest of their time together. They had both needed this holiday affair. They had both needed each other, to heal, to see light. That didn't happen nearly enough in life and she wasn't about to throw that away.

She pulled Alex into a hug. "Come here." She settled her head on his shoulder and ran her hand back and forth across his back, soaking up his warmth, never wanting this to end. "You can always tell me the ugly stuff. Always. Honestly, you can't scare me. Just tell me the worst. I promise I won't run away."

Alex laughed and reared his head back. "Thank you for that. It means a lot. Truly."

She smiled, feeling so much better. They'd had such an amazing day. "Ready to go inside?"

He nodded. "With you? Always."

Nine

Joy watched Alex put on his clothes. He was half-asleep, fumbling a bit, which made him exceptionally adorable. Most of the time he was perfect while making zero effort. She loved his human moments.

"You okay? You're staring," he said, standing up from the spot where he'd been sitting on the edge of the bed.

Of course I'm staring. You're astounding.

"I'm good. Just not totally awake. Last night wore me out."

"That was a pretty rigorous tree lighting." He snickered to himself.

"Not what I meant, Mr. One More Time. Your stamina is exhausting."

He stepped closer and kissed her on the corner of her mouth. "That's not what you said last night."

"True. I guess I just have to accept that I'm going to be a step slow today."

Except there was no room in Joy's day for being a step slow. If she and Alex were going to spend Christmas together, she would need to buy him a gift. She'd thought about doing something homemade, making him a basket of his favorite pastries and maybe a jar of jam, and although it was somewhat romantic, it wouldn't last. Plus, Alex was a guy accustomed to the best of everything, and although he was sweet and she doubted he would ever, ever be unhappy about receiving some of her scones or muffins, she wanted to give him something of permanence. She would feel better about parting from him if she knew he might be walking around with something she'd given him. He could have a reminder of her, of everything they had shared—the passion, the good times, the laughter.

The only hitch was the most perpetual and pervasive problem in her life—money. She wouldn't get paid by the bakery until the end of the week, and even then, it wouldn't be enough to buy him something truly spectacular, something worth holding on to. She needed a chunk of money, real cash.

"Just about ready to go?" he asked.

"I am. I just need to get a few things. You should run downstairs and grab a cup of coffee. I just made it."

He smiled and grasped her elbow. "You're a savior." He pecked her on the nose.

As soon as he was out of sight, Joy went to the closet and grabbed a box from the top shelf, which was hidden under a pile of sweaters. This cardboard box, soft and smashed in at the corners, was filled with the most important things Joy owned. It had her grandmother's recipe cards, faded shades of pink, mint green and canary yellow, a precious bundle wrapped up in a rubber band. It also contained pictures of her family, some of which were in small frames.

She'd gotten so settled in Santa Barbara at the Marshall estate that she'd actually put the photos on the dresser in her room in the staff quarters. That was a leap she didn't make often. Once she was out of culinary school, she never stayed in one place for very long, moving from cooking job to cooking job, city to city. That was when she was on a roll, climbing the ladder of success and actually making leaps. It was a magical time that would hopefully resume at some point.

In one corner of the cardboard carton sat a small jewelry box. Not the clamshell kind from a fine jeweler, but rather the paper kind for earrings from a gift shop. Inside that was a burgundy felt pouch with her grandmother's most prized possession: a gold locket on a slender chain, a gift from the family her grandmother had spent most of her adult life cooking for.

Her grandmother had loved the family and they loved her right back. Joy's grandfather had died when Joy was just a little girl and her grandmother had taken the job, moving in with the family, as her only means of survival. Joy was the only grandchild, her mom the only child. Her grandmother's world might have been modest, but she'd filled it with love and incredible food for everyone who had been lucky enough to have been a part of it.

Joy was not about to let this necklace go forever. No way. But she had pawned it once before, to buy a ridiculously expensive textbook for culinary school, and she'd worked doubly hard to make the money to buy it back. She would do that again—she planned to ask Bonnie for extra hours at the bakery. Surely no one in a town like Vail would give one hoot about her grandmother's necklace. It was too old-fashioned, too sentimental. It wasn't flashy or showy. It was simple and unassuming, and Joy hoped that meant it could sit in the case in the pawn shop for just long enough for her to get paid and buy it back.

"Thank you for taking me to work. I realize it's not fun to get up at 6:00 a.m."

"I admire your dedication. Most people who are using a space to research a book would just show up when they feel like it."

She shrugged it off playfully, feeling nothing close to lighthearted. "I don't just talk the talk. I like to walk the walk, too."

The new day was just dawning when Alex drove her into town. Joy tried not to focus too much on the uneasy feeling in her stomach when she thought about pawning her grandmother's necklace. She tried to focus on her true goal—Alex meant something to her and she wanted him to remember her. Somewhere in the world, she wanted someone special to think of her from time to time, and maybe, for an instant, think that Joy had made their world a better place. It was the sort of thing her grandmother had done in her life, and Joy wanted the satisfaction of having accomplished at least a fraction of that.

"Here we are," Alex said as they pulled up on the side street. "Sure you don't want me to walk you in? I can get a parking spot no problem this early."

"No. It's okay. I know you have things to do."

"I do have things to do. Like going back to bed. Then shopping."

"Nothing too big. We agreed on that."

"Yes, ma'am."

"Thank you for the ride." Her lips were instantly drawn to his for a soft and gentle kiss.

His eyes were half-open when their lips parted, that look that made Joy's stomach do somersaults. Knowing he was still savoring their kiss was a wonderful feeling. "You're more than welcome. And you know, I sort of like getting up this early in the morning. It helps me imagine what it's like to be a farmer."

Joy swatted him on the arm. "Very funny. I'm guessing that nowhere in your family lineage is there a single farmer."

"You would be right about that. I think the Townsends have always been bankers."

Of course they have. "Probably even in prehistoric times when they were trading rocks and shells."

"Probably. I'm guessing your ancestors were baking scones?"

And scraping for every penny. "Not until there was baking soda and butter in the world, but at some point, yes."

Alex feigned a shiver. "I don't even want to think about a world without butter. You would be so unhappy and I don't want that."

"Me neither."

"So, tomorrow? Christmas Eve dinner? Do you need me to pick anything up? Can I do the shopping for you? I know you're busy and my enthusiasm for work is pretty slim."

Joy had forgotten about paying for groceries. Alex had picked up the tab the last time. "Actually? That would be wonderful, if you're okay with that."

"If it means I get to watch you cook, then yes. Absolutely. Text me a list and I'll get everything taken care of."

"You're the best."

"I try."

She gave him a final kiss and ventured into the cold, rushing down the cobblestone walk and ultimately into the warm safety of the bakery. The aromas that hit her nose every time she walked in the door were such a pleasant comfort, although she'd felt that way about every food-related job she'd ever had, even the bad ones. Probably because she associated the scents with her grandmother and the happiest parts of her childhood.

"Morning," Natalie said, coming in right behind Joy. "I see that the guy with the fancy car gave you a ride again. Have a good night?"

Joy looked over in time to catch a wink. Heat and embarrassment crept over her, even when it was a good seventy-five degrees in the bakery. She was past the point of pretending that Alex was just a ride. "Yes. We had a very nice time."

"Are things getting serious?" They walked to the back and put away their coats and bags in the employees' locker room, then stepped out into the hall where the stacks of clean, folded aprons sat.

Joy looped the string over her head and wrapped the tie around her waist, knotting it in the front. It gave her enough time to come up with a good answer.

If things were different between her and Alex, they might actually be getting serious. They felt serious. Whatever it was between them felt very real. But reality was so far removed from those feelings, it was ridiculous. They weren't simply residing in different states, they were on different planets, and it all boiled down to one sad truth: she had lied to him about who and what she was. There would be no coming back from that.

That meant no future for them.

"No, not serious. We're just having fun. He lives in Chicago anyway. He'll be heading home after Christmas."

Natalie drew her hair back into a high ponytail and put on a bandana to keep everything out of the way. "I wouldn't mind having fun with a guy like that. You're a lucky woman."

"I know."

And my luck is just about to run out.

Just then, Bonnie stepped out of her office.

"Hey, Bonnie. Can I talk to you for a minute?" Joy asked.

"Sure. Of course."

"I'll get the scones started," Natalie said.

"I promise I'll only be a minute," Joy countered.

Bonnie nodded in the direction of her office doorway and Joy followed her inside, taking a seat next to her desk.

"What can I do for you?" Bonnie asked, settling into her worn wooden chair.

Joy sat a little straighter. She wanted Bonnie to know how serious she was. "I know I'm new here, but I could really use some more hours, even if it's just for a few weeks."

"Strapped for cash at the holidays?"

"Something like that. I was thinking, the bread team is short one person, right?"

"I need you on pastries. You know that."

Joy nodded. "I do. But what if I started coming in early after Christmas? I could help on bread for four hours, then switch to my regular job."

Bonnie picked up a pen and tapped it on her desk. "We're talking brutal twelve-hour days."

Joy forced a smile. "I know. I figure I can do anything for a few weeks."

"If you're up for it, it's a deal. You'll really be helping me out until I can hire a new person." Bonnie got up from her seat and shook Joy's hand. "You aren't in some sort of trouble, are you?" Bonnie asked, seeming genuinely concerned.

No more than usual. "No. I just need to get some things squared away."

Bonnie sighed. "Okay. Let me know if anything changes."

Joy smiled wide, relief washing over her. "Thank you so much. Really. I appreciate it. I'd better get to work or Natalie will never let me hear the end of it."

Joy flitted into the kitchen, and she and Natalie worked together like a well-oiled machine, knocking out scones, muffins, cookies and Danish like they were nothing. As much as Joy hadn't loved her pastry courses in culinary school, she was starting to suspect her reaction had been more about her professor, who was a real wet fish and not much fun to be around. She actually loved baking. It had all the same pleasures of preparing main dishes. Maybe she really would write a baking cookbook one day. After she had a few new recipes under her belt, of course. Dreams were important, even ones of the pipe variety.

After the morning pastries were all out in the front cases, Joy and Natalie went to work on the rest of the day's tasks—cakes, pies and tarts. They had restaurant orders to fill, as well as a few special requests from customers. It was as busy and frantic a morning as they'd had since she'd started working there. When it came time for lunch, she was exhausted and wanted nothing more than to get off her feet for thirty minutes and have something to eat. But she had that errand to run.

"I need to go take care of something," Joy said, taking off her dirty apron and chucking it in the laundry. "I'll see you after lunch?"

"You need me to come with you?" Natalie asked.

Joy delivered a tentative smile. "No. It's okay. I need to do this on my own. I'll be back in a few." She rushed out of the bakery. It was a good ten-minute walk down a side street to the tiny pawn shop she'd spotted a few weeks ago.

The bell on the door rang when she walked inside. Leave it to this lovely hamlet to have a high-class pawn shop. It might have been called an emporium, but Joy knew exactly what she was dealing with. No regular store had glass cases filled with fine jewelry and musical instruments ringing the room. Joy reasoned that being in a place that wasn't the slightest bit seedy might help her get more money, which was exactly what she wanted.

"Hello, there," the man behind the counter said. He was tall and particularly thin, wearing frameless glasses and a tan pullover sweater. "What can I help you with today?"

"I have a necklace I need to pawn." Joy pulled the small pouch out of her purse, her hand trembling. She tried to focus on positive things to keep her mind off how much this necklace meant to her—she'd made her plan with Bonnie to earn the money quickly to buy it back. In the end, it would all be worth it if she made Alex happy.

He'd changed her entire mindset while she was here. A few weeks ago, she'd been as down as could be. Her Prince Charming, although he wasn't meant to be hers forever, represented a turning point, and for that, he deserved a reward.

The man pulled out a small board covered in black velvet, seeming unfazed by the way she tapped her fingers on the case. He was probably used to customers who were on edge. Joy draped the necklace across the fabric, then busied herself by browsing the other items in the store. The man was remarkably quiet while he examined the piece, leaving Joy to hum what was stuck in her head—the song that had been playing in the bakery when she left.

"I can give you two-fifty," he said, placing the necklace back on the board.

Joy took a second to think it over, but she knew this was a yes-or-no proposition. She didn't want to haggle for more money; it would only mean more to pay back in order to return it to her possession. It was far less than the necklace was worth, but the man had to have some room for profit. "Great. Thank you."

The man pulled out some paperwork, and after procuring some information from her and making a copy of her driver's license, she signed away the necklace. "You have until the 27th to buy it back for three hundred," he said.

"That's it? The last place I pawned it gave me two weeks."

The man grimaced and shook his head. "Sorry. I'm not a bank and we don't get a lot of customers. If you're in a real jam, you can come in that day and pay me ten percent for an extension."

Forget that. Like Joy had extra money to expend. "Are you open for regular hours that day?"

"Every day but Christmas."

This still was making her far too nervous. "You have my cell phone number. Can you call me if you put it out before I get back here? I don't want to take a chance that someone else might buy it."

The man sighed. "I'll make a note of it. No promises, but you seem like a nice person, so I'll do my best."

That made her feel a whole lot better. The man had a kind face. She had to believe in the goodness of strangers. "I'd really appreciate it. I'm definitely going to buy it back."

"Of course you are." His voice had a distinct edge of skepticism.

"I'm sure people say that to you all the time, but in my case, it's true. I have to have this necklace. It means too much for me to ever let it go."

"You must be in a tough spot."

Yep. I'm the queen of the tough spot.

"It's okay. I'll get out of it just fine."

Ten

Alex pulled up to Joy's place and killed the engine. Stealing a second to look in the car's visor mirror, he straightened his tie—the dark blue one. Did he look like he was walking into a business meeting? He didn't want to look like that. Not for Joy. Was his hair okay? He didn't dare mess with it too much without a comb, so he just flattened the spot in the back that never seemed to co-operate. One deep breath and he flipped up the visor. He just wanted tonight to be perfect. That was all.

He grabbed the gifts he'd bought for Joy from the pas-senger seat and scaled the steps to the front door. This would likely be his last time in this house. No matter how she reacted to the most important of the gifts tucked under his arm, tomorrow was Christmas Day and his last full day in Colorado. The meeting with his dad on December 27 could not be rescheduled and he needed

December 26 to get back in the office and prepare. Alex realized that this was a convenient out for him. If the big gift, the important one, fell flat, he could make a graceful exit and kick himself later for thinking that a woman like Joy might want more than a fling.

He rang the doorbell, remembering very well that first night when he'd stood out on this stoop and wondered if he was crazy for returning. Yes, it had been the responsible thing to do, but there had also been a great deal of curiosity woven into his thought process, whether he'd been willing to admit it to himself at the time or not. He'd wanted to know more about the beguiling Joy Baker. How much he had learned since then.

The door latch clicked and his pulse picked up, although he wasn't entirely sure why. It hadn't been that long since he'd seen her. They'd talked on the phone that morning.

The door flew open. "Oh, my God. Dinner is a disaster." Joy smiled thinly, lunged for him, kissed him on the cheek and ran off down the hall into the kitchen. "Just come in. I have no idea when we're eating."

Alex stepped into the foyer and closed the door behind him. What had just happened? He took off his coat, slung it over his arm and strode into the kitchen. Normally, Joy had everything under control. She made Martha Stewart look messy and disorganized. Today, not so much. The kitchen counter looked like a crime scene, bowls everywhere, a significant flour spill, a carton of eggs still sitting out.

"What happened?" He tossed his coat over the back of one of the chairs in the living room and casually slipped his gifts under the tree.

Joy was shaking her head and peeking through the

window in the oven door. She was wearing a long red dress with a decidedly unsexy plain black apron over the top of it. He really wanted to see the rest of the gown though—the back had a deep V, showing off a glorious stretch of her creamy skin. "I wanted to make a cheese soufflé, but I forgot to make the adjustments for the altitude, and it fell on one side. I don't know if it's going to recover. It was so dumb. I do it every day at the bakery. I did it when I baked you all those damn scones, but when it's really important, like our last big dinner together, I blow it." Her voice did something then he'd never heard—it cracked. Right in half. Strong, feisty Joy was losing it.

He approached, careful to be calm, and pulled her into his arms. "Joy, come on. Take a breath. It's going to be fine. I really don't care about dinner. I just want to be here with you."

She sucked in a sharp breath, but the exhale was a shuddering gasp. She was crying. She clung to him so hard, digging her fingers into his back. "I know. But I wanted tonight to be perfect."

He grasped her shoulders, dropping his chin and forcing her to look at him. "Tonight is perfect because you're here. I'm here. We're together. That is all that matters."

She just looked at him as a tiny tear rolled down her cheek. She was absolutely gorgeous, even with misty eyes, but it broke his heart to see her like this. She chewed on her lower lip, her head bobbing. "You're so sweet. It almost makes it worse."

He laughed and shook his head. "Worse? How could I possibly make it worse by being understanding?"

"I don't know, Alex. Maybe because I'm waiting for you to commiserate with me."

"Well, sorry. As much as I love your cooking, I really don't care that much about dinner. I care way more about everything else."

The timer buzzed and Joy snatched a pair of hot pads from the counter. She pulled the soufflé from the oven and set it down next to two plates, which already had side salads waiting on them. "If this was culinary school, I would be getting chewed out right now, big time."

"Luckily, it's not." He grabbed a piece of lettuce from the plate closest to him and popped it into his mouth. "Mmm. Good vinaigrette."

"Thank you. Hopefully the salad makes up for everything else." With a large spoon, she scooped a portion of the soufflé onto each plate. She then reached behind her and untied the apron, lifting it over her head and tossing it onto the counter behind her. "Can you get the forks?"

"Sure." Alex never should've agreed to the request. He was not capable of simple tasks right now. All he could do was drink in the vision before him—Joy in that dress. Forks were the exact last thing on his mind. "Wow."

"You haven't even tasted it yet. Let's sit in the dining room. I put out a bottle of wine, but I still need to light the candles."

"Hold on a second." He ran his fingers down the back of her bare arm as he admired her. The deep V of the gown's back was matched in the front, the neckline dipping low enough to show off the swell of her beautiful breasts. There was no way she was wearing a bra. Apparently, she was trying to kill him. With the apron gone, he could truly see how stunning she was in red, with her long chocolate-brown hair falling behind her shoulders and her eyes as warm as ever. "You are so beautiful. I mean, seriously." He wanted to say more, to be poetic, but had no clue where his command of the English language had gone. "Can I just tell you that?"

She cocked her head to the side as a smile crossed her lips, only making him want to kiss her more. "You like the dress?" She turned once and the floor-length skirt swished behind her, but when it came to a stop, he saw a flash of her leg. The dress had a very high slit. "It's not too much?"

Alex was surprised he didn't need to physically put his eyes back into his head. "Too much? No. I'm just lucky I get to look at you in it." It was official. He had zero interest in food. He'd never been less hungry. He placed his hands on either side of her neck and tilted her chin upward. "I'm just lucky I get to kiss you right now."

His lips fell on hers and there was this magical moment where the world around them fell away—no messy kitchen, no life circumstances holding them back. Only Joy's warm and giving kiss, the way her tongue sought his, was of importance now. He didn't give a damn about anything but this.

She popped up on to her tiptoes, stretched out her arms onto his shoulders and dug her delicate fingers into his hair. She deepened their kiss. He countered, and she whimpered, a sound he would never tire of hearing. He wrapped his arms tightly around her, but one hand caressed the bare skin of her back, her silky skin. He wanted to touch every inch of her more than he'd ever wanted to, which was saying a lot. He dropped one hand to her hip and gathered the skirt upward, taking a fistful of the soft fabric. His fingers reached her bare thigh and she gasped like he'd just seared her skin.

"The soufflé will get cold," she said, breathless. Gladly, there was an edge to her voice that said she didn't care, either.

"I promise I'll make it up to you." With that, he reached down and swept her into his arms, holding her tight.

She wrapped her arms around his neck and set her head against his chest. He tried not to stare down into her cleavage, reminding himself he needed to get her upstairs safely. Then he could have his reward.

He wasted no time getting up to her bedroom. He planted a knee on her bed and set her down gently.

She swished her hands across the duvet. "I love this bed. It feels so amazing."

You are amazing. Not taking his eyes off her, Alex dispatched his suit coat and tie. Why he'd ever worried about the damn color was beyond him. It clearly hadn't made a blip of a difference to Joy.

She propped up on her elbows and raised her knee, allowing the slit of her dress to fall open. He unbuttoned his shirt as fast as he could.

"I like watching you take your clothes off," she said.

He tossed the shirt aside. "I like *taking* your clothes off." He stretched out on the bed next to her, wishing he'd been smart enough to ditch his damn pants—they were entirely too confining right now—but he just wanted to touch her. That had seemed most important.

They went right back to kissing like their lives depended on it. He flattened her against the bed, she dug her fingers into his back, hitched her leg up over his hip, tracing the back of his thigh with her foot. Her other leg slipped between his and she pressed against his crotch, raising a groan from the depths of his belly and bringing it to his lips. The heat inside him was building like a wildfire on a sunny day. A windy, sunny day, at that. This was an all-new level of longing for Joy. If this was their last time together, he wanted to make it count.

He pulled one dress strap off her shoulder. Thankfully his earlier assumption had been right. No bra. He cupped her breast with his hand, her velvety skin impossibly soft against his. He lowered his head, flicking his tongue against her nipple. He loved feeling the way heat surged beneath his palm, and her skin tightened beneath his touch. She moaned softly, rubbing her leg more convincingly against his crotch as his lips closed in on the firm bud.

He lowered his hand and found the gap in the skirt, his fingers roaming higher on her thigh and lifting the voluminous fabric. When he reached her hip, he moved to her belly, and his fingers slipped beneath the silky fabric of her panties. He took his time getting to her center, teasing with a delicate touch. One well-made loop with his fingers and he knew exactly how ready she was. He didn't think he could stand the wait much longer.

She clamored for his belt buckle, unhooking it and the front of his pants. When she unzipped them and slipped her hand inside, molding her hand around his erection, he was blinded with need. All he could think about was what it was like to be inside her, to experience every inch of her. He scrambled off the bed and shucked his pants and boxers. Joy got up as well, turning her back to him and pulling her hair aside. He unzipped her dress and she pulled it forward from her shoulders. It fell to the floor in a beautiful red puddle.

Taking her hair in his hand and pulling it aside, he wrapped his other arm around her waist and pulled her snug against his body. He wanted her to feel just how turned on he was, grinding his hips against her. He kissed his way from her nape to one shoulder, then back to the other side. Joy turned in his arms, planted a hot, wet kiss on his lips before dropping to her knees. He nearly fell over from the anticipation.

She dragged her hands down his chest and stomach, then shot him a white-hot look before gripping his erection and taking him into her mouth. His eyes clamped shut, his own mouth so agape he thought he might not ever close his jaw again. It felt so impossibly good, the tenderness of her tongue, the firm hold of her lips, the attention she put into pleasing him. It would've been one thing to have this treatment from any woman, but from Joy, it was so beyond mere physical gratification. She was a rare and beautiful creature. He was lucky and he knew it.

Joy had to admit—she loved having Alex at her mercy. She paid special attention to every noise he made, every subtle twitch of the muscles in his firm thighs. She'd messed up dinner, but she was pretty sure she could get this right. Judging by the deep groans he kept unleashing, she was on the right track. Knowing they were parting tomorrow made her charge even more important. She wanted him to remember this. She knew she would. She shut out the sad feelings that threatened to take over. They had been encroaching on her thoughts all day, and she'd had enough. She would enjoy him if it was the last thing she did.

Alex caressed her shoulders, dug his fingers into her hair. "You are so damn sexy," he muttered.

She would've smiled if it wasn't going to ruin the rhythm she'd so carefully established, the one that had elicited the words in the first place. Instead, she gripped his hips a little harder and flicked her tongue from side to side, keeping as much suction as she could. The tension in his body only grew. If she didn't slow down, Alex was going to need recovery time before he could make love to her. She didn't want to wait.

He grasped her upper arms. "Come here. I need you."

Now she could smile. That was exactly what she'd been thinking. She rose to her feet and he gathered her in his arms, planting a fast and loose kiss on her lips. She opened the drawer in the bedside table and took out a condom, ripping it open and putting it on him. One more kiss and she climbed on to the bed, rolling to her back, sinking into the plush bedding and waiting for him.

He had that cocky grin on his face, the one that made her want to roll her eyes, except in this setting, it only meant she was in for a treat. He was so stunning standing before her, and even better looking when he descended on her, kissing his way up her belly and moving his attention to her breasts. He positioned himself at her entrance and drove inside.

Time stopped. Her breaths stalled. Her heart was the only thing talking as her body molded around him. It wouldn't stop saying all sorts of implausible things. *You need him. You can't let him go.*

Alex settled his weight on her, driving her crazy in the best possible way. He knew exactly what she liked, the perfect amount of pressure to send her into oblivion. How he had figured out in little more than a week what a fair number of men had *never* figured out was a mystery; she only knew that Alex had a way of getting to the heart of all matters, her body included. They moved together in the rhythm that was their own, her legs wrapped around his hips to have him as deep as he could go. Their kisses were slow and careful, and she tried once again to stop thinking of the lasts that were coming for them—the last time they would make love, the last kiss. She didn't want this to be a countdown, but it was hard not to think of it that way. And if she did, the tears would come.

The pressure of pleasure was warring in her body with the melancholy. She had to fight for the good, cling to the beauty of two people who understand each other and want to please each other. She let her thoughts go and opened her eyes, soaked up the beauty of Alex.

His breaths were tearing from his chest now, and hers were nearly the same. Tension doubled in her belly, then doubled again, and just as she felt herself teetering on the edge, she tumbled into the release and gave herself up to it. Alex's torso froze for a moment as he reached his own climax, his shoulders and hips shuddering when he relaxed and let it wash over him. He collapsed into her and she wrapped every limb she had around him as tightly as she possibly could.

A million kisses followed, or at least it felt that way—an embarrassment of riches. Dinner was a distant thought. Alex got up and used the bathroom, then Joy, and they retreated to bed, wound around each other and silent.

There wasn't much more to be said. Talking about what was coming wouldn't solve a thing. Sometimes, just giving in to the inevitability of something could be freeing.

You can't fight every last thing in life. Eventually, you'll lose.

Alex fell asleep while they were still entwined. The warm flickers from the fire lit up the side of his handsome face. Joy let her eyes roam, taking in every inch of perfection. She had to remember everything—the exact curve of his mouth, the way his lashes skimmed his cheeks when his eyes were closed, the dimple in his chin.

She was going to be so disappointed with herself in the years to come if she wasn't able to conjure up this image and make him seem real. Her memories were the only things she had left to cling to. He was about to walk out of her life. She'd known all along this was coming, and although it already hurt—although it already made a pit in her stomach and her chest blaze with a flame that might never go out—she refused to regret her time with Alex. He had given her so much. He had reminded her of the things she still loved about herself—her passion, her heart.

There had been a time in her not-so-distant past when she'd hated herself. That entire drive from Santa Barbara to Vail had been a long running dialogue about what a failure she was, how she'd created every terrible thing in her life that she hated. She'd been knee-deep in the reverberations of that self-loathing when Alex came down the hill that night. He'd lifted her out of it and shaken her into her better state, one where she didn't question her abilities, her talents, herself.

She'd thought about telling him that she was falling in love with him, but that didn't make any sense now. What good would it do? It would only make parting that much harder. It would make it painfully awkward. She wasn't about to ruin yet another good thing. She had to take the fleeting moments they had together and hold on to them in her heart forever. That was the best she could possibly do. For both of them.

She snuggled closer to him and set her head against his chest. She let his warmth seep into her, trying to ignore the worry that when he was gone, she might be left a cold and empty shell. She turned her face into his skin, inhaled his comforting smell as tears rolled down her cheeks.

He deserved to know the truth. "I'll always love you, Alex Townsend. Even after we say goodbye."

Eleven

Joy had to make up for the disaster that had been last night's dinner. They hadn't eaten until after midnight, when Alex had woken up, his stomach growling. Even then, they'd only made grilled cheese sandwiches. That flopped soufflé? Sadly, it had ended up in the trash.

She'd gone with apple cinnamon muffins—Alex had mentioned the other day how much he loved anything with cinnamon. The kitchen smelled amazing and she hoped that her perfect vision of Christmas morning would come to fruition.

She walked into the living room with a tray of coffee and breakfast. "I hope you're not disappointed, but I made muffins this morning. I can't serve you scones forever." She slid the tray onto the coffee table.

He stood and went to her, seeming exceedingly happy. "I already know I love your muffins." He gave one butt cheek a gentle squeeze and kissed her softly.

She laughed, their lips still brushing against each other before they were naturally drawn into a deeper kiss. She grasped his shoulder and bowed into him, then realized how close she was to getting pulled off track. As much as she loved sex with Alex, this morning was important for other reasons. "If we aren't careful, it'll be a repeat of our first tree lighting ceremony, right here in this room."

That day had been such an amazing turn of events. She loved reliving every moment—the flirting, the longing, the moment when they'd been unable to fight their attraction anymore and she'd finally just kissed him. It had been one of the best days of her life.

"After presents. And breakfast." He sat on the couch next to her and sipped his black coffee. If she wasn't mistaken, that was contentment on his face.

Joy handed him a muffin. "Apple cinnamon. Pretty basic, but they're still really good."

"I would say you're full of yourself, except that I know you're not." He removed the paper baking cup and took a generous bite. "Absolutely perfect."

"Thank you. That's sweet."

"Just telling you the truth." He finished off his muffin and sat back, trailing his fingers up and down Joy's back. "When do you want to open gifts?"

"I'm worried you won't like what I got you."

"Not possible. No way. You could just give me the recipe for these muffins and I'd be happy."

She knocked her fist against his knee. "I never said I was going to give you something that good." She took another sip of her coffee and got up from the couch. "Now is as good a time as any." Kneeling down, she pulled a small box out from under the tree. "You first."

The gift was wrapped in gold foil, with a red ribbon he untied. He slipped the box from the paper and lifted the lid. Inside, on a bed of cotton fluff, sat the silver money clip she'd bought him at a men's store in the village with the money from her grandmother's necklace. He picked it up and held it in the palm of his hand. She'd worried that it wouldn't make a grand enough impression, but he truly seemed to like it. "It's beautiful. What is this embossing on the top?" He ran his thumb over the irregular texture, a series of short diagonal lines.

"Do you not recognize it?" She snickered. "It's supposed to look like tire tracks. I thought it would be a fun reminder of the way we met."

He shook his head and laughed. "I'm never going to live that down, am I?"

"Just like I'll never live down diving into a snowbank." She sucked in a deep breath, but the weight of the moment lodged in her throat. That had been the beginning and they were now wedged in the end. She hated the end. She hated goodbyes. There was never a single fun thing about them, but this one was already especially painful. "I just wanted to give you something that you could remember me by. Something to carry in your pocket."

"Well, thank you. I love it. I will always keep it with me. Always." His comment was only confirmation that they really would be parting. There wasn't the slightest hint of staying another day. He was ready to say farewell. He got up and retrieved more than one box from under the tree. "I know we said we were only going to do one gift, but I cheated and got you three."

"Alex. You weren't supposed to do that. It's so mean. I only got you one."

"I know, but I just couldn't decide. I literally could've bought out the whole store when I went shopping."

"And then you would've had nothing for your money clip, so I'm glad you kept things in check." She desperately wanted to keep the tone light and fun, even when it was the opposite of what she was feeling. She just had to hold it together a little longer.

He set the packages on the coffee table, setting one apart from the others. "This one gets opened last."

"Okay." She took the first of the two remaining and tore open the paper. The instant she saw the famous red and black checks on the camel cashmere background, she knew exactly how extravagant he'd been. "A Burberry scarf? I love it. I've always wanted one of these." She'd actually fantasized about it, but never thought she'd ever actually own one. She wrapped it around her neck and bunched up her shoulders. "It's so soft."

"You were complaining about your scarf the day of the tree lighting and I thought it would look gorgeous against your dark hair. And it does."

"Well, thank you. I love it. I will keep it forever." *Forever.* She needed to avoid that word. It was only going to take its toll later. She took the second package and opened that one just as quickly. "Oh. Perfume. I never buy myself perfume." She removed the top and spritzed some on her wrists. It smelled like vanilla and sugar cookies. "Ooh. Yummy."

"This one might be stupid. I bought it because it reminded me of the way you smell when you've been baking. I just thought it would be nice." He swiped the final gift from the table. "Now this one, you're just going to have to tell me to take a hike if you don't want it. I'm not trying to make you feel hemmed in or anything."

Her brows drew together. She couldn't imagine what it could possibly be. The box was smaller than the scarf box, but the same shape—long and flat. "Now you really have me curious." She was much more careful with the paper this time, knowing this was the final part of their Christmas morning together. The tape popped free and she carefully set aside the wrapping intact. She opened the box. A folio was inside, but she still had no guess as to what this was. She opened the front flap. Inside was a plane ticket. To Fiji.

"Oh, my God. A trip."

For a moment, her heart performed the most ridiculous routine—jumping around like it wasn't attached to anything.

"Yes. Fiji. I just, I think one thing we both learned over the last few days is that we could use a vacation. A real vacation where nobody worries about work at all. And I thought that the farthest we could go away, the better. I've been to this resort and it's beautiful."

She didn't say a word. She just stared at the tickets, frozen. A tear rolled down her cheek.

"It's okay if you don't want to go. I just…" He closed his eyes and pinched the bridge of his nose.

She looked up to see him warring with himself. Was he changing his mind?

"I don't want this to end," he said.

It was the sweetest thing anyone had ever said to her. And now Joy was tangled in a web of her own making.

In her wildest dreams—or more like nightmares—she couldn't have come up with a scenario like this one. She wanted to cry and scream. She wanted to kiss Alex for being desperately romantic. She wanted to be in his arms and tell him that she loved him.

But there were about one hundred things that had to be said before that. And she was reasonably sure she'd never get that far. The tears—oh, boy, did they come, like she'd never cried in her entire life and had been waiting for this moment.

Because the truth was that the name printed on her ticket was Joy Baker. Her fake last name might as well have been Betrayal. That was what she'd done. She'd betrayed him. And for someone who'd made a zillion mistakes in her life, this one was definitely the worst.

An hour ago, Alex was sure he hadn't been this excited about Christmas morning since he was a kid. He'd certainly been nervous about how his gifts would go over with Joy. Now she was crying and hadn't said a single thing that sounded like yes.

Why had he been so stupid? How had he read it so wrong? It was too big a leap. They'd only known each other for a little more than ten days. This was not the same as asking a woman out to dinner on the fourth or fifth date. Sadly, he couldn't undo it now.

"Why are you crying?" Alex gently rested his hand on her shoulder. In some ways, touching her only made it worse. She didn't respond like she normally did. She nearly recoiled.

"I have to tell you something. I have to tell you a lot of something." She gulped for breath. She kept looking at the floor. "This isn't my name. My name is Joy McKinley. I made up Baker because I'd just spent the whole day working at the bakery and I was trying to hide my identity because nobody can know that I'm here."

Alex felt as though she had just plunged a knife into his heart. She wasn't who she said she was?

"I don't understand. Hide your identity? Is someone trying to hurt you?"

"Not exactly. I'm not really supposed to be staying in this house. It's not owned by friends of mine—it belongs to my former employer. I quit after she and I had a huge argument, and she said that if I ever gave her reason to, she would destroy my career. She and her husband are immensely powerful in the food world. If she wanted to, she could make it impossible for me to get any job as a chef, let alone pursue anything else with cooking."

"How powerful could these people be?"

"Harrison Marshall, the celebrity chef. The house belongs to him and his wife, Mariella."

"Oh, wow." Alex didn't know the ins and outs of the culinary world, but he did know who the Marshalls were. Joy's story was becoming more and more complicated. Alex was struggling to keep up. None of it made sense. "So why wouldn't you just go somewhere else? Do you not have permission at all?"

"My boss's son said I could stay here until mid-January, but nobody could know about it because his mom hates me. I had nowhere else to go. I have no money. I haven't been able to find a place I can afford. And you know I can't go home."

"You didn't have a friend you could stay with?"

"Not here. I have some in other parts of the country, but I couldn't get that far. That pile of junk under the tarp in the garage is my car. It doesn't work. That's why I need a ride everywhere."

Alex put his elbows on his knees and ran his hands through his hair. What in the hell was happening? Was fate playing some cruel trick on him? She kept launching lie after lie at him and he didn't know what he was supposed to do about any of it.

"Say something, please. I am so sorry. I never would've lied to you if I'd known what was going to happen between us. It was just one little lie after another, piled on top of the first one."

He then turned to her, his head hung low. The hurt in his heart was unfathomable. He wasn't sure he knew how to breathe anymore, or if he even wanted to. He wanted to disappear. "You couldn't bring yourself to tell me the truth before now? When you were basically backed into a corner? What about the day we went to the tree lighting? Or last night when I came over?"

"Are you serious? That would've been better? If I had ruined those beautiful, romantic moments we were sharing? For all I knew, you and I were never going to see each other again after today. You've only mentioned your departure date a dozen times, like you wanted to remind me that there was an expiration date on our affair."

His vision narrowed on her and the hurt faded, giving way to anger. "It was a fact. Nothing more than that. And it was the truth, which seems to be a big problem for you. No wonder my private investigator couldn't find anything about you. It was almost as if you didn't exist. Now I know that Joy Baker from Santa Barbara, California, doesn't actually exist. She's fake."

Joy's eyes blazed with fury. "You called your private investigator about me? Is that what you do with all women?" She got up from the couch and stared down at him. "You probably don't want to risk getting involved with anyone too messy. The perfect Alex wouldn't want to look bad."

"You want to know why I called my private investigator? Because my ex-fiancée was actually a career criminal. A con artist, trying to get at my money. Maybe you two know each other." That was a low blow, but he refused to take it back. He was too mad right now. Every happy, hopeful thought he'd dared to have over the last week had been destroyed with her version of the truth.

Joy picked up the tickets and threw them at him. "You can take your fancy Fiji trip and shove it. I wouldn't get on an airplane with you if my life depended on it. Just go by yourself and find some anonymous woman to sleep with, like you did with me. If you keep it short and sweet, you won't even have to call your PI to do a background check."

Alex picked up the money clip and tossed it in his palm. "Where'd you get the money for this? Did you steal it?" He had to know the full extent of her deception.

She started crying again, which just felt manipulative. "No. I did not steal it. I pawned the only thing I own of my grandmother's. A gold necklace that she'd gotten from one of her employers. She was a cook. Just a plain old regular cook, Alex. She worked for almost nothing, cooking for families like yours. That's why my parents didn't want me to pursue my dreams. They didn't want me to have the life I have right now, but that's just the way things are. I know I messed up. I lied to you. I fully own up to that. But you have accused me of things today that I can't live with. Because no matter what, I know now that you never trusted me. From the very beginning. That's no basis for happiness."

Alex's jaw was set firmly. He really hadn't trusted her. He'd only convinced himself that he did. Now he knew that he'd been right. "I don't think you understand what

I went through. A woman literally tried to trick me into marrying her, just so she could get my money. Do you have any idea how awful that was for me? And how this feels like more of the same?"

"I'm sure it does feel terrible. And I'm sorry. But I think you and I both know that this wasn't going to work out. You were suspicious of me all along. You just told me as much. So I think it's best if you just go. Go back to Chicago and live your life. I'm sorry I hurt you."

Alex got up from the couch, looking around the room. He didn't know what to do. He was still reeling.

"Just go, Alex. Get your things and leave."

The money clip was still in his hand. He wasn't sure he could ever look at it again. "Here. Take this back." He tried to hand it to her, but she wouldn't take it.

"No. I don't want it. I'm about to get paid. I'll get my grandmother's necklace back on my own."

"Joy. You're being ridiculous."

"I'm not. I don't want your charity. I bought you that money clip because I cared about you. You should keep it to remind yourself that somebody did. Maybe someday you'll be ready to accept that from someone." She crossed her arms and walked to the other side of the room, facing the windows, looking out at the snow.

He didn't know what to say. Was that true? Had she really cared about him? If they could rewind and undo her lies, would she have said yes to the trip? Would she have said yes to not wanting it to end? Now he would never know.

He ran upstairs and gathered his things, put on his shoes. She wanted him out and he wanted the same, if only to clear his head. He'd arrived last night with so much hope in his heart and now it was filled with nothing but black clouds and misery. He had to leave. He had to go home.

Downstairs he went. He took only one step into the living room before Joy turned to him.

"I'm going." His voice was only a trace of its normal strength. He was too hurt to muster anything with more force. "For the record, I never said I wanted things with any woman to be easy."

She closed her eyes then turned away. "Well, then, you got your wish."

Twelve

Alex left for Chicago Christmas night.

He couldn't spend another hour in Colorado. He'd normally call for the corporate jet, but there was no time for it to get to him, so he flew commercial, snagging a first-class seat on the last flight out of Denver. There was no reason to stay in Vail. There were only painful reminders of Joy there and that was the last thing he needed. The wound was plenty deep. He didn't need to claw at it. Maybe he'd just sell his place there. Or let his brothers use it. He couldn't fathom wanting to go back anytime soon.

The lights in the cabin were off as the plane began to descend. Alex stared out the window, watching the city below, pin dots of light scattered on an inky black canvas. Somewhere down there, somebody was happy. They'd had the best Christmas they'd ever had. Certainly there were children being tucked into bed, exhausted from the most incredible day they could remember. Even though he'd only had the chance to do so for a few days, he'd held out a lot of hope for this Christmas, that it would finally be the kind of day he'd always imagined—filled with love and cheer. It had certainly started out promising. He just hadn't known how badly it would crash and burn.

"Mr. Townsend. Your coat."

Alex turned to see the flight attendant handing him his jacket. She was wearing a Santa hat and jingly earrings, with long brown hair similar to Joy's. As if he needed more reminders of how much this Christmas had sucked, or of how badly his heart had been broken into two. Again. "Thank you." He took it from her and laid it across his lap, returning his sights to the city. Soon enough he'd be home.

The next day was Wednesday and Alex was up with the sun, unfortunately. Sleeping had been impossible. He just rolled around in his bed, unable to keep the thoughts of Joy out of his head. Had he been too hard on her? His gut was telling him that he hadn't. He'd been duped before, and he'd sworn to himself he would never, ever let it happen again.

He stepped on the scale after brewing a pot of coffee. He'd gained two pounds while he was away. Scone weight. He really should've been working out more while he was in Colorado. You'd think all that sex would've burned off some calories. Apparently not.

Luckily, he had a home gym in Chicago. He hopped on the treadmill and ran until he couldn't run anymore—more than an hour, listening to loud music in his earbuds, just trying to get out the anger and pain and resentment built up inside him. He sat on a weight bench when he finally gave in to exhaustion, rubbing his wet hair with a towel and sucking down water. He didn't feel any better, and all his stupid mind wanted to fixate on was what Joy was doing. At least he was fairly certain he'd sleep that night.

After a shower, he went into the office to prepare for his meeting with his father, even though no one was expecting him for another day. Striding into the offices of Townsend & Associates Investments, he knew that work was the only way to get through this. He had to put in the hours. Bury himself in numbers. He needed to blow his dad's expectations out of the water, continue to wow the world of finance. In a few months, people could gossip about him, try to guess what had gotten into him and given him such superhuman strength when it came to work.

He'd never tell a soul that it had all been fueled by a broken heart.

"Morning, Barb," he said to the receptionist.

She was on the phone, so she nodded and gave him the cursory smile. He was the boss and most people were afraid of him, so he didn't tend to get much more than that. He might need to see about changing that, too. Maybe if he spent more time with the lower-level employees, he could create an even tighter company culture. His father would be horrified by the sheer idea.

It was relatively quiet as Alex walked down the hall to his corner office. He'd given many of their employees the option of taking off the week between Christmas and New Year's. Another initiative his father did not like, but this was a slow time of year. Best to have everyone up and running at full strength after the holidays. Alex unlocked his door and got straight to work, answering

emails, typing up ideas for initiatives for the new year.
A little after ten, Paul poked his head into his office.

"Hey there." Paul knocked on Alex's open door.

Alex didn't believe in keeping his door closed unless absolutely necessary. It made him feel like a caged
animal. He sat back in his chair. "Have a seat. How was
your Christmas?"

Paul had a huge grin on his face. A mile wide, no ex-
aggeration. "It was fantastic. I got my grandson that action figure we were talking about. I have never seen a
kid so happy in my entire life. My wife loved her gifts,
and she was in a great mood because both kids were
there. She and our daughter made this pastry on Christmas morning that my wife hasn't made since the kids
were little, a Swedish tea ring. Have you ever had one?"

Alex shook his head, while visions of scones and muffins materialized before him. "No. I haven't."

"It's delicious. Like a giant cinnamon roll. The whole
house smelled amazing." Paul nodded and laughed quietly to himself. Surely he was recalling some happy moment from Christmas that he didn't feel needed to be
shared. "So? How about you? What happened with that
woman you wanted me to check out? Joy Baker?"

Thankfully, Alex didn't need to sugarcoat things with
Paul. He could just come right out and tell him. "She lied
to me about her name. It's not Baker. It's McKinley. And
she's from Ohio, not California." He didn't quite know
how to read the expression on Paul's face—it almost
looked like remorse.

"I am so sorry. I should've dug a little deeper. So she's
not a baker, either, I take it."

"No. No. That much was true. And she worked in

Santa Barbara for a while, so that was where she'd lived most recently."

"How did you find out? See her driver's license or something?"

"She told me. On Christmas morning, no less. I'd bought her tickets to Fiji. That's the thing that's so pathetic about this whole story. I really liked her. I wanted to take her away. She saw her fake name on the ticket and started to cry and she told me everything."

Paul drew in a deep breath through his nose. "Wow. That's tough. I'm so sorry. Did she say why she'd waited to tell you?"

Alex shrugged and rocked in his chair. "Well, she knew I was leaving the day after Christmas, so I guess she didn't see the point. I was coming home to Chicago. She wasn't sure where she was going next because she doesn't really have a place to live."

Paul lowered his chin and looked down his nose at Alex. "So she's homeless."

"Sort of. Not really. She was staying in the house of her former employer and she lied about her name because she didn't want me to know. She couldn't afford to go anywhere else."

"Sounds like a real mess."

"Yes. Exactly. Thank you. Her story steamrollered from there. One lie basically led to another lie, until I didn't know what was what anymore. The whole thing is a disaster and just hits way too close to home. I know you know what I mean."

"Can I speak freely?"

"Of course. You know that. I trust you. What?"

"I know you have no idea what it's like to be poor. And I'm not blaming you for that, but let me tell you, I do know. I know it very well. My family struggled when I was a teen. I had a hard time making ends meet in my twenties." Paul spoke in his characteristic calm voice, but it was even more measured than usual. "It's not fun to live your life feeling like you're up on a high wire about to fall off. You definitely reach a point where you will pretty much do anything to keep your life together. That's why it's called a survival instinct."

"So what are you saying? That I was wrong to be upset about being lied to?"

Paul shook his head. "Absolutely not. Of course not. You had every right. I'm just trying to give you some perspective, because I have a sneaking suspicion that what you were thinking in that moment when she told you the truth was that this was Sharon all over again."

"Well, it is. Isn't it?" It had felt just like Sharon when Joy had told him the truth. Although, he had to admit that he'd gone straight to feeling sad much more quickly than the first time.

"Did Sharon confess? No. I had to find out about it and you had to confront her. And what did she do when that happened?"

"Denied everything." Alex could see where Paul was going with this, but he wasn't convinced he was right. Alex had been lied to and there was no good excuse for it. He didn't care for explanations.

"Then what?"

A grumble left Alex's throat. "She stole stuff out of my apartment and tried to say that I had given it to her."

"Is that how it went down with Joy?"

"No. Not at all. She even apologized. But that still doesn't change the way I felt. That still doesn't make what she did okay."

"Of course it doesn't make it okay. And you were justified in being upset. But now that you've had time to cool down, maybe you should at least try to think this through."

Paul scooted forward to the edge of his seat. This was as close as Alex would ever get to receiving fatherly advice. "Obviously, I don't know this Joy woman. But let me just say this. That last time I talked to you, you were genuinely happy. I could hear it in your voice. And you were never like that with Sharon. Never."

"I was happy then. I just had a lot of stuff going on at work. It was a stressful time." Now he was even more confused. "I sort of thought I was happy."

"And this isn't a stressful time in your life, Alex? You're running the company now, for God's sake. The buck stops with you and you turned your phone off for twenty-four hours. You want to know what that says to me? That stress was the last thing on your mind. You met someone who was enough to take your eye off the prize. Which makes me think that she might be the real prize."

"You don't even know her."

All Alex could think was that the words he'd uttered would not have the intended effect. The truth was that he would love for Paul to meet Joy. He would love to know that he wasn't crazy, that there was a spark between the two of them that other people could see and feel. He wanted someone to tell him it was real.

"No. I don't. And there's a chance I'm totally off base."

"That doesn't help me. At all."

Paul got up out of his chair. "Look, I didn't come into your office to play psychiatrist. But I don't like what Sharon did to you. And I think you're still processing some of it. It's not fair to this other woman that you're making her pay for someone else's lies, especially when those other lies were designed to hurt you." Paul knocked his knuckle against Alex's desk. "Intent is important."

What had been behind Joy's lies? She'd been trying to protect herself. She'd been trying to survive, in a world Alex had never had to live in. "What do I do now? About Joy? I said some truly awful things to her. Terrible things." His stomach hurt just thinking about it. He'd accused her of stealing. Could he ever come back from that?

"You'll figure it out. You're a smart kid."

"I'm a few months from thirty-five, Paul. And I'm your boss."

"Hey. To me, you're still that pimply thirteen-year-old you were when I started working here. I'll always worry about you."

Alex shook his head in disbelief. How Paul could see so much was beyond him. He only knew that he did.

And now, Alex had to figure out what to do about it.

Joy had given herself one day to be sad, but now she had a sad hangover. She was also more than a little bit pissed off at herself. She had quite literally done everything she'd sworn she would never do again. Why did she keep putting herself in these situations? How did she have such a talent for creating her own unhappiness? She wasn't sure. She only knew that she couldn't allow herself to live like this anymore. She'd thrown away what she had with Alex, and he might have been the best thing that had ever happened to her. That mistake would haunt her forever. No more doing things that she couldn't stand to live with.

First thing on the day after Christmas, she called Natalie. "Hello? Joy?" Natalie sounded more than a little sleepy.

"Natalie, hey. I'm sorry if I woke you. I just figured you were up and at 'em like I am on a day off."

"Not usually, no. But I do have some stuff I need to do today."

"Okay. Well, I need to tell you some things. And I need a couch to sleep on."

Joy then launched into the entirety of the truth—where she was living, why she shouldn't be living there anymore, and that she needed help coming back down to Earth, where she belonged.

"I'll call my brother and have him come up to look at your car. I'll get him to fix it for free. You're welcome to stay on my couch for as long as you like," Natalie said.

"You're not mad I lied about the house? I asked you to drop me off at a house that I wasn't even living in. I feel horrible."

"No, I'm not mad. I don't judge people. We all have to do what we can to survive and I've been in a few jams in my life. I know you're a hard worker, a talented baker, and a good friend. You're definitely the most fun person I've ever worked with."

"We do have fun, don't we?" Joy smiled to herself. Natalie was a blessing she was so thankful to have.

"Rolling dough all day long." Natalie laughed. "Okay. Let me get some coffee and we'll get this show on the road. Text me the address."

"Will do. But you'll know it when you see it. It's the house you never would've believed I belong in." Joy hung up and got to work, collecting her things from Elana's closet, washing bedding and making the beds, cleaning the kitchen and the bathrooms, even sweeping ashes from the fireplace. She was careful to put everything exactly as it had been before. And to think she'd spent so much time worrying that Mariella Marshall would find out she was living there and would end up kicking her out. In the end, Joy was evicting herself. She never should've come here in the first place.

With every task complete, she waited to feel closer to closure, but the feeling wouldn't come. Perhaps it was because the Christmas decorations were still up. She managed to remove the first few ornaments from the tree before she started to cry. The tears streaked down her face, she gasped for air, but she kept going. Every pretty glass bauble was returned to its box, the tiny tree all packed up, and along with it, her memories of Alex.

Her tears weren't about sentimentality over the things that they'd done together—those were nothing but good and pleasant memories. The remorse was for what might have been—a chance at happiness. She'd fallen in love with him. Someday, he might've fallen in love with her. She'd had no idea he'd wanted more. She'd never expected it. And she couldn't stop asking herself why she'd never dared to think it. But now, she was starting to see the answer.

She'd doomed them from the start. She'd lied. With that first untruth, she'd made it impossible for them to ever have more—what person could ever see past that? She'd taken one look at his perfect face, his finely tailored wool coat, and his expensive car and decided they were from different worlds and that meant there was no reason to treat him with anything other than wariness and skepticism.

She'd let her circumstances harden her and turn her into something she wasn't, all because she was afraid.

When things got bad, she was allowing herself to feel just as small as Ben used to make her feel. Just as small as Mariella Marshall had made her feel. She needed to stop reacting that way when life pushed against her. Everyone had their trials. She needed to do a better job of standing up to hers. Alex would have to be the one who got away—it would always hurt. No amount of time would remove him from her head or her heart.

Late that night, she was settled at Natalie's. The couch was not as comfortable as Elana's bed, but that was fine. Joy was sleeping on this couch with full permission, with no fear of anyone discovering her whereabouts. There was a lot to be said for the peace of mind of that. But she still had unfinished business.

Things with Alex had not ended the way they should have. As upset as she'd been about the fact that he'd called his private investigator, the truth was that he was absolutely right to have done it. If he'd gotten any sort of strange vibe from her, it was completely her fault. And for that reason, she had to call him and apologize one more time. This was part of making everything right with the world.

She got his voice mail. It wasn't entirely surprising that he hadn't answered. He had every reason in the world to hate her. And she had to take some comfort in the fact that he hadn't blocked her number.

This is Alexander Townsend with Townsend & Associates Investments. Please leave a message. His voice filled her with so much regret.

"Hi, Alex. It's Joy. I'm calling to apologize. It was never my intention to lie to you. I was in a jam, and I did some things I'm not proud of. But I'm out of the Marshalls' house now and about to start working extra hours at the bakery to get my head above water." It occurred to her that he might not care about any of this, but she had to keep going. She had to get it off her chest. "I want you to know that I will always fondly look back on our time together. You're an amazing man, and any woman would be lucky to have you in her life. I hope you find happiness. I hope you live a good life." *And I love you.*

The words were threatening to burst forth from her lips, but she couldn't saddle him with that burden. This phone call was not about pulling at heartstrings. It was about making things as right as she could. "Goodbye, Alex."

She pressed the button to end the call and muted her phone, stuffing it under her pillow. She snuggled up under the blanket, closed her eyes, and willed herself to sleep. Hopefully the tears wouldn't last for long.

Joy and Natalie went into work together the next morning. Natalie took her break at eleven thirty. Joy took hers right after, just as the clock struck noon. She had to hurry. She had something important to do. Now that she was staying with Natalie, she had a brief reprieve on finding a place to live. And since her car had been fixed by Natalie's brother, Joy could use her paycheck to buy back her grandmother's necklace.

The bell on the pawn shop door rang when Joy pushed it open. It was just as dead quiet in there as it had been the first time she walked in. That seemed like a lifetime ago. When she was sure she knew how things with Alex would end. Her version would've had the same net result, but at least he would've thought well of her. He wouldn't have known the truth, but hopefully a smile would've come to his face when he remembered her.

That would've been the closest she and Alex could have come to a happy ending.

But it hadn't happened like that, and she had to continue with the baby steps toward acceptance. That was the only way to heal.

"Can I help you?" the man behind the counter asked. He wasn't really looking at her, preoccupied with polishing up an old pocket watch.

Joy pulled her paperwork out of her purse. "Yes. I'm here to buy back a necklace I pawned." She scanned the glass case but didn't see it with the other jewelry. That stuff was all more contemporary. Maybe he'd put it in another section. Joy whipped around and rushed to the other side of the store, hands on the glass, searching.

"I remember you," he said. "It's gone. A woman came in about a half hour ago to buy it."

"What? A half hour? You told me you'd call me. We talked about it."

The man shrugged. "Sorry. I guess I forgot."

Joy closed her eyes and dropped her head back. The loss shuddered through her body. How much more could she possibly lose in this world? Alex. Her pride. The necklace. What next? "Do you have the woman's information by any chance? Do you remember what she looked like or where she was going?"

"She was blonde. She mentioned something about the bakery."

"Really?"

"Yes."

Joy didn't waste another minute, hitching her bag over her shoulder and bolting out into the cold. Around the corner and down the side street she ran, as fast her impractical brown boots would carry her. When she finally stumbled through the door of the bakery, the only customer inside was an older gentleman buying a loaf of bread.

Shoot.

Joy went back out on the sidewalk and looked both ways down the street. No sign of a blonde woman. Maybe this just wasn't meant to be. She went back inside, feeling defeated, but deciding it was not the time to feel broken about anything. Her grandmother wouldn't want her to do that. She'd figure out something. She'd go back to the pawn shop tomorrow and tell the owner to call her if it turned up again. People who bought things at pawn shops often ended up taking them back.

Just then she heard a man's voice from the back hall. It made the hair on the back of her neck stand up, but not in a bad way. It was more like she was convinced that she was hearing things. It had to have been one of the bread bakers. Except that it was after noon, and they were usually gone by then. She shook it off and went in search of Natalie. The hall was now empty, just stacks of flour bags lining the walls, and the apron hooks half-empty. Natalie's laugh rang out from the front kitchen.

When Joy pushed through the aluminum swinging doors, she nearly fell over from what she saw. Alex, standing there in a baker's apron, sleeves rolled up, hair back in a bandana no less. When he turned and his eyes met hers, she thought she had died and this was the dream on the other side, the one where things work out and you get everything you always wanted. And that was before he'd said a single word.

"Hi, Joy."

"Alex. What are you doing here?"

He held up the rolling pin in his hand. "Learning how to make scones."

Natalie smiled. "He just got here a little while ago. I told him you were at lunch, so he said he'd wait."

"I tried to call you."

"You did? I didn't get any calls." Joy slapped her forehead. She'd forgotten to take her phone off mute after last night. It wasn't like she'd been expecting any important calls. She pulled her phone from her bag and sure enough, five missed calls, all from Alex. "I'm so sorry. I put my phone on mute after bed last night and totally forgot to turn it back on."

Alex stepped closer to her and Joy did the same, until they were nearly toe-to-toe. "Can we talk?" he asked.

"I can leave you two alone, if you want," Natalie offered.

"No. It's okay. I know you're busy," Joy answered. "We'll go out in the hall."

She led the way and Alex followed. She wasn't sure what to think right now. Had he listened to her message? Would he accept her apology?

He untied the apron and hung it back up on the hook, then removed the bandana from his head.

"Here. Your hair is a mess." She popped up onto her tiptoes and brushed flour from his hairline. Their lips were so close. She could smell his warm cologne. This was too much like things used to be. It was starting to hurt to look at him, like her heart was being pulled out of her chest. "I can't believe you're here."

"I had to come back. I hate the way I left things on Christmas morning."

She shook her head so fast she was surprised she didn't dislodge some brain matter. "Don't apologize for that, Alex. You were absolutely right. I'd left this gray cloud hanging over our time together and it wasn't right.

I should've said something as soon as I realized that I was romantically interested in you."

That clever smile of his crossed his lips. "The moment down by the pool?"

"The moment you didn't kiss me. That's when I should have told you that I wasn't Joy Baker, the baker."

"Which was the most adorable fake name you could've given yourself, by the way."

"It was dumb. And terribly unoriginal. I was panicked. And it wasn't fair to you." She reached for his hand. "I'll say I'm sorry every day if it means you'll give me another chance. Even if it's just one dinner."

"One kiss?"

Was that all he wanted? Even if another goodbye might kill her, she had to take this. She gripped his shoulders and leaned into him, planting her mouth on his. The second his lips parted and his tongue touched hers, she flattened him against the bakery wall. It was too good not to keep it going. It was too perfect. She could've melted right into him then and there.

Alex was the one to end it. "Wow."

She dropped down to her heels. "Sorry. I get carried away." She gazed up at his eyes knowing this was the moment when she had to lay it on the line, again. "You do that to me. Nobody else has ever done that to me. I don't know what made you come back, but I don't want you to leave. Not until we've had that dinner and we've had a chance to talk everything out."

"To start over?" His beautiful blue eyes nearly knocked the breath right out of her.

"That would be amazing." She planted one hand on his chest, watching it rise and fall with his breaths. "What made you come back?"

"Well, I needed to get a grip. That was first on my list. Second was some shopping. For jewelry." He reached into his pocket. Joy gasped when she saw what was in his hand.

"The locket." She watched as Alex draped it into her hand. "But the guy at the pawn shop said a blonde woman bought it."

Natalie poked her head out of the kitchen and waved. "Did I tell you I went to the pawn shop on my break? Not that I was eavesdropping or anything." Just like that, she ducked out of sight.

"I called the pawn shop yesterday and gave them my credit card number so I could get it back. Then I called the bakery this morning after I couldn't get through to you on the phone. Natalie answered and at that point, I figured I might as well make it a surprise, so I asked if she'd go pick it up for me."

Joy shook her head in amazement. "You did all that for me?"

"I did that for the woman I love." He smoothed back her hair with his fingers. "I'm in love with you, Joy. As crazy as that sounds, it's true. The minute I walked out of that house, I only wanted to go back in. But I also had to clear my head. I needed some perspective. Luckily it didn't take long for me to get it."

Joy grabbed his hand and squeezed it. "I love you, too. As crazy as that sounds. I do."

He nodded. "Okay. Well then, you and I have some talking to do and some decisions to make. I don't want to ask you to leave your job here, but I think you know my whole life is in Chicago. We could try long-distance for a while if you want to."

Joy looked at Alex and knew one thing—she was

done making mistakes. "I love the bakery, but I love you more."

"Yeah?" The happy lilt in his voice filled Joy's heart with contentment.

"Yeah. I think that means your scone lesson is over, mister. We need to pack up my things and head to Chicago."

Epilogue

Joy stepped on to the beach and curled her toes. She would never get over how soft the sand was in Fiji. "This is pure heaven."

Alex took her hand, his flip-flops in the other. "Agreed. Let's never leave. Ever."

They embarked on their nightly post-dinner walk. Another thing she would never get over was how beautiful the Fijian sunset was, either. "Is it just me or is it a particularly perfect night?"

"I don't think it could get much better, that's for sure."

In some ways, it felt as though the sun was putting on a command performance just for them, in ultra vivid shades of orange and gold, nothing else but the big blue ocean stretching out beneath it. She and Alex had watched the sunset every night from the deck of their private bungalow, holding hands, savoring their time together. Joy couldn't recall ever feeling so lucky, not even the day she'd landed the job with Harrison Marshall.

Colorado was a distant thought now, although it would always be in the back of her mind. She'd gone there, not realizing she was trying to escape her life, and ended up finding an entirely new one.

"It sure doesn't make me miss Chicago in January," he added.

"I don't know about that. As beautiful as it is here, I'm eager to get back home." Home—that was a concept which Joy had only toyed with over the past few years. Now she was living with Alex. His penthouse apartment in the River North neighborhood of Chicago was unbelievable—spacious, elegant, and most important, it felt like home. Of course, she'd added some of her own touches, mostly to the kitchen, but it was otherwise perfect. Every night, Joy would experiment with new recipes, they would enjoy a lovely meal together, and they would, of course, end up falling into bed. Alex had quipped about how Joy was really helping him get over his bad habit of watching too much TV. Apparently she was enough of a distraction.

Being in Chicago had also brought Alex's family into their lives. His father, Alexander Townsend II, was pretty much what Joy had expected, and he'd been kind, but she wasn't sure how much warmth she'd ever get out of the man. There wasn't a lot there, and that made her sad. Alex deserved better. Alex's brothers, Matthew and Jonathan, helped to fill that void, though. Affable and nearly as handsome as their big brother, they both clearly idolized Alex and gravitated toward him for everything from jokes to advice. Joy could see that the sibling bond fed Alex's soul, and that Alex wouldn't be leaving Chicago anytime soon.

And that meant she'd had to start looking for a job. Yes, Alex had more than enough money and hadn't asked for a cent from her, but they were a committed couple with only six weeks of togetherness under their belts. It was still early days, and Joy didn't want to be caught without a safety net if things didn't stay as wonderful as they were right now. Luckily, her career prospects were shaping up nicely.

Alex had introduced her to several friends who owned restaurants, and Joy would be going for interviews when they returned to Chicago in a few short days. He'd also touched base with a friend who worked for a big New York publisher. He was keen on her getting her foothold in the world of cookbooks if she was ready to do that as well. It was all moving so fast, but she was trying to sit back and take her good fortune as it came. She figured she'd saved up her whole life for it.

They'd made one final weekend trip before getting on the plane for Fiji, a trip for which Joy had been extremely nervous. Alex had taken her to Ohio so he could meet her parents. Of course, Joy hadn't worried about whether or not her mom and dad would like her new beau. They took to him right away. Alex was such a down-to-earth guy, he'd had no problem grabbing a beer with her dad and hanging out in the TV room watching football. He'd been very sweet with her mom, as well, complimenting her cooking and commenting that she was clearly where Joy got her beautiful, long hair and her equally long legs. Thankfully, Ben had not made his presence known, although that was likely due to Alex. Overkill or not, he'd hired two off-duty police officers to stand sentry outside her parents' house the entire time they were there. When she'd wondered aloud if it had been too much, Alex had replied that it had done the job and that was all he cared about.

It was all like a dream, but that did not mean she'd suddenly retired to the land of zero worries. She had big news for Alex, and she had no idea how he was going to react to it. Keeping secrets from him the first time had backfired and she wasn't about to do it again. The question was when the right moment would arise. Alex had been on edge all night.

"Let's get our feet wet," she said.

"Okay." Alex kneeled down and rolled up his pant legs. She'd told him one hundred times she didn't care if he wore shorts to dinner, but he'd insisted that it didn't feel right.

"Ready?" She grabbed his hand and flitted down to the water, moaning softly when her feet reached the gentle waves. "It feels so good tonight. Maybe we should go swimming." She pulled him closer and kissed him gently. "I doubt anyone would notice if we went skinny-dipping." Indeed, the resort they were staying in was so private, they could go for hours without seeing a soul.

"Maybe later. Okay?"

Joy twisted her lips and stifled a sigh. There was definitely something up with him. The man did not turn down an opportunity to be naked together. "Is everything okay? Did you not enjoy your dinner?"

"Dinner was great. It's not your food, but it was really, really good. And I'm fine. I just have a lot on my mind."

"Did your dad call you or something?"

Alex shook his head and they resumed their walk, ankle deep in the warm and tranquil water. As the sky darkened, the moon came into view, casting a moody glow. "No. I haven't dared turn on my phone. I'm here to enjoy my time with you and nothing else."

"Good. I'm glad." She felt a little better now, but only a fraction. There was still an awkward silence between them, which was not their normal dynamic. Usually, the words flowed freely. Maybe she just needed to come out with it. Tell him what was going on. Maybe that uncomfortable feeling was coming all from her. "I have something to tell you," she blurted out, surprising even herself.

Alex came to a stop. "I have something to tell you."

Oh. Was that good? Or bad? "Do you want to go first?"

"You said it first. You can go."

She sucked in a deep breath. *Here goes nothing.* "Okay—"

"Wait." He shook his head. "I'm really sorry, but the thing I have to say has literally been on the tip of my tongue all evening, and I just feel like I have to get it out or my head is going to explode."

Joy stood there, not knowing what to say. It wasn't like Alex to get flustered. "Yes. Of course."

He cleared his throat and looked at her. As beautiful as the moon was that night, his eyes put it to shame. She would've said something if the look on his face wasn't so pained and tortured. "You make me happy, Joy. Really happy. Are you happy?"

She almost laughed—wasn't the answer obvious? "Yes. Extremely."

"Okay, good." He took her other hand and then he did the most inexplicable thing—he dropped down on one knee. Which was odd enough in its own right, but they were still in the water, which meant he was now kneeling in the South Pacific. "Dammit. I didn't really plan this out very well, did I?"

Joy giggled nervously. Was this why he'd been so on edge? "It's my fault. I suggested we get our feet wet."

Alex shrugged and gazed up at her. "I'm down here, so I might as well just go with it." The most sincere smile she'd ever seen crossed his face. "I love you, Joy. And I'm happy and you're happy and I know that the world says we're supposed to be together for a few years before you go off and do something crazy like get married, but I think we should. If you want to." His vision narrowed on her. "Do you want to? Get married?"

Again, Joy wanted to laugh. Alex was so adorably out of his element right now. She also couldn't believe the timing. His question certainly segued well into her announcement. "Alex. I couldn't care less what anybody says about what we're supposed to do. We met because you nearly hit me with your car. I feel like the universe was telling us we belong together. Of course I will marry you. I love you more than anything."

Alex grinned like she'd never seen him do before, then let go of her one hand and reached into his pocket. "This is why I couldn't wear shorts. I needed bigger pockets." He opened the jewelry box and presented her with the sort of ring she never thought she'd get—a big sparkly diamond on a platinum band. Still, Alex was kneeling in the ocean and she could just imagine where this ring was going to end up if they weren't careful.

"Can I get my ring on dry land? I think it would be better."

"Yes. It's weird being in the ocean with your pants on." He clapped the ring box shut and stood, immediately planting a soft and steamy kiss on her lips. "You're sure?"

The tears she almost never shed? They were starting up. "Yes, I'm sure. One hundred percent."

Hand in hand, they walked up on shore, where he tried a second time with the ring. He took it from its velvet box and placed it on her finger. "Do you like it?"

She nodded, more fixated on him than on the ring, however beautiful it was. He was a miracle. And she was the luckiest woman in the world. "I love it."

He sighed and the perma-grin on his face grew even wider. "So what were you going to tell me?"

She still wasn't sure how to approach this. Alex had clearly been sweating the proposal. She wanted to give him his moment to bask in the sun. Still, there were no secrets between them anymore. She took his hand and flattened it against her belly. Not a word came from her lips as their gazes connected. The wonder that flickered in his eyes was everything she could've hoped for—such a pure and sweet reaction.

"You're pregnant?"

She nodded, choking back the tears, overwhelmed by the beauty of their surroundings, their perfect moment, her unbelievable man.

"But when? How?"

"I'm pretty sure we got pregnant that night the condom broke. Not that we weren't basically messing with the gods of contraception that whole time."

"True. I think we destroyed the margin for error." He laughed. "It's such amazing news."

She couldn't contain her smile. "I'm only about six weeks along. It's early. But I had to tell you as soon as I was sure."

He pulled her into his arms and kissed her forehead, then her cheek, and finally, her lips. "A baby. I'm going to be a dad. You're going to be a mom." He ran his hand through his hair. "You know what? You are going to be the best mom."

Good Lord, she was going to perish from Alex's sweetness. "And you're going to be the best dad."

He put his arm around her shoulders and they started walking back to their bungalow. Each step felt different now, like they were walking toward their happy future. "My only question is this," he said. "At what point do we teach our child how to bake scones?"

* * * * *

A sexy smile touched the corners of his lips.

"I've wanted to kiss you from the moment I saw you."

Bristol drew in a deep breath and stared at him. "I just can't believe you are alive. Someone in the State Department checked into it and told me you'd died."

"When was this?"

"A month after I last saw you."

He nodded. "I was presumed dead, so the person was right. I was rescued just days before Christmas the following year."

"That was a long time."

"Yes, it was." Only his close friends knew about the nightmares he'd had for months following his rescue. Nightmares he still had at times.

"Why were you trying to reach me, Bristol?"

Drawing in another deep breath, she met his gaze and said, "I wanted to let you know I was pregnant."

* * *

His Secret Son
is part of The Westmoreland Legacy—
Friends and relatives of the legendary
Westmoreland family find love!

HIS SECRET SON

BY
BRENDA JACKSON

First Published in Great Britain 2017
By Mills & Boon, an imprint of HarperCollins*Publishers*
1 London Bridge Street, London, SE1 9GF

© 2017 Brenda Streater Jackson

ISBN: 978-0-263-92848-8

51-1217

MIX
Paper from
responsible sources
FSC™ C007454

This book is produced from independently certified FSC™ paper to ensure responsible forest management.

For more information visit: www.harpercollins.co.uk/green

Printed and bound in Spain
by CPI, Barcelona

Brenda Jackson is a *New York Times* bestselling author of more than one hundred romance titles. Brenda lives in Jacksonville, Florida, and divides her time between family, writing and traveling.

Email Brenda at authorbrendajackson@gmail.com or visit her on her website at www.brendajackson.net.

To the man who will always and forever
have my heart, Gerald Jackson Sr.

To Cozett Mazelin and Tamira K. Butler-Likely.
Thanks for your assistance in my research of
two-year-olds. Your information was invaluable
and I hope I did the character of "Little Laramie"
justice! I could tell from your responses
that you are great moms!!

To my readers who continue to love my
Westmorelands, this book is for you.

For none of us lives for ourselves alone,
and none of us dies for ourselves alone.

—Romans 14:7, NIV

Prologue

Bristol Lockett hurriedly moved toward her front door, wondering who would be visiting this late in the afternoon. Although it was still light outside, this particular Paris community was on the other side of town from the famous city center, where most people hung out on Friday nights and weekends. Normally, she would be there herself, but her habits had changed in the last couple of months.

She was one of those pregnant women who experienced morning sickness in the morning and at night. Smells alone would send her running to the nearest bathroom. Most morning sickness lasted until the twelfth week of pregnancy. She was in her sixteenth week and there didn't seem to be an end in sight. Her doctor had even placed her on a special diet to make sure she was getting sufficient nutrients into her body for her baby.

A glance out the peephole indicated her visitor was her best friend, Dionne Burcet. She and Dionne had met when Bristol first arrived in Paris four years ago to attend Académie des Beaux-Arts, which was considered one of the most prestigious and influential art schools in all of France.

Dionne also attended the art academy and with so much in common, they'd hit it off immediately.

Dionne, who'd been born in Paris, had introduced Bristol to French culture, and Bristol had taken Dionne home with her to America last Christmas to meet her aunt Dolly and to experience New Year's Eve in New York. A feeling of sadness fell over Bristol whenever she remembered that was the last holiday she and her aunt had spent together. Her aunt, her only relative, had died a few days later in her sleep.

Bristol opened the door smiling. "Dionne! This is a surprise. I thought you were leaving for—"

"I have something to tell you, Bristol."

Bristol heard the urgency in Dionne's voice, which resonated in her eyes, as well. "Okay, come on in. Would you like a cup of tea? I was just about to make a pot."

"Yes, thanks."

Bristol wondered about Dionne's strange demeanor as she led her friend to the kitchen, which wasn't far from the front door. She loved her studio apartment. It was small but just the right size for her. And it held a lot of memories. Her baby was conceived here, in her bed. She would miss this place when she moved back to the United States next month after graduation.

"Sit and tell me what's wrong. Did you and Mark have a fight?"

Dionne shook her head as she sat down at the table. "No. It's not about me, it's about you."

"Me?" Bristol said in surprise.

"Yes. You remember what you shared with me last month?"

"Yes. I told you I was pregnant." Telling Dionne hadn't been easy but she'd felt the need to confide in someone. The baby's father was a man she'd met one day at a café. He had been a US navy SEAL out with a few of his friends and he'd flirted with her outrageously. She'd done something she had never done before and flirted back. There had been something about Laramie Cooper that had made her behave like a different person and for the next three days, over the Christmas holidays, they had enjoyed a holiday fling. It was a period in her life she would never forget. Her pregnancy made certain of that.

"Yes, from that guy. The American soldier."

"Not just a soldier, Dionne. Laramie was a navy SEAL," Bristol said, smiling proudly.

"Yes, the navy SEAL Laramie Cooper," Dionne said.

From the time they'd been introduced, Bristol had liked his name and he'd said he liked hers. Laramie had told her very little about his work or even about himself. She knew he was an only child and his parents were still living in the US. He hadn't said where.

Bristol regretted that Dionne had been away visiting her grandparents in Marseille for the holidays and hadn't been around to meet Laramie. She believed her friend would have liked him. "What about him?"

"You told me how the two of you spent time together over the holidays and since finding out you were pregnant, you've been trying to locate him to let him know."

Since she'd known very little about Laramie, other than his name and age, she had mailed a letter to him in care of the US Navy. The letter had been returned weeks ago stamped UNABLE TO LOCATE.

"Yes, and like I told you, it doesn't matter to me that our time together was a no-strings affair, I believe he has a right to know about his child. I refused to do to him what my mother did to my father."

For years, Bristol never knew her father and, according to her mother, she never told her father about Bristol. It was information her mother had taken with her to the grave. It was only after her mother's death that Bristol's aunt Dolly had given her the man's name. She had met Randall Lockett at sixteen. He had been surprised to find out about her and had welcomed her into his life.

"Yes, I know. That's why I decided to help you."

Bristol raised a brow. "Help me?"

"Yes."

"How?"

"Remember I told you about that guy—an American—I dated years ago? The one who worked at your embassy?"

"Yes, I remember."

"Well, he was recently reassigned back to the embassy here and I ran into him. I gave him your SEAL's name and asked if he would try locating him and forwarding him a message to contact you."

Happiness eased into Bristol and spread to all parts of her body. Although it might have been nothing more than a holiday fling for Laramie Cooper, it had been a lot more for her. She had fallen in love with him. "Was your friend able to find him?"

Dionne slowly nodded her head. "Yes."

Bristol stared at her friend, knowing there was more. The happiness she felt earlier began dissipating at the sadness she saw in Dionne's eyes. "What is it, Dionne? What did you find out?"

All sorts of things began rushing through her mind. What if Laramie hadn't been the single man he'd claimed to be and had a wife and children somewhere? When Dionne didn't say anything, but looked down at the cup of tea Bristol had placed in front of her, Bristol slouched her shoulders in disappointment. "I think I know why you're hesitating in telling me."

Dionne looked back at her. "Do you?"

"Yes. He's married. Although he told me he wasn't, you found out differently, didn't you?"

"Bristol."

"It doesn't matter. He has a right to know about his child

anyway. If he decides never to be a part of my baby's life, it will be his decision and—"

"That's not it, Bristol," Dionne cut in to say.

Bristol frowned. "Then what is it?"

Dionne took a sip of her tea, hesitating. The dawdling was driving Bristol crazy. "For Pete's sake, Dionne, will you just get it out and tell me what you found out about Laramie?"

Dionne held her gaze and drew in a deep breath. "Some mission he was on went bad and he was killed. He's dead, Bristol."

One

"Let me get this straight, Lieutenant Cooper. You actually want to give up your holiday leave and remain here and work on base?"

Laramie "Coop" Cooper forced his smile to stay in place while answering his commanding officer's question. "Yes, sir. I actually want to do that."

He wouldn't tell anyone that he'd looked forward to going home for the holidays, because honestly, he hadn't. The phone call he'd gotten from his parents that they would be jet-setting to London again this year was expected. They'd done so every holiday for as long as he could remember. He doubted they'd even canceled those plans that Christmas three years ago when they'd thought him dead.

At thirty-two, he had stopped letting his parents' actions affect him. As far as Ryan and Cassandra Cooper were concerned, the universe revolved around them and nobody else. Especially not a son who, at times, they seemed to forget existed. It wasn't that he thought his parents didn't love him; he knew they did. They just loved each other more. He had long ago accepted that his parents believed there were different degrees of love, and that the love they shared for each other outweighed the love for their child.

In a way, he should be glad that after thirty-five years of marriage his parents were still that into each other. They shared something special, had this unbreakable bond, and some would even say it was the love of a lifetime. But on the other hand, that love never extended to him in the same degree. He knew their lack of affection had nothing to do with his deciding to become a navy SEAL instead of joining his parents' multimillion-dollar manufacturing company. His father had understood Laramie's desire to make his decisions based on what he wanted to do with his life, and he appreciated his dad for accepting that.

More holidays than not, for as far back as Laramie could remember, he'd been packed up and shipped off to his paternal grandparents' ranch in Laredo. Not that he was complaining. His grandparents had been the best and hadn't hesitated to show him the degree of love he'd lacked at home. In fact, he would admit to resenting his parents when they did show up at his grandparents' ranch to get him.

So, here he was volunteering to give up his holiday leave. It wasn't as if he hadn't received invitations from his SEAL teammates to join them and their families for the holidays, because he had. Bane Westmoreland—code name Bane— had been the first to invite Laramie to spend the holidays with his family in Denver. But given the fact that Bane's wife, Crystal, had given birth to triplets six months ago, Laramie didn't want to get underfoot.

Same thing with Thurston McRoy—code name Mac— with his wife, Teri, and their four kids. Gavin Blake—code name Viper—would be celebrating his first Christmas as a married man so Laramie didn't want to intrude there, either. The only other single guy in the group was David

Holloway—code name Flipper. Flipper came from a huge family of four brothers, who were all SEALs, and a father who'd retired as a SEAL commanding officer. Laramie had spent the holidays with Flipper's family last year and didn't want to wear out his welcome.

"I'm denying your request, Lieutenant."

His commanding officer's words recaptured Laramie's attention. He met the man's gaze and tried to keep a frown off his face. "May I ask why, sir?"

"I think you know the reason. SEAL Team Six, of which you are a vital member, has been pretty damn busy this year. I don't have to list all the covert operations successfully accomplished with very few casualties. You deserve your holiday leave."

"Even if I don't want to take it?"

His commanding officer held his gaze. "Yes, even if you don't want to take it. Military leave is necessary, especially for a SEAL, to recoup both mentally and physically. Don't think I haven't noticed how much you've been pushing yourself. It's like you're trying to make up for the time you were a captive in Syria."

Laramie remembered all eleven months of being held prisoner in that guerilla hellhole. He hadn't known from one day to the next if he'd survive that day. The bastards had done everything in their power to make him think every day would be his last. They'd even played Russian roulette with him a couple of times.

It was on one of those particular days when he'd been rescued. Leave it to Bane, who was a master sniper, to bring down the four men from a distance of over a hundred feet. Laramie was convinced there was no way he would have survived if his SEAL team hadn't shown up.

During those eleven months he'd fought hard to stay sane and the one memory that had sustained him was the face of the woman he'd met in Paris just weeks before the mission.

Bristol Lockett.

It had been a three-day holiday affair. Sadly, there was little he knew about her other than sharing her bed had been the best sexual experience of his life.

"However, since I know you're going to insist," his commanding officer said, reclaiming Laramie's thoughts again, "I've got an important job that I want you to do. However, it means traveling to New York."

Laramie raised a brow. "New York?"

"Yes. An important delivery needs to be made to a member of the United Nations Security Council."

Laramie wondered what kind of delivery. Classified documents no doubt.

He'd heard how beautiful Manhattan was when it was decorated for this time of year. He'd been to the Big Apple a number of times, but never around the holidays. "Once I make the delivery, sir. Then what?"

"That, Lieutenant, is up to you. If you decide to take your holiday leave, then you won't have to report back here until the end of January as scheduled. However, if you still want to give up your leave, then you're free to come back here and I'll find more work for you to do."

Laramie nodded. He might take a week off to enjoy the sights and sounds of New York, but there was no doubt in his mind that he would be returning to San Diego for more work.

Bristol glanced around the art gallery. She always felt a sense of pride and accomplishment whenever she saw one of her paintings on display. Especially here at the Jazlyn Art Gallery of New York. She wanted to pinch herself to make sure she wasn't dreaming.

She had worked so hard for this moment.

"Looks good, doesn't it?"

She glanced up at her manager, Margie Townsend. "Yes, I have to admit that it does."

Margie's tenacious pit bull–like skills had landed Bristol a showing at this gallery, one of the most well-known and highly respected galleries in New York. She and Margie had met last year on the subway and struck up a conversation. When Bristol discovered what Margie did for a living, she felt their chance encounter must have been an omen. She'd invited Margie to her home to see her work, and the excitement reflected in the woman's eyes had been incredible. Margie promised to change Bristol's life. She promised that Bristol would get to the point where she could quit her job as an assistant magazine editor and make her living as the artist she was born to be.

Less than eight months later, Margie had sold one of Bristol's paintings. The buyer had been so taken with her work that he'd also purchased several others. The money had been enough to bring about the change in Bristol's life Margie had guaranteed. She had turned in her resignation and now painted full-time in her home.

Bristol was happy with the direction of her career. She got to spend more time with her son since she kept him with her every day instead of taking him to day care like she used to do.

Her son.

She smiled when she thought about her rambunctious two-year old—the most important person in her life. He was her life. Every decision she made was done with him in mind. She'd already started a college fund for him and couldn't wait to share the holidays with him. Last night they had put up their Christmas tree. Correction, she thought, widening her smile. She had put up the tree. Laramie had gotten in the way with his anxiousness to help.

Laramie…

It was hard not to think of Laramie's father whenever she

thought of her son. She had named him after his biological father, Laramie Cooper, who had died way too young, and without knowing about the child they'd created together. Sometimes she wondered what he would have done had he lived and gotten the letter she'd tried to send him.

Would he have been just as happy as she'd been? Or would he have claimed the child wasn't his? She might not have known Laramie Cooper long, but she wanted to believe he was a man who would have wanted to be a part of his child's life. The way her father had wanted to be a part of hers. The two years she'd shared with the man who'd fathered her had not been enough.

"Are you ready to go? You have a big day tomorrow and I want you well rested."

She chuckled as she tightened her coat around her. "And I will be."

Margie rolled her eyes. "I guess as much as you can be with a two-year-old running around the place."

She knew what Margie was hinting at. Bristol was spending less and less time painting now that Laramie was in the terrible twos. It was also the get-into-everything twos. The only time she really got to paint was during his nap time or while he slept at night.

"Did you give any more thought to what I said?"

Margie had suggested that she send Laramie to day care two to three days a week. "Yes, but I'm thinking of hiring someone to come to my home instead of me having to take him somewhere."

"That might work, but he has to start learning to interact with other kids, Bristol." As they walked toward the waiting private car that was compliments of the gallery, Margie changed the subject. "Have you decided to go out with Steven?"

Bristol shrugged. Steven Culpepper was nice enough, and good-looking, too. However, he was moving too fast.

At least, faster than she liked. They'd met a few weeks ago when she'd closed a huge deal for a commissioned piece. He was the corporation's attorney. He'd asked for her number and, without thinking much about it, she'd given it to him. Since then he'd called constantly, trying to get her to go out with him. So far, she hadn't. She hated pushy men and Steven, she thought, was one of the pushiest.

"No."

"I like him."

Bristol grinned. "You would. You have a thing for wealthy businessmen." She knew Margie had been married to one. Or two. She was on her third marriage and not even fifty yet. But the one thing all three men had in common was the size of their bank accounts.

"Well, I know you still have a thing for Laramie's father and—"

"What makes you think that?"

"Bristol, you make it quite obvious that you haven't gotten over him."

Did she? The only thing she'd told Margie about Laramie's father was that he'd been in the military and had died in the line of duty without knowing he'd fathered a son. She'd even fabricated a tale that Laramie had been her deceased husband and not just her lover.

It had been pretty easy. Dionne's fiancé, Mark, had helped. Mark worked for a judge in Paris and had falsified the papers before Bristol left France. It was a way to make sure her son had his father's last name without people wondering why her last name was different. It wasn't as if she was trying to cash in on her son's father's military benefits or anything.

"If you ask me, I think you should finally move on… with Steven," Margie said, interrupting Bristol's thoughts.

Bristol wanted to say that nobody had asked Margie. But deep down, a part of her knew Margie was right. It was time for Bristol to move on. However, she doubted very seriously that it would be with Steven.

A short while later she was entering her home, a beautiful brownstone in Brooklyn that she'd inherited from her aunt Dolly. She loved the place and knew the neighborhood well. She'd come to live here with her aunt ten years ago, when she was fifteen. That had been the year her mother died.

She didn't want to think sad thoughts, especially after her positive meeting with Maurice Jazlyn, the owner of the gallery. The man was excited about tomorrow night's showing and expected a huge crowd. He loved all the artworks she would be exhibiting.

"How did things go tonight?"

She turned toward the older woman coming down the stairs to the main floor. Charlotte Kramer lived next door and had been a close friend of her aunt Dolly. With her four kids grown and living in other parts of New York, Ms. Charlotte had thought about moving to a condo not far away, but had decided she'd rather stay put since she'd lived in the area close to forty years and loved her neighbors. Ms. Charlotte said there were a lot of memories of Mr. Kramer stored in that house. He'd passed away eight years ago, a couple of years after Bristol had come to live with her aunt.

Bristol appreciated that Ms. Charlotte loved watching Laramie for her whenever she had meetings to attend. And Ms. Charlotte had offered to watch him again tomorrow night when Bristol attended the exhibition.

"Everything went well. Everyone is excited about tomorrow. Mr. Jazlyn thinks he'll be able to sell all my paintings."

A huge smile touched Ms. Charlotte's lips. "That's good news. Dolly would be proud. Candace would be, too."

She doubted the latter. Her mother had never approved

of Bristol becoming an artist. It was only after she died that
Bristol learned why. Her father had been an artist who'd
broken things off with her mother to study in Paris. It was
only after he'd left the country that her mother discovered
her pregnancy. She'd known how to reach him but refused
to let him know about his child. She had resented him for
ending things with her to pursue his dream.

Bristol had been sixteen when she'd met her father for
the first time. She would not have met him then if it hadn't
been for her aunt's decision to break the promise she'd
made to Bristol's mother years ago. Aunt Dolly wanted
Bristol to know her father and vice versa. When Bristol
was given the man's name, she had been shocked to find
that the person whose art she'd admired for years was really her father.

She'd finally gotten the courage to contact him on her
sixteenth birthday. Randall Lockett was married with a
family when they'd finally met. He had two young sons—
ages ten and twelve—with his wife Krista. Bristol was
his only daughter and she favored him so much it was uncanny. She was also his only offspring who'd inherited his
artistic gift.

When he'd died, he had bequeathed to her full tuition
to the school he himself had attended in Paris as well as
the vast majority of his paintings. He'd felt she would appreciate them more than anyone, and she had. She'd heard
that Krista had remarried and sold off all the artworks that
had been left to her and their sons.

Paintings by Randall Lockett were valued in the mil-
lions. Art collectors had contacted Bristol on numerous
occasions, but she had refused to sell. Instead her father's
paintings were on display at the two largest art museums
in the world, New York's Metropolitan Museum of Art and
the Orsay Museum in Paris.

A few months before her father had died, they had completed a painting together, which was her most cherished possession. It was so uncanny that when it came to art she and her father had possessed identical preferences. They even held their brushes the same way. On those days when she felt down and out, she would look at the portrait over her fireplace and remember the six weeks they'd spent together on his boat while painting it. That was when they'd noticed all the similarities they shared as artists. She hadn't known he was dying of cancer until his final days. He hadn't wanted her to know. He was determined to share every moment he could with her without seeing pity and regret in her eyes.

Forcing those sad thoughts from her mind, she glanced back over at Ms. Charlotte. "Did Laramie behave himself tonight?" she asked, placing her purse on the table.

The older woman chuckled. "Doesn't he always?"

Bristol smiled. "No, but I know you wouldn't tell me even if he was a handful."

"You're right, I wouldn't. Boys will be boys. I know. I raised four of them."

Yes, she had, and to this day Ms. Charlotte's sons looked out for her, making sure she had everything she needed and then some.

After Ms. Charlotte left, Bristol climbed the stairs to her son's room. He was in his bed, sound asleep. Crossing the bedroom floor, she saw he had put away all his toys. That was a good sign that he was learning to follow instructions.

Approaching the bed, she sat on the edge and gently ran her fingers through the curls on his head. He favored his father. Laramie Cooper's features were etched in her memory. Whenever Laramie smiled, he displayed his father's dimples in both cheeks. Then there was the shape of his mouth and the slant of his eyes. Like father, like son. There was no doubt in her mind that one day Laramie would grow up and capture some woman's heart just as quickly and easily as his father had claimed hers.

As she sat there watching her son sleep, she couldn't stop her mind from going back to that time in Paris when she'd met US Navy SEAL Laramie Cooper…

Two

Paris, France, three years ago

Bristol glanced up from her sketch pad when she heard the male voices entering the café. Military men. All five of them. That was easy to deduce, even though they weren't wearing military attire. They were wearing jeans, shirts and dark leather jackets. The five walked confidently and were in perfect physical condition. Boy, were they ever! She wondered what branch of service they represented. It really didn't matter. Whichever one branch it was, they were representing it well.

The group took the table not far away from where she sat and one of the men, as if he felt someone staring at him, glanced over at her. Bam! She'd been caught. She hadn't averted her gaze back to her sketch pad quickly enough. For some reason, she knew without glancing back up that he was still looking at her. She could feel his gaze, just as if it was a physical caress. It made her heart beat faster. It seemed that every single hormone in her body had begun to sizzle. Nothing like that had ever happened to her before.

Okay, Bristol, concentrate on your sketch, she inwardly

admonished herself. Her father hadn't paid her tuition at
one of the most prestigious art schools in France for her to
get all hot and bothered by a bunch of military men. Although the five were extremely handsome, it was only one
of the men who had caught her eye. The one who'd stared
back at her.

"Excuse me, miss."

She glanced up and the man was now standing at her
table. Up close he was even more gorgeous. Definitely eye
candy of the most delectable kind. Hot. Sexy. You name it
and this man could definitely claim it. That had to be the
reason intense heat was plowing up her spine.

Bristol swallowed deeply before saying, "Yes?"

"I was wondering if…"

When he didn't finish but kept looking at her, she asked.
"Wondering what?"

"If I could join you?"

She wished he could but unfortunately, he couldn't. She
glanced at her watch then back at him. "Sorry, but I work
here and happen to be on my lunch break, which will end
in less than five minutes."

"What time do you get off today?"

She tilted her head to look at him. "Excuse me?"

"I asked what time you get off today. I'll wait."

She figured that he had to be kidding, but the look in
his eyes showed that he wasn't. "I get off in four hours."

"I'll wait. What's your name?"

This guy was definitely moving fast. But she couldn't
ignore the scorching hot attraction between them, even if
she wanted to. And for some reason, she didn't want to.
She liked it.

"My name is Bristol Lockett."

"The name Bristol is unusual. It suits you well. I like it."

And she liked his voice. It was deep and husky. The
sound made heat curl inside her. OMG! What on earth

was wrong with her? She'd never thought such outlandish things in her life. She might not have always been prim and proper but she'd been pretty close to it. She'd been in Paris close to four years and although she'd dated, most of the time she did not. She preferred curling up with her sketch pad and working on her watercolors than going out with any man. But now this ultrafine specimen was making her rethink that decision.

"Are you American or French?"

She blinked at his question. "I'm American."

"So am I."

She smiled. And what a good-looking American he was, with a body to die for. She felt as if she could draw her last breath just from looking at him. This guy was tall, at least six foot two or three. And his skin was the color of lightly roasted almonds. His dark eyes appeared somewhat slanted, and as far as she was concerned his lips were perfectly shaped. His hair was cut low on his head and his ears were just the right size for his face. But what captured her attention more than anything were those dimples in his cheeks. Doing absolutely nothing but standing there, he was arousing something within her that no other man ever had.

"And who are you?" she asked, deciding not to let him ask all the questions.

"I'm Laramie," he said, stretching out his hand to her.

She took it and immediately a spike of heat seemed to burst from his fingers and hit her dead center between the thighs. And when she stared into his eyes and saw the dark heat in his pupils, she knew he'd felt something, as well.

"Are you married, Laramie?"

"No. I've never been married. What about you? I approached you because I didn't see a ring on your finger."

At least he didn't hit on married women. Some men didn't care. "No, I'm not married, either, and never have been."

"So, Bristol Lockett, do I have your permission?"

She licked her lips. "For what?"

That sexy smile widened. "To be here when you get off."

Then what? she wondered but decided not to ask. "Sure, if that's what you want."

His chuckle made desire claw at her but it was his next words that sealed her fate. "There are a lot of things I want when it comes to you, Bristol."

Jeez. If he wasn't standing there she would close her eyes and moan. This man presented a temptation she shouldn't even think about yielding to. Too bad her best friend, Dionne, was out of town for the holidays and not around to talk some sense into her.

"What about if we share a drink at one of the pubs first?" she asked, and then frowned. Why had she made it sound as if she would be willing to move to the next stage once they shared a drink?

"That's fine. I'll be back in four hours."

When he walked off she glanced at her watch. Her break was officially over but she knew her encounter with this military man was just beginning.

She hurried behind the counter to put on her apron while watching Mary-Ann, another waitress, head over to the table to serve the five guys. More people entered the café, and Bristol was about to cross the room to serve a couple with a little girl when Mary-Ann stopped her.

"They asked for you," Mary-Ann said, smiling.

"Who?"

"Those soldiers. I've given them menus but they want you to serve their table. That's fine with me. Then I don't have to commit a sin by forgetting I've been married to Joel almost twenty years. Those five are too much temptation," she said, fanning herself. "I hope you can handle it."

Bristol hoped she could handle it as well, as she made her way to the table where all five men sat. Hot and heavy testosterone was thick in the air surrounding them. Drawing in a deep breath she approached them with her notepad in hand. "Have you guys decided what you're having?"

"Apparently, Coop has," one of the men said, grinning at her. "We're still deciding."

She nodded. "Okay, and who is Coop?"

"I am," the guy who had introduced himself to her earlier said.

She met his gaze. "I thought your name was Laramie."

He smiled again and she tried not to feel weak in the knees. "It is. My real name is Laramie Cooper. They call me Coop."

"Oh."

"Let me introduce everyone," Laramie said. "First off, guys, this is Bristol," he said to his friends.

"Hello, Bristol," they all said simultaneously as they stood to their feet, showing they had manners.

"Hello."

"I'm Bane," one of the men said, extending his hand to her.

She smiled at the very handsome military man as she shook his hand. "Hi, Bane."

"Is that a New York accent?" Bane asked.

"Yes, you would think after being in France for almost four years it would not be so easily detected."

Bane's smile widened. "Some things you can't get rid of."

"Apparently," she said, chuckling.

"I'm Flipper," another one of the guys said, offering his hand. He was definitely a hottie, with blond hair and the bluest eyes she'd ever seen. The color reminded her of the ocean and she wondered if that was why his nickname was Flipper.

"Nice meeting you, Flipper," she said, shaking his hand, as well.

"Same here, Bristol."

"I'm Mac," another one of the men said, leaning across to take her hand. This man appeared older than the others by at least three or four years.

"Hi, Mac."

"And I'm Viper."

She glanced at the man who introduced himself as Viper. He was taller than the others and just as handsome. His eyes seemed sharp and penetrating. "Hi, Viper," she said, shaking his hand.

"Hi, Bristol," Viper returned, smiling.

"And you know me," Laramie said, taking her hand.

And just like before, a spike of heat hit her. "Yes, I know you." She quickly pulled her hand away. "It's nice meeting all of you and I like all your nicknames," she said as the men all sat back down.

Bane chuckled. "They aren't nicknames. They're our military code names."

"Oh. And what branch of the military?"

"We're navy SEALs," the one named Flipper said, grinning proudly.

He had every right to feel that way. She'd heard about navy SEALs. Some considered them the American government's secret weapon against any enemy force.

"So, Laramie, I'll start with you. What will you have?" she asked, getting ready to write on her notepad.

"For now I'll take a juicy hamburger, a large order of French fries and a huge malted strawberry shake."

For now? She wondered what he planned to have later. From the way he was looking at her, she had an idea. And why didn't realizing this guy evidently thought she was on his menu bother her?

Bristol went around the table and took everyone's order. Apparently all five were big eaters and she wondered where they would put all that food and how they stayed in such great physical shape. After turning their orders in to the cook, she began waiting on other tables, but felt the heat of Laramie's gaze on her the entire time. Every time she glanced over in his direction, he was staring at her. Blatantly so.

Maybe it hadn't been a good idea for her to agree to have a drink with him when she got off work. She knew nothing about him, other than his name was Laramie Cooper, his military code name was Coop, he loved juicy hamburgers and he was a navy SEAL.

She delivered their food a short while later and watched them eat all of it. She could tell that the five were more than just members of the same military team. They shared a close friendship. That much was obvious from the way they joked around with each other.

Mac was married and had no problem showing her pictures of his wife and kids. It was evident he was proud of them. Bane, she'd discovered, was also married, but from the way the others teased him she could only assume he hadn't seen his wife in a while, which meant the two were separated. Like Laramie, Viper and Flipper were single and from the sound of things they intended to stay that way.

At the end of the meal when they paid their bill, she was shocked at the tip they left her. She would not normally have earned that much tip money in a week. "Thanks, guys."

"No, we want to thank you," Flipper said standing, like the others. "It was nice meeting you, Bristol, and the food was great."

The others shared the same sentiments as they moved to leave the café. Laramie hung back. "I'll be here when you get off work."

She knew now was a good time to tell him that she'd changed her mind about that. However, there was something about Laramie Cooper that made her hold back from doing so. It might have been his smile, or the way he was making her feel, or just the fact that she deserved to have some fun for a change.

For four years she had worked hard at the art academy and come spring she would be graduating. The café would be closing for the holidays and she had the next ten days off work. As far as she was concerned, there was nothing wrong with Laramie being there when she got off. They would just grab drinks at one of the pubs nearby. Besides, after today, she probably wouldn't see him again.

"I'll be waiting," she heard herself say.

She didn't have to wait. Laramie arrived a half hour before she was due to leave work. He ordered a croissant and coffee while he waited for her. She hung up her apron, wished everyone a Merry Christmas and then headed toward the table where he sat. He stood, smiling down at her.

"Ready?" he asked her.

"Yes" was her reply, although she wasn't sure what he had in mind and if she should be ready or not.

He surprised her by taking her hand, as if they both needed to feel the sexual chemistry between them. He led her through the doors and onto the sidewalk. Holiday decorations were everywhere. It was hard to believe tomorrow was Christmas Eve. Last year she had gone home for Christmas and had taken her best friend, Dionne, with her. But not this year. Her aunt Dolly had died in her sleep four days into the New Year.

She needed to stop thinking that she didn't have any living relatives when she had two brothers and a stepmother. She knew they'd only tolerated her while her father was alive and now, with him gone, they had let her know—by not returning her calls or letters—that they didn't have to put up with her anymore. That was fine. She'd adjusted to being a loner. At least she had Dionne and Dionne's family. The thought had even crossed Bristol's mind that she should not return to the United States after graduation and make Paris her home.

"Which pub are we going to?" she asked the man who was walking beside her and still holding her hand.

He smiled down at her. "Which one do you suggest?"

"Charlie's is a good one. It's right around the corner."

They didn't say much as they walked to the pub. They talked about the holidays. He told her that he and his team would be headed out in four days and they were in Paris for a little R and R.

"Your friends are nice," she said.

He smiled down at her as they continued walking. "They said the same thing about you."

She smiled at that, while trying to ignore all that desire she saw in his eyes. She figured if they kept talking it would go away. "The five of you seem close."

"We are. In fact, we're like brothers. Viper, Flipper, Bane and I attended the naval academy together and immediately became the best of friends. Mac is four years older and finished the academy ahead of us. He's been a SEAL longer and likes to think he's looking out for us."

They reached the pub and saw it was crowded with no tables available. It seemed everyone had decided to begin celebrating the holidays early. "I have an idea," Laramie said, tightening his hand on hers.

"What?"

"Let's go someplace private."

An uneasy feeling crept over her, but it was overpowered by exciting sensations that settled in her stomach. Their hands were still joined and his fingers felt warm and reassuring.

"I want to be honest with you about something."

She swallowed. "About what?"

"Usually I spend the holidays alone, but I want to spend them with you."

She held his gaze a minute and then asked, "What about your friends?"

"They'll be in touch with their families."

"But you won't?"

He didn't say anything for a moment and then he said, "My parents are still alive. I'm their only child. But we've never spent the holidays together."

She found that odd. Christmas was the one holiday she never had to worry about being alone. Her mother had always made it special and after her mother's death, her aunt Dolly had been there for her. She'd even spent one Christmas with her father. It had been the first and last holiday they'd spent together. This would be the first Christmas that she had no one. She thought it sad that Laramie had never really spent his holidays with family.

She saw the sincerity in his eyes, in what he'd told her. He wasn't trying to feed her a pity line but was telling her the truth. She felt it in her heart.

"I can think of a place we can go," she suggested.

"Where?"

She knew it would be crazy to invite him, a perfect stranger to her home, but she was about to issue the invitation. "My place. It's not far from here. Just so happens I was going to be alone for the holidays as well and would love some company."

His hand tightened on hers. "You sure?"

Was she? She had never done anything so daring in her life.

She wasn't a child. She knew the obvious signs. Desire was thick between them. Spontaneous combustion as volatile as it could get. She dated infrequently and most guys who'd hit on her had tried to work her. But she would say that Laramie was the first guy who'd tried and managed to elicit her interest. He was also the first guy she was trusting to this degree. She had never invited a man to her home before. There had to be a reason for her doing so now.

"Yes. I'm sure," she said.

From the way his lips spread into a smile, she knew her response had pleased him. "All right then. Lead the way."

That smile made her heart miss a beat as they continued to walk along the sidewalk. Like she'd told him, she didn't live far and they arrived at her studio apartment in no time. "It's small," she said, opening the door. "But it's the right size for me."

She stepped aside and he entered. She immediately thought her apartment might be just the right size for her, but with him inside it, it suddenly appeared small.

"Nice place," he said, glancing around.

Bristol was glad she was a neat freak. There was nothing out of place. "There's a bottle of wine over there if you want to pour us a glass," she said, removing her coat and hanging it in one of the closets.

"Okay," he said, removing his jacket. She took it and hung it in the closet, as well. She tried not to notice how perfect his abs were and what a broad chest he had. She also tried not to notice the sexual chemistry between them, which had increased now that they were alone and behind closed doors.

"Do you need to let your friends know where you are? Won't they be worried when you don't return to your hotel?" she asked him.

He shook his head as he grabbed the wine bottle and glasses off the rack. "No. They'll figure things out."

"Okay." She sat down at the table while he poured the wine into their glasses. And then he joined her there. "I know this isn't champagne but let's make a toast."

"To what?"

"To what I believe will be the best holiday I've ever had."

Deep down she believed it would be the best she ever

had, too. Their glasses clinked and then they took a sip. She
met his gaze over the rim and immediately, a deep sexual
hunger flared to life in her midsection. From the hot, penetrating look in his eyes, the same hunger hit him, as well.

Bristol placed her glass down the same moment he did.
And then he stood and reached out to her. She went into his
arms willingly and he lowered his head and captured her
mouth in his. The moment she felt his lips on hers, a deep,
drugging rush of desire filled her to the core.

He was using his tongue in the most provocative way,
making shivers of need course through every part of her.
She had never been kissed like this before and he was an
expert.

He deepened the kiss and her mouth became locked to
his. She couldn't hold back the moan that erupted from
deep within her throat. Nor could she hold back the sensations overtaking her. She had been kissed before, but never
like this. Never with this much possession, this much overwhelming power.

Moments later he ended the kiss and pulled back slightly
to look down at her. A sexy smile touched the corners of his
lips and the arms around her tightened, bringing her closer
to him. "I wanted to kiss you from the moment I saw you.
I had a deep yearning to know how you tasted."

Wow! She wasn't used to having such carnal conversa-
tions with a man. "Is that why you kissed me the way you
did just now?"

"Partly."

"And the other reason?"

"I just wanted the feel of my tongue in your mouth."

And then as if he hadn't gotten enough of doing that
the last time, he lowered his head and captured her mouth
again. On a breathless moan she parted her lips, giving him
the opening he needed. He slid his tongue inside, mating it
with hers, over and over again.

When he finally released her mouth, she looked up at him with glazed eyes. "What are you doing?" she asked, barely able to get the words out. Never had a kiss left her so off balance.

"Starting our celebration of the holidays."

She could feel blood rushing through her veins with his words. She hadn't expected this so soon. She figured they would share a drink today and then tomorrow he could come back for lunch. But it seemed he had other plans, plans she was giving in to. She couldn't help it. So many sexual sensations were taking over her mind and body just from his kiss. She knew there was no way she could stop from wanting him. He sealed her fate when he began kissing her again and she felt herself being lifted into his arms.

He was carrying her someplace and she knew where when he placed her on the bed. What happened next was amazing. In record time he had removed both of their clothes, as if needing to be skin to skin with her was paramount. As if needing to see her naked body was essential.

In a way she understood, since seeing him standing there without a stitch of clothing was doing something to her, as well. He represented such virility and masculinity, and coiling arousal was throbbing deep in her core. Never had she wanted to make love to someone so badly. Never had she felt this filled with need. And she could tell from his huge erection that he wanted her. His desire for her was obvious.

She watched as he put on a condom before heading back to the bed. She reached out and glided her hands up his tight, sculpted abdomen and chest, loving the feel of his skin. Heat curled inside her with the contact.

"You touch me and I will touch you," he warned, grazing his jaw against her ear, while growling low in his throat. It amazed her that he would respond to her touch this way.

"I want you to touch me, Laramie."

She couldn't believe she'd said that. But there was something about Laramie Cooper that she didn't understand. Namely, how he could make her lose her common sense. How he could make her nerves dance and her brain race. How he had the ability to make her want to have things she'd done without in the past. And how he made her want him with a passion.

She needed to make him aware of something. Make him understand and she heard herself saying, "I've never brought a man here before."

She felt the intensity of his gaze all over her body.

"There's a first time for everything, don't you think?" he replied, slowly moving back toward the bed.

With each step he took, she felt her womb contract. He was staring at her with dark, penetrating eyes and her body heated under his intense regard. She'd never had a one-night stand in her life. Always thought she was above that. But at that moment the only thing she wanted was this man, who had the ability to mess with her mind and senses.

There was something else she needed to tell him and it was best if she did it now. "Laramie?"

"Yes?"

"I'm not on any type of birth control."

If she thought that revelation would stop him dead in his tracks, she'd been wrong. He kept moving toward her. "I have condoms. Plenty of them. Around a dozen or so. And if we need more we'll get them," he told her.

Get more? Did he honestly think they would use more than a dozen? Her heart began beating way too fast as she wondered just what kind of stamina he had. Would she be able to keep up?

She was about to find out.

He joined her on the bed and began kissing her again while touching her all over. Sexual excitement churned inside her, sending an intense throb through her veins. She slipped her arms around his muscled back, loving the manly feel of him.

"I'm dying to taste you," he whispered, just moments before shifting his body to place his head between her legs.

She gripped tight to his shoulders as she felt his hot tongue inside her, stroking and licking. He was unwavering in his determination to taste her like he wanted. Sensations she'd never experienced before rushed through her and instinctively, she made sinfully erotic movements with her hips against his mouth.

Over and over he laved her womanly core with greedy intent, making her whisper his name over and over. Suddenly, her body exploded like a volcano erupting and she surrendered to the pleasure he'd given her.

Before the last spasm left her body, he had shifted to position his body over hers, and then she felt him enter her, stretching her to accommodate his size. She inhaled the scent of him—the scent of them—and then used her tongue to lick his shoulder, needing to taste the texture of his skin.

He pushed his shaft as deep inside her as he could go and then he locked their legs together. He began moving, thrusting back and forth, in and out. He established a rhythm that sent sexual undercurrents all through her body.

He looked down at her, held her gaze as he made love to her. She clung to him, holding tight to his shoulders as if they were a lifeline. His languid, deep, hard thrusts were driving her over the edge and making every nerve ending in her body zing brutally to life.

He threw his head back and growled her name as he continued to make love to her, indulging her with his words. Her skin sizzled where their bodies connected and the more he stroked inside her, the more her body awakened to the aching hunger he was feeding.

And then he called her name again. Together they were slammed with another orgasm. He gathered her in his arms, touched the side of her face with his fingers as they rode the tidal waves of ecstasy together.

The next morning it had felt odd waking up with a man in her bed. They had made love practically all evening, only to get up around eight and eat some of the soup she'd made the day before with French bread. Then they had gotten back in bed and made love all over again. All through the night.

No personal information was exchanged. None was needed. She knew the next three days would be considered one and done. Chances were, they would never see each other again. They were taking advantage of the now.

"You're awake?"

She glanced over at him and saw desire in the depths of his dark eyes. "Yes, I'm awake."

"Good."

He got out of bed to put on a condom then returned to her. "And what if I wanted breakfast first?" she asked, grinning.

He grinned back. "And do you want breakfast first?"

She shook her head. "No. I want you, Laramie."

And she did want him. She had to keep telling herself this was just sex and nothing more. When he left here the day after Christmas he wouldn't be coming back, nor would they stay in touch. The only thing she would have were her memories. Regardless, she could not and would not ever regret any time spent with him.

After making love that morning they dressed and went out to grab breakfast. He surprised her with his suggestion that they get a Christmas tree. That meant they had to purchase ornaments, as well. He refused to let her pay for anything. Like kids, they rushed back to the house and decorated the tree. Their tree.

Since most restaurants were closed for the holidays, she decided to prepare Christmas dinner for them. That meant grocery shopping, which she told him she wanted to do alone. She knew from their earlier shopping trip how he liked to spend money and she wanted Christmas dinner to be her treat.

When she returned to her apartment he was waiting for her. The minute she opened the door and glanced over at him, heated sexual attraction consumed them. She couldn't put her grocery bags down fast enough before he was ripping off her clothes, making love to her against the refrigerator.

He surprised her on Christmas Day with a gift, a beautiful scarf and a pair of earrings. The gift touched her deeply. He'd apparently gone shopping when she left to get groceries.

She surprised him with a gift, as well. A pair of gloves, since she'd noticed his were well-worn. He said he enjoyed Christmas dinner, but most of Christmas was spent in bed making love rather than eating.

The next morning, the day after Christmas, she awoke to find him dressed and ready to go. Ready to walk out of her life. She hadn't expected it to be so hard, but it was. She knew she had fallen in love with him. Not with the sex but with the man.

He kissed her deeply, wished her the best in her artistic dreams and thanked her for making this one of the best holidays for him, ever. And then he turned and walked out the door...without looking back.

She'd quickly gotten up and stood at the window to watch him leave. He'd called a cab and, as if he'd known she would be there at the window, before getting into the cab he looked over his shoulder, saw her, blew her a kiss and then waved goodbye.

She blew him a kiss and waved back. And as the cab drove away she knew at that moment that Laramie Cooper had taken a piece of her heart with him.

Three

"I'm glad you guys are finding this entire thing amusing," Laramie said as he moved around the hotel room to dress. He had placed the mobile call on speaker while engaging in a five-way conversation with his teammates.

"Hey, Coop, we can't help but think it's pretty damn funny," Bane Westmoreland said. "I can just imagine the look on your face when you discovered what you were delivering to that member of the Security Council wasn't top secret documents like you thought, but her pet cockatiel."

Laramie couldn't help but smile as he slid on a T-shirt. "No, Bane, you can't imagine."

"Well, just think positive," David Holloway said. "You got a free trip to New York."

"Damn, Flipper, it's cold as the dickens here. I prefer California weather," Laramie said.

"Stop whining, Coop," Gavin Blake said, laughing.

"Kiss it, Viper."

And then he said, "Hey, Mac? You still with us? You're kind of quiet."

"I'm still here," Thurston McRoy said. "I'm trying to keep up with you guys and watch the game, too. In case none of you realized, it's Thursday night football."

That led to a conversation about their predictions for what team would make it to the Super Bowl. By the time Laramie had ended the call, he was completely dressed and ready to leave.

And go where? He figured that since he had a taste for a juicy hamburger, he would grab a meal at Xavier's. Flipper had recommended he dine there and said he wouldn't be disappointed.

A short while later, Laramie entered the restaurant and was shown to a table. It was busy and there had been a fifteen-minute wait but he didn't mind. This wasn't his first visit to Times Square, but he did note a lot of changes since he was here last.

"What would you like tonight?"

He glanced up at the waitress. No one could credit him with being slow and he immediately knew the double meaning behind her question. "A menu would be nice," he said, hoping that would defuse any ideas she had.

Maybe another time, but not tonight. He just wasn't feeling it. He chuckled and wondered if he was running a fever. There hadn't been too many times when he'd turned down sex. And there was no doubt in his mind the woman was offering.

"I'll make sure you get a menu…as well as anything else you might want," she said, smiling.

He smiled back. "Thanks. The menu will do for now and a beer."

She walked off and returned with the menu and his beer. "Thanks."

"You can thank me later." Then she sashayed off.

He wondered why he wasn't taking advantage of those

curves and long gorgeous legs. His excuse had to be that this place sort of reminded him of that café in Paris. The one where Bristol worked.

Bristol.

He'd been thinking about her a lot lately. Maybe because it was around this time—during the holiday season three years ago when they'd met. Whatever the reason, Bristol Lockett was on his mind.

After his rescue from Syria, one of the first places he'd gone had been to Paris to see her, a woman he hadn't meant to ever see again. But something had compelled him to seek her out, only to be told by the manager of the apartment complex where she'd lived that she had returned to the United States a couple of years ago and had not left a forwarding address.

When he noticed the waitress looking over at him, he decided to place his order, eat and then leave. He wasn't up for any female company tonight and didn't want the woman to get any ideas.

An hour or so later, he left the restaurant a pretty satisfied man. The food had been delicious but he'd had a hard time deflating the waitress's flirtation. By the end of his meal, she'd all but placed her apartment key in his hand.

Instead of catching a cab back to his hotel room, he decided to walk off the hamburger and fries he'd eaten. Although he'd complained earlier about the cold weather, it really wasn't too bad. He'd endured worse. Like that time his team had that mission in the Artic.

He was about to cross the street when a sign ahead stopped him. It was an art gallery and the poster said:

TONIGHT
SPECIAL SHOWING OF ART BY BRISTOL

Bristol…

He shook his head. He was losing it. He hadn't thought Bristol was a common name. Was it?

What if it wasn't? Could it be his Bristol?

He dismissed the idea that Bristol was his. She was merely a woman he'd had a three-day fling with while relaxing in Paris before a mission.

Merely a woman he hadn't been able to forget in three years.

The name was unusual. He'd told her so when they'd met. He knew she was an artist. She'd shown him some of her art.

There was no way she could be here.

But then, why not? She was a New Yorker. He'd gathered that much from a conversation she'd had with Bane. Laramie hadn't asked her anything. His main focus had been sleeping with her.

What if the Bristol on the sign was the same Bristol from Paris?

His chest pounded at the possibility. He watched all the well-dressed people getting out of their limos and private cars to enter the gallery. He glanced down at himself. Jeans, pullover shirt, leather jacket, Stetson and boots. Definitely not dressed to mingle with the likes of the high-class crowd entering the gallery. But at that moment, he didn't give a royal damn.

He had to find out if this Bristol was the same woman he hadn't been able to forget.

"Would you like some more wine, Bristol?"

Bristol glanced up at Steven Culpepper, forced a smile and said, "No, thanks. I'm fine."

He nodded. Looking over her shoulder, he said, "Excuse me for a minute. A few of my clients just arrived."

"Sure."

She let out a deep sigh when he walked off. Why was he hanging around as if they were together when they weren't?

She glanced around. There was a huge crowd and she appreciated that. A great number of her paintings had been sold already.

"I see Steven is quite taken with you tonight, Bristol."

She turned to Margie. "I wish he wouldn't be. He's barely left my side."

Margie lifted a brow. "And you see that as a bad thing?"

Bristol shrugged. "I just don't want him getting the wrong idea."

"Oh, I see,"

Bristol doubted it. Margie was determined to play matchmaker.

"A lot of the people here tonight are ones he invited. People with money. Need I say more?" Margie then walked off.

No, in all honesty, Margie didn't have to say anything. Steven had told her several times tonight just how many people were here because of him. It was as if he'd assumed Bristol would not have gotten anyone here on her own. Although he was probably right about that, he didn't have to remind her of it every chance he got.

"Hello, Bristol."

She turned to an older gentleman. His face seemed familiar and after a quick study of his features, she remembered him. "You're Colin Kusac, a close friend of my father's."

He smiled. "Yes, that's right. I haven't seen you since the funeral and the reading of the will."

That was true. Her father had named Colin as executor, and the scene hadn't been nice that day, especially when all her father had left her was revealed. Krista had accused Bristol of looking for her father only to get his money. Her stepmother had been wrong about that.

Her father had told her that he and Colin had attended high school together and over the years had remained the best of friends. Before Randall died, he'd also told her to contact Mr. Kusac if she ever needed anything. Since there was nothing she'd needed, there had been no reason to call him.

"How have you been?" she asked him.

"Fine. And you? I understand you have a son."

She wondered how he'd known that. She lived a quiet life and it hadn't been highly publicized that she was Randall Lockett's daughter. Although, at her father's request, she had taken his last name. At sixteen it had taken a lot of getting used to, going from Bristol Washington to Bristol Lockett.

Although she'd taken her father's name, she'd never flaunted it to influence her own career. And in the art community her father had used the pseudonym Rand, so very few people had made the connection anyway. However, over the years, people had mentioned how much her paintings resembled those of the renowned artist Rand. Although Margie was aware of her father's identity, Bristol had sworn her manager to secrecy. Bristol wanted to make it on her own and not use her father as leverage.

And now she was Bristol Cooper...

"Yes, I have a beautiful two-year-old son. His first name is Laramie, after his father. His middle name is Randall, after my father. He has the names of two good men."

"Randall would have liked that. He would have been proud of his first grandchild." Colin didn't say anything for a minute and then added, "I miss my good friend. He was there for me more times than not. When I first saw your work, I was taken back by just how much you and he painted alike."

She smiled, thinking how wonderful it was that on this very important night, although her father wasn't here, a man she knew to be his closest friend was. "Yes, we discovered that before he died."

"Randall was a gifted artist and so are you."

"Thank you."

"There's a beautiful landscape over there that I'm thinking about buying. I wonder if you can tell me what inspired you."

She knew exactly which one he was talking about. It was the first painting she'd done after her father died and a lot of her pent-up emotions had been poured into it. "Certainly."

And then she and Colin moved toward the huge painting on the wall.

"May I help you, sir?"

Laramie wasn't surprised someone had approached him the minute he walked into the gallery. All he had to do was look around the room to see he seemed obviously out of place. He really wouldn't have to stay a minute longer if the man could answer one question. "The artist on the sign. Bristol. What's her last name?"

When the older man, who he suspected to be someone in charge, gave him a strange look, Laramie added, "I once knew someone by that name."

The man nodded his understanding. "Oh, I see. Her last name is—"

"I will handle this gentleman, Jazlyn," an authoritative voice said behind him.

Laramie didn't turn around. He figured whoever had spoken would make himself known soon enough. Besides, he hadn't liked the emphasis the man had placed on the word *gentleman*. As if he thought Laramie was anything but a gentleman. And what had he meant by "handle him"?

Laramie inwardly smiled. He would like to see that happen.

"Yes, of course, Mr. Culpepper." And then the older man walked off.

The guy who'd spoken came around to stand in front of Laramie and quickly sized him up. Laramie didn't have a problem with that since he was sizing up the other man, as well. And Laramie didn't like the arrogant glint in the man's eyes, like he assumed he was better than Laramie just because he was dressed in a designer suit.

A quick assessment told Laramie what he needed to know. The man was in his upper thirties, probably a Harvard or Yale graduate, a Wall Street type, most likely CEO of his own corporation.

"May I help you, Mr...?"

Evidently no one had explained to this man the proper way to introduce oneself. It wasn't by asking a question. Therefore, Laramie didn't intend to give his name unless this ass gave his. Besides, his name was irrelevant to what he wanted to know. "Like I was saying to the older man a moment ago, before we were interrupted—I once knew a woman name Bristol and was wondering, what is the artist's last name?"

The man's smile didn't quite reach his eyes. Who was this man and what business was it of his that Laramie was inquiring about the artist?

"I'm sure it's not the same person."

How the hell would you know? he wanted to say. Instead he said, "Let me decide that."

He could tell his response hadn't gone over well. The man's eyes darkened in irritation. Evidently, he wasn't used to being put in his place. "I won't let you decide anything. In fact, I'm almost certain Bristol doesn't know you."

Laramie was beginning to read the signs. This man was territorial. Evidently, there was something going on between him and the artist. "You sound sure of that, Mr..."

The man smiled. "Culpepper. Steven Culpepper. And

the reason I sound certain is because I know Bristol. We are well acquainted."

"Obviously. So what's her last name?" He tilted his Stetson back to stare down at the man, wondering why Steven was giving him a hard time.

"What's the name of the woman you're looking for? Just in case you haven't noticed, you're drawing attention."

And he was supposed to give a damn? Laramie drew in a deep breath, tired of playing this cat-and-mouse game. The man was probably right, it wasn't the same Bristol, but there was something about this man's attitude that rubbed Laramie the wrong way. "Lockett. Her name is Bristol Lockett."

The man smiled. "Lockett? Then I was right all along. Her last name isn't Lockett."

"So what is it?"

Evidently tired of this conversation as well, the man said, "It's Cooper. Bristol Cooper."

Laramie frowned. He and the woman had the same last name? What a coincidence. But then there were a lot of Coopers out there. "You're right. It's not the same woman. Sorry I took up so much of your time."

"No problem. Let me see you out."

"No need. I know my way." Laramie had made it to the door when he heard it. That laugh.

It was a distinctive sound that could only come from one woman. He turned and glanced around the room. He didn't see her. Had he only imagined hearing her laughter?

"Is anything wrong?"

That Culpepper guy was back. Laramie looked at him. "Not sure. However, I'd like to meet the artist, Bristol Cooper, after all."

"That's not possible."

Laramie was about to tell the man that with him anything was possible, when he heard the sound again. His gaze sharpened as he looked around the room. The sound had come from another part of the gallery. He was certain he hadn't imagined it twice.

He began moving toward the sound, not caring that people were staring at him.

"Wait a minute! You need to leave now."

When Laramie kept walking, he heard the Culpepper guy call out, "Mr. Jazlyn, I suggest you call for security."

They could call for security all they wanted. He wasn't leaving until he made sure...

He entered another area of the gallery and immediately felt it...that undisguised pang of longing and desire he hadn't felt in three years. He swallowed hard against the deep yearning in his throat as his gaze swept around the room.

And then he saw her.

Her back was to him. She stood beside an older gentleman as the two of them studied a landscape. Laramie knew without even seeing her face that the woman was his Bristol.

He'd only spent three days with her, but he knew that body, even if it was now draped in a beautiful gown. There were a few curves that hadn't been there before, but he was certain everything else belonged to Bristol Lockett, right, front and center. Especially that shapely backside.

He remembered the feel of his hand on that backside as well as the brush of his fingers along her inner thighs. He felt an immediate tightening in his gut at the memory.

Every muscle in his body tensed as he quickly moved in her direction. When he came within a few feet of her, he inhaled her scent. It was the one he remembered from Paris. Hurried footsteps were headed in his direction. Security was coming. Let them come. But not before he made his presence known.

"Bristol?"

She must have heard her name but she seemed almost afraid to face him. And when she slowly turned, she looked as if she was staring at the face of…a ghost?

She took a step forward. She whispered his name. And then she crumpled.

Four

Laramie managed to grab her before she passed out on the floor, sweeping her into his arms. People were staring, some had begun moving in their direction, no doubt wondering what the hell was going on.

"Put her down!"

He recognized Culpepper's voice. Laramie turned to see Culpepper flanked by several security guards and the owner of the gallery. Then suddenly a woman pushed through the crowd. "What happened?"

Laramie thought it was obvious but answered anyway. "She fainted."

"Fainted? How? Why?" She then narrowed her gaze at him. "Who are you?"

"Laramie Cooper."

"Laramie Cooper?" The woman gasped.

He wondered why hearing his name had such an effect on the woman. "Yes, Laramie Cooper. I need to take Bristol somewhere to lie down. And I need someone to get a wet cloth."

"Wait a damn minute," Culpepper was saying. "He has no right to be here. Who is he supposed to be?"

He heard the woman whisper something to the bastard that sounded like "He's her husband."

Laramie wondered why the woman would make such an outlandish claim. He wasn't anyone's husband. Then he recalled what Culpepper had told him earlier. Bristol's last name was Cooper. Now he was more confused than ever and confusion was something he didn't deal with very well.

Suddenly, the older gentleman Bristol had been talking to said, "Will someone do as this man asks and get a wet cloth? Jazlyn, where is your office?"

"Right this way, Mr. Kusac."

"Kusac?"

Laramie ignored the flutter of whispered voices repeating the man's name as if it meant something. Even the woman who was moving ahead of them stopped to look at the man in awe. Who was this guy Kusac? Was he a celebrity or something?

Laramie moved quickly toward the back of the gallery while carrying Bristol in his arms. He recalled the last time he'd carried her, from her kitchen to her bed.

Entering the gallery owner's office, Laramie laid Bristol on the sofa. The man who'd been identified as Kusac closed the office door, only admitting the three of them along with the woman. Laramie couldn't determine who she was studying more, him or Kusac. There was a knock on the door and Kusac opened it: Wet cloths were handed to him and he passed them over to Laramie.

"Is she all right?" the woman asked nervously.

"Yes" was Laramie's response as he began wiping Bristol's face with a cloth.

"By the way, Mr. Kusac, I'm Margie Townsend, Bristol's manager. I appreciate you coming out tonight and giving your support. You and Bristol seem to know each other."

"We do. I was a close friend of her father's."

"Oh." And then out the corner of his eye, Laramie noted

the woman moving closer to him. "And are you really Laramie Cooper?" she asked.

He didn't take his gaze off Bristol as he continued to wipe her face. She was even more beautiful than he'd remembered. Her chocolate brown skin was smooth and soft. He'd always liked the shape of her lips. They had the perfect bow. He recalled kissing them. How he'd licked them with his tongue.

Bristol was three years older now. Twenty-five. But you couldn't tell it by her features. It was as if she hadn't aged at all.

She still was the most beautiful woman he had yet to meet.

He switched his gaze to the woman who'd introduced herself as Bristol's manager and who'd asked him a strange question. "Yes, I'm Laramie Cooper."

"B-but you're supposed to be dead."

Laramie frowned. Bristol must have told her that. But then, how had Bristol known?

Deciding he would get all the answers he wanted from Bristol when she came to, he said, "Yes, I'd been captured, and they presumed I was dead."

"And you decided to show up after all this time?" the woman snapped. "Fine husband you are!"

Before he could ask her what in the hell was she talking about, Bristol made a sound. She whispered his name just moments before her eyes fluttered open.

And then she stared up at him. Tentatively, she reached up and touched his face, as if to make certain he was flesh and blood. Tears fell from her eyes when she whispered, "You're alive."

He nodded. "Yes, I'm alive."

"But they told me you were dead."

He nodded. "They thought so for a while, before I was rescued."

"Rescued?"

"Yes. Almost a year later."

From the look in her eyes, he saw something was bothering her. Maybe it was the fact that she was using his last name and claiming they were married.

"We need to talk privately, Laramie," she said, barely above a whisper.

She was right. They needed to talk. He nodded and then glanced at the other two people in the room. Before he could say anything, Kusac said, "We heard." He opened the door. When Margie Townsend hesitated, Kusac said, "They need time alone."

Margie nodded. "Yes, of course." She then said to Bristol, "If you need me I'll be right outside the door."

When the door closed behind them, Laramie helped Bristol sit up. She drew in a deep breath and stared at him. "I can't believe you are alive."

Laramie didn't say anything. He was trying to make sense of what he'd learned and was failing miserably. He needed answers to help him understand. "How did you know I was supposedly dead?" he asked, sitting beside her on the sofa.

She nervously licked her lips. "I tried to find you. I sent you a letter, through the navy, and it was returned. A friend of mine knew someone who worked in the State Department. They checked into it and that's what I was told."

"When was this?"

"A few months after I last saw you."

He nodded. "I was presumed dead, so the person was right. I was rescued just days before Christmas the following year."

"That was a long time."

"Yes, it was." Only his close friends knew about the nightmares he'd had for months following his rescue. Nightmares he still had at times. His enemies had tried to break him and he'd refused to be broken. But their attempts had become lasting scars.

"Why were you trying to reach me, Bristol?"

Bristol drew in a deep breath, not believing that Laramie was alive, not believing that he'd shown up here tonight. How had he known where she was? Had he been looking for her? If he had, that would make what she was about to tell him easier. But what if he hadn't been looking for her? What if he had forgotten all about her and moved on? For all she knew he could be married, although there was no ring on his finger.

She studied his features. He was even more handsome than she remembered. He looked slightly older and there was a hardness in the lines of his face that hadn't been there before. Instead of taking away from his striking features, the hardness defined them even more. And the look in his eyes reflected experiences she couldn't come close to imagining.

Even if those experiences had changed him, it didn't matter. He still had a right to know about her son. His son. Their son.

He could accept it or question whether Laramie was truly his, but he had a right to know. How he handled the news was up to him.

Drawing in another deep breath, she met his gaze and said, "The reason I tried reaching you was because I wanted to let you know I was pregnant."

Five

Laramie froze. He stared at Bristol. He'd heard what she'd said but he needed to verify it. "You were pregnant?"

"Yes," she said in a soft voice. "And you're free to order a paternity test if you need to confirm that my son is yours."

He had a son?

It took less than a second to go from shock to disbelief. "How?"

She lifted a brow, indicating she'd found his question as stupid as he had, but she answered nonetheless. "Probably from making love almost nonstop for three solid days."

They had definitely done that. Although he'd used a condom each and every time, he knew there was always the possibility something could go wrong. "And, where is he?" he asked, still trying to wrap his mind around the fact that he had a son.

"At home."

Where the hell was that?

It bothered him how little he knew about the woman who'd given birth to his child. At least she'd tried contacting him to let him know. Some women wouldn't have.

If his child had been born nine months after their holiday

fling, that meant he would have turned two in September. Laramie recalled that September. Although it had been hard keeping up with the days while being held hostage, somehow he'd managed, by counting each sunrise. He'd been lucky to be held in a cell with a tiny window.

He hadn't known that while being a pawn in his enemies' game of life and death that somewhere in the world Bristol was giving life.

To his child.

Emotions bombarded him with the impact of a Tomahawk missile. He'd been happy whenever Mac became a father again and had been overjoyed for Bane at the birth of his triplets. And now Laramie was a parent, which meant he had to think about someone other than himself. But then, wasn't he used to looking out for others as a member of his SEAL team?

"Have you gotten married, Laramie?"

He frowned at her question. Marriage was the very last thing on his mind. "No, I'm still single."

She nodded and then said, "I'm not asking you for anything, if that's what you're thinking. I just felt you had a right to know about the baby."

He stared at her while conflicting emotions warred inside him. She wasn't asking him for anything? Did she not know that her bold declaration that he'd fathered her child demanded everything?

"I want to see him."

"And you will. I would never keep Laramie from you."

"You named him Laramie?" Even more emotions swamped him. Her son, their son, had his name?

She hesitated, as if she wasn't sure how he would like her response. "Yes. His first name is Laramie and his middle name is Randall, after my father. I thought you were dead and I wanted him to have your name. So I named him Laramie Randall Cooper."

He didn't say anything for a full minute. Then he asked, "So, what's your reason for giving yourself my name, as well?"

Oh, boy. Bristol wondered why so much was happening to her tonight of all nights. When she'd left home she'd hoped for a great night for the showing of her work at the gallery. She hadn't counted on a lover—specifically, her son's father—coming back from the dead.

And now he wanted answers.

Although she knew he deserved to have them, she wasn't ready to tell him any more than she had already. She just wanted to go home and hug her son. Tomorrow, she would tell her son that the father he thought had become an angel was now a mortal.

She was about to tell him she was tired of talking for now when there was a knock on the door. "I'll get that," he said, standing.

She still appreciated the way he walked. Spine ramrod straight, steps taken in perfect precision with the best-looking tush she'd seen on a man.

When Laramie opened the door he practically blocked the doorway, but she heard Margie's voice. "How is Bristol?"

"I'm fine, Margie," she said. Thankfully, Laramie shifted aside so Margie could see for herself.

"Do you need anything?"

"No, I'll be out in a minute."

"No rush. Most of the people have left anyway. But the good thing is that all your paintings were sold. Tonight was a huge success."

Was it? As far as her manager was concerned, it had been a successful night. But Bristol saw beyond the money her paintings had earned. She saw the man standing by the door. Her heart slammed against her ribs. Already she was wondering what changes were about to be made in her life.

"And Steven is worried about you."

Bristol saw Laramie's body stiffen at the mention of Steven's name and wondered why. She became even more curious when he said, "Tell Culpepper she's fine and is in good hands. Now if you will excuse us, Bristol and I need to finish talking." He then closed the door.

How had Laramie known Steven's last name? Had the two of them met? If so, when?

Laramie slowly turned away from the door to stare at her. It was a good thing she was sitting down because her knees began shaking. The intensity of his gaze sent sensuous chills through her body. How was that possible when she hadn't seen him in three years?

The sexual chemistry that had drawn them to each other from the first was still there. She wanted to deny its existence, but she couldn't. She wanted to break eye contact with him and look away, but she couldn't do that, either. She sat there and endured the moment, hoping it would quickly pass. It didn't. It seemed to extend longer than necessary.

She decided to use it to her advantage; checking him out wasn't a hard thing to do. He wore a pair of jeans, a dark blue pullover shirt, a dark leather jacket, a Stetson and boots. He looked like a cowboy, ready to ride off into the sunset. He seemed to have gotten taller and his body appeared even more fit. Was he still a navy SEAL or had he given it up after that mission that had obviously gone all wrong?

Her gaze moved to his shoulders. She remembered them well. She could easily recall how she clutched tight to them when they made love. How she would cling to them while he thrust inside her. What she remembered the most was that Laramie Cooper was a very physical man, filled with an abundance of strength and virility.

She sighed as her gaze returned to his too-handsome face and stared into his eyes. And she saw it again, that hardness. Pain he refused to show. Ravaged secrets. A wounded heart. A damaged soul.

He probably didn't want her to see any of those things, but for a quick moment, she'd seen them anyway. She wondered what he'd endured during those months when everyone thought he was dead. Would he share the details of that time with her if she were to ask? Was it any of her business?

He didn't say anything as he continued to study her as intensely as she was studying him. What was he seeing? Besides a few extra pounds she hadn't shed after her pregnancy. Some men would think of them as curves. She thought of them as a nuisance that wouldn't go away no matter how much she exercised.

"Are you ready to answer my question?" he asked in a deep, husky voice that seemed to resonate inside her. "Because I have even more."

She'd been afraid of that. She also knew they couldn't stay holed up in Mr. Jazlyn's office forever. She understood she needed to fill Laramie in on so much that had happened but now was not a good time. "I suggest we meet tomorrow and—"

"No. I need to know tonight."

Tonight? "That's not possible," she said, glancing at her watch because she needed to stop looking into his eyes. His dark gaze wasn't just directed at her, it was assessing her in a way she knew too well. During those three days in Paris, she had been able to—most of the time—interpret what he was thinking from his eyes. Namely, she knew when he was ready to make love again by the desire she would see in them.

"Why tonight?" she asked.

"Why not tonight?" he countered.

Drawing in a deep breath, she said, "My neighbor, Ms.

Charlotte, is keeping Laramie and I don't want to get home too late."

He nodded. "And where is home?"

"Brooklyn."

He nodded again as he continued to stare at her. She couldn't help wondering what he was thinking. She found out when he said, "I want to see my son tonight, Bristol."

Why did him saying her name, no matter the tone, make an unexplainable warmth spread through her? "It's past his bedtime and he'll be asleep."

"Doesn't matter. I want to see him."

She eased up off the sofa. "Why?" she asked, not sure she was ready for him to come to her home, invade her space and meet Ms. Charlotte, who was the closest thing to a family she had now. "Don't you believe me?"

"Yes, I do. I just want to see him."

It was similar to her father's wish when she'd first made contact with him. She hadn't known what to expect when she'd first spoken with him. To break the ice, her aunt Dolly had spoken with him first. By the time Bristol had gotten on the phone, he had been eager to talk to her. Nervously, she'd blundered out the words, "I'm your daughter." And he'd said, "I believe you and I want to see you." He'd flown out that same day from Los Angeles and in less than eight hours was knocking on her aunt's door.

Bristol studied Laramie. Noticed his stiff posture. Was he expecting a fight? Hadn't she told him that she wanted him to know about their child? "Fine, you can see him tonight. A private car is taking me home."

She nervously nibbled her bottom lip. There was something she had to tell him before they left the office. It was the answer to the question he'd asked regarding her use of his name. "And to answer your question about me taking your name."

"Yes?"

"Before leaving Paris, I had already made up my mind to name my son after you, first name and last. But I didn't want people asking questions about why we had different last names. My friend Dionne came up with the idea. She had a friend who was an assistant to a judge in Paris who was willing to help with our plan. We did a fake marriage license where I listed you as my husband. It was then filed with the courts in Paris."

He didn't say anything for a minute before he asked, "Giving birth to a child without the benefit of a husband drove you to do that?"

She looked away for a second to figure out how to make him understand. "Yes. More so for Laramie than for me." She paused. "My mom was a single parent and I never knew my father. All my life the stigma of being born illegitimate bothered me because there were those who never let me forget. I got teased a lot about not having a father. I know having kids out of wedlock is more acceptable these days, but still, I didn't want to take a chance and put my child through that."

Although her mother had never said so, Bristol believed it bothered her mother as well, not only for her daughter but for herself. While growing up, there had been organizations Bristol's mother had tried to sign up for that had rejected their application because they hadn't met what was considered normal family dynamics. In other words, she didn't have a father and her mother didn't have a husband.

"I assume your manager believes we're married. She practically accused me of deserting you and my child."

Bristol rubbed her hands down her face, feeling bad about that. "I'm sorry. I'll tell her the truth."

"Don't bother doing that. At least I know why she's been acting like I'm scum. And I also now know why that Culpepper guy was acting like an ass when I asked about you."

"Steven?"

"Yes, I take it he's your boyfriend."

Where would he get an idea like that? "No, he's not my boyfriend. Steven and I have never even gone out on a date."

Laramie held her gaze, apparently finding it odd that the man would act so territorial under those circumstances. "But he has asked you out though, right?"

"Yes, but I've always declined. He's not my type." She checked her watch again and then looked up at him. "Are you going to deny you're my husband? People might question you about it."

"Don't worry. I won't give your secret away."

Six

When they walked out of the office, the first person Laramie noticed was Steven Culpepper and how the man's eyes narrowed when they got closer. If the guy had gotten word that Bristol's supposedly dead husband wasn't dead after all, then what the hell was he still hanging around for?

Laramie detected Bristol's nervousness. Did she think he would rat her out, expose her for lying about their marriage when he'd told her he wouldn't? He slowed his pace and she slowed hers. He glanced down at her. "You okay?"

"Yes. I'm just surprised to see Steven still here."

That made two of them. "You want me to ask him to leave?"

"No. I guess he was concerned. I see Mr. Kusac is still here, too. I can understand his concern since he was a good friend of my father's."

Laramie didn't say anything. He recalled how people had jumped into motion when the man named Kusac had barked out orders earlier. Even the owner of the gallery was quick to do the man's bidding.

Margie left the group to walk toward them, a smile on

her lips. "Well, did the two of you get things straightened out?" she asked.

Laramie answered before Bristol did. "Yes, and we're leaving."

The woman lifted a brow. "Leaving? To go where?"

Laramie was tempted to tell the woman that he didn't think it was any of her business, but Bristol answered, "I'm going home, Margie. Is the car ready to take me there?"

"Yes."

"Good." She then turned to Laramie and said, "I need to say good-night to everyone."

"Okay, let's do that."

Her eyes widened, probably in surprise that he'd included himself in the goodbyes, but she didn't say anything as he walked with her over to the three men. "I would like you to meet Laramie Cooper."

Laramie was sure it didn't go unnoticed how Bristol had introduced him. She hadn't referred to him as her husband. He figured these people assumed he was her back-from-the-dead husband, but she wasn't allowing anyone to presume anything about the nature of their relationship.

She thanked the owner of the gallery for hosting the event and apologized for all the commotion she'd caused by fainting.

Maurice Jazlyn waved off her words and said, "I would have passed out, too, had I thought my husband was dead and then he suddenly appeared out of nowhere."

Laramie didn't speak. If they were waiting for him to explain his absence for the past three years, they could wait on.

Then Jazlyn's face broke into a smile. "But then, I certainly can't complain since every last one of your paintings sold and you being here brought Kusac out tonight. It's been years since I've seen him."

"And I was glad to see him, as well," Bristol said, smiling at the man. "Thanks for coming."

Colin Kusac smiled. "Your first art show in New York—I would not have missed it for the world."

Then Bristol's attention went to Steven Culpepper. Laramie didn't like the vibes he was picking up off the man. He hadn't liked them from the first. "Steven," he heard Bristol say. "Thanks for inviting all those people here tonight. It was a nice turnout thanks to you."

"No need to thank me, but I'd like for us to meet sometime this week. Several of my clients here tonight were impressed with your work and want to see more. A few are willing to commission some of your future projects."

"That's wonderful! I'm sure we can arrange a meeting," Margie said excitedly behind them. "Just give me a call, Steven. I'll work out a date and time when Bristol is available."

A tight smile touched Culpepper's lips. "Yes, of course, Margie." Laramie had a feeling Culpepper had wanted a private meeting with Bristol and her manager had ruined those plans.

"I'll call you tomorrow to discuss your availability, Bristol," Margie said.

"That's fine," Bristol said, smiling. She then turned to him. "I'm ready to go, Laramie."

He nodded and took her hand, leading her toward the door.

"I don't bite, you know."

Bristol glanced across the back seat at Laramie and had to admit there was a lot of space between them. He might not bite but she could vividly recall a lot of other naughty things he could do with his mouth.

Jeez. Why was she remembering that now?

"I know you don't bite, but I figured you would want your space."

She thought the chuckle that ensued from his throat sounded way too sexy for her ears. "Is that a way of letting me know you like yours?"

She shrugged. "I guess I've gotten used to it." No need to tell him that she hadn't had another man in her life since him, serious or otherwise. After her son was born, he had become her whole world and there hadn't been room for anyone else. Some women needed a man to feel like a female; she didn't.

He didn't say anything for a minute and that was fine with her as the private car carried them through the streets of Manhattan and toward the Brooklyn Bridge. When they'd left the gallery she'd noticed the temperature had dropped. Forecasters had predicted a heavy snowfall before Christmas and with this cold snap being less than two weeks before Christmas, she could see it happening.

"Tell me about him. My son."

Laramie's words intruded into her reverie and she glanced over at him. The bright lights from the tall buildings they passed illuminated his features and she could see why she'd been taken with him from the first. Any woman would have been.

In Paris, Laramie Cooper had been handsome and charismatic all rolled into one. He was still handsome, she would give him that, but he had yet to unleash any of the charm that had swept her off her feet and into the nearest bed. But then she figured when a man was told he was the father of a child he hadn't known he had, his secret son, shock might put a damper on the charm.

Bristol settled her body against the leather seat. Talking about her son was one of her favorite subjects. "He's perfect."

There was that sexy chuckle again from him. "Besides

that. How about starting off telling me about your pregnancy. Was it a hard one?"

She could vividly recall all nine months of it. "Not after my sixth month. I was one of those unusual women who had morning sickness in the morning and at night. I could barely keep anything in my stomach, and the smell of some foods would send me rushing for the nearest bathroom."

"Sounds pretty bad."

"I thought so at the time. I had planned to leave Paris in my fifth month but my doctor restricted air travel until I was better. I'd lost a lot of weight. I wasn't eating much and what I was eating my baby was getting. That's why it doesn't surprise me now that Laramie is a big eater."

"When did you leave Paris?"

"In my sixth month. I wanted my baby to be born in the United States. Thank God for online shopping and for Ms. Charlotte, who lives next door to my aunt. The house was cleaned out and baby furniture delivered, which made things easy for me when I finally arrived back in New York. Once the morning sickness stopped and I could retain food, I blew up overnight but the weight gain was mostly all baby. Laramie was born weighing close to nine pounds."

"And during all that time you thought I was dead."

He'd said it not as a question but as a statement. "Yes. I had no reason not to believe what the State Department had reported. A part of me wished I'd known more about you so I could reach out to your parents. I recall you'd mentioned they were alive but you never gave me any personal information about yourself."

"And you never gave me any personal information about yourself, either," he said. "Though I do remember you telling Bane you were from New York."

No, they hadn't exchanged any of those details. She doubted if it would have mattered anyway. It was not like he'd intended to one day pick up where they'd left off.

There was no doubt in her mind that after he'd been rescued he'd gotten on with his life and hadn't given her a second thought.

"How did you stumble across me tonight?" She was certain now that he hadn't been looking for her.

"I came to New York on military business. After dinner I was headed back to my hotel room when I saw the sign at the gallery with your name. I figured there couldn't be too many artists with that name."

"So you came into the gallery on a hunch?"

"Yes, although I knew from the way I was dressed I would stand out like a sore thumb. And then I encountered your Steven Culpepper, who—"

"He's not my Steven."

"He tried to paint the picture that he was. Appeared pretty damn possessive, too. He'd convinced me you weren't the Bristol I was looking for, but then I heard your laugh."

"My laugh?"

"Yes. I was less than a foot from the door when I heard you laugh. Twice."

She nodded. "Colin Kusac was sharing something with me about how he and my father used to get in trouble in high school."

"Your laugh is what let me know you were the same Bristol. I remembered it."

Those three days they'd spent together had been memorable in so many ways. And it hadn't been all about the sex. They'd had fun sharing breakfast in bed, sharing jokes. They'd even watched movies together. She had enjoyed waking up in his arms and going to sleep the same way.

Those memories were what had held her sanity together while she carried his child and believed he'd been lost to her forever. Those memories were what she'd remembered when the labor pains had hit. She'd drawn comfort from them.

The car came to a stop and she glanced out the window. She was home. The place she'd escaped to when she needed to heal from the grief she'd endured when she thought Laramie had died. It was the place where, months later, she had brought her son. Because her baby had been so large, at the last minute she'd had to deliver by C-section. Luckily, Dionne had made plans to be with Bristol as her delivery coach and ended up being a lot more. Her best friend was a godsend during the weeks following the delivery.

The first time Bristol had seen her son she'd been filled with so much love. She'd been given a special gift. She'd immediately noticed how much he looked like his father. It was uncanny. Her son's coloring, the shape of his eyes, the tilt of his mouth, had all come from the older Laramie. And the older her son got the more he looked like his father. Would Laramie notice? There was no way he couldn't.

"Are you okay, Bristol?"

She looked over at him. "Yes, I'm fine." A part of her wondered if that was true.

The driver came around and opened the door. Laramie slid out, and she couldn't help noticing how his masculine jeans-clad thighs slid with ease across the leather. Then he stood by the door and extended his hand out to her, to help her out.

The moment she placed her hand in his, she felt it. That spark, that tingling sensation she'd felt the first time they'd touched. She glanced up at him and met the darkness of his eyes and knew he'd felt it, too. Knew he was remembering.

Then she decided she wasn't fine after all.

Seven

Laramie considered what had passed between him and Bristol a few moments ago. He was fully aware of the strong sexual chemistry that was still between them. Even when they weren't trying, they pushed each other's buttons. No surprise there. But what he found surprising was the intensity of what he'd felt from her touch.

Shoving his hands in his pockets, he turned to look at the line of brownstones, especially the one in front of them. The SEAL in him quickly surveyed his surroundings, took in every nook and cranny. It was a nice neighborhood of older well-kept homes on a tree-lined street with sufficient lighting. Even the sidewalks in front of the homes looked as if they'd been scrubbed clean. It was easy to see this was a block that took pride in their neighborhood.

He followed as Bristol walked ahead of him. Several live plants lined the steps to her front door. Had he told her how nice she looked tonight in that long, flowing black gown with a split on the side? The male in him couldn't help but appreciate how those curves filled out the gown. She was a beautiful woman and he could understand Culpepper's interest. What man wouldn't be interested?

She took the key out of her purse and looked at him. Had she sensed he'd been staring at her backside? "Nice neighborhood," he said, in case she had.

"Yes, it is." She paused. "I will have to tell Ms. Charlotte who you are, as well. She will be shocked."

He nodded. "She also assumes we're married?"

"Yes. The only person who knows the truth is my best friend in Paris. Dionne."

Laramie didn't say anything as she unlocked the door and opened it. Then she stepped aside. "No, after you," he told her. "I'm used to bringing up the rear."

She nodded and entered her home. He followed, closing the door behind him. Her place had a cozy air. It felt small and intimate compared to the monstrosity of a house his parents owned, where he'd grown up as a child.

He stood in a foyer with stairs on one side and a living room on the other. The lit fireplace reminded him of how cold it was outside. The heat in here felt good. She had decorated for the holidays. A Christmas tree sat in front of the windows and he couldn't help noticing that several of the ornaments were the ones he had bought for her in Paris. It made him feel good to know she had kept them.

"Nice place," he said, glancing over at Bristol as he removed his Stetson and placed it on a nearby hat rack.

"Thanks."

"I thought I heard voices. You're home."

An older woman came down the stairs and he figured her to be Ms. Charlotte. She smiled when she saw them. Then suddenly, the smile seemed to freeze on her face and she stopped walking to stare at him.

"Sorry I'm late, Ms. Charlotte. How was Laramie tonight?"

The older woman answered Bristol, without taking her eyes off him. "He was fine as usual."

It was then that Bristol said, "Ms. Charlotte, I'd like to introduce—"

"I know who he is," the older woman said, still staring at him.

The woman's words gave Laramie pause. "How can you know?" he asked, lifting a brow.

"Your son looks just like you."

His son looked like him? "Does he?" he heard himself asking.

"Yes, your spitting image," the older woman said.

"That's one of the first things I noticed after he was born," Bristol added.

The woman finally continued down the stairs. When she reached the bottom step, she said, "I know you're not a ghost, so I can only assume you weren't dead as Bristol thought."

Laramie stared into the older woman's eyes. He admired their sharpness. He had a feeling you couldn't hide much from those eyes. "No, I wasn't dead, although the government thought I was. I was missing in action for almost a year before being recused."

For some reason he felt he should provide her an explanation. She nodded and her lips creased into a smile. "I'm glad you came back alive. You're going to love that little boy up there. He's a sweetheart."

Bristol groaned. "You shouldn't say things that aren't true, Ms. Charlotte. You and I both know he's just gotten the hang of the terrible twos."

"Like I've always said, boys will be boys. I should know after raising four of my own." She then glanced at her watch. "Time for me to leave. I'm sure the two of you have a lot to talk about," she said, heading for the door.

She glanced back at them, specifically at Laramie, and said, "I'm glad you're here." The older woman then opened the door and closed it behind her.

Laramie saw Bristol was focused on the painting that hung over her fireplace. He'd seen it before. In Paris. In her bedroom. It had hung directly over her bed. She'd told him it was one she'd painted with someone. He'd been amazed how the beauty of the Point Arena Lighthouse had been captured so magnificently on canvas. The painting was so vivid it seemed that the waves from the Pacific were hitting the shoreline. He recalled visiting the actual lighthouse years ago with his parents.

"Bristol?"

She switched her gaze to him. "Yes?"

"Are you okay?"

She stood beside a lamp and the light illuminated her. He was thinking then what he'd thought when he'd first seen her. She was beautiful. In the bright light, he could study her. See more. Her dark hair was swept up and away from her face in a way that seemed to make her features even more striking. Especially with those earrings in her ears...

It was then that he remembered. He'd given her the earrings as a gift. It seemed the Christmas ornaments weren't the only thing she'd kept.

"You're ready to see him?"

"Yes."

She nodded. "He's asleep, so whatever you do, try not to wake him. Laramie can be a handful when awakened from his sleep. He doesn't like that very much."

"I won't wake him."

"Okay. Then follow me please."

She headed up the stairs and he followed, feeling his stomach knot with every step. This was crazy. He'd faced bitter enemies without flinching. Yet knowing that at the end of these steps was a child he'd helped to create had nervous tension flowing through him.

The moment they reached the landing she turned to him.

"This way. His bedroom is next to mine so I can hear him at night."

He nodded, inhaling her scent. It was soft, subtle—jasmine. He recalled that was her favorite fragrance and for those three days they'd spent together it had become his.

He hung back when she opened the door and entered the bedroom. She turned on a small lamp. His gaze raked the room. It had bright yellow walls and a mural of zoo animals gathered around an image of someone reading a book.

Then there was the toy box in the corner. He smiled, remembering how he would pull all his toys out of the box at the beginning of the day as a boy, only to have to put them back at the end. His parents always had a full-time housekeeper and undoubtedly, she'd figured the more she taught him to do in his playroom, the less she would have to do.

He watched Bristol move toward the bed. From the doorway he could see the small sleeping form beneath the blanket. A mop of dark curly hair peeped out and he instantly recalled the pictures he'd seen of himself as a child with the same mass of curly hair. His parents hadn't given him his first haircut until he was about four.

When Bristol stopped by the bed, he moved to where she stood as blood pounded in his temples. He looked down and his heart stopped. Suddenly, he was bombarded with emotions he couldn't keep in check. He was looking down at his child. His son.

His son.

A son he and Bristol had made together during their three days of heated passion. Three days he hadn't been able to forget. Three days, the memory of which had helped him maintain his sanity when any normal person would have lost it.

He had expected to feel something. But not this. Not this overflowing of emotions filling him to capacity, taking hold of his mind and heart. He might not have been interested in fathering a child before, but the thought that he'd fathered this one had intense pride tightening his shoulders then spreading all the way down to his gut.

Since his child was lying on his stomach, he could only see one side of his face. That was enough. His mind rang out with the words... *He's mine. All mine.*

Um, not quite, he thought, glancing at the woman by his side. His son was hers, too. That was a fact he couldn't forget.

She met his gaze. At that moment, something passed between them and this time it wasn't sexual in nature. It was an unspoken understanding that no matter what, this child—their child—would always come first. He understood and accepted the pledge.

"Does he sleep through the night?" he whispered. He had to say something. He wanted to know so much. He wanted to know everything.

A smile touched her lips. "If you're hoping he'd awake anytime soon, no such luck," she whispered back. "He usually fights sleep tooth and nail, but when he's out, he's out until the next day."

"May I come back tomorrow to see him? Spend time with him?"

She didn't answer. Why? All he needed was a yes or no, preferably yes. Instead, she whispered, "Let's go back downstairs and talk about it."

Talk about it? Did she think her answer would make him yell and risk waking up his son? What was there to talk about? This was his son. She'd said so. He'd believed her even without seeing all of him. Drawing in a deep breath, he hoped like hell there was not about to be any drama. The only true drama he enjoyed was of the SEALs kind.

He followed her out the door and back down the stairs. "Would you like a cup of coffee or a beer, Laramie?"

"A beer will be fine."

"I'll be right back."

In a way, he was glad she'd left him alone for a few moments to deal with all these emotions. Was she deliberately stalling? Would she try to deny him rights to his son? She'd said the reason she'd tried writing to him three years ago was because she'd wanted him to know she was pregnant. He'd just seen his child. Now what? Did she expect him to walk away? Should he consider obtaining an attorney so he could know his rights as a father? All he knew was that his son had his name. Bristol even had his name, although they weren't legally married.

He rubbed a hand down his face. The hour was late. Was he overthinking things? If he was, it wouldn't be the first time. He was a suspicious bastard by nature. He rarely took anything at face value.

She returned with a beer for him and a cup of tea for herself. He remembered how she would drink a cup of tea every morning and every night before bedtime. He would get all turned on just watching how she sipped her tea.

"Let's sit in there," she said, indicating the living room. "Although I loved my studio apartment in Paris, it's nice to have more room here, especially with Laramie."

She sat down but he remained standing. Her calmness kicked up the uncertainty inside him even more. Was this when she would tell him he could have no part in his child's life or that he would only get whatever part she chose to give him?

He opened his beer and took a huge swig. The cool liquid felt refreshing going down his throat. He glanced over at her and saw she was looking at him. It was as if she wanted to say something but was too nervous to do so. In that case, he needed to just come out and squash whatever ideas were formulating in her head here and now.

"I asked you upstairs if I could come back tomorrow

and you never gave me an answer. So I can only assume you have a problem with me doing so. In that case, I think you need to hear me out, Bristol."

He moved to stand a few feet from where she sat and met her gaze. "I want to see my son again. Every chance I get. I want to know him and I want him to know me. I want to be there for him. I want to be a part of his life. I'm not a man who will walk away from my child. I have rights as a father."

He paused before adding, "And just so you know, if you deny me those rights, I will fight you legally with every penny I have."

Eight

Bristol knew she needed to do something before she began crying. Already it was taking everything within her to fight back the tears glistening in her eyes. She doubted Laramie knew just how much his words meant to her.

A part of her had known that she'd fallen in love with him during their holiday fling for a reason. Although she hadn't gotten to know him in the way she would have liked, in her heart she'd believed he was a man with character. A man of honor. A man who believed in doing the right thing.

When she discovered she was pregnant, letting him know had been automatic because of what her mother had done to her father. But Bristol hadn't known, until this very minute, how Laramie would feel about their son. Whether he would accept him or walk away. Even when he'd said he believed Laramie was his and had wanted to see him, there hadn't been any guarantees as to what his reaction would be. But she could not deny him the right to see his son and if he'd walked out the door after doing so, it would have been his loss. Not hers or her child's.

But from what he'd just said so passionately, he didn't plan to walk out the door. He wanted to be a part of his child's life…just like her father would have wanted to be a part of hers had he known about her sooner. Laramie Cooper was proving there were decent men out there. Just like her father.

Tears she couldn't contain any longer wet her cheeks. Why was she getting so emotional? Especially now? She blamed it on the fact that the man she'd fallen in love with three years ago, the man she'd thought was dead, was not only very much alive but was here, in her home, standing in front of her and accepting his child without any hesitation. Of course that didn't mean he wanted to renew a relationship with her or anything; she understood that. That was fine. The most important thing was that he wanted a relationship with his son.

"Hell, Bristol, you're crying over what I said? Just because I want to be a part of my child's life?" Laramie asked in an incredulous voice.

More tears she couldn't control flooded her eyes, and she saw both anger and confusion in his features. She wasn't handling this very well and now she had him thinking the complete opposite from what she was feeling.

"I need to get some tissue," she said, quickly getting up to go into her kitchen to grab a few. Moments later, when she returned, Laramie was standing in front of her Christmas tree with his back to her. His hands were shoved into the pockets of his jeans. She wondered if he'd noticed the ornaments. She doubted he would ever know how much she'd come to treasure them. How each time she looked at one she was reminded of Paris.

"Laramie?"

He turned around and met her gaze. She could tell from his stance and his brooding expression that he was still angry, even more so. She needed to explain and the only way she could do that was to tell him everything. "I think we need to sit down and talk."

The look in his dark, piercing eyes said that as far as he was concerned, there was nothing to talk about, but he nodded anyway. She took a seat on her sofa again, but he said, "I'd rather stand."

She wished he would sit down. Then she wouldn't have to stare up at him. Wouldn't have to notice just how well-built he still was. How sexy he looked in jeans and a leather jacket. And she wouldn't have to notice how his eyes were trained on her. But she said, "Okay, if you prefer standing."

The room was quiet but she was convinced she could hear the pounding of her heart. "I might have confused you about a few things, Laramie," she said. "I would like to explain and hope in the end you'll understand."

She paused before saying, "Growing up, I never knew my father. Other kids had daddies and I didn't understand why I didn't. It was just me and my mom. One day... I believe I was eight at the time... I asked her about it. I wanted to know where my daddy was. She got angry with me and said I didn't have a daddy, that I didn't need one and not to ever bring up the subject of a father again. Her words were final and I knew it."

Bristol picked up her teacup and took a sip although the tea had cooled. "It was only after my mother died when I was fifteen that I moved from Houston to—"

"You lived in Texas?"

"Yes. I was born in Houston and lived there until I was fifteen."

He nodded. "I'm a Texan, as well. I was born in Austin."

She nodded and then continued her story. "When Mom died, I moved here to New York to live with my aunt Dolly. She was my mother's only sibling."

Bristol took a breath and then continued, "It was only then that I got up enough courage to ask my aunt about my father. I knew nothing about him. I didn't even know his name. But Aunt Dolly did. However, my mother had sworn her to secrecy. According to my aunt, my father and mother dated while in high school in Dallas but he broke things off with my mom to pursue his dream of studying art in Paris. My aunt said he asked my mother to go with him, but she refused, saying she didn't want to live in another country."

"Your father was an artist, as well?" Laramie asked as he leaned against a bookcase.

"Yes." Now might have been a good time to tell him her father was the famous artist known as Rand, but she didn't. Her father's identity wasn't important to this story.

"Imagine how excited I was when I found that out. When I learned where my artistic abilities had come from. It also explained why my mother never wanted me to pursue my art. I guess me doing so reminded her of him. Once I found out who he was, I wanted to connect with the man I never knew. The man my mom had kept from me."

She took another sip of her tea. "According to my aunt, my mother never told my father she had gotten pregnant. He didn't know he had a daughter. The reason Mom kept it from him was because she resented him for choosing Paris over her."

She paused again before saying, "I convinced my aunt that I needed to see my father. To let him know I exist. She prepared me by saying that he might not want a child, that he might question if I was really his. Aunt Dolly didn't want me to get hurt. But I didn't care. I needed to meet him."

She recalled that time and how desperate she'd felt. "One of the men at my aunt's church was a detective with the NYPD. He tracked down my father and discovered he lived in Los Angeles. I made the call to my dad the morning of my sixteenth birthday. Aunt Dolly talked to him first, to break the ice and introduce me. Then she handed the phone to me."

"What did he say?"

No need to tell Laramie it had practically been the same

thing he'd said when she'd told him about their child. "He said that he believed I was his and that he wanted to see me. To prove that point, he flew out immediately. In fact, he knocked on my aunt's door in less than eight hours." She smiled. "That was the best birthday present ever."

She fought back the tears that threatened to fill her eyes again as she said, "On that day, I began what was the happiest two years of my life. He told me that he wrote my mother but she refused to write him back. His letters were returned. She stopped all communication between them. When he returned to Dallas from Paris that first year for the holidays, he'd tried finding my mother but no one knew where she had moved to. Later on, he met someone else. He was still married to that woman when we met. They had two young sons. None of his sons were interested in art and he was glad that I was. We discovered we had quite a lot in common."

"Was he upset that your mom kept your existence from him?"

"Yes, very much so. He saw that as wasted years. Years when I could have been spending time with him. We tried to do everything we could together during those two years because that was all we had."

A bemused look appeared on Laramie's face. "Why was that?"

She swallowed, feeling the lump in her throat. "Because, although I didn't know it, my father was dying of cancer."

She drew in a deep breath as she held Laramie's gaze. "So as you can see, my actions regarding you and my son were based on my own experiences with my dad. That's why I wrote to you as soon as I found out I was pregnant. I didn't want to make the same mistake my mother made. You had a right to know about him, even if you rejected him. It would have been your decision. Your loss."

He didn't say anything for a minute. "I'm sorry about your father."

"Me, too. But we got to spend two years together. He made me feel so loved. So very special. He even asked me to change my last name to his, and I did. He also asked if I would come spend my last two years in high school with him in California. That meant leaving Aunt Dolly and I was torn about doing that, but she was fine with it and encouraged me to go. Although she never said, I think he confided in her and told her he didn't have long to live."

"And nobody told you?"

"No. Very few people knew about his condition. In his final days, I saw him getting weak and asked him about it, but he said he'd caught some kind of a virus. He only told me the truth during his last days. That's when he told me what was wrong and if I ever needed anything to contact Colin Kusac, his close and trusted friend." There was no need to tell him how much her father's wife had resented her presence and how mean she'd been at the reading of her father's will.

"So you ended up in Paris to study like he had?"

"Yes. He made that possible before he died. He wanted me to study at the same art academy." She had worked at that café in Paris not because she had to, but because she had wanted to. Her father had taken care of her tuition as well as provided her with a generous monthly allowance. Then there had been the proceeds from her mother's insurance policies. She had put all the money in a savings account. While growing up, her mother had taught her the importance of being independent and not wasteful.

"I had a wonderful father. I just wish I'd had more time with him."

Laramie didn't say anything for a moment, then he asked, "Do you resent your mother for standing in the way of that happening?"

She drew in a deep breath. "Not now, but for years I did. She wanted to hurt my father by keeping my existence a secret from him. She knew him and had known he would have wanted to become a part of my life, but she never gave him that opportunity. In the end, she not only hurt him but she hurt me, as well. I could never do that to my child. That's why I would never stand in the way of you developing a relationship with Laramie. I know the pain and heartbreak it could cause."

The only noise in the room was the sound of the logs crackling in the fireplace. "Thanks for sharing that with me, Bristol."

Telling him the story of her parents and her relationship with her father had drained her. Slowly standing to her feet, she said, "Now that we've gotten that cleared up, what time would you like to come meet Laramie tomorrow?"

An anxious smile touched Laramie's lips. "How soon can I come?"

She chuckled. "Laramie is an early riser so I'm usually up preparing breakfast around eight. You're welcome to join us if you like."

"I would love to."

She glanced at her watch. It was late. Almost midnight. "Do you want me to call you a cab?"

"No, I should be able to get one on the corner."

"Okay." She walked him to the door and watched as he put on his Stetson, while thinking how much more cowboy than SEAL he looked at that moment. "I'll see you in the morning then."

"Yes. In the morning. Oh, by the way, does Laramie have a favorite toy?"

She shook her head. "No. Like most kids his age he likes stuffed animals. He does have this thing for airplanes and he likes to color so he has a ton of coloring books. For his birthday one of Ms. Charlotte's sons, who also has a two-year-old, gave Laramie an electronic tablet. I'm trying to teach him how to play educational games on it."

He nodded. "What kind of tablet is it?"

Bristol told him the brand. Her heart missed several beats when Laramie stood in front of her, holding her gaze. As if to get her mind off what she was feeling, she thought of something. "It might get confusing with you and Laramie having the same first names. Can I start calling you Coop, or is that name restricted to just your team members?"

"No, it's not restricted so that's no problem."

"Good."

He shoved his hands into his pockets. "If there's a change of plans or if you need me for anything, you can contact me at the Marriott Hotel in Times Square. I'd like for you to have my personal number," he said, pulling out his cell phone. "What's yours so I can call you? That way you can have it."

She rattled off her phone number and when she heard her phone ringing in the purse she'd placed on the table earlier, she said, "I got it."

He nodded. "Now you have mine and I have yours."

She dismissed any significant meaning to that. He was merely providing her his number because of Laramie. "Good night, Laramie… Coop. I am so glad you are alive."

He smiled. "Me, too."

He stood there for a second, staring at her, before saying, "Good night, Bristol. I'll see you in the morning."

He turned and quickly moved down the steps.

Laramie entered his hotel room, feeling a happiness he hadn't felt in a long time. In addition to that, a rush of adrenaline was pumping furiously through his veins. What were the chances of the one woman he thought he would never see again, the one woman he thought about often, the one woman who'd helped him retain his sanity while being held hostage, would be here? In New York? And that he would run into her?

Well, he hadn't exactly run into her, but the circumstances surrounding their chance encounter still seemed unreal. And not only had he found out he had a son tonight, but he'd seen him. What a feeling! It was exhilarating, and he couldn't wait to share it with the guys.

He glanced at his watch. It was late. Almost midnight. But he knew Bane, Viper, Mac and Flipper would be up. However, Bane had triplets and Mac had four kids Laramie didn't want to wake up. To be on the safe side, he would text the four to call him.

Laramie also knew he needed to contact his commanding officer to let him know he would be taking his military leave after all. He wondered what would have happened had he not been in New York tonight. No telling when his and Bristol's paths would have crossed, if ever. He'd already missed two years of his son's life and he didn't plan to miss any more.

At some point he also needed to call his parents to let them know they were grandparents. He wondered how they would feel about that. They'd never hinted one way or the other if they wanted grandchildren. They hadn't ever nagged him about settling down or marrying.

After sending the text off to the guys, he removed his jacket and hung it in the closet before the first call came in. He recognized the number as Bane's. "You okay, Coop?" Bane asked with deep concern in his voice.

"Yes, I'm fine. But I do have some news to share. Hold on, I hear another call coming in."

The others began calling and they connected to their conference number so they could all be on the phone at once. "Okay, Coop, what kind of news do you want to share with us?" Viper asked.

"Don't tell us the commander gave you another top secret job. Another cockatiel for you to deliver to some very important person?" Flipper teased.

"Maybe it will be a dog this time," Mac kidded. "Or maybe a pet monkey."

Laramie took their jokes in stride; nothing could put a damper on his mood. "I ran into Bristol Lockett here in New York."

"Bristol Lockett? That woman we couldn't tear you away from in Paris three years ago?" Viper asked.

"If I recall," Bane said, "you went missing for three days because you were with her."

"And we couldn't wipe that damn smile off your face for almost a month," Mac interjected.

"So how was the reunion?" Flipper asked. "She still look good?"

"Yes, she's the same woman, Viper. I didn't know you were missing me so much during those three days, Bane. I don't recall smiling for almost a month, Mac. If I did, I had a good reason for it. And yes, Flipper, she still looks good and the reunion was great once she recovered from fainting."

"Why did she faint?" Bane asked.

Laramie settled down on the edge of the bed. "Bristol thought she was seeing a ghost. She'd assumed I was dead."

"Why would she assume that? Had she contacted your parents or something?" Viper asked.

"No. I never gave her any information about my family."

"Then why would she assume you were dead? No agency had the authority to release that information. Our mission in Syria was a top secret, highly classified covert operation," Mac said.

"Bristol tried writing to me and the letter was returned. She knew someone who had a friend at the State Department who told her I'd gotten killed in Syria."

"Someone breached classified information?" Flipper asked.

"The person who did it felt she needed to know. Like I said, she was trying to reach me."

"Why was she trying to reach you?" Viper asked.

Laramie paused before saying, "She wanted to let me know she'd gotten pregnant."

Everyone got quiet and Laramie knew why. They were trying to digest what he'd said. A smile touched his lips when he added, "Yes, what you're thinking is right. I have a child. A two-year-old son."

Nine

"Hungry, Mommy."

Standing at the stove while preparing breakfast, Bristol couldn't help but smile. Each morning her son woke up in a good mood. Hungry, but good. It didn't matter that he usually had a bedtime snack. He evidently slept that off every night.

"Mommy is almost done, Laramie. Please color me a picture."

"Okay."

She'd discovered early that Laramie liked marking up things, preferably with his crayon. When her walls became a target, she'd purchased him a coloring book. Now it was the norm for him to color her a picture in the book while he waited for breakfast. And since he was home with her every day, she used any free time she had to teach him things. He already knew his primary colors, how to count to ten and since she knew fluent French, she made that his second language by identifying things in both English and French. So far he was mastering both.

She had just finished cooking the eggs when the doorbell rang. Laramie ceased his chatter long enough to say, "Door, Mommy."

Wiping her hands on a kitchen towel, she turned and said, "Yes, I heard it." And from the way her heart was pounding in her chest, she knew who it was. Laramie... Coop. "I'll be back in a minute, sweetie."

Refusing to acknowledge the fact that she'd taken extra care with her looks this morning, she headed for the door. Coop was here to see Laramie and not her.

Before opening the door, she looked through the peephole. There was no way on earth she could dismiss just how incredibly handsome her son's father was. With his striking masculine looks she found it hard to believe some woman hadn't snatched him up by now. He'd said he wasn't married, but he didn't say whether or not there was a special woman in his life. She tried to push the thought out of her mind; it wasn't any of her business.

Their only connection, the only reason he was standing on her doorstep a little after eight in the morning, was Laramie. And from the looks of it, he was bearing gifts. She had a feeling her son would be getting an early visit from Santa.

Inhaling deeply, she opened the door. "Good morning, Coop."

Bristol looked even more beautiful in the daylight. Today her dark brown hair was flowing down her shoulders. And although she wasn't wearing lipstick, she'd put something on her lips to make them shine. Another thing different from last night was her outfit. Today she was wearing a pair of jeans and a pullover sweater. Was it a coincidence or had she remembered him once telling her that red was his favorite color?

The color really didn't matter because the woman standing in the doorway was too stunningly beautiful for words. He drew in a deep breath and pulled in her scent. She was wearing the same perfume from three years ago, from last night. He tried to keep memories of their holiday fling at bay so he could focus on their son. But then how could he, when the result of that fling was why he was here?

He recalled Mac's lecture. Mac, being the oldest of the group and the one who'd been married the longest, had given him advice last night. If Laramie's only interest in Bristol was his son, then he needed to make that point clear up front. Mac had known a lot of men who hadn't. Because of that, the women in those relationships assumed romance and the baby were a package deal.

As he tried to regain control of his senses, it occurred to Coop that while he'd been checking Bristol out, she'd been doing the same with him. He cleared his throat. "Good morning, Bristol. I hope I'm not too early."

"No, your timing is fine," she said, stepping aside to let him in. "I just finished cooking breakfast. I hope you're hungry."

Boy, was he ever, and it had nothing to do with food. The moment she'd opened the door, he'd felt it. The sizzle of attraction had been bad enough outside, but now, within the cozy confines of her home, it was stronger than ever. Did she feel it, too?

"Yes, I'm hungry."

He couldn't recall ever being swept away by a woman except for once in his life. And she had been that woman.

"Good, because I've made plenty. Laramie is up and as usual for this time of morning, he's in a good mood."

"Is he ever in a bad mood?" he asked, placing the gift-wrapped packages on her sofa.

She smiled and he wished that smile didn't cause a stirring in his gut. "Yes, whenever he's sleepy and tries like the dickens to fight it. That's when he becomes cranky."

She took in the numerous gifts he'd brought. "Looks like you went shopping."

He smiled. "I did. I was there when the gift shop at the hotel opened. I plan to do more shopping later today. It's hard to believe Christmas is in less than two weeks."

"Yes, it is."

They reached the kitchen and Coop stopped dead in his tracks. The little boy sitting at the table staring at him was a miniature of himself. The emotions he'd felt when he'd seen his son last night came back to hit him tenfold. Ms. Charlotte and Bristol were right. His son resembled him so much it was uncanny.

They shared the same skin tone, eye color and shape of nose, lips and ears. And then there was that mop of thick curly hair. Although Coop wore his hair cut low now due to military regulations, for years he'd worn it long, even during his teen years. His parents hadn't had a problem with it as long as he kept it looking neat. And he could tell, even though his son was sitting down, that he was taller than most two-year-olds. But then Cooper men were tall. He was six foot two and so was his father. His grandfathers on both sides had been six foot three.

"Who's that?" Laramie asked his mother loudly, pointing at Coop.

"It's not nice to point, Laramie." The little boy put his finger down but kept an I-am-sizing-you-up look on his little face.

"Laramie, this is your daddy. Can you say Daddy?"

"Daddy?" his son asked his mother, as if for clarification.

"Yes, Daddy."

The little boy nodded, looked back over at Coop and said, "Daddy."

Coop's heart missed a beat at hearing his son call him

that for the first time. He watched as Laramie began waving his hand, and then said, "Hi, Daddy."

Coop waved back. "Hi, Laramie."

And then as if Coop was being dismissed, Laramie picked up a crayon and began coloring in the book in front of him.

"You can go ahead and sit down, Coop."

Laramie snatched his head back up and scrunched up his face and said, "He Daddy, Mommy. Not Coop."

Bristol smiled. "You, and only you, can call him Daddy. I can call him Coop. You call him Daddy. Understand?"

Laramie nodded his head up and down. "Yes, Mommy."

Then to explain further she said, "I can also call him Laramie."

Laramie's face scrunched up again. "But that's me."

"Yes, but his name is Laramie, too."

Laramie then looked at his daddy. "You got my name?" he asked.

Coop decided not to say it was the other way around. Instead he would let Bristol handle this since she seemed to know how much their son could understand. "Yes, I have your name."

"But Mommy calls him Coop so he'll know when I am talking to him and not to you. Okay?"

Laramie nodded. "Okay." He then went back to coloring in his book.

Coop moved to the table and sat down. That got his son's attention again. Laramie looked over at him and with a stern face asked, "Clean hands, Daddy?" And to show what he meant, he held his hands out in front of him. "My hands clean."

"Oh." Coop got the message and glanced over at Bristol. "Where can I wash my hands?"

He could tell she was fighting back a smile when she said, "There's a bathroom right off the living room."

He stood. "Thanks." He headed to the bathroom to wash his hands. He had a feeling his two-year old son planned to keep him on his toes.

"Be still my hormones," Bristol muttered under her breath as she watched Coop leave the kitchen and head for the bathroom. Today he was wearing a pair of khakis and a pullover brown sweater. She was convinced that no matter what he put on his body, he was the epitome of sexy. There wasn't a single thing about him that didn't start her heart fluttering and send her female senses into overdrive. Then there was that self-assured walk he'd mastered. The man was true masculinity on legs.

"Daddy gone?"

She glanced over at her son as she placed the plates on the table. Was that sadness she saw in his little eyes? Of course, she had to be imagining things since Laramie had just met Coop. He couldn't have gotten attached already. She'd known Laramie would like Coop since he liked everybody.

"No, Daddy went to wash his hands."

Laramie nodded and then said, "Good." He then added, "Me got clean hands, Mommy." And just like he'd done for Coop, as proof of how clean they were, he held them out and flipped them over a few times.

She smiled and said, "Yes, you have clean hands, Laramie."

At that moment Coop returned and sat back down at the table. "Daddy back," Laramie said, smiling.

Coop returned his son's smile. "Yes, Daddy's back."

"Daddy, want to play some more?"

Coop, who was stretched on the floor, wondered how one little boy could have so much energy. He glanced at his watch. It was almost noon. Had he been here nearly four hours already? Breakfast had been delicious and he'd discovered just what a great cook Bristol was. When he'd complimented her she credited her aunt for making sure her culinary skills were up to par before she'd left New York to live in Paris.

After breakfast he helped Bristol tidy up the kitchen, although she'd said his help was unnecessary. But he'd wanted to help. Laramie had sat at the kitchen table, ignoring them while he colored.

Afterward they had gone to the living room. They'd placed most of the presents under the tree but there had been a few he'd let his son open now. Namely, more coloring books. To give him time alone with Laramie, Bristol had gone upstairs to her studio and closed the door. He felt good knowing she trusted him to take care of Laramie.

For a two-year old, his son was pretty darn smart. He spoke in understandable sentences and even knew how to speak French. During breakfast Bristol would lapse into French with Laramie. Coop appreciated that fact since he himself spoke several different languages, including French, and he enjoyed conversing with them in the language.

"Play games, Daddy."

Coop pulled himself up and looked at Laramie. He knew that his son didn't know the true meaning of the word *daddy*. To him it was just a name, but Coop hoped when Laramie got older it would come to mean a lot more. He wouldn't be around his son 24/7 because of the nature of his work as a SEAL. But he would be with him every chance he got.

That meant after every mission, he would head to New York. It no longer mattered that he liked California's weather better. His son was in New York and that's where he intended to be.

"He hasn't worn you out yet?"

He glanced up and saw a smiling Bristol standing in the entryway to her living room. He chuckled. "No, not yet."

"Well, you get a break since it's lunchtime."

As if Bristol had said a magic word, Laramie jumped up off the floor. "Lunch, Mommy?"

"Yes, Laramie. Lunch."

He was about to race for the kitchen when Coop stopped him and asked, "Clean hands?"

Laramie's small eyes widened. He then looked down at his hands. "No."

Coop nodded. "Come on, let's wash our hands."

Bristol watched them go, walking side by side. Father and son. It was a vision she'd thought she would never see, and seeing it now pulled at her heart. She recalled the telephone call she'd made to Dionne last night, to let her know Laramie was alive. It had taken her a full hour to tell her best friend everything, including how she'd fainted.

Then Dionne had asked her some tough questions. Namely, how she felt about Laramie and if she still loved him. Bristol had to explain that of course she still loved him but now her fears were greater than ever. She had taken news of his death hard and the grief had been so deep she'd sworn never to get that attached to another person again. It seemed all those she loved eventually died. Her mother. Her father. Her aunt Dolly. Was that why she was sometimes overprotective with her son? At least Margie thought that she was.

The work Coop did was dangerous. He risked his life constantly. Most of the time his whereabouts were unknown because the nature of his work was highly classified. There was no way she could make such a person a permanent part of her life. She couldn't imagine going through that sort of grief again. He'd beaten death once but the next time he might not be so lucky.

Dionne had asked Bristol the one question she couldn't answer. How could a woman stop loving a man like Coop?

She had no idea but she was determined to find out. She and Coop hadn't had a chance to sit down and talk, other than the discussion they'd had last night. She had no idea how long he would be in New York or what his plans were while he was here. He had said he wanted to spend as much time with Laramie as he could, and she didn't have a problem with that. She wanted her son to get to know his father.

She needed to get to know him, too. There was a lot of personal information about Coop that she wasn't privy to. She'd just learned last night that he was born in Texas. He rarely spoke of his parents but she knew they were alive. At least they had been alive three years ago.

"Mommy, hands clean now."

Coop and Laramie had returned. Now he was sitting high on Coop's shoulders with a huge grin on his face. "Okay, then, let's head into the kitchen for lunch."

Coop put Laramie down and as soon as his little feet touched the floor he took off toward the kitchen. He paused at the kitchen door long enough to look over his shoulder to say, "Come on, Mommy. Come on, Daddy. Laramie is hungry."

Coop burst out laughing as he walked beside her. "Did I imagine it or did he eat a huge breakfast a few hours ago?"

She chuckled. "No, you didn't imagine it. You'll find out just how much food he consumes. You'll never guess how much I spend on groceries."

He stopped walking and touched her arm. She couldn't contain the surge of sensations that settled in the middle of her stomach from his touch. "I will help you with that."

She shook her head. "Thanks, but I don't need your help. I told you last night that I don't want anything from you and I meant it." All she wanted was for him to have a relationship with his son.

"I don't agree with that."

She frowned, detecting his anger.

"We'll discuss this later, Coop. When Laramie takes his nap."

Coop nodded. "Okay. Do you need help with lunch? I can fix a mean peanut butter and jelly sandwich."

"No, thanks, I've got it covered. Today it's tuna sandwich and chips. He loves anything with seafood."

"So do I."

Bristol wondered if it would be the same way with Coop and Laramie as it was with her and her father. They had discovered so many similarities. She headed for the refrigerator, trying not to notice Coop's sexy walk as he moved to the table, where Laramie was already seated. She couldn't push to the back of her mind how he'd looked stretched out on her living room floor with Laramie. He had made himself at home and removed his sweater. No man had a right to such a sexy chest covered only by a T-shirt. She knew SEALs stayed fit, but he seemed to be working overtime doing so. And she tried not to think about how comfortable it felt having him here in her home with them. It was as if he belonged.

Air was nearly snatched from her lungs at the thought. How could she even think such a thing? There was no way Coop could be a permanent fixture in their lives. At least not hers. He was only here because of Laramie. Had there been more between them, he wouldn't have just stumbled across her the way he had. He would have looked for her after his rescue. But he hadn't. That reinforced her assumption that their holiday fling had been just that, a fling. Afterward he had moved on and not looked back. She knew she'd been out of sight and out of mind. He hadn't expected or probably hadn't wanted to ever see her again.

Like she told him, they would talk when she put Laramie to bed for his nap. There was a lot she and Coop needed to discuss. She had to reiterate that she wanted nothing from him. Hopefully, that would put him at ease that she wasn't going to hit him up for child support payments. However, she had a feeling he would want to pay them anyway, just because of the responsible person he was.

But she didn't intend to let him.

They also had to talk about her fake marriage to him. They needed to resolve that. Yes, she thought, as she began pulling the items out of the refrigerator for lunch. They definitely needed to talk.

Ten

Coop would be the first to admit that he'd been somewhat nervous upon arriving this morning, not sure of how his son would react to him. So far things were going great and he knew he had Bristol to thank for that.

As he settled back on the sofa, he thought about what she'd told him about her childhood. Specifically, growing up without knowing her father. And then only getting to spend a couple of years with him before he'd died.

After hearing her story, he wasn't sure what was worse. Having parents who were bitter toward each other or having parents like his who were obsessively into each other. If he had to choose, it would be the parents who were obsessively into each other. As far as he was concerned, her mother's resentment, bitterness and anger had only hurt Bristol. It was sad how one person's decision could change the lives of so many. He was glad Bristol had learned from her mother's mistake.

He couldn't help but smile when he remembered lunch. Laramie had cleaned his plate in record time. More than once, Bristol had to tell him to slow down so his food could digest. Coop hadn't been sure if Laramie knew what that meant until the boy began taking smaller bites of his sandwich.

It was obvious Bristol and Laramie had a routine. He hadn't put up a fuss when she'd mentioned it was time for his nap. Instead, he'd waved goodbye to Coop. But not before he'd asked if Coop would be there when he woke up. Before Coop could answer, Bristol had told Laramie not to expect him to be there because he had things to do. Was that her way of letting Coop know he was wearing out his welcome?

Hell, he hoped not. He'd placed a call to his commanding officer letting him know that he would be taking his holiday leave and would remain in the New York area. Like he'd told Bristol last night... He planned to spend as much time with his son as he could.

"I think he was asleep before his head hit the pillow. What did you do to tire him out?" Bristol asked, grinning as she returned to the living room.

He looked at her and thought those jeans she wore definitely displayed all her curves. Not all women could wear jeans and exude that kind of effect on a man. The kind that could shoot his libido into overdrive. The kind that made him remember, whether he wanted to or not, how things had been between them in Paris. How easily they'd connected. How insatiable their hunger for each other had been.

With effort, he brought his mind back to the conversation. Coop smiled. "He wanted to play hide-and-seek."

"Oops. I should have warned you about that."

In a way, Coop wished she had. Then he would have given his son restrictions about not hiding in certain areas. Coop hadn't set any rules, and Laramie had found a good place to conceal himself in his mommy's bedroom. He hadn't felt comfortable going into Bristol's room but since she'd left the door open he had seen enough to know it was neat as a pin and decorated in colors of mauve and gray.

And he had seen her bed.

It was the same one she'd had in Paris. Seeing that bed had made him recall everything they'd done and how they'd done it. It also made him realize that his son was conceived in that bed. Or it could have been the time he'd taken her against the refrigerator.

"How many times did you find him?"

Bristol's question interrupted his reverie. "Every single time."

No need to tell her that he'd had to coax Laramie out of his hiding place in her bedroom so he wouldn't have to go in there looking for him. That hadn't been easy. A promise to take him to the park one day soon cinched it.

He watched Bristol sit down on the chair and somehow she did it in a way that was a turn-on. He inhaled deeply, remembering for the umpteenth time that Bristol was off-limits. His presence here had nothing to do with her but everything to do with their son. No matter how many good memories he had of them together, no matter how hard he'd tried to find her in Paris, and no matter how attracted he was to her now, the bottom line was that Laramie was his focus.

A relationship with his son was the only thing that mattered. That meant he and Bristol needed to talk about a few subjects they'd skirted around.

Deciding not to beat around the bush, he said, "So let's talk, Bristol."

He could tell she was nervous. But whatever they discussed would be with the intent of putting their son's needs before their own. Unfortunately, Coop had plenty of needs.

He hadn't bedded a woman since his last assignment nearly eight months ago. No particular reason he hadn't done so other than the fact he'd been too busy trying to hire more men to help run the ranch in Laredo that he'd inherited from his grandparents.

Cooper's Bend was his favorite place in all the world and when he retired from being a SEAL, he planned to move there and make it his permanent home. He could retire after his twenty years with the military, which was what he planned to do. He had less than ten years left. Six more to be exact, since he'd entered the military at eighteen and could officially retire at thirty-eight. Then he would become the full-time rancher his grandfather had been. In the meantime, he had a good group of people running the place and went there from time to time to check on things.

It might be a good idea for him to consider moving there now. That would eliminate his need to find housing in San Diego to accommodate him and Laramie. The ranch, which sat on over six-hundred acres, was plenty big. He would love for Laramie to visit him at the ranch that held so many wonderful childhood memories for him. Hell, when his son got older, he could have his own horse.

"Yes, I think we need to cover a few things and come to an agreement," Bristol said, interrupting his thoughts.

"Okay. What do you want to cover?" he asked her.

She paused and then said, "I meant what I said about not needing anything from you where Laramie is concerned."

Already Coop knew that wouldn't fly. "I can't agree to that because Laramie is my responsibility, too. A responsibility I take seriously."

She opened her mouth to argue the point and he held up his hand to stop her. "Not negotiable, Bristol. It doesn't matter if you're able to take care of him yourself. What sort of man would I be if I didn't contribute to the welfare of my child?"

She didn't say anything and broke eye contact with him to gaze down at the floor. He knew she was thinking, probably of a way to counter what he'd said. As far as he was concerned she could think all she wanted, he wouldn't change his mind. As the only grandchild, he had inherited trust funds from both sets of grandparents. Also, his parents had established an endowment for him that he'd been eligible for when he'd turned thirty. He was yet to touch any one of them. In addition to all that money and the ranch, he was heir to RCC Manufacturing, Inc., a corporation founded by his parents over thirty-five years ago upon their graduation from Harvard. Considering all of that, there was no way in hell he would not contribute to his son's upbringing. In fact, he'd already left a message with his attorney to contact him. He intended to list Laramie's name on all his legal documents as his heir.

"I think we should compromise," she finally said.

He lifted a brow. "Compromise how?"

"You can provide for his future, such as setting up a college fund. I'll take care of any expenses for his well-being now."

Coop shook his head. "No. I still won't agree to that. I want to provide for my child's present and his future."

A frown marred her features. "Why are you being difficult?"

He returned her frown. "Why are you? Most men who father a child and are separated from them are required to pay child support."

"But usually only until they are eighteen. All I'm doing is asking you to start the support at eighteen."

He had news for her. He intended to take care of his child for the rest of his life. The trust funds he planned to establish for Laramie would assure that. The age of eighteen had nothing to do with it. He couldn't believe he was even having this conversation with her. Most women would want his monetary offering. Was he missing something here? "Can I ask you something?"

She nodded slowly, almost reluctantly, before saying, "Yes."

"You said you only met your father at sixteen. I don't

know anything about him, but did he wait until you were eighteen to begin providing for you?"

She stiffened. "He paid my entire tuition at the art school in Paris."

Cooper figured tuition at that school hadn't been cheap. "That's all he did? He actually waited until you were eighteen before doing anything?"

"Of course not."

"Then why would you expect me to? Evidently being an artist has you rolling in dough since you feel you don't need my help. That might be all well and good for you, but not for me. For me it's the principle of the thing. It's about doing my share in providing for a child I helped to create. So please don't ask me to consider doing otherwise."

Bristol's gaze held Coop's and she could tell from the determined look in his eyes that he would not back down on this. She wasn't privy to his income as a SEAL but she was certain he could use his money for better things...

Like what?

She drew in a deep breath when she suddenly accepted something. It was apparent that as far as Coop was concerned, nothing was better than taking care of his son. For Coop, it wasn't about the money. It was about taking care of his own. She'd gotten the impression three years ago that he wasn't extremely close to his family. But what she'd failed to realize was that her son was now his family and he wanted to not only be there for him but also contribute toward his well-being. For Coop, the contribution was essential. She got that now.

He'd been saying it all along, so why hadn't she been listening? Probably because, like her mother, she was determined to be independent and not depend on anyone for anything. She didn't have a problem with Coop being a part of his son's life physically, but she was trying to stop him from being a part of Laramie's life financially. Most men would have jumped at the chance to get out of paying some form of child support. But Coop wasn't one of those men.

Neither was her father.

And Coop was right. Randall Lockett hadn't waited until her eighteenth birthday to be a father to her. He'd immediately stepped in and, like a whirlwind, he'd changed her last name to his, bestowing upon her all the rights of being his offspring. He had taken her under his roof, adding her to his household.

She had enjoyed living with him in Los Angeles, even if it had meant moving out west, attending another school and making new friends. To her it had been worth it just to spend time with her father. He'd made sure she hadn't gone without anything. But the most important thing was the time they'd spent together. Nothing else mattered. Not the closet filled with new clothes, the private school or the international vacations. Not even the new sports car he'd given her.

"Okay, Coop," she finally said.

"Okay, what?"

She released a deep sigh. "Okay, we will share in the cost of raising Laramie."

"You don't have to sound so overjoyed about it."

She narrowed her gaze at him before she saw his lips tilt into a smile. He'd been teasing. Releasing another sigh, she said, "I'm not trying to be difficult, Coop. But when I had Laramie I knew he would be my entire world and that I would be the one he would depend on for everything. I thought you were dead. For the past two years, I've made it work. There hasn't been a decision I made without considering him. Even when I decided to quit my position with that magazine publisher to become an artist full-time. I'm doing okay financially."

No need to tell him about the ridiculously high com-

missions she received every month from her father's art.
"I was raised by a single mother who worked hard and
made sure we didn't waste money on frivolous things. I
knew the difference between getting the things I really
needed and denying myself those things I wanted that
weren't essential."

She didn't say anything for a brief moment then added,
"The reason I suggested you handle Laramie's future is
because I think that's what upset my father the most with
my mother…besides her keeping my existence from him.
Knowing she hadn't adequately prepared for my future.
I had to explain to him that it hadn't been her fault since
there was no extra money to set up a college savings account for me. Mom was a teacher, not a six-figure-salary
engineer. She had student loans to pay back. But still, we
lived in a nice house in a good neighborhood. I thought we
lived pretty good."

She smiled. "Mom said we were a team and always
would be one. I was happy. I was content. At the time. I really didn't think of life being any better. It was years later
that I found out just how complicated life could be."

Coop nodded. "Our son's financial well-being is something you don't have to worry yourself with anymore because I'm here to help." He leaned forward and rested his
arms on his thighs. "There is that other item we need to
discuss before I leave today, Bristol."

She lifted a brow. "What other item?"

He held her gaze. "The issue of our fake marriage."

Eleven

Coop could tell from the look in Bristol's eyes that she'd forgotten about that complication. That was unfortunate for her, since he clearly remembered. A woman claiming to be your wife was something that pretty much got stuck in your mind.

"I told you why I did it," she said in a defensive tone.

He leaned forward. "Yes, you did. But that doesn't mean we don't need to talk about it. Spinning that tale might have been okay when you assumed I was dead, but as you can see, Bristol, I'm very much alive."

When she didn't say anything, he asked, "What do you think we should do?"

She shrugged. "Why do we have to do anything? It's not as if anyone knows the truth but my best friend, Dionne, and her husband, Mark, who was working for the judge at the time."

"It's a lie, Bristol. And one thing about a lie, it can come back to haunt you when you least expect it."

She stood and began pacing. He watched her, trying to keep his mind on the issue at hand, but found it difficult to do so. Especially when her body was in motion. He should be noticing the sound of the wooden floor creaking beneath her feet or the way her hair brushed against her shoulders as she moved. However, he wasn't attuned to either of those things. Instead his total concentration was on her body. A body he remembered so well.

Coop couldn't watch her move those jeans-clad thighs without recalling a time he'd been between them. Recollecting a time when he'd tasted her. Touched her all over. He was so damn aware of every damn inch of her.

She suddenly stopped pacing and looked over at him. Why? Had she detected him staring? Should he sit there and pretend he hadn't been? He doubted he could, even if he wanted to. That would be trying to do the impossible where she was concerned.

"What do you suggest?" she then asked him.

Right now he thought about suggesting they go upstairs to her bedroom and get it on. Rekindle those days in Paris, if for no other reason than to prove he hadn't imagined it, that it had been as good as he'd remembered.

"There are only two options, Bristol. Either we pretend to get a divorce to end the fake marriage or we make the marriage real."

She came and sat back down. "There's absolutely no reason to make the marriage real, so getting a pretend divorce sounds good to me. All that involves is us saying we're getting a divorce. No paperwork needed." A huge smile touched her lips. "Great! That was an easy solution."

"Not quite."

She lifted a brow. "And why not?"

The muscles in his jaw tightened. "Because in the end you'll emerge smelling like a rose, but I'll be the scumbag. A man who deserted his wife and child for nearly two years, and then who turns around and divorces her."

His harsh description had her lifting a brow, which

meant she knew he didn't appreciate the position she was placing him in. "But I told you why I did it," she said.

"And now you want to take the easy way out."

Coop wondered why he was taunting her, especially when he truly didn't give a royal damn what people thought. They didn't know him. No, it wasn't the people he was concerned about. It was his son. When Laramie grew into manhood, what story would he hear about and believe? No matter how much quality time Coop would spend with his son, he ran the risk of Laramie one day wondering why he hadn't been there for them when it mattered the most. Hadn't Bristol said she'd wondered about it when she didn't know the real deal with her own father?

And, if he was honest, there was another reason he was suddenly thinking this way. It was about those memories he just couldn't shake. It was his attraction to Bristol that had been there from the start. This deep sexual chemistry they'd given in to in Paris.

He'd always prided himself on being a person who exuded total control. His SEAL friends often referred to him as the quiet storm. There was a coolness about him. Always calm. Always composed. Levelheaded to a fault. And beneath all that equanimity, he was watching, waiting, always on the lookout for the unknown. Considering the possibilities while fighting off the restlessness. But when he was provoked, all bets were off and he would kick ass like the best of them. Even more so. When pushed into a corner, he came out fighting.

What if at some point down the road Bristol met someone and decided to marry? How would that impact his relationship with his son? Would he have to stand in line for his son's attention? His affection? Was there a way to assure that didn't happen? Was he being a selfish bastard for wanting to make sure it never did?

"Coop?"

He blinked. Had he been staring at her while all those crazy thoughts rushed through his brain? And were they crazy? His steady gaze held hers. No, they weren't crazy. Irrational, yes. Crazy, no. There was a difference.

When she said his name again he answered, "Yes?"

"Are you okay?"

Now, that was a good question. Was he? To her he said, "I just realized how little we know of each other. How very little information was exchanged between us in Paris."

"We didn't do much talking," she blurted out. From the look on her face he knew she hadn't meant to say that. It didn't matter since what she'd said was true. Her hormones and his testosterone had been working overtime and the only thing they'd wanted to do was assuage the desire flowing between them. He hadn't wanted to know anything about her and she hadn't wanted to know anything about him. For those three days, pleasure had been the name of the game and they'd played it well.

"No, we didn't," he said. "And now we have a son to show for it. I want to get to know you."

"Why?"

"Because you are the mother of my child and there is a lot I don't know."

She lifted a chin. "Don't sweat it. The only thing you truly need to know is that I love him, will always take care of him and put his interests first."

He wondered if that was really all he needed to know. Maybe. Then maybe not. It had been one thing to arrive in New York a few days ago without a care in the world. His only thought had been how soon he could return to California. Now things had changed. He had a son. A real flesh-and-blood son. He also had a fake wife, who was the one woman he desired most. He could admit that no other woman had ignited his passion as quickly and as easily as Bristol.

Thoughts of her had sustained him. He recalled every single time he had touched her. How he had touched her. He remembered tasting her and how she'd tasted. How it felt to experience heaven while inside her. Their bodies locked together and hurtling into one orgasm after another.

"I'm not sure that's the only thing I need to know, Bristol," he said, finally addressing her earlier statement. "I need to know you."

She frowned. "No, you don't."

"Yes, I do. And you need to know me. Laramie needs to know me. He has grandparents that he needs to get to know and vice versa."

"I have no problem with that."

No, she might not. But would everything be on her terms? What if that guy Culpepper decided to come back around sniffing behind her the minute Coop was gone? His mouth pressed into a hard line at the thought.

"Can I ask you something, Coop?"

He looked over at her. "Yes."

"How do you feel about having a son? One you didn't know you had?"

He thought about her question, wanting to answer as honestly as he could. "I always liked kids well enough, Bristol. I get along fine with Mac's four. They call me Uncle Coop and all. But to be quite honest with you, I never intended to have any of my own because marriage wasn't on my radar. And having one out of wedlock was something I never intended to do. But now he's here. I've seen him and knowing he's mine and that you and I made him is so overwhelming. It's caused emotions I didn't think were possible to feel. It's not just about me anymore. Now it's about my child and you."

He saw the frown that touched her lips. "You don't need to concern yourself with me, Coop."

Boy, was she wrong about that. As far as he was concerned, she and his son were a package deal. The kind Mac had warned him about. But them being a package deal was Coop's choice, since it obviously wasn't hers. Nevertheless, he knew better than to try to convince her just yet. They would finish their conversation regarding their fake marriage later.

"When can I come back?"

"You're always welcome here, Coop. You're Laramie's father and like I told you, I would never keep you from sharing a relationship with him."

However, if she were to marry one day, a future husband might. He'd heard stories from Flipper about how one of his brothers had to constantly take his ex-wife to court for visitation rights. Just because this guy she'd married hadn't felt comfortable with Flipper's brother coming around whenever he'd wanted to see his daughter.

Coop didn't want to deal with that kind of problem. "I'd like to take you and Laramie to dinner tonight," he said.

"Dinner?"

"Yes, dinner. Is that a problem?"

"No, but other than McDonald's, I've never taken Laramie out to eat."

He liked the idea that his son's first time going to a restaurant would be with him. "There's a first time for everything, don't you think?"

Bristol recalled another time he'd told her that. It had been in Paris after he'd stripped her naked and she'd told him that no other man had been in her apartment before.

"So will you and Laramie have dinner with me tonight?"

"Where?"

"You pick the place."

She drew in a deep breath. Maybe going out to dinner wouldn't be so bad. "Laramie loves spaghetti and there's an Italian restaurant not far from here."

"I happen to like spaghetti, too, so that will work for me, if it works for you," he said.

"It will work for me if it's early. I need to have Laramie back here with a bath and into his pajamas no later than eight."

He nodded. "Will reservations at five o'clock be okay?"

"Yes. That's the time he usually eats dinner anyway."

Bristol was wondering why on earth she was paying so much attention to Coop's mouth when they should be figuring out details regarding Laramie. Why was she paying so much attention to his captivating eyes? To his masculine body? She saw men all the time but had never focused on any of those things. Why him? She knew the answer. Mainly because she knew how that mouth felt connected to hers.

She knew how it felt to be held within the scope of those eyes while desire streamed through her. And she knew all about that masculine body. How it felt to be beneath it. To feel the weight of it on her. To feel him inside her. Her breathing became choppy and she forced her gaze away from him.

"Are you okay, Bristol?"

Was she? She wanted to think she was, but honestly she wasn't sure. He'd been the last man she had slept with and now all those hot, delicious and wanton thoughts were trying to take over her senses. They really hadn't finished figuring out how to end their fake marriage. For some reason, she found the discussion draining and really didn't want to go back to it right now. There was no doubt in her mind he would bring it back up again.

However, there was something that had been on her mind since last night that she did want to discuss. "I'm fine, Coop, but there is something I've been wondering about."

"What?"

"Your friends. Those four guys I met who were with you in Paris. Mac, Bane, Viper and Flipper. Are they okay?"

A smile touched his lips. "Yes, they're okay. I'm surprised you remembered them."

"They were nice and—" she said, chuckling "—unforgettable. I liked them. I often wondered if they had gotten captured with you and if they'd lost their lives."

"No, in fact they were part of the team that rescued me. If you recall, Mac was married when you met him. He and his wife are doing fine. Bane and his estranged wife renewed their vows and Viper is married now."

"He is?"

"Yes, and happily so. Reminds us of that every chance he gets. Flipper is still Flipper. Happy-go-lucky and cheerfully single. Bane and his wife had triplets this year, almost six months ago."

"Triplets?"

"Yes. Two boys and a girl. They want a huge family so I guess you can say they're off to a good start."

"I'm glad they're all okay. When I got word that you'd been killed, I wondered about them. I take it the five of you are still close friends."

"Yes, and we're closer than ever. Even while I was being held hostage a part of me believed they would find me and get me out. And they did. We stay in contact even when we're not on a mission. I talked to them just last night and told them I had seen you."

"You did?"

"Yes. They remembered you, as well. I also told them I had a son. They're happy for me."

"Even though fatherhood wasn't anything you asked for?"

"Doesn't matter. I used a condom. Close to a dozen if you recall. Evidently one was defective. I regret that." He paused and then said, "But under no circumstances do I regret Laramie."

She nodded. "Neither do I."

He inclined his head and looked at her. Under his close scrutiny she was tempted to cross her arms over her chest. She could feel her nipples hardening. "I keep thinking that things could have been different. You could have made another decision and not had him," he said.

She knew what he was hinting at. "Not having him wasn't an option for me. I admit becoming a mother was the last thing on my mind, but when I found out I was pregnant I knew I would keep my baby. When I mailed that letter to you, I had no idea how you would respond. It really didn't matter. I was doing what I thought was the right thing by letting you know. I was prepared to go solo regardless."

"And now you don't have to because I'm here."

For how long? she wondered. He was still a navy SEAL and could get called away on a mission at any time. A mission he might not return from. She'd already had to deal with news of him dying once; there was no way she could go through it again. That meant she had to fall out of love with him. But how could she do that?

He had made it pretty clear that he wanted to see Laramie as often as he could. So she'd be seeing him often, too. In that case, how could she begin the process of removing him from her heart? There had to be a way and she was determined to find it. She had lost her mother, her father and her aunt. The three most important people in her life were gone. Now she had Laramie. She lived for her son and that would be enough.

"I'll leave now so you can get some things done while Laramie is taking his nap. I'll be back around four-thirty."

"All right."

She moved to walk him to the door, but he just stood

there. Staring at her. More specifically, his gaze was fixated on her mouth. She saw it. Felt it. Her lips suddenly felt warm. Sensitive.

She knew she should turn away so her mouth wouldn't be the object of his focus. But the truth was, she couldn't. His assessing gaze was getting to her, and she couldn't do a single thing about it.

Bristol knew what he planned the moment he took a step in her direction but she didn't back up. She couldn't. It was as if she was rooted in place. Then he was standing directly in front of her. His eyes penetrating hers. His features fierce.

"I thought about you a lot, Bristol. During those eleven months while being held hostage."

His words made her heart flip several times. He had thought about her? "You did?"

"Yes. Thinking of you kept me sane…especially during those times I was being tortured," he told her quietly.

Oh, God! Tortured? There was an intense searing in the pit of her stomach. She couldn't imagine what he'd endured.

"I would close my eyes and remember each and every time I made love to you. Every single time I kissed you. We shared a lot of kisses over those three days."

Yes, they had. They'd shared a lot of things, including their bodies. He hadn't been the only one who'd remembered, although her situation hadn't been as difficult as his by any stretch of the imagination. Every time her child, their child, had kicked or moved within her womb, she would think of him. Mourn him. Grieve for him. She would also thank him for giving her his child.

"I need to kiss you," he said in a husky tone, reclaiming her attention. "I need to kiss you as much as I need to breathe."

And she needed to kiss him, as well. That was the shocking truth. No matter how independent she wanted to be, she needed to kiss him. Her eyes were focused on his lips with the same intensity that his had been on hers. She needed to feel the heat of her body against his.

She was succumbing to everything male that he represented.

"As you wish," Bristol whispered. She was the one who made the first move, standing on tiptoe, leaning in close and placing her mouth against his.

Twelve

Coop wrapped his arms around her and took over the kiss. The moment their tongues touched, getting reacquainted in the most passionate way, liquid heat seemed to spread through, burning him from the inside out.

His body leaped to life. He was now a man very much aware and filled with a yearning so deep it ached. Yet at the same time the yearning calmed the beast within him. Made him accept that Bristol could affect him in ways no other woman could.

He hadn't counted on her kiss being as greedy as his, her need just as insurmountable. Their tongues were mating in ways that sent a crackle of energy escalating between them. From the very first, he'd known she was different. He just hadn't known what role she would eventually play in his life. He had no idea that one day she would become the mother of his child.

He had given more of himself to her than he had to any woman. Even now he felt a need for her in every cell, in every pore. How could she get under his skin this way? To the point where he confessed to thinking of her while being held captive. Remembering her while being in pain.

He'd never shared that much about one of his missions with anyone. There had been no one to tell. His parents hadn't wanted to hear the gory details. And he hadn't been able to open up to the psychiatrist the military had ordered him to see. Only his SEAL teammates had known the hell he'd gone through. And now Bristol knew. Not everything but enough.

They needed to come up for air, so he slowly ended the kiss, pulling his mouth away on a guttural moan. Still needing a connection, he used the tip of his tongue to lick her lips from corner to corner, before grazing his jaw against her ear.

He dropped his hands and couldn't recall at what point his fingers had become buried in her hair. Now it looked unruly. Sexy as hell. The sight of her kiss-swollen lips made him even more aware of how much he wanted her. Desire pulsed through him and he felt hard as a rock.

He took a step back, because otherwise he would be tempted to sweep her off her feet and carry her upstairs to that bedroom he'd refused to enter earlier. "I'll be back to get you and Laramie around four thirty."

And then he headed for the door. He came close to making it out without looking back. But temptation was too much. Overpowering. He stopped and glanced over his shoulder. Bristol was standing there looking more beautiful than any woman he'd ever seen. There was heat in her eyes.

A hungry throb stirred inside him and he drew in a wobbly breath before forcing himself out the door and closing it behind him.

Bristol released a breath before burying her face in her hands. What on earth had she done? What on earth had she started? That kiss had made her come unglued. No, she'd lost her composure long before that kiss. The intensity of her sexual need had begun to affect her the moment Coop had walked into her house that morning.

She could no more deny the carnal attraction between them than she could refrain from breathing. And today, just a few moments ago in her living room, they'd both unleashed pent-up, held-back desires. Her body knew him, desired him, ached for him. Closing her eyes, she felt a surge of yearning trying to take over her senses again.

Opening her eyes, she refused to let it. At that moment she heard her cell phone ring and wondered who was calling. Coop had her number. Would he be calling her? There was no way he'd made it to the corner already. Maybe he'd decided dinner wasn't a good idea after all and was canceling. If that was true then she agreed with him. Sitting in a restaurant across from him might push temptation to a new level. She wasn't certain if their son would be enough of a buffer.

Pulling her phone out of the back pocket of her jeans, Bristol saw the caller wasn't Coop but Margie. She quickly clicked it on. "Yes, Margie?"

"You okay? You sound kind of breathless."

She swallowed. Did she? "I'm fine."

"I called to see how things turned out with your soon-to-be ex."

Bristol frowned, confused. "My soon-to-be ex?"

"Yes. You can divorce him on the grounds of desertion, you know. I can refer a good attorney you can use."

"Desertion?"

"Yes. At least that's what I call it. You thought he was dead. Granted I understand the military made a mistake, but if he had cared anything about you—even if he didn't know about your son—you were his wife. He should have moved heaven and earth to find you. Showing up now after all this time won't cut it."

Bristol didn't like what Margie was saying. But then her

manager didn't know the whole story. "Laramie and I have things to work out."

"What's there to work out? I talked to Steven and he's concerned about a dead husband reappearing. But I explained things to calm him down. I told him it was all a mistake and you would send your ex packing in no time. I assured him that there was no way you would hook up with Laramie again."

Frissons of anger ignited in Bristol's spine. Margie was believing just what Coop said people would believe about him. And it was all her fault. Furthermore, who gave Margie the right to tell Steven anything?

"Look, Margie, I have to go." It was either end the call or end their relationship, Bristol was just that mad.

Her manager didn't say anything for a moment, then added, "You sound upset, Bristol, and I hope it's not with me but with him. I'm aware you loved your husband. And I can understand you having feelings for him now. But I hope you're not thinking about tossing aside a chance with Steven for a man who didn't come looking for you."

Bristol lost it. "I don't know how many times I have to tell you that I'm not interested in Steven. Now goodbye."

She then hung up the phone.

Coop released a deep sigh the moment his hotel room door closed behind him. What a day. It had started out with him enjoying breakfast with his son and then it had ended after lunch with him kissing Bristol like he couldn't get enough of tasting her mouth.

He licked his lips. He still hadn't.

He never knew a woman's taste could mess with your taste buds and block out your other senses. But he had found out today. He just didn't understand it. Once he'd returned to his team to hang out for New Year's, after spending those three days with her, he'd been fine. She hadn't totally consumed his mind.

But he had thought about her...

And he had thought about her even more while being held hostage, because when your thoughts were filled with orgasmic pleasure it could erase the pain. The more those bastards tried to break him, the more he'd thought about Bristol.

Was that why he was so consumed with her now? He had thought about her so much that the memories of the time they'd shared in Paris were now a part of him? He rubbed his hand down his face. Maybe he was thinking way too hard.

He was removing his jacket when his cell phone rang. He recognized the ring tone. It was Bane. He pulled his phone from his pocket, chuckled and said, "With triplets, don't you have more to do with your time these days?"

Bane laughed. "No. That's where the benefits of belonging to a large family kick in. Everyone wants to help out. There haven't been triplets in the family since Quade's babies and everyone's excited. I couldn't tell you the number of visitors we've had. And more of them are planning to visit for the holidays. I told the family about your son. They're ecstatic and want pictures, so I need you to text me a few. You know the routine so get with the program."

Yes, he knew the routine. He had pictures on his phone of Mac's four kids. His phone was also filled with pictures of Bane's triplets. In the beginning, it seemed like Bane would text him a new picture every other day. Now it had decreased to only one a week. "No problem. I'm taking them to dinner and will take a photo then."

"I take it things are going well. I assume you had that talk you said you were going to have with her."

"Yes, I had it. She wasn't keen on the idea of sharing

support for our son. I had to explain that I don't operate that way. She didn't like it but she finally gave in."

"That's good. What did the two of you decide about the fake marriage?"

Coop rubbed the back of his neck when he remembered that particular conversation. "Bristol doesn't want to be married any more than I do. But we have Laramie to consider now. She suggested we just tell everyone we're getting a divorce. That will release her from the fake marriage. She sees that as the easiest and simplest way out."

"Is that what you want?"

Coop dropped down in the wingback chair. "No. But then marriage isn't what I want, either. At least it wasn't until I met my son. At first I convinced myself being a single dad wouldn't be a big deal since I'd be gone on missions most of the time anyway. But then I began thinking about those times I would be around. What if she began seeing someone who didn't want me to have access to my child the way I wanted?"

"You can work out visitation rights with an attorney, so there shouldn't be any problems with that. Why do I get the feeling there's more, Coop?"

Because there was more. It was at times like this that a part of him wished Bane didn't know him so well. He, Bane, Viper, Flipper and another friend by the name of Nick Stover had gone through the naval academy together. Mac had been a SEAL several years before any of them. For the longest time, Mac had come across like the big-brother SEAL looking out for them, like he figured they couldn't take care of themselves. Over time they'd learned how to look out for each other. A few years ago Nick had given up being a SEAL to take a job with Homeland Security after his wife had triplets.

He, Mac, Viper and Flipper had wondered if Bane would do the same thing because of his triplets. But Bane had assured them he wouldn't. Whereas Nick and his wife didn't have any family to help out, Bane had more family than the law allowed. Bane's triplets were the third set born in the Westmoreland family. There were Westmorelands all over the place. In several states, including Alaska.

Coop was close to all his team members but he and Bane shared a special bond because they'd been roommates at the academy.

"Yes, there's more," he finally said. "It's Bristol."

"What about her?"

"I'm more attracted to her than ever, man. She's beautiful. She's also headstrong, independent and a wonderful mother to Laramie."

"Sounds like you're falling for her all over again."

Coop leaned back in the chair. "To be honest, I don't think I ever stopped falling. I told you how she was constantly on my mind while I was in Syria and how those memories of us together were how I held on to my sanity."

"Did you tell her that?"

"Yes."

"And did you tell her that the minute the hospital released you to travel that you headed to Paris, hoping to see her?"

"No, I didn't tell her that. Maybe one day I will."

"Women like to know they were thought of. Remember how I kept all those cards and letters over the years for Crystal. It meant a lot to her."

He and Bane talked a little while longer. When they ended their conversation, he glanced at his watch. He needed to make another call, namely to his parents. He also needed to follow up with his attorney. Afterward, he would go to the hotel's fitness center and work off that delicious breakfast and lunch Bristol had prepared.

He thought about their kiss again. What he'd told Bane was the truth. He was attracted to her more so than ever.

Visitation rights with his son weren't the only thing he was concerned with. Visitation rights with his son's mother were also on his mind. The thought of her marrying someone else bothered him.

If it bothers you so much, then maybe you should marry her yourself.

What the hell! Why did an idea like that pop into his head? Anyone who knew him would attest to the fact that he wasn't the marrying kind. He liked his freedom. He enjoyed not answering to anyone but himself. He…

Loved his son.

His lips firmed in a straight line. Yes, he loved his son, but what did that have to do with desiring Bristol? Suddenly, he knew the answer. His love for his son affected everything. Even his son's mother.

He groaned in frustration. He had suggested the option of making the marriage real. She had immediately rebuffed it. At the time, it hadn't bothered him one iota. That idea hadn't been at the top of his list anyway.

So why was he thinking about it now?

Once again the answer was the same. He loved his son. Unlike his parents, who believed their love for each other weighed more than the love for their child, he didn't hold such beliefs. Although he'd seen his child for the first time only last night, more love than he thought he could ever have for any other human being had seeped into his heart and it was going to stay there.

He loved his parents. He loved his SEAL teammates as brothers. But the love he had for his child was so amazing that more than once today he'd had to pause to make sure he hadn't dreamed the whole thing.

That little face looked so much like him it was uncanny. Maybe the next time they would have a girl and she would look more like Bristol. Coop went still.

How could he even think what he just had? A daughter? With Bristol as the mother? Jeez.

He stood and began pacing. He was really losing it to even think such a thing. He needed to stay focused. The only person he needed to be thinking about was his son. But how could he think of his son and not think of his son's mother? The woman who'd given birth to him? The woman who made sure he got all the things he needed? The woman who was already teaching him a second language?

Hadn't he decided earlier today that they came as a package deal? But that had only been regarding financial support and nothing more. Hadn't it? Then why was he thinking all crazy? Why was he thinking beyond the financial to something even more? To marriage?

Because she's the woman you want.

Want and not love.

He knew love had nothing to do with it. Whatever feelings he had for Bristol were purely physical. That kiss today proved it, as well as the sexual chemistry surrounding them whenever they were together. That conclusion about the nature of their relationship didn't bother him and he doubted it bothered her.

Coop stood and checked his watch. He needed to go to the fitness center to work off his sexual frustrations, and he had plenty. When he arrived at her house to take them to dinner, maybe he would have worked some sense back into his brain.

Thirteen

"Daddy is back, Mommy?"

Bristol couldn't ignore the excitement in her son's voice. He had been disappointed when he woke up from his nap to find Coop gone. The light had come back into his little eyes only when she'd told him Coop would be back and would take them out to dinner to eat spaghetti.

Laramie had jumped with anticipation when he heard the sound of the doorbell. Now he was right at her heels as she moved toward the door. He was ready and she didn't want to admit it, but so was she. Her lips were still tingling from her and Coop's kiss earlier and she hadn't been able to paint for thinking of him.

And that wasn't good. She needed to get more than a grip. She needed to put things in perspective. When she did, that kiss would be placed on the back burner, where it belonged.

Looking through the peephole, she confirmed it was Coop. He looked handsome, just like the Texan he was proud to say he was. She opened the door and tilted her head to look up at him. Before she could say anything, Laramie, who'd managed to squeeze between her legs, said, "Daddy, you left me."

Her son's words had been spoken with such heartfelt pain that she understood why Coop reached down and pulled Laramie into his arms. She stepped back for him to enter. She was amazed at how quickly Laramie had taken to Coop. Maybe it was a male thing. Maybe he would get attached to any man. She wouldn't know because he rarely saw other men. Ms. Charlotte's sons came around every so often and Bristol hadn't dated since Laramie was born.

"I'll get his coat so we can go," she said, when Laramie sat down on the sofa.

"No rush," Coop said, glancing at her. "We have time."

She started to tell him that he couldn't get all emotional whenever Laramie flashed those sad brown eyes at him. Besides, due to the nature of Coop's job as a SEAL, there would be plenty of times when Laramie wouldn't see him. It was not like this would be Coop's address. He lived heaven knew where. But not here.

She crossed the room to the coatrack to get Laramie's jacket and heard what Coop was telling their son. He was being as honest as he could. "There will be days when Daddy will have to go away. Sometimes for a long time."

"How long?" Laramie asked his father. "This long?" Laramie then stretched his little arms out wide.

"Maybe even this long," Coop said, stretching out his own arms even wider.

"Oh." A disappointed pout curved Laramie's tiny lips.

Coop gathered his son close. "Just remember, I will always come back."

Bristol stopped. She had gone along with everything Coop had said until now. But considering the type of job he did, he couldn't promise that he would always come back. How dare he make such a promise to Laramie?

"Where you go, Daddy?"

"Far away. To keep you safe."

"Keep me safe?"

"Yes. Always."

Of course Laramie had more questions but Bristol had heard enough. She grabbed his coat off the coatrack, determined that she would have a talk with Coop when they returned from dinner, after she put Laramie to bed.

"Here's his coat," she said, returning to the living room to hand the coat to Coop.

There was no need for her to try and put on Laramie's coat since he was determined to stick to Coop like glue. The thought didn't bother her and she wasn't filled with even an ounce of jealousy. There was enough of Laramie to go around for the both of them. She thought it was sad her mother hadn't thought that way when it came to Bristol's father.

"Ready?"

She glanced over at Coop as she buttoned up her own coat. "Yes."

"I rented a car for us to use," Coop said, picking up Laramie.

"Just to go to the restaurant? We could have taken a cab."

"I plan to be in New York for a while and figured I would need one for you and Laramie."

She frowned. "Why would you need it for me and Laramie? If we need to go anywhere, we can take the subway like we always do."

"Not while I'm around," he said, heading for the door with Laramie.

Bristol didn't move for a moment, trying to push feelings of annoyance away. She was not used to depending on anyone except Ms. Charlotte. She should just accept what he'd offered as a kind and thoughtful gesture and let it go. Besides, her mother had always told her to pick her battles. What was foremost on her mind right now was the lie he'd told their son a few moments ago—that promise to always come back.

* * *

"Are you okay?" Coop asked Bristol, after she opened the front door. They were returning from dinner and he was carrying a sleeping Laramie in his arms.

"I'm fine. Why do you ask?"

"You were quiet at dinner."

She shrugged as she closed the door behind them. "I think Laramie did enough talking for the both of us."

Coop couldn't help but chuckle. That was true. His son had definitely been the life of the party. Their waitress had fallen in love with him and had been surprised at how well he conversed for his age. Laramie had eaten all of his spaghetti and clapped his hands afterward, saying how good it was.

Keeping his word to Bane about sending a picture, Coop had given their waitress his cell phone and asked her to take one of them. At first Bristol hadn't wanted to participate, saying it was about him and his son, and that his friends wouldn't want her included. He'd dismissed that assumption by reminding her how much they'd liked her when they'd met her in Paris.

The picture was perfect. They had looked like a family dining out together, enjoying their meal and each other's company. In addition to Bane, Coop had texted the photo to the others. Within minutes, his phone had blown up with their responses. They all thought Laramie was a mini-Coop just as he assumed they would. They also thought Bristol looked good. Really good. And texted him to tell her hello. They also said how good the three of them looked together. Funny, he'd thought the same thing.

He couldn't help but notice how little Bristol had said all evening. Was something bothering her? He knew she hadn't been keen on him renting a car just to have it available for her and Laramie, but surely she wasn't upset because of that.

"You want him upstairs, right?" he asked to make certain.

"Yes. I need to undress him for bed," she said, removing her coat. "It's past his bedtime. He lasted longer than I thought he would."

Carrying their son, he followed her up the stairs, trying not to notice the sway of her hips and the curve of her backside. But he did notice. He was a man after all, and didn't intend to feel guilty about checking her out.

He placed Laramie on the bed then watched while Bristol removed his clothes and put him in pajamas. Laramie opened his eyes once and gave his mother a droopy smile. "Love you, Mommy."

"Love you back, Laramie. See you in the morning." She leaned over and kissed him on the cheek. Then he drifted back to sleep.

Coop felt like an intruder to what was probably a usual bedtime exchange between mother and son. An exchange he was witnessing for the first time, one he felt no part of. He would have loved to dress his son for bed. But he hadn't been asked. Instead, he'd been delegated to the sidelines.

Bristol then glanced over at him and whispered, "We need to talk."

There was something in her tone. Whatever she wanted to talk about, he wasn't going to like it. "Okay."

She moved out of the room and he followed. In spite of his mixed emotions while watching Laramie's bedtime routine, Coop enjoyed walking behind Bristol. She helped keep his libido healthy. He thought now what he'd thought a number of times before. She looked good in jeans. He wondered if his son's birth was the reason behind all those curves that now looked even more delectable to him.

"Coffee or beer?"

Bristol's question thrown over her shoulder drew his attention. He had a feeling he would need something stronger than coffee. Probably even stronger than beer, so he would take the alcohol. "Beer."

She kept walking toward the kitchen while he remained in the living room. With her no longer in sight, he turned his attention to the Christmas tree. He might be wrong but it looked like she'd added more ornaments than were there yesterday. The tree looked all bright and festive, recalling to his mind how perfunctorily the tradition was observed in his own family. His parents, or rather the housekeeper, put up a tree every year. And it remained up until New Year's whether anyone was there to enjoy it or not.

He couldn't help but recall his telephone call to his parents earlier today, to let them know about Laramie. They were surprised he'd been so careless with protection and his father had strongly suggested Coop get a blood test before claiming anyone. His mother had stated that if Laramie was truly his, then they would give the little boy all the love they'd given to Coop. He'd had to chuckle at that.

When his mother asked what was funny, he'd respectfully said nothing. They just didn't get it, but at this point in his life, he didn't care. His parents weren't going to change and he was used to their behavior.

A part of him wondered if he would one day find his soul mate, like his father had. Coop knew well the story of how his parents had met in college and fallen in love, apparently at first sight. He often wondered if his parents had really planned for him, although they claimed they had. One thing was for certain, if Coop ever did meet his soul mate, he wouldn't get so wrapped up in her that he wouldn't love with equal intensity any child they'd made together.

He drew in a deep breath. Why was he thinking about soul mates? As far as he was concerned, one didn't exist for him. Laramie would most likely be his only child. He was satisfied with that.

"Here you are."

He turned and Bristol handed him his beer. It was cold, but what he felt was the warmth of her hand when they touched. She had a beer for herself, as well. This was the first time he'd seen her drink beer instead of tea.

"I didn't know you drank beer," he said, tempted to reach out and touch that lone dimple in one of her cheeks.

"There's a lot you don't know about me, Coop."

She had him there. "What do you want to talk about?" he asked.

She moved past him to sit down on the sofa and, as usual, he watched her movements. He wanted to go sit beside her, but knew he shouldn't. For two people who'd made a baby together, they were as far apart as ever. He felt it. She was upset about something and he couldn't wait to hear what it was. He moved to sit down in the chair across from her.

"I want to talk about what you told Laramie."

He lifted a brow. "And what did I tell Laramie?"

The lamp in the room cast a soft light on her features. She wore her hair up in a ponytail with little curls fanning her face. He remembered her wearing a similar style three years ago. He'd taken the band out of her hair so it could fan around her shoulders. His fingers itched to do the same thing now.

"That you would always come back to him."

"I will."

She frowned. "You don't know that."

Now he was the one who frowned. "Do you think I'd deliberately stay away after seeing him? After getting to know him? You think I'd shuck my responsibilities? Even worse—that I could stop loving him and forget about him?"

"That's not what I'm insinuating, Coop. You're missing the point."

He leaned forward, needing to study her expression. To

try deciphering what the hell she was talking about. "So what is the point? Why don't I know that I will always come back to him?"

"Because."

He lifted a brow. "Because what?"

He watched her bury her face in her hands and draw in a deep breath before looking back up at him. The anguish he saw in her gaze made his insides clench when she said, "Because you could die."

Coop didn't say anything. Flashes of a time when everyone thought he had died, when he'd lived each day extremely close to death, filtered through his mind. He pushed the memories back and concentrated on the real fear he saw in Bristol's eyes. That was what he would address. "Yes, I could die. But so could you."

He saw the shiver pass through her before she lifted her chin. "Don't even try to compare what I do with what you do. I paint. You and others like you carry the weight of the world and all of the country's problems on your shoulders. You constantly put your life in danger, Coop. Do you deny that?"

He shook his head. "No, I don't deny it. But whenever I leave for any mission, I have every intention of coming back. Would you have preferred me to tell my son I won't be coming back?"

"No, but I wish you wouldn't make promises you might not be able to keep. If anything ever happens to you, I will be the one who has to explain what happened."

Why were they talking about him dying? Thanks to his son, he had every reason to live, not that he'd ever taken life lightly. But now he had someone in his life who made living doubly important. "I think you're going to the extreme with this, Bristol."

It was clear his words angered her. "You think I'm going to the extreme? You aren't the one who got word while four months pregnant that the father of her child was dead. Dead, Coop. I thought you'd died like all the others."

He frowned. "What others?"

"It doesn't matter. I prefer you don't make promises to Laramie you might not be able to keep."

He stood, feeling angry now, as well. "Then I suggest you do the same. Stop telling him at bedtime that you'll see him in the morning. Anything can happen to you overnight. You could even die in your sleep."

She narrowed her gaze at him. "Stop being ridiculous."

His jaw tightened. "Then I suggest you stop being ridiculous, too. There are no guarantees in life. People die every day. When your time comes, there's not a damn thing you can do about it."

She took a step forward. Got in his face. "I guess of all people you should know, since you had a chance to beat death."

Not good, he thought, meeting her eyes. He wished she didn't smell so good and he definitely preferred her not standing so close. As if it had a will of its own, his gaze moved from her face to her body. She was beautiful even when she was angry.

"And just what are you looking at?" she all but snapped.

Since she asked, he had no qualms in telling her. "You. Did I tell you how good you looked tonight?"

Fourteen

Bristol suddenly realized she might have made a mistake by getting in Coop's space. How had they gone from discussing his death to how good he thought she looked?

She angrily crossed her arms over her chest and then wished she hadn't when his gaze shifted to her chest. As if on cue her nipples hardened right before his eyes. She drew in a deep breath and took a step back. "I think it's time for you to go."

"Is it?"

"Yes."

"I thought you wanted to talk," he said, reclaiming the distance she'd put between them.

"I think we've said enough for tonight."

"Do you? Have you ever noticed we never seem to resolve anything when we talk?"

"And whose fault is that?" she snapped.

"Both of ours." A smile touched the corners of his mouth. "I agree that we've said enough for tonight."

"Good."

"No, Bristol, this is good." And then before she realized

what he was doing, he pulled her into his arms and lowered his mouth to hers.

Shivers of pleasure, the kind she only experienced with him, shot through every part of Bristol. Her eyelids fluttered shut, too overtaken by desire to remain open. When Coop slipped his tongue into her mouth, tasting of the peppermint candy he'd been sucking on earlier, she shuddered. More enjoyable shivers ran up her spine. Sensations consumed her. When his hands wrapped around her middle, she was pulled close to the fit of his hard, masculine body.

When she felt his engorged erection nestled in the juncture of her thighs, she couldn't help but moan. How could they have been talking about serious stuff one minute and kissing the next?

Heated pleasure nearly melted her where she stood. She should be fighting to hold on to her sanity, but she couldn't. Even thinking of it was almost impossible. His assault on her mouth was sensuous and unhurried. It was mind-blowing. It had awakened needs long ago forgotten. And when she thought she couldn't possibly handle anymore, he deepened the kiss and new sensations overtook her.

Suddenly he broke away and she moaned in protest. Looking into his eyes she saw a naked desire that nearly tripped her pulse. Thickened the blood rushing through her veins. The air shimmered around them with sexual undercurrents.

"I want you, Bristol."

His words, spoken in a deep voice, stroked over her skin like a warm caress. Her breathing became as rapid as her heartbeat. And she knew at that moment that kissing wasn't enough. Especially now that they'd been reminded of how it felt to become so enmeshed in each other. Sexual excitement curled her stomach at the memory. It wasn't about love…at least for him it wouldn't be.

For him, it was physical desire driving what was happening between them.

She, on the contrary, was driven by deep, never-ending love.

Two different drives. One final destination.

No need to deny what she truly wanted. "I want you, too, Coop."

As soon as the words left her lips, she was swept off her feet into strong arms and carried up the stairs.

Coop practically took the stairs two at a time with Bristol in his arms. He'd been unable to endure her form of passion any longer. Desire was clawing at his insides, making his need for her palpable. His need to make love to her was a pulsing, throbbing necessity he couldn't fight.

Entering her room, he went straight to the bed and placed her on it. Then he stood back and began removing his clothes while watching her remove hers. She pulled the sweater over her head and tossed it aside. He inhaled a sharp breath when he saw her breasts encased in a sexy black lace bra. Breasts his tongue had known and wanted to know again.

She unhooked the front clasp of her bra and his erection throbbed harder when the twin globes were freed. He'd always liked her breasts—their shape, size and texture. Coop was convinced if given the chance, he could devour those nipples 24/7.

He stopped taking off his own clothes just to watch Bristol finish taking off hers. He was mesmerized, captivated, so damn fascinated. When she removed her jeans, leaving herself only in undies, his erection got harder. She was wearing black panties that matched the bra.

Three words immediately came to mind. Gorgeous. Hot. Awesome.

"Is there a problem, Coop?"

Her voice snapped him back. He swallowed when he shifted his gaze to her face. "No, there isn't a problem."

"I was just wondering."

He didn't want her to wonder about anything. Especially about him being anxious to make love to her. He was convinced that somehow during those three days they'd spent together in Paris, Bristol had gotten into his blood. That had to be the reason he hadn't been able to forget her. The reason why thinking of her had kept him sane. What other reason could there be?

He quickly removed the rest of his clothes and then pulled out a condom from his wallet. He sheathed himself, knowing she was watching. It wouldn't be the first time she'd seen him do this and he didn't intend for it to be the last.

Bristol frowned when he got closer to the bed. Her fingers touched the scars that hadn't been there the last time they'd made love. From the look on her face he figured she knew where they'd come from. And then she did something he hadn't expected. Something that touched him deeply.

She leaned close and showered kisses over the scars. It was as if she wanted to kiss away any pain they might have caused him. When her mouth came close to his erection, he pulled back. He didn't want a reason to take off his condom. That was probably how she'd gotten pregnant the last time.

"I want to be inside of you, Bristol. I need it," he whispered hoarsely, climbing on the bed to join her.

"And that's where I want you, Coop," she said, wrapping her arms around his neck. "Inside of me."

Maybe she shouldn't have said that, shouldn't have so openly admitted her desire. Maybe she should not have been so brutally honest. But what else could she say when the juncture of her thighs throbbed for him? When her nipples were hard? When her heart was beating fast? When every nerve in her body shrieked with excitement and anticipation? When the moment she'd kissed his scars it was as if they'd become hers?

There was still a lot they didn't agree on and they truly needed to be downstairs talking instead of in her bedroom doing this. But then, maybe this was needed before they could have any sensible discussions. It was hard to sit down and talk like adults when said adults wanted to tear each other's clothes off, roll on the floor in front of the fireplace and mate like rabbits.

There was nothing that could hold her back from this. From giving herself to him like she'd done three years ago. So much had happened since then, but she didn't want to remember any of it…except for the birth of her son. That would always be a spot of joy in her life. But right now, at this instant, she wanted to be transported back in time. She wanted to experience once again how it felt when their bodies joined. When he proved to her just how much vitality he had. How much stamina.

When he showed her just how much he desired her. She could never get enough of that. His open display of need made sexual excitement curl her stomach. She felt light-headed with the effect of his masculine power.

"I plan to take this slow, Bristol."

His words had a shock effect to her system. Slow? He had to be kidding. She was so enthusiastic she was convinced that slow would kill her.

He touched her, using his fingers to unhurriedly skim across her skin, right beneath her breasts. His fingertips elicited sensations that made parts of her tingle. Lighting her up like a flame he intended to let burn gradually before sensuously snuffing it out.

The intensity of his gaze took her breath. She wasn't sure what emotions she saw in his penetrating look—except for one. The sexual vibes between them. They were stronger than they'd been in Paris. That was hard to believe because what they'd shared in Paris had been mind-blowing at minimum.

While his fingers were intent on driving her insane with lust, he increased her pleasure by leaning over and whispering, "I need to taste you."

She knew what he meant. He'd already kissed her. She knew he was referring to tasting her in another way. A way she remembered so well. A way that made the throbbing between her legs intensify. The one thing she remembered about Coop was that he never did anything without telling her beforehand, to make sure she was comfortable with what he wanted to do. He was not a man who exploited a woman's weak moments. There hadn't been any surprises in what he did, only in the magnitude of the pleasure his actions delivered.

She nodded. He took the motion as consent. Before she could draw her next breath, he lowered his head to her chest and slid a nipple into his mouth.

She purred. Of course he would start here, knowing exactly what he was doing to her and how he was making her feel. He was well aware that he could push her into an orgasm just from his mouth devouring her breasts. He'd done it before and, from the feel of things, he intended to do it again.

Suddenly, he pulled his mouth away and looked up at her. "Did you breastfeed our son?"

His question took her by surprise. "Yes."

He smiled as if the thought pleased him. She didn't have the mind to ponder why when his mouth went back to her breasts. Then, as if with renewed energy, he began sucking hard. Her womb contracted with every draw of a nipple into his mouth and her purr got louder.

She needed to touch him. She slid her hands over his shoulders and down his arms before bringing them back to cup the side of his face. Tingling sensations built between her legs. She was certain she was about to be pushed over the edge when he pulled back, lifted his head and said, "Not yet. Remember what I told you. I intend to make this slow so you can remember me for a long time."

She felt his body shift lower. Then he was touching her stomach, caressing it with gentle strokes. His hands moved lower and his fingers stilled when they touched the thin line of a scar.

"Because Laramie weighed so much I had to have a C-section," she said, explaining the bikini cut that was barely visible. Of course someone as observant as him would detect it.

He didn't say anything, but she felt his mouth when his tongue traced a path over the scar. He was kissing her scar like she'd done for his.

The air surrounding them became even more charged. And she was suddenly filled with so many emotions she felt completely out of whack.

Then he lifted her legs to fall over his shoulders while her hips were elevated with his hands. He nudged her knees open and then as if it was the most natural thing to do, eased his face between her legs and slid his tongue inside.

He kissed her with an expertise she found utterly amazing. His tongue went deep. It was thorough. And it was excruciatingly slow. It was as if he had all the time in the world to drive her mad with desire. The more she moaned, the more he tortured her, delving deeper with powerful strokes.

Then she had to fight back a scream when her body exploded into a gigantic orgasm.

Shivers ran through Coop as the thighs encasing his face quivered. He knew what that meant but he refused to stop. In fact, he needed to keep going because her taste was more potent now. Her taste was what he'd remembered, what he'd longed for, yearned for. His shaft throbbed with an urgency he hadn't felt since the last time he'd been with her.

He felt her tremors subside but he refused to let up. Doubted he could even if he wanted to. The taste of her juices flooded him with even more desire. When her thighs began trembling again, he knew she was reaching climax again.

When he'd seen that scar he had been filled with such profound emotion. They both had scars to show from their time apart. Hers had been a celebration of life, his had been a prologue to a death that never happened.

Those days were over. He was free and back in the land of the living. Back in Bristol's bed. The same bed where memories had been made before. The same bed where his son was created. Same bed, same woman.

He couldn't get enough.

When the last of the spasms wore off, Bristol wondered how she'd had mulitple orgasms so close together. Had she been that needy? That greedy? That hard up for sex?

If she'd just wanted sex she would have dated Steven, or any of the other men who'd hit on her over the years. But none of them had enticed her to open herself up this way. To invite them to her bed. To tell them she wanted them inside her. Only with Coop could she behave so boldly. And she knew why.

She was still in love with him.

Coop smiled down at her as his body straddled hers. Surely he didn't think she had the energy for another round of anything. Especially intercourse of the most intense kind. She was so tired she would probably fall asleep in the middle. But then she'd had two orgasms in less than twenty minutes. She owed him something and would fake it if she had to. He deserved his pleasure, as well.

She'd only faked it for one guy, her first time in high
school. With Coop she'd never needed to fake a thing. He'd
kept her blood pumping. Kept the primal attraction between
them so real that she'd been ready whenever he'd been
ready. She'd even been tempted to wake him up for more.
But not this time. There was no way her body could endure
another orgasm tonight. But for him, she would pretend.

"You're not about to go to sleep on me, are you?" he
asked her, staring down at her.

She looked into his eyes and her body warmed under
his intense regard. She lowered her gaze to his lips. Lips
that were wet with her juices. Why did that cause a deep
stirring in the pit of her stomach? Maybe it was because
she recalled how his tongue had lapped her into consecu-
tive orgasms.

"Ready to taste yourself?" he asked in a low whisper.

Blood rushed through her veins. He'd never asked her
anything like that before. Taste herself? She knew how he
would do it and imagining it aroused her enough that a low
moan escaped her lips.

"Is that a yes?"

A sensual force seemed to overtake her. Where was his
sexual aura coming from? Hadn't she thought of faking it
just a minute ago? Now he was arousing her all over again
with mere words. Laramie Cooper was too compelling for
his own good. Definitely too sexy.

She should have known she couldn't fake anything with
him because he had the ability to turn her on, even when
she thought such a thing wasn't possible.

"Yes," she said.

Then he lowered his mouth to hers. The moment their
lips touched, every hormone in her body crackled. She
knew it was more than their combined tastes driving her
over the edge. It was the masterful way his tongue domi-
nated her mouth.

Her nerves did a pirouette, her brain sprinted and her stomach flipped.

He ended the kiss and looked down at her in a way that made moisture gather between her thighs. "You're ready for me again, Bristol?"

Yes, she was ready, even when she'd thought earlier there was no way she could go another round. Not only could she go, she intended to participate to the fullest and there wouldn't be anything fake about it. "Yes, I'm ready."

Her legs opened automatically, as if her body needed what he was giving. It had been three years since she'd done this and the last time had been with him. She slipped her arms around his neck and felt the large length of his erection touching her feminine mound.

Then he eased inside, inch by inch. His fullness encompassed her as he went deeper, filling her to the hilt. Her body stretched to accommodate him.

"You okay?"

She looked up and met his gaze. "Yes, I'm okay."

And honestly, she was. It was like a homecoming. The man she'd thought lost to her forever, the man she'd believed would never make love to her again, was doing just that. It was more than she could have hoped for.

"Thank you for my son," he whispered hoarsely.

And then he began moving while still holding her gaze, as if daring her to look away. She stared into his eyes while his body thrust inside her with a rhythm that released a sensual throb of desire in her veins. The sinfully erotic movement of his hips drew everything out of her, while at the same time demanding that she take as much of him as she could. Each hard thrust made her moan.

He kept moving at an unhurried pace, as if he wanted her to feel every single stroke. And she did. They were a perfect fit. She felt intense pleasure all the way to her bones.

The undercurrent flowing between them was explosive, hot with passion of the most mind-blowing kind.

Her body moved with his. Her inner muscles tightened around him. Together they were creating a sensual heat like she'd never felt before…not even the last time. She'd thought nothing could be more powerful than what they'd already shared. Bristol was proven wrong.

Then he increased his pace, refined his strokes and pumped into her with a vigor that made her entire body respond. She exploded the same time he did, and he covered her mouth to keep the scream from her lips.

They seemed to flow into each other. Her hips were connected to his. Their bodies were perfectly aligned as they experienced the throes of ecstasy together. When he finally released her mouth, she drew in a deep breath and clung to his shoulders. They rode the waves of pleasure together.

Moments later, he rolled off her and gathered her in his arms. His thumb stroked her cheeks. The last thing Bristol remembered before sleep overtook her was whispering his name.

Fifteen

Coop wasn't sure what awakened him, but he jerked upright in bed and glanced around before remembering where he was. Bristol's bed. He drew in a deep breath and rubbed his hand down his face before looking at the clock. It was three in the morning. The spot beside him was empty. He'd been sleeping so soundly that he hadn't noticed when Bristol got out of bed.

Where was she? He lay back down thinking she was probably in the bathroom. A few minutes later, when she hadn't returned, he got up and checked. She wasn't there. Had she gone to see about Laramie? Coop pulled on his jeans and left the bedroom to go to his son's room. He found his son sleeping, but Bristol wasn't there, either.

He was about to head downstairs when he heard a noise coming from the attic. He knew from playing hide-and-seek with Laramie that she'd converted the attic into her studio and that was where she did most of her painting. Was she painting this time of morning?

Coop walked up the six steps and found the door open. And there she was, standing in front of an easel. Was she wearing anything under that artist's cape? It was short and hit her at midthigh, which gave him a good view of her legs. She had a nice pair and like him, she was in her bare feet. He watched the look of concentration on her face. Her full attention was on whatever she was painting. Considering what they'd done tonight she should be exhausted. Obviously, she had a lot of energy.

She hadn't noticed him and he decided not to disturb her. Coop took in the room. It was huge. There were several built-in cabinets for her supplies. There was also a love seat, as well as a sink and counter that he figured she used as a cleanup station. The room had only one small window and he figured she wanted the least distractions possible while painting.

Coop was about to leave when he noticed several framed photographs on the wall. One was a photo of her and an older man. They favored each other and he figured the man was her father. He studied the man's features and tried to recall why he seemed so familiar.

Coop leaned in the doorway and recalled bits and pieces of what she'd told him about her past. Their son's middle name had been her father's first name. When they'd first met, her last name had been Lockett. He also remembered the story she'd told him about the two years she and her father had spent together before he'd died.

"That's a picture of you and your father, isn't it?"

His words had her swinging around so fast she almost dropped her paint brush. She released a nervous breath. "Coop, you scared me."

"Sorry," he said, entering the room. "I woke up and found you gone and wondered where you'd taken off to." It hadn't been his intention to stay the night at her house, but after making love that first time, they'd slept and had awakened to make love once more. Then they'd fallen asleep again.

She smiled over at him. "I didn't want to wake you. In

addition to painting during Laramie's nap time, I often paint late at night when he's asleep." She then broke eye contact and glanced at the framed photograph. "Yes, that's my father," she said proudly. He could hear the love in her voice.

"Randall Lockett was your father."

She snatched her gaze to him. "How do you know that?"

He could see the surprised look on her face. Was her father's identity supposed to be a secret or something? "I recognize him. I'm familiar with his work thanks to my parents, namely my mother. She owns several of his paintings."

"She does?"

"Yes."

He glanced at her easel and back at her before saying, "I even met him once when he came to Austin for an art show to benefit one of my mother's charities. I liked his work. I should have made the connection in Paris with your last name being Lockett and the two of you having similar styles. But it never crossed my mind." There was no need to tell her that the only thing that had been on his mind was getting her to the nearest bed.

"I can't believe you actually met my father."

He heard the excitement in her voice. "Yes, I was seventeen at the time and a senior in high school. It was the last event my mother sort of forced me to attend with her and my dad. In the end, I'm glad I went. He was a nice man. Very personable. Like I said, Mom has quite a few of your father's paintings and it was nice meeting the man who was getting so much of her money. I'm sure you know his work isn't cheap."

She chuckled. "Yes, I know."

"I remember that time well," he said. "I'd gotten word a few days before of my acceptance into the naval academy and was going away with my parents' blessing. I was relieved they hadn't placed any pressure on me to follow in their footsteps and take part in the family business."

"And what business is that?"

"RCC Manufacturing Company."

She lifted a brow. "RCC? I'm familiar with them. They're a huge operation based in Texas. I order a number of my art supplies through them."

He chuckled. "My parents would be happy to hear that."

"And you decided to become a SEAL instead of going into your family business?"

"Yes, that's right. I knew early on I wasn't cut out for the business-suit-and-tie crowd."

Coop glanced back over at the framed photograph and then back at her. "You seemed surprised that I knew Randall Lockett was your father, like it was supposed to be a secret or something. Was it?"

Bristol looked away from Coop to glance at the picture she'd taken with her father, one that she'd proudly hung on her wall. She wished Coop wouldn't stand there shirtless and in his bare feet. In jeans riding low on his hips and not quite zipped up all the way, with the snap undone. He looked way too sexy for her peace of mind.

She'd yet to answer Coop's question and she realized how little they knew about each other, even with all the intimacy they'd shared. She blamed it on the fact that whenever they were together they did little talking due to all the sexual chemistry surrounding them. Like now. She could feel it and she knew he did, as well.

She hadn't known so much need had been bottled up inside her. All it had taken was Coop unleashing it and she'd become a mad woman wanting to make up for lost time. Luckily for her, he'd been the same way. It was as if they hadn't been able to get enough of each other.

"It's not a secret per se. I just don't go around broadcasting it, so few people know. I don't want to use his name to build my own career as an artist, although I am proud to have been Randall Lockett's daughter."

"And I'm sure he was glad he was Bristol Lockett's father."

His words made her feel good. More than once, her father had told her how proud he was of her and all she'd accomplished. "Thank you for saying that."

"No need to thank me."

He moved around the room, looking at the easels showing various paintings she had done. She wasn't used to anyone invading her space, especially in here. For some reason his presence didn't bother her.

Another thing that didn't bother her, when maybe it should have, was how quickly they'd become intimate again. Had it been just the night before when he'd shown up at the gallery? She had wanted him immediately. Had needed him sexually. And he'd delivered, satisfying her.

It wasn't his fault that she had fallen in love with him years ago. Nor was it any of his concern that she was trying to fall out of love with him now. Sleeping with him hadn't confused the issue for her. She knew he didn't love her back.

She needed to get her mind off Coop, namely off his body, and transfer her thoughts to something else. She walked over to the coffeepot she kept in her studio and poured a cup. She then turned to him. "Would you like some?"

Her insides heated when his gaze roamed over her, making her realize just what she'd asked. She swallowed, thinking he'd had some already. A lot actually. But if he wanted more…she was game.

Drawing in a deep breath, she clarified, "Would you like a cup of coffee, Coop?"

He nodded slowly. "Yes, I'd love a cup."

She poured his coffee and he walked over to take the cup from her hand. Their fingers brushed and her stomach curled with pleasure.

"Thanks," he said.

"You're welcome."

They both took a sip of their coffees. Despite trying not to love him, she wanted to get to know him. Like she'd told him earlier, she was very familiar with his parents' company. It was on the Fortune 500 list, which meant he came from money. He'd said the reason he'd wanted to become a SEAL was that the work was a better fit for his personality. And he'd become a SEAL with his parents' blessing. She knew things didn't always work that way for the sons of important families.

"It's late. I hadn't intended to impose on you by spending the night. I'll leave now if you want me to."

She looked at him over the rim of her cup. Did she want him to leave? No, she didn't. "There's no need, unless you want to go. You'll probably be back in the morning for breakfast anyway."

He chuckled. "Only if I get an invitation."

"You have an invitation, Coop. I told you, you can spend as much time with Laramie as you want."

He nodded and took a sip of his coffee. "In that case, I'd like to ask you something."

"What?" she asked.

"What plans do you and Laramie have for the holidays?"

She thought about his question. "Just a quiet time at home this year. It will be Laramie's first Christmas where he understands that the holidays are special. I've been telling him that if he's a good boy, Santa will bring him something nice. He's been keeping his toys put away and getting better with potty training." She paused before asking, "Why did you want to know about my plans for the holidays?"

"Because I'm hoping I can join the two of you." He drew in a deep breath. "And before you ask, the answer is no. I had no plans to spend Christmas with my folks."

Bristol remembered the last holiday they'd spent together. At that time, he'd given her the impression that he and his parents weren't close. Now was just as good a time as any to ask him about it. After all, his parents were her son's only living grandparents. In fact, the only living relatives Laramie had besides her and Coop, as far as she knew. If anything were to ever happen to her or Coop…

She suddenly needed to know about the people who might one day be responsible for her son. "You're welcome to join us, but I want you to tell me about your parents, Coop. Laramie's grandparents."

He leaned against her art table, avoiding her stacks of supplies. "What do you want to know?"

She shrugged. "Mainly, why you never want to spend the holidays with them?"

A part of Coop wanted to think her question was simple enough. But when it came to his parents, nothing was simple unless you accepted them for who they were. He'd done that a long time ago.

"Come on, let's sit on the sofa and I'll tell you about them."

"Okay."

Together, they sat down. To be on the safe side, since she was too desirable for her own good, he sat at the other end of the sofa. He took a sip of his coffee and said, "I think my parents are swell people who after nearly thirty-five years of marriage still love each other deeply."

He chuckled. "I wouldn't be wrong if I were to say they were obsessed with each other. I was told by both sets of my grandparents—who are deceased now—that it had been that way from the first, when they'd met at Harvard.

Dad was from Laredo, Texas, and Mom from Laramie, Wyoming."

She lifted a brow. "Laramie?"

"Yes, and before you ask, the answer is yes. She named me after the city where she was born. She loved it that much and tried getting my father to move there after they were married. But he was a Texan through and through. He'd come from generations of ranchers, but he gave up that way of life, deciding not to follow in his father's, grandfather's and great-grandfather's footsteps as a rancher. He was the suit-and-tie kind. After college, he and my mom lived in Austin and started a business. Less than a year after graduating from college, the two of them were married. I was born three years later."

"No wonder your parents were so understanding about allowing you to have the career you wanted. They'd faced the same challenge."

"Yes, but my paternal grandparents weren't as understanding. They thought Dad was throwing away his legacy. Especially since my father was their only child."

He paused to take another sip of coffee. "I'm told that my mom's pregnancy with me was difficult. At one point, they thought she would die. My father was even told he might have to choose to either save his wife or his child. He picked his wife. But a top specialist arrived and assured my father he could save us both. He did. However, I think I was still a stark reminder to my dad of how close he came to losing Mom."

Bristol frowned, and he thought it was cute. "Surely, he didn't hold you responsible and mistreat you in any way."

"No, not at all. Dad was good. However, my parents' relationship took a turn. They were always close, but I think nearly losing Mom freaked Dad out. After that he was determined to spend every moment he could with her... for the rest of their lives. They take more trips than I can count every year, and they have a tradition of spending the holidays together somewhere—usually with friends in England. Like I told you before, I've never spent the holidays with my parents. I've always spent them with my grandparents on their ranch. And trust me, I had no complaints. My grandparents were the greatest. I loved being out on their ranch."

"Did you ever feel resentful of your parents for not spending time with you?"

He knew it was hard to understand his relationship with his parents, but for her he wanted to try to explain. "It's not that my parents never spent time with me, Bristol, because they did. They were very active in my life while growing up and there were a number of trips we took together."

He took another sip of coffee. "Thanks to them, I saw most of the world before my sixteenth birthday. There was never a time I didn't think my parents loved me. However, I always knew they loved each other more."

"And you didn't have a problem with that?"

"No. I had friends whose parents didn't even like each other, couldn't stand to be in the same room together. Some of their parents divorced as soon as they finished school and my friends knew they had been the glue that held their parents' unhappy marriages together. That wasn't the case with my parents. There was never any doubt in my mind that Dad and Mom loved each other to the moon and back."

He didn't say anything for a minute, then he added, "When they thought I was dead, they went bonkers. I think they got even closer, if such a thing is possible with them. When I was found alive, they refused to let me out of their sight at first. They even questioned if I should continue being a SEAL. I knew they were worried, but I wasn't used to all the attention, at least not from them. I couldn't wait until I finished my recuperation period to return to work."

She spun her cup in her hands and asked, "What happened to your grandparents' ranch?"

"They willed it to me, although they were fully aware of my career as a SEAL. But my grandparents also knew I would manage the ranch as well as become a SEAL. For the ranch, I hired the right people to take care of it until I retire from the military, which will be in about six years. Some of the men working at the ranch for me used to work for my grandparents and can be trusted."

She nodded. "What kind of ranch is it?"

"It was always a cattle ranch but thanks to Bane's family, the Westmorelands, I've added horses. Several of his family members own a horse breeding and training company. They needed another holding depot before shipping the horses off to be trained. That's where my ranch comes in. So, I guess my ranch is a horse ranch, as well."

"Do you go there often?"

"Not as much as I would like. When I do go there it's mainly to check on things. My men have everything pretty much under control."

"I'm glad."

A part of him believed she was, which made him say, "I want to show you and Laramie my ranch one day." He would tell her that much. He wouldn't tell her yet that he planned to make it his primary home for whenever Laramie visited.

She smiled and he felt a stirring in his stomach. "I'd love to see it, Coop. I know Laramie will, too. He loves horses."

"Then it's settled. I will take the two of you there after the holidays." Standing, he said, "I've kept you from your work long enough."

She smiled, standing, as well. "I'm okay. I was about to come to a stopping point anyway."

"You do this every night? Paint while Laramie sleeps?"

"Not every night. Just whenever the urge hits."

Funny, she should mention urges. At that moment, he was swamped with another urge. "Speaking of urges, Bristol," he said, setting his cup aside.

"What about them?"

"I feel one coming on myself."

She smiled. "You want to try your hand at painting?"

He chuckled. "No. It's not an urge to paint."

"Oh? What kind of urge is it?"

He leaned over and whispered in her ear. She smiled and placed her own coffee cup on the table. She moved closer and wrapped her arms around his neck. "In that case, I think we need to deal with these urges of yours."

"I agree." He swept her off her feet and headed toward her bedroom.

Sixteen

Coop felt something poke him against his nose and he snatched his eyes open. He saw a miniature pair of eyes and a little hand right in his face. "You in my mommy's bed," his son all but accused.

Yes, he was in Laramie's mommy's bed. Before Coop could open his mouth to assure his son that everything was okay, Laramie had pulled himself up on the bed and crawled over him, saying, "Move over, Daddy." The little boy then planted himself in the middle of the bed, unceremoniously separating Coop and Bristol like the parting of the Red Sea.

"Laramie!" Bristol said, quickly sitting up after coming awake. "Be nice."

"He in your bed, Mommy."

Bristol yawned and ran a hand through her son's curls. "I know and it's okay. Good morning, Laramie."

He wrapped his arms around his mother's neck. "Good morning, Mommy."

Then, as if satisfied, Laramie slid beneath the covers and closed his eyes.

Bristol glanced over at Coop and smiled. "Sorry about that."

"Hey, don't apologize. I take it he does this every morning."

She nodded, pushing a mass of hair back from her face. "Yes. And as you can see it's not quite six o'clock. He comes in here, gets in my bed and will go back to sleep for another hour or so, then he'll wake up hungry. That's how we start our day."

For Coop that was a bummer because he'd planned to start his day by making love to her. Now, thanks to their son, those plans would be canned. But son or no son, Coop intended to get a good morning kiss. He leaned over and placed a kiss on her lips. "Good morning, Bristol."

She smiled. "Good morning, Coop."

He returned her smile. He'd liked waking up with her while in Paris and he liked waking up with her now. Even after making love to her multiple times last night, he still had a lot of sexual energy to work off and he knew only one other way to do so besides making love to Bristol.

"I'm going to the fitness center."

She lifted a brow. "The fitness center?"

"Yes, back at the hotel. I'm used to working out every morning." Usually he worked out twice a day. "I'll be back for breakfast if that's okay."

"That's fine. We'll be here."

"I'm counting on it." He leaned over and kissed her again, this time a little longer, before easing out of bed. He slid into his jeans and went into the connecting bathroom. When he returned a few moments later, he saw she had drifted off to sleep with Laramie cuddled close.

As he finished dressing, he couldn't stop looking at them. Something deep tugged at his heart. He wasn't sure how to deal with all these emotions. For years, he'd stayed in control of all relationships he was involved in. Usually, none were for the long-term. He'd been determined that no woman would ever rule his heart.

He liked his freedom. Besides, his work as a SEAL wasn't conducive to a normal family life. He didn't know from one month to the next where a mission might take him or for how long he'd be gone. He'd always enjoyed the adventure, the excitement, the quest and, yes, even the danger. Definitely the danger. It was enough to get your blood pumping and your adrenaline flowing.

But, he thought, studying Bristol while she slept, she got his blood pumping and his adrenaline flowing, as well. And when he thought about what they'd shared last night, he couldn't help but smile. Then his smile widened and he knew why. He was happy. Truly happy. And the two people responsible for his happiness were sleeping in that bed. In the last forty-eight hours, his life had changed.

Already, he could admit he wouldn't want it any other way.

When he finished dressing, he walked back over to the bed to stare down at them. At her. He wondered if she had any idea what she did to him, what she had done to him three years ago. Resisting her hadn't been an option.

Bristol had gotten next to him without much effort and there hadn't been anything he could do about it.

Other than to fall in love with her.

That admission shook him to the core. He hadn't seen that coming. But now that he knew the truth, he had to accept it.

He loved her.

He drew in a deep breath. If he analyzed his behavior over the past three years, he probably would have realized he'd fallen in love with her the moment he and the guys had walked into that café in Paris. He'd seen her staring at him. He was certain he'd lost his heart then and there.

He'd left everyone at the table to approach her, determined to introduce himself before they could. Now his actions made sense. Love explained everything. Including the importance of those memories to his survival as well as why he'd returned to Paris looking for her as soon as he'd recuperated. When he'd accepted that she had been lost to him forever, he'd moved on. He'd been living a satisfied life but not a truly happy one.

There had to be a reason their paths had crossed in New York after all this time, a reason they had a child, who would always be a bond between them. And more than anything he also believed, whether she agreed or not, there was a purpose behind her decision to concoct a fake marriage and take his name.

He wanted Bristol and Laramie to always be a part of his life. He might not have planned for the recent turn of events, but now that he was faced with this little family of his, he had no regrets.

He was well aware that Bristol harbored reservations about making their marriage real, but he intended to get rid of whatever roadblocks stood in their way.

She didn't love him yet, but in the end she would. He was a determined man and when he came to a decision there was no stopping him.

He turned and walked out of her bedroom.

Bristol was in the middle of preparing breakfast when her phone rang. Was it Coop letting her know he wouldn't make it back for breakfast? Upon waking up again, Laramie had seemed a little disappointed that Coop had left. She had to admit, she was, too.

As she put the biscuits in the oven, she thought about how he'd found her in her studio working. He had been a distraction, but a welcome one. They had talked. But the one thing he hadn't said was whether or not he'd told his parents about Laramie. And about their fake marriage. If so, what did his parents think of all this?

When she grabbed the phone, she saw from the caller ID that it was Margie. "Yes, Margie?"

"Are you in a better mood today?"

Bristol raised a brow. "Was I in a bad mood yesterday?"

"I thought so. I might have upset you with those things I said about your husband. If I did, I'm sorry."

Bristol drew in a deep breath. Margie's words from yesterday had annoyed her. "There is a lot about my relationship with him that you don't know." And one of them was the fact he was not really her husband.

"Then enlighten me. Let's do lunch today."

Bristol nibbled on her bottom lip. Today was not a good day. She didn't like having to ask Ms. Charlotte to keep an eye on Laramie at the last minute. There might be a chance Coop would be available to watch him, but she couldn't depend on that. On top of those conflicts, she and Coop still had more to work through. They needed to decide how to move forward. He wanted to spend the holidays with them and she was fine with that. What she didn't want was what they'd shared last night muddying the waters.

She didn't want him to think that just because she'd allowed him in her bed she'd allow him into her life. That wasn't the case.

"Tomorrow will be better, Margie," she heard herself say.

"Okay, and tomorrow would it be a good time for you and Steven to talk?"

Margie's words got her attention. "Talk about what?"

Margie chuckled. "Honestly, Bristol, have you forgotten he represents a company who's a client? A client who made it possible for you to leave that boring job to stay home with your son and paint every day."

No, she hadn't forgotten, mainly because Margie refused

to let her. She just didn't understand why Margie couldn't see that Bristol and Steven didn't click. "Fine, as long as this is strictly a business meeting, Margie."

"What other kind of meeting would I arrange? You don't like Steven, I get that now, although for Pete's sake, I don't know why. But it's your choice. Call me later and tell me when would be a good time to get together tomorrow."

"All right. I'll talk to you later."

As soon as she clicked off the phone and placed it aside, her doorbell rang. "Daddy's back, Mommy!"

The excitement in her son's voice touched her. At least he wasn't annoyed like he'd been this morning when he'd discovered his favorite spot in her bed already occupied. Once he'd gone to sleep and woken back up, he'd been team Coop all over again. "Yes, sweetheart, I think your daddy is back."

Putting the kitchen towel aside, she left the kitchen and headed toward the door.

"Good morning. I got you this," Coop said, handing her a huge poinsettia. There was a florist shop by the hotel and when he'd seen it this morning he knew he wanted to get it for her.

"Thanks. It's beautiful, Coop."

"You're welcome. I liked it when I saw it. It looks healthy and there are leaves that will be turning red in a few days."

She smiled. "Come on in." She stepped aside. "I just put the biscuits in the oven."

"Biscuits? You can make biscuits?"

"Yes, thanks to Aunt Dolly."

He entered, pulling off his Stetson and hanging his jacket on the coatrack. "I knew you could cook but claiming you can make biscuits has elevated you to another level."

She smiled. "That's good to know."

He watched as she placed the potted plant on a small

table not far from the Christmas tree. It was hard to believe it was a week before Christmas, but in New York it was hard to forget the season. There seemed to be a Santa on every corner and all the light posts were decorated with wreaths.

"So, what do you think?" she asked, turning to stand beside the plant he'd given her.

His focus was on her when he said, "I wish I could have seen you pregnant."

"Where did that come from?" she asked, smiling.

"You asked what I thought and those were my thoughts while seeing you standing there, knowing my son is in the kitchen sitting at the table."

"Coloring."

He chuckled. "Yes, coloring."

She didn't say anything for a minute. "While pregnant, I looked like a blimp."

He crossed the floor to stop in front of her. He cupped her chin in his hand. "I bet you looked beautiful." He leaned down and brushed his lips across hers.

Then, as if she needed time to compose herself, she said, "The biscuits are about ready to come out the oven."

She hurried to the kitchen.

A couple hours later, Bristol stood in front of her easel. The sound of her son's laughter could be heard all the way upstairs, letting her know he was enjoying another day of Coop's company.

Her thoughts shifted back to breakfast. Laramie had been glad to see his father and had talked a mile a minute. Just like yesterday, after breakfast Coop had volunteered to help clean up the kitchen. Although she'd told him his help wasn't needed, he'd given it anyway. And she would inwardly admit there had been something comfortable about him helping with kitchen chores.

Her thoughts shifted to the poinsettia he'd given her. It was big and beautiful and looked like it belonged right in the spot she'd placed it. It had been so thoughtful of him to bring it for her, and it made her feel special, although she wished it didn't. The only other man who'd given her flowers had been her father. He had arrived at their first meeting with flowers and had given her flowers on her birthday ever since. Even after his death the flowers were delivered. They were always a beautiful bouquet and the card always said, "You are forever loved, Dad."

She wiped the tears from her eyes that always sprang up when she thought of her father and the little time they'd had together. But he was still making a positive impact on her life. The same way she believed Coop would make a positive impact on Laramie's life. He was spending time with their son and that meant a lot. Laramie would miss Coop when he left but he would look forward to his father's return.

If he returned...

She drew in a sharp breath as fear gripped her. She didn't want to think of the risk Coop took whenever he left on a covert operation, but she couldn't push it from her mind. Although he'd told her little about his work, he had explained to her in Paris that most of his missions were classified and couldn't be discussed. She wondered how families of navy SEALs dealt with not knowing from one day to the next the whereabouts of their loved ones and when they would return.

The sound of her cell phone snapped her out of her reverie. She grabbed it off the table and smiled when she saw the caller was Dionne. "Hi, what's up?"

"Just calling to check on you. Are you and my godson okay?"

Bristol smiled. "We're fine. Just getting used to having a male presence around." She thought of how Coop had looked, standing on her doorstep that morning wearing a Stetson, jeans, suede jacket and boots. You could take the man out of Texas but you couldn't take Texas out of the man.

"A hot male presence, right?"

She thought about what had taken place in her bed last night and hot was just one adjective she could use. Other descriptions definitely came to mind but since Dionne had said hot... "Um, you can't imagine just how hot."

"*Oui!* Tell me!"

Bristol laughed. "No details for now. I need to prepare Laramie's lunch."

"Okay, but you will tell me later."

"Yes, later."

"You sound happy, Bristol."

Did she? "It's the holidays. Of course I sound happy."

"Usually you're not cheerful this time of year. Those memories of your aunt..."

Yes, there would always be memories of her aunt, who'd died over the holidays. "I know. At least I was here when it happened."

"Yes, I was there, too. I got to meet her. She was so nice."

"She was super."

They talked about other things while Dionne brought Bristol up to date on her family and the other friends Bristol had left behind in Paris. "Bristol?"

"Yes?"

"Have you decided what you're going to do?"

Bristol frowned. "About what?"

"Your fake marriage. We went to a lot of trouble to make it seem real."

Bristol didn't say anything at first. She and Coop still hadn't decided how to proceed. "A fake divorce makes sense then, doesn't it? But then why waste money undoing something that wasn't real anyway?"

"Is that what he wants? To undo it?"

"I don't know what he wants. It only came up once. We need to talk about it again and make a decision," she said. "Everyone here thinks I was a widow and then out of the clear blue sky my husband reappears. It placed him in an awkward situation since he had no idea everyone thought we were married until I told him."

"Why not make it a real marriage under the pretense of renewing your vows?"

"Because there is no love between us."

Bristol knew what Dionne was going to say before she'd even said it. "There is love, Bristol, at least on your part. You loved him after Paris. Remember, I'm the one who told you he had died. I saw what that did to you and the grief you endured. You loved him too much. That much love doesn't just go away. There's no way you don't still love him."

Bristol opened her mouth to say that wasn't true, that she didn't still love Coop, but she couldn't lie to Dionne. "It doesn't matter. I intend to fall out of love with him."

"Why?"

Bristol drew in a deep breath. "You just said the reason. You saw the way I handled the news of his death and the grief I suffered as a result. I couldn't risk going through something like that a second time. I can't and I won't."

Seventeen

For the second night in a row Coop stood aside while Bristol tucked their son into bed. Today had been a full day of activities. After breakfast he'd stretched out on the floor and helped Laramie put Lego blocks together. Then after lunch he had bundled his son up in his boots and coat and they'd walked to the park.

Bristol had invited Coop to stay for dinner and now he couldn't help wondering if she would invite him to stay the night. She really hadn't invited him last night, but their need for each other had pretty much made the decision for them.

There was a strong possibility she might send him packing after they had the little talk he intended for them to have. It was time he forced her hand on a few things.

"Laramie wants to tell you good-night."

Bristol's words broke into Coop's thoughts and he moved from leaning in the doorway to where his son lay, barely able to keep his eyes open. His son, who had captured his heart the moment he'd heard he existed.

"Daddy, you stay. Sleep in Mommy's bed, okay?"

He couldn't help but smile. His son was giving him

permission even though Bristol hadn't done so. Instead of agreeing with Laramie, Coop said, "Good night, Laramie."

"Stay, Daddy. Sleep in Mommy's bed. Okay?"

Evidently Laramie wasn't going to let him off that easy. Was this the same kid who'd pushed his nose in this morning when he discovered Coop was in Bristol's bed? The same little fellow who'd crawled over him to claim his spot beside his mother?

"He will stay, Laramie. Now you need to go to sleep."

He glanced over at Bristol. Was that her way of giving him an invitation? But then all she'd assured their son was that he would stay, not necessarily that he would stay in her bed. Did that mean she planned to make him sleep on the sofa?

He'd tried deciphering her mood today. Although she'd been friendly enough, it had seemed as if she had a lot on her mind. That was fine. He had a lot on his, too. But still, he couldn't help wondering if she regretted the intimacy they'd shared last night. She hadn't mentioned it and neither had he.

"Love you, Mommy."

"Love you back, Laramie. See you in the morning." And just like the night before, Bristol leaned over and kissed him on the cheek. However, unlike last night, before drifting off to sleep Laramie said, "Love you, Daddy."

Coop felt a tug at his heart and a tightness in his throat. It boggled his mind how a child could love so easily. "I love you back, Laramie."

He and Bristol watched as their son drifted off to sleep.

When they left Laramie's room, Coop told her they needed to talk.

Did he regret sleeping with her last night? The morning had started off well…at least she'd thought so, when he'd returned and surprised her with that beautiful plant. However, since then he'd seemed quiet. More than once she'd noticed him studying her like she was a puzzle he was trying to put together. Why?

She looked across the room at him. He was staring at the Christmas tree. What was he thinking? She'd invited him to spend Christmas with her and Laramie. Then what? When would he be leaving New York for his next mission?

"Ready to talk?"

She wondered why he was asking her when he was the one who initiated the meeting. "I'm ready if you are."

He nodded and sat in the chair across from her. He looked at her for a few moments then he said, "I spoke with my attorney today."

"Oh? Why did you feel the need to do that?"

He leaned back in the chair and the fabric of his jeans emphasized his masculine thighs. She wished she didn't notice such things, but she did.

"Laramie is my heir and I wanted to include him in all my important documents."

"I see."

"I also needed legal advice on my rights as his father."

Bristol raised a brow. "Your rights?"

"Yes."

She frowned. "I don't understand. I thought I made it clear that I would never deny you access to Laramie and you could spend as much time with him as you want."

"Yes, but what if you decide to marry one day and your husband feels differently?"

"I don't ever plan to marry, so you have nothing to worry about."

"You don't know that."

"I don't know what?"

"That you never plan to marry. Things happen. You might change your mind."

Her frown deepened. "That won't happen."

"You can't be sure," he countered.

"Yes, I can."

He shook his head. "No, you can't. And because you can't, my attorney suggested that I take steps to protect my rights as Laramie's father by filing for joint custody."

Coop watched her lean forward in her seat, at full attention. Her eyes widened. "Joint custody?"

"Yes."

"That's crazy. You're not in this country most of the time. How can you even think about joint custody?"

"How can I not think about it, Bristol? In a way, it will make things easier on you."

"How do you figure that?" she asked, glaring at him.

"You will know what times during the year he will be with me and when he will be with you. One thing I'd like is to swap holidays every year."

"Swap holidays?" She asked the question like what he was requesting was the craziest thing she'd ever heard.

"Yes. I told you about the ranch I inherited from my grandparents. I want him to spend the holidays with me there next year. That will free you up to do whatever you want to do."

"Free me up? To do. Whatever I want. To do?"

She had enunciated each phrase. He could tell from the sound of her voice that her anger was increasing. "Yes. I figure with me pitching in, you'll be able to paint more. While I'm away as a SEAL, I plan on hiring a full-time nanny who—"

"A full-time nanny? You've got to be kidding." She inhaled and exhaled a few times and he knew she was trying to get her anger under control. "What's going on, Coop? What are you trying to do?"

He had no problem giving her an answer. "I'm trying to give you a reason to make our marriage real."

* * *

Bristol's pulse jumped a few notches as she inhaled deeply. "Why?" she asked him. "Why should we make our marriage real?"

He shifted again in his seat and she wondered if he'd done it on purpose to distract her. Did he have any idea how his movements always increased her hormone level?

"The foremost reason is our son. I just cited complications that could arise if we aren't married. Knowing I have a child is a game changer for me. It was never my intent to father a child until later in life, and like I told you, I don't regret him, Bristol. I appreciate everything you went through to bring him into this world. And just so you know, if the situation had been different and I hadn't been held hostage, if I had gotten your letter, you would not have been alone. I would have come to you. I would have been there for you and for my child."

"But how would you have been there, Coop? You're a part of the military's special services. When you leave on one of your missions you have no idea when you'll get back."

"True, but I would have taken the time off. The entire nine months if I had to. I would have made sure I was there for you. You would not have gone through your pregnancy alone."

He didn't say anything for a few moments. "I believe in accepting my responsibilities, Bristol, but, just so you know, I would not have asked you to marry me just because you were having a baby. I would have done right by my child and by you, but I would not have suggested marriage between us unless I thought it would work."

At least he was honest, she thought. "So given that, why do you think it will work now? We don't even know each other."

"We know enough and over the past couple of days

we've found out more. We could be together for years and not know everything. Besides, I enjoy getting to know you."

He shifted again and her gaze followed the movement. "I know you are a good mother. As far as I'm concerned, you're the best. I can't think of anyone else I'd want to be the mother of my child. I watch you with Laramie and I know how much you love him and will always put him first. A part of me wants to envy that closeness, but I can't. I want to be a part of it, Bristol. You've given Laramie something special. A home."

His words reminded her of something her father had said. Even though her mother had robbed him of time with Bristol, in the end, he couldn't resent her mother when his heart was filled with gratitude to her for shaping Bristol into the woman she was. One who was loyal and independent. Not spoiled or selfish. Although her father had never said so, she knew he'd compared her to his other two kids. After living in their household for almost two years, she could plainly see that his wife's parenting skills had been vastly different from her mother's. Krista Lockett hadn't known how to tell her sons no.

"To me marriage is more than a piece of paper," he said, interrupting her thoughts. "I can't help but believe that, especially when I see my parents together and how they interact with each other. Even if there wasn't all that love, I believe there would still be trust, respect and friendship between them."

Unfortunately, Bristol thought, she'd never witnessed any such thing between a married couple. It had always been just her and her mother, and her mother had rarely dated. The few times she had, Bristol hadn't been introduced to the men. When she'd asked her mother about it, all she'd said was that until she met someone special, there was no reason to introduce her dates to her daughter. Evidently her mother never met anyone special. And as for her father's marriage to Krista, Bristol could honestly say she'd never felt any love in their relationship. They'd shared the same bedroom but that was about all. They'd lived separate lives.

Bristol drew in a deep breath as she thought about what Coop had said. Yes, there was trust and respect between them. She'd trusted him enough three years ago to invite him into her home and she still trusted him. She also respected him. In just two days he had made an impact on his son's life. And there was his love for his country and his willingness to put his life on the line to protect it. There was no doubt in her mind they could be friends as they got to know each other. Sex between them was good.

But what about the love?

That was something he hadn't mentioned. He didn't love her, whereas she'd loved him almost from the start. A part of her truly believed she'd fallen in love with him the moment she'd seen him in Paris. There was no way she would have agreed to an affair if she hadn't loved him.

But none of those feelings mattered because all the love, respect, trust and friendship in the world couldn't erase how she'd felt when she'd thought he'd died. That was a period in her life she couldn't relive. Somehow, she needed to make him understand that.

"What you said might be true, but there's a reason I can't marry you, Coop, and it's one I can't get beyond."

He lifted a brow. "And what reason is that?"

She met his gaze, held it and said, "You might die."

Eighteen

"You might die…"

Coop stared at her, recalling their conversation last night when she'd said the same thing. Why was she so hung up on the possibility of him dying?

Something else he recalled her saying last night was that three years ago she'd thought he'd died like the others. At the time, he'd wondered what others she was talking about. Now he had an idea who they were. Her mother, father and aunt. All the people she'd ever cared about and loved.

His heart pounded hard in his chest. Did that mean she cared deeply for him, that she loved him?

What if he was right? The thought that she could love him as much as he loved her was more than he could have hoped for. There was only one way to find out.

"I vividly remember having this conversation with you last night. Why are you so obsessed with the possibility of me dying, Bristol? Why are you so convinced I won't come back to you and Laramie?"

He watched her closely, saw how she went still, saw the stark look of fear come into her eyes. Their gazes locked for a minute longer and then she rubbed her hand down her face before meeting his eyes again. Then he saw the tears she was fighting to hold back.

"Talk to me, Bristol. Tell me," he said softly.

Bristol's mind shifted to that day when Dionne had arrived at her apartment and told her what she'd found out about Coop. How could she make him understand how she'd felt and why there was no way they could have a real marriage?

There was no way she could go through something like that again.

"When I thought you had died," she said, trying not to choke on the words, "I thought I was going to die, as well. It came as such a shock. I experienced pain like I'd never felt before. It was deeper than when I lost my mom, my dad and Aunt Dolly. And I felt so alone."

She fought back her tears to continue. "Then I suddenly felt my baby…our baby…move for the first time. It was like he was trying to reassure me that things would be all right. But the thought that I'd lost you was more than I could bear. Even when I told myself that I never had you, that all we'd had was a holiday affair and that I probably would not have seen you again anyway, it didn't matter. The thought of you dying like the others nearly destroyed me. It was only when I finally came to grips with the fact that I was having a baby…your baby…a baby that would always be a part of you, that I was able to move on with my life."

Coop stood and walked over to her, extending his hand out to her. She took it and he gently tugged her off the sofa and into his arms. It was only then that she realized she hadn't been able to hold back all her tears. A few were streaming down her face. How awful it was for him to see her like this, crying over a man who'd meant more to her than she'd meant to him. But when he tightened his arms around her, pulling her deeper into the warmth of his embrace, it didn't seem to matter.

"Knowing you cared that much means a lot to me, Bristol. Like I told you, you were never far from my thoughts when I was captured. Thoughts of you are what helped me survive."

"Why?" she asked, wanting to know why he'd thought of her.

"Because during those three days we were together, you made a lasting impression on me."

Like he'd made on her, she thought. However, he'd gone a step further in making her fall in love with him.

He pulled back and looked at her, forcing her to meet his gaze. "And as you can see, I am very much alive. No matter how much torture they inflicted on me, I refused to let those bastards break me—because of you."

She lifted a brow. "Because of me?"

"Yes. I convinced myself that I had to survive for you. That once I was rescued I had to get back to you."

Too bad he hadn't meant that, she thought.

"By the time I made it to Paris, you had left."

Bristol went still as she stared at him. "What did you say?" She was convinced she'd heard him wrong.

"After getting rescued I had to comply with military procedures and get both physical and psychiatric evaluations. That took about three months. Then I flew to Paris to see you. Your landlord said you'd moved back to the States and hadn't left a forwarding address."

Bristol's head began spinning. "You went to Paris looking for me?"

"Yes."

"But why?"

He gently cupped her chin in his hand. "I had to see you again and let you know those three days with you meant everything to me."

"They did?"

"Yes, and I just didn't know the depth of what they meant until I saw you again the other night. But it really hit me this morning when I saw you and Laramie in bed, sleeping. Then I knew for certain."

"What did you know?"

He dropped his hands from her face to wrap them around her waist. "That I had fallen in love with you."

His words made her head spin even more. "What did you just say?"

He smiled down at her. "I said I fell in love with you, during that time in Paris. I tried to convince myself it was about the sex, and maybe it was at first. But by the time I left your place I felt an attachment to you I've never felt to any other woman." A smile touched his lips. "Who knows? Maybe my body knew I'd left something behind with you that I've never left with another woman, my baby."

"Oh, Coop," she said, feeling more tears well in her eyes. "I love you, too, but I'm so afraid I might lose you again."

He pulled her into his arms and tightened his hold on her. "Shh, sweetheart, it's okay. In life there are no guarantees, we know that. That's why it's important to enjoy our time together. If nothing else, being close to death so many times has taught me not to sweat the small stuff and to appreciate life. Living it to the fullest is what I want to do with you and our son. Please don't deny me that."

He paused before adding, "You gave me the hope and the will to live before, which was how I survived that hellhole. And you will continue to give me hope whenever I go out on any covert operation, Bristol. Now I have two people to come back to. Both you and Laramie. The two people I love the most."

His words meant everything. They were what she'd needed to hear. But could she get past the thought of losing him again?

She tightened her arms around him knowing she had to get beyond those fears. For her sake, for his sake and for their son's. She had to be strong and believe there was a reason their lives had reunited after all this time.

She pulled back and went on tiptoe to place her lips to his. The moment their lips touched, intense heat consumed her. She felt it spreading to him. He tightened his hold on her.

His masculine scent invaded her nostrils as he took her mouth with an urgency that made her weak in the knees. When she shifted she felt the hardness of his erection pressing against the juncture of her thighs.

Bristol released pleasured moans with every stroke of his tongue. She needed this. She had to think positively and believe they'd been reunited for a reason. For a purpose. They would do what her parents didn't do and raise their child together.

He deepened the kiss and she felt it all the way to the bone.

Suddenly, he pulled back and looked deep into her eyes. "I need more."

She needed more, too. "Then take more. Give me more."

Nothing else needed to be said. He swept her off her feet and into his arms and carried her up the stairs.

"I love you, sweetheart," Coop said, after making love to Bristol again.

He pulled her into his arms and glanced over at the clock. They'd made love three times since coming upstairs and had gotten little sleep in between. If the other morning was anything to go by, he figured his son would be invading this room in a couple hours, and Coop and Bristol still needed to talk.

Coop knew she was about to drift off to sleep and he needed to get her attention. "Bristol?"

"Um?"

"Will you marry me?"

She didn't say anything at first, then she looked up at him. "I can't let fear have power over me, right?"

He nodded. "Right."

A smile touched the corners of her lips. "Then yes, Coop. I will marry you."

A huge smile touched his features. "How soon?"

She chuckled. "Can we get through the holidays first?"

He shrugged. "I guess we can."

She kissed him on the cheek. "Thanks for being so accommodating." Then she asked, "When do you have to leave for another mission?"

"End of January, and I want us married before I leave."

"That shouldn't be a problem," she said.

"As far as anyone knows, we are renewing our vows. There will only be a few who know the truth."

"Your teammates?"

"Yes, and my parents. I told them I loved you and if nothing else, they understand the love between two people and how strong it can be. They can't wait to meet you and Laramie."

She eyed him skeptically. "You sure about that?"

"I'm positive." And he was. Once the initial shock wore off, his parents had called him back. They were excited and happy to have a grandchild. Coop figured they must have decided Bristol couldn't be all bad since she hadn't shown up trying to claim any of his inheritance on behalf of her child after she'd gotten word he was dead.

"And since we won't have time for a real honeymoon until later, I thought it would be nice if I took you and Laramie to my ranch for a week or two before I head out. We can hire an interior decorator to spruce the place up while I'm gone."

"I'd love that. Would you prefer living there more so than here?" she asked him.

"Wherever you want to live is fine with me. We can even do both if you like."

"Yes, that might be best. But for some reason I think I'm going to like your ranch."

He hoped she did. He wanted Laramie to love Cooper's Bend as much as he had while growing up.

"You will check out of the hotel and move in here with us, right?"

He chuckled. "Yes, I'll move in here with you and Laramie and we will spend the holidays together."

"Good."

He pulled her closer. She was right, all was good, and as long as he had her in his life, everything would continue to be good.

Everything would be perfect.

Epilogue

"I now pronounce you husband and wife. Laramie Cooper, you may kiss your bride."

Coop pulled Bristol into his arms and all he could think about was that she was now truly his. Legally so. When he felt a pull on his pants he broke off the kiss to glance down at his son.

"I want to kiss Mommy, too, Daddy."

Everyone laughed when Coop lifted his son up to kiss Bristol, as well.

He then glanced around. It had been a small wedding at the church Bristol attended. All his teammates had arrived yesterday with their wives, including Bane and Crystal. Coop's parents had gushed all over their grandson and Laramie enjoyed being the center of their attention.

Ms. Charlotte and her four sons attended and Coop was glad to meet them. Bristol hadn't told him that all four worked for the New York Police Department. They assured Coop that whenever he was gone they would keep an eye on Bristol. It wouldn't be a problem since she lived next door to their mother and they routinely checked on her anyway.

Coop's mother had walked into Bristol's home that

morning and her gaze had immediately latched on to the huge painting over her fireplace. When she asked Bristol about it, Bristol confessed it was a painting she and her father had done together. It was then that she'd told his mother who her father was. Coop thought he was going to have to pick his mother up off the floor. His very sophisticated mother had gotten giddy at the thought that her future daughter-in-law was the daughter of the famous artist, Randall Lockett.

The reception would be held in the church's dining hall, and tomorrow the three of them would fly to his ranch in Laredo. He couldn't wait to introduce his wife and son to ranch life at Cooper's Bend.

They would take a honeymoon when he got back from his next mission. Ms. Charlotte had agreed to watch Laramie for a week while they went to Jamaica.

"Ready to go to the reception Ms. Charlotte set up for us?" Bristol asked him.

Holding their son in his arms, Coop smiled at her. "Yes, sweetheart, I am ready. When it comes to you, I will always be ready."

"Thanks for inviting me, Bristol."

She smiled up at Colin Kusac. They had exchanged phone numbers that night at the gallery when she'd reunited with Coop. When Mr. Kusac had called to check up on her a few days later, she'd learned that just as she'd suspected, he was the person carrying out her father's wishes to make sure she got flowers every year on her birthday. He had explained that Randall had asked that of him before he'd died and Mr. Kusac had promised he would do so.

He'd also told her that he'd promised her father he would check on her from time to time. He confided that he knew how she'd been while living in Paris; and that when she returned to the United States to have her baby, he'd known about that, as well. He'd seen that night at the gallery as an opportunity to talk to her himself. She had discovered that Mr. Kusac—Colin—was one of the wealthiest men in New York and had come from old money.

"Thanks for standing in for Dad and giving me away."

"Thanks for asking me. I was honored to do so. Randall would have been proud of you today."

"Thank you."

They talked for a while longer and then the wives of Coop's teammates came up to say hello. She liked all the wives—Crystal, who was married to Bane, Layla, who was married to Viper, and Teri, who had been married to Mac from the start. They assured Bristol that she wasn't the only one with fears—that was part of being a SEAL wife. They would be part of her support team and would be there whenever she needed them. They even invited her to visit them at their homes. Everyone was excited when Viper and Layla announced they would be having a baby come early summer. They exchanged numbers with her and she knew they were women she would get to know as friends.

No sooner had the women walked off than Margie appeared, all smiles. Bristol knew why.

"I can't believe your husband is connected to so much wealth. Who would have thought his parents would be *those* Coopers. And that he's their heir."

"Yes, who would have thought?" Bristol smiled, knowing how Margie's mind worked.

"You did good, choosing him over Steven."

Bristol decided not to say that Steven hadn't even been in the running. When Margie left, Coop appeared at Bristol's side. "A car will be picking us up in a few minutes for the airport."

His parents' jet would fly them to Texas, where they

would stay for a week on a short vacation with Laramie. After Coop had told Laramie about the horses, their son had been bubbling over with excitement to visit the ranch.

Not caring that they had an audience, Coop pulled his wife into his arms and whispered, "I love you."

She smiled up at him. "And I love you, too."

And she meant that from the bottom of her heart.

* * * * *

Don't miss where the legacy began...meet the
Westmorelands from the very beginning...
THE WESTMORELANDS
Any of the titles can be read as stand-alone novels,
but the entire Westmoreland experience
is not to be missed!

***

DELANEY'S DESERT SHEIKH
A LITTLE DARE
THORN'S CHALLENGE
STONE COLD SURRENDER
RIDING THE STORM

JARED'S COUNTERFEIT FIANCÉE
THE CHASE IS ON
THE DURANGO AFFAIR
IAN'S ULTIMATE GAMBLE
SEDUCTION, WESTMORELAND STYLE

SPENCER'S FORBIDDEN PASSION
TAMING CLINT WESTMORELAND
COLE'S RED-HOT PURSUIT
QUADE'S BABIES
TALL, DARK... WESTMORELAND!

WE'RE HAVING A MAKEOVER...

We'll still be bringing you the very best in romance from authors you love…all with a fabulous new look!

Look out for our stylish new logo, too

MILLS & BOON

COMING JANUARY 2018

MILLS & BOON®

Desire™

PASSIONATE AND DRAMATIC LOVE STORIES

A sneak peek at next month's titles...

In stores from 14th December 2017:

- **Taming the Texan** – Jules Bennett *and* **Little Secrets: Unexpectedly Pregnant** – Joss Wood

- **The Rancher's Baby** – Maisey Yates *and* **Claiming His Secret Heir** – Joanne Rock

- **Contract Bride** – Kat Cantrell *and* **Pregnant by the CEO** – HelenKay Dimon

Just can't wait?
Buy our books online before they hit the shops!
www.millsandboon.co.uk

Also available as eBooks.